THE
HUNT FOR
FREDERICK DOUGLASS

The Last-Chance, Secret Mission to Avoid the Civil War

i

"*The Hunt For Frederick Douglass* is a powerhouse of a first novel. Beautifully written and expertly crafted—author, Terry Balagia, tells the tale of Texas Ranger, Rip Gatlin, who is ordered to capture Douglass for the South to use as a pawn to avoid the outbreak of the Civil War.
Historically accurate and full of Frederick Douglass quotes, *The Hunt For Frederick Douglass* is a thrilling read."

~ Maxine Paetro
Novelist, NYTimes best-selling author,
and co-author of more than thirty thrillers with James Patterson.

"Balagia has uncovered a remarkable story that history somehow looked past. A brilliant read."

~ Cameron Day
Author of *Chew with Your Mind Open* and *Spittin' Chiclets*

"The unconventional alliance of a Texas Ranger and legendary abolitionist Frederick Douglass in this fictional *what if* mission to change history also challenges assumptions about the civil war and today's racial-cultural realities and social injustices. Big plus: it's a thriller action novel about a covert operation by an unexpected duo on a wild-ride adventure."

~ Jay Levin
Founder and former editor-in-chief of LA Weekly.

"I struggle to find the right words to express how thoroughly I enjoyed this book! As a debut author, Terry Balagia hit a home run! It gave me pause to consider how young our nation was during these growing pains and drove me to reconsider our history and how it carved our culture and sense of humanity. Balagia's characters are strong and tell a compelling story; a story that does not end as one might imagine. I can't wait for the author's next book; I am glad he was prompted to pursue a path he was sure he would not take!

~ T. R. Stearns
Retired Superintendent of Schools

THE
HUNT FOR
FREDERICK DOUGLASS

The Last-Chance, Secret Mission to Avoid the Civil War

A Novel

By Terry Balagia

*To my mother
who taught us to love
books.*

*To my father
who taught us to love
people.*

*To Jackie, Dorice,
Jimmy, and Suzy
who gave me their love
and support.*

"The only thing necessary for the triumph of evil is for good men to do nothing."

~ Edmund Burke

CONTENT

The Hunt for Frederick Douglass
Terry Balagia

The Hunt for Frederick Douglass
Terry Balagia

The Hunt for Frederick Douglass
Terry Balagia

ACKNOWLEDGMENTS:

MAXINE PAETRO: A brilliant writer and supportive friend. The perfect mentor, always inspiring and making me better. You had me take the Robert McKee seminars; you had me listen to the ever-brilliant James Patterson on Masterclass—which was masterful. Thank you, Max, for your generosity of time, thought, love, true friendship, and guidance.

SUSAN SEMBER: Where would I be if I had not met Susan Sember? My publisher, contributor, coach, support system, and miracle worker all in one. I said a prayer and hit 'send' and the Universe responded with you. Lucky me. It was meant to be. I am excited about what's coming next!

BECKY HILLIKER: My writing was much improved by many; first by you. A great writer and brilliant editor who always came through. Thank you for your comments, changes, improvements, ideas, and brilliant suggestions, which I always took.

ANNA WEBER: Indebted thanks for the final mastery of editor extraordinaire, Anna Weber, and the invisible hand of genius which you wield so deftly. Thank you for being a big part of this book. You made it so much better. Anna, please stay close at hand.

Thank you to the MANY EARLY READERS who made great insightful comments, including many of my students who were kind enough to give it a read at many stages of the creative process; and whose comments, critiques and criticisms made significant changes and improvements in my final work.

To FRIENDS AND OTHER WRITERS who read different iterations at different times and commented I thank you, including Eric

Gardner, my daughter Rebecca and brother, Jimmy. I took all your suggestions to heart, and to paper.

An extended thank you to Susan's ENTIRE DESIGN, PR, AND PRODUCTION TEAM, including Randy Scott Goad and Tom Morrissey.

A special thanks to TEACHERS SERVING STUDENTS IN PUBLIC SCHOOLS everywhere. Especially those I had at Lee elementary, Baker and Austin High Schools—in particular, Mr. Bernard K. Owen, my senior year.

Thank you, Jody Hotchkiss, for your encouragement through the years.

Thank you, Jay Penske, and Dragon Books.

Thank you to my old friend, Hugh Forrest, for your support.

Thank you, FeliciteApparel.com

And thank you, Walt Harris.

Thank you TO MY ASSISTANT, MARIA ISABEL RODRIGUEZ, for her masterfully managed author-side social media and promotional efforts, from content building, creation, production, placement, and management.

To my FAVORITE FOUR PEOPLE IN THE WORLD, Terence, Sarah, Rebecca, and Adam, whom I love more than anything.

And to my SWEETHEART AND LOVE OF MY LIFE, Venay. For all her love, support, and belief.

BEING A TEXAS RANGER

A LARGE PROPORTION was unmarried. A few drank intoxicating liquors. Still, it was a company of sober and brave men. They knew their duty, and they did it. While in town, they made no braggadocio demonstration. They did not gallop through the streets, shoot, or yell. They had a specie of moral discipline. They did right because it was right.

~ Texas Ranger Captain John Ford (1819–1897)

Cherokee Prayer

Ga lu lo hi gi ni du da
Sky our grandfather

Nu da wa gi ni li si
Moon our grandmother

E lo hi gi ne tse
Earth our mother

Ga li e li ga
I am thankful

Si gi ni g'e yu
We love each other

O sa li he li ga
We are grateful.

Prologue

THEY WERE HERE to follow Frederick, so I decided I better follow them, too. I spotted them hiding outside the storehouse and immediately recognized them as the two we had run into on the trail coming up here the night before. The Ranger man and the young one he called Cadence.

At first, I wondered what they were doing here. But the minute Frederick exited the storehouse, I saw them take notice and follow him from the shadows. That's when I realized I had best be following them.

I watched them spy on Frederick as he walked with the small group to the muddy boat launch and said his goodbyes to his son and the other young Negro recruits. As he politely and correctly thanked and bade goodnight to the group of well-wishers and family members who had gathered there. I saw them lurk in the shadows, following behind Freddie as he walked alone across the promenade.

I followed all three of them for a good while. I stayed hidden in the shadows myself and watched as Frederick was recognized by many of those parading about on the lovely March evening. Some had been in the audience at the Ford Theater earlier when Frederick gave his rousing speech. Others recognized him after hearing people call out his name. Some approached to shake his hand or to ask him to sign his name on their program guide or their ticket stub. Many had copies of his book or issues of Douglass' *Monthly* newspaper. It seemed like practically everyone in Washington, D.C. recognized his distinct hair, his imposing presence, his commanding baritone voice, and contagious laugh. The things I had grown to know and love so much myself.

I observed how the Ranger man and Cadence stayed well behind Frederick, at a consistent distance, and at a casual pace. I noted how deliberate they were. I knew they were up to no good.

But I did not know that the Ranger man was so deep in his own thoughts he wasn't paying no mind, and when he looked around, he suddenly realized Frederick was gone. They had lost him.

"Dammit, Little Cade! Where did he go?" I heard the Ranger man get all frantic.

"Shit, I don't know! You were the one that was watching him," his little puppy dog, Cadence, responded.

I could see that set the Ranger man off. He turned on the little one. "You and all your damn questions about your damn father. Now go down that way." He pointed down one of the streets. "I will head back this way. Then, when we come back together, we will sandwich him between us. Now go! Hurry!"

I watched as they turned the corner and suddenly bumped right into Frederick coming the other way. Cadence was in front, and his head hit Freddie about chest high. Cadence bounced back. Frederick hardly noticed but apologized immediately.

"Excuse me, gentlemen." I saw Frederick stare down at them. He seemed to recognize the two and stepped back to take another look. I did not realize at the time, but Frederick had encountered them earlier that evening, before his speech. "The bad hombre with the match," I heard Frederick say. I could see him smile warmly. "I recognize those scruffy clothes. You gentlemen really stood out earlier."

The Hunt for Frederick Douglass
Terry Balagia

Then I saw Freddie stiffen his back and stand straighter and stronger, towering above the other two. "Since you are following me, I should ask—are you my supporters or my assassins?"

He quietly looked down at them.

That was when the Ranger man must have realized they had not lost him. Frederick had ditched him and Cadence, then had come back around to get the jump on them both. The Ranger man could see that Frederick didn't have a gun. He seemed unsure of his next steps. I could sense this was an unusual situation for the Ranger man to find himself in.

That's when 'ol foolhardy Freddie broke the tension by letting go with one of his obnoxious booming laughs. It was so loud it could be heard two blocks away and so startling it nearly made me jump out from where I was hiding as I spied on them.

He immediately apologized for his joke.

"Please forgive me, gentlemen. Laughter helps me to let off tension after a long speech. It has been an exhausting day."

I could see the little one fidgeting around like a nervous fanatic. "Actually, if you wouldn't mind," I heard Cadence ask with shakiness in his voice, "I would like for you to sign my *Douglass' Monthly*. I bought it at the theater before your speech."

"My pleasure..." Frederick started to reach into his pocket for his pencil.

"But it's in my saddlebag. Would you mind walking to the livery barn near Ford's Theater with us?"

They waited for Freddie to answer.

The Ranger man did not move but seemed surprised by his little companion's resourcefulness. Even I had to admit, it was a perfect way to get Frederick out of everyone's sight and nearer to their horses.

"Well, seeing as I'm headed back that way anyway, certainly." Frederick nodded with a smile.

What a fool! I thought. I loved Frederick with all my heart, but sometimes he could be such a trusting buffoon! From the shadows, I was tempted to run out there and slap his foolish face. But I didn't.

Instead, I followed as the three men walked the two or three blocks to the livery. I saw the Ranger man and young Cadence make brief eye contact with each other. They were probably thinking this was perfect. Their horses were at the livery. It would provide them with a quick getaway. I moved in to get closer so as to hear them better.

"We, ah, enjoyed your speech," I heard the Ranger man say, looking up and staring eye to eye with Frederick. I saw Frederick nod as he bowed his head slightly. "Very kind of you, Sir."

Freddie can be so gullible sometimes, I thought as I followed behind. I decided to cut across the back streets so I could get to the livery ahead of them.

They made it to the theater. I could see them as they turned down the alley behind it. The Ranger man was behind Frederick, looking around to see if there were any late-night stragglers still roaming the sidewalks or streets. Cadence walked ahead, leading them right toward the livery stable and the large open barn at the end of the alley.

I was already there, peeking out from inside the barn. A single lantern hung over the outside of the barn door, making it dark and full of shadows inside. I noticed the Ranger man seemed preoccupied—as though he were considering the plethora of possibilities in how the next two minutes might transpire.

The Hunt for Frederick Douglass
Terry Balagia

As they entered the barn, Cadence approached his horse and pretended to mess with his saddlebag, keeping his back to Frederick and the Ranger man. Once all three were inside, I seen Cadence turn effortlessly, his gun drawn. His movement was smooth and perfect.

Freddie was caught completely off guard. I knew he would be. I could tell his feelings were hurt a little bit, too. He slowly raised his hands as the Ranger man grabbed a huge empty burlap feed sack from the floor of the barn and threw it over my tall and elegant friend, Freddie, from behind. The Ranger man tried to reach for the cuffs on the back of his gun belt while keeping Frederick's arms pinned down. But Frederick was a big, strong man, and the Ranger man could not hold him long.

Frederick was about to get away, when the little one, Cadence, holstered his Colt, grabbed a large cast-iron pan hanging on the side wall of the huge barn, and smashed Frederick in the head with it, knocking him out cold. The Ranger man fell to the ground with him, his arms still wrapped around Frederick's torso.

Then I heard the Ranger man say, "Quick, Kid, ride over to the smithy and get the wagon before he comes around."

The little one jumped on his pony and rode away as Frederick regained his consciousness and he and the Ranger man tussled again.

Frederick still had the grain sack over his upper half, but he managed to get to his feet and spun around and butted the Ranger man hard with his head, sending them both to the straw-covered ground. As the Ranger man hurried to get back up, I could see Frederick still struggling with the sack.

The Ranger man stood tall and slowly drew his gun. "I'm Rip Gatlin...Texas Ranger," he said, as they both gasped for air. The

The Hunt for Frederick Douglass
Terry Balagia

Ranger's voice echoed through the old barn. "And you...Frederick Douglass...are now under arrest!"

The Ranger man failed to realize that they were not alone. His old mare had sensed it. But the Ranger man had no idea the huge barn was full of my people. My runaways were hiding in the shadows of the dark, cavernous structure. Everyone had kept perfectly still as we watched the men struggle.

I was there with them. Standing in the shadows, I was their leader, their Moses. The Ranger man did not see me as I stepped out from the shadows and into the light. But all my people did. I reached for the door of the blacksmith's furnace. I grabbed the handles to the tongs whose opposite end was buried deep in the smoldering coals. I pulled the tongs out of the burning forge, revealing the red-hot ends, and held them high above my head.

His wise old mare made a loud snort to warn the Ranger man, but it was too late. I slowly turned. My motion was smooth and perfect, too. In one graceful arching move—just as the Ranger man realized I was there—I shoved the iron tongs directly into his face. His skin sizzled as it burned on contact with the red-hot metal, melting one of his eyeballs instantly and singeing most of his mouth shut.

All the while, I sensed the power of the Holy Spirit take hold of me. The Lord suddenly commanded the full power of my lung's breath, as if the Angel of God Himself was speaking through me, reciting from Acts, Chapter 9, Verse 4. "Saul, Saul, why do thou persecute me?"

It was then I felt the beginning of one of my falling spells coming over me. But before the darkness overtook me, I looked down at the Ranger man, as he collapsed to his knees, howling in excruciating pain.

The Hunt for Frederick Douglass
Terry Balagia

Steam rose from his burning skin and flowed in wafts around him and me. The smell of his burning flesh stung my nose. I imagined that Rip Gatlin could not help but wonder how he, a legendary Texas Ranger who had no business even being in these parts, had ever gotten involved with a plan to capture Frederick Douglass in the first place.

The Hunt for Frederick Douglass
Terry Balagia

THE
HUNT FOR
FREDERICK DOUGLASS

The Last-Chance, Secret Mission to Avoid the Civil War

The Hunt for Frederick Douglass
Terry Balagia

PART
ONE

March 1861

LINCOLN TOOK OFFICE on March 4. All he wanted…was to heal the country.

All the northerners wanted…was to re-supply Ft. Sumter.

All the southerners wanted…was to secede from the Union. In fact, some already had.

All the Texas Ranger wanted…was to do his duty. And then to go home.

The Hunt for Frederick Douglass
Terry Balagia

CHAPTER 1

FIVE DAYS EARLIER, Rip Gatlin was riding back to Richmond on his cream-colored palomino mare. Rip and Blade had been with each other for over twenty-five years. They had escaped the Alamo together. The old girl was still every bit as dependable as she had been when they escaped that day, but Rip knew this would be their last job together. He looked forward to finding a Texas pasture for them both to retire. The sun was high, and the dust hung in the air.

Rip took one long look around at the flat highland plane of northwest Virginia, knowing they were on the road back to Richmond for the last time. *We'll collect the reward for the runaway we've spent the previous five days and nights tracking, and then Cadence and I will head back to Texas.* Or such were his thoughts. Rip was eager to get back. He had been to Virginia once before, fifteen years ago, and things had not gone well then, either.

That first time, it was in pursuit of an escaped convict. This time, Rip was in Richmond after having escorted a convoy of supplies as a gift from Texas Governor Sam Houston to the newly formed Confederacy.

Slavery was against the law in Texas when it was part of Mexico. But when Texas won its independence, slavery slowly seeped across the Sabine River to the cotton fields in East Texas.

Since Lincoln's election five months earlier, four southern states had seceded from the Union and formed the Confederate States of America. The Texas state legislature pressured Governor Houston to join the Confederacy, which he staunchly refused to do.

The Hunt for Frederick Douglass
Terry Balagia

Houston hoped that by sending the convoy of money, guns, and supplies, he would placate the state legislature while keeping Jeff Davis and the Confederate States of America at bay, even if only temporarily.

To further sweeten the deal, he assigned his most renowned Texas Ranger, Rip Gatlin, to escort the convoy; and then stay in Richmond for a month following the delivery of the convoy to 'help maintain law and order during these troubled times.'

But now the month is over. After this, Cadence and I are headed back to Texas. At least, that is what I plan.

Rip's weathered face stretched in a smile at the thought. His face resembled dried, cracked leather left outside too long. He might have been considered handsome if he were sixty-five. But he was only forty-five. Life as a Texas Ranger had been hard on him. In return, Rip had been hard on life.

Dangling from Rip's saddle were all the accouterments of the slave hunter's trade: a large bullwhip, a set of iron handcuffs, leg shackles, a large Bowie knife, a ring of skeleton keys, and a rolled-up blood-stained bedsheet. Within Rip's grasp were guns of various sizes, gauges, and calibers. Everything from a single-shot derringer wedged inside his left boot to a .44-caliber Henry Rimfire in his saddle gun-sleeve, with a hinge-breeched 12-gauge scattergun jammed into the bedroll behind his saddle for good measure. And, as always, Rip had his government-issue Walker Colt revolvers—one on each hip. Rip never took off his gun belt, unless he slept or took a bath, which was rare—or when he was handling the buckboard wagon. In which case, he would take his gun-belt off and set his Walker Colts under the bench seat for easy access.

Riding behind Rip and handling the buckboard was Rip's young deputy, Cadence. He was a stout and strong, good-looking twenty-year-old with blond hair and warm brown eyes and stood half a foot taller than his horse's withers. The young deputy was sitting on the bench seat of the buckboard wagon with his own personal arsenal. Besides his two six-shooters, he also kept an 8-gauge scattergun under the bench seat within easy reach.

Little Cade's black and white pinto mustang, Paint, was pulling the small wagon. Unlike Rip, Cadence wore both his revolvers on his hip, even when he handled the wagon reins. He kept them anchored to his thighs with leather strings that hung down from each holster.

Mounted on the buckboard behind Cadence was an iron cage large enough for a man to squat in. A thin, wiry, dark-skinned man sat anchored to the bottom of the cage with an iron chain. He was not wearing a shirt and was sitting with his arms wrapped around his knees. The man had on a pair of old leather britches that were tattered, torn, and stained; sable skin was covered in goose bumps from the harsh elements.

His name was Jonas, and he pleaded in a shivering voice, "Sir, please don't take me in. Sir, please don't take me in," over and over, repeating it like a mantra. As he grew more delirious, huddled up in a ball at the bottom of the cage, he began to chant.

"Your road to Damascus is coming," Jonas called out. "The Lord just done told me so. He says, 'Jonas, behold that man who cages you. I will place the wrath of wisdom upon him like a sword of light and blind him for three days and three nights, like I done to Saul. For this man, who exchanges your freedom for a reward, will be called upon to answer for his sins upon his fellow man. That will soon be his reward!'" The captured runaway then grew silent as he gradually lost consciousness.

The group continued to Richmond.

They were crossing a flat, open plain when Blade stopped so suddenly, Cadence, on the buckboard behind them, struggled to bring Paint and the wagon to a halt. Rip looked straight ahead, studying the road in front of them. He slowly and carefully scanned the horizon from one side to the other. In his head he repeated the Cherokee mantra, *Listen to the wind, it talks. Listen to the silence, it speaks. Listen to your heart, it knows.*

Rip became still and quiet. His attention focused on the rock and the wind spirits, as White Elk had taught him.

When Rip was a young boy, some kids at the mission orphanage in San Antonio were from local Cherokee tribes. Often, Rip would go live with the Cherokee for the summer harvest or for the hunting season in the fall. The summer he was twelve, Rip left the orphanage and never came back. He spent those years learning the way of the Cherokee with White Elk as his mentor and his spiritual sponsor of sorts.

Rip listened between his breaths...between his heartbeats. He held his breath. He listened more. All was silent.

Then he heard it. Or rather, sensed something from the spirits in the shadows. Blade opened her nostrils and smelled the air. She sensed it, too. She reared her head slightly. Rip reached down, took the derringer out of his boot, and stuffed it behind him between the saddle cantle and his bedroll. Just in case, Rip nudged Blade, and they started up again.

Cadence loosened the reins on Paint, who pulled the wagon forward. Rip fixed his eyes on the turn up ahead, cautiously watching a blind bend in the road with dense woods and dark shadows on both sides—the perfect place for an ambush.

Cadence was oblivious. He reached under his wagon seat where he kept his small library of books: one or two novels, *The Columbian Orator*, and some law books. He brought out a large book and laid it down on the bench seat next to him. As they entered the bend, handling the wagon required Cadence's full attention and that of both of his hands.

"I think I'll read some more of that book you like, Rip, just as soon as I—whoa!"

Suddenly, four horsemen darted out from the shadows with their guns drawn. Blade reared up instinctively. Cadence pulled back hard on the reins, stopping Paint and the wagon abruptly, and sending the book flying forward. In an instant, the armed men surrounded Rip, Cadence, and their captured runaway, who had been jolted awake. They were trapped. Nowhere to go.

A fifth man rode out from the shadows to join the others. Rip recognized the slave-hunting gang of Foster Nelson. Rip knew Nelson. They had ridden together fifteen years ago when Rip came to Virginia tracking an escaped convict from a Texas prison.

"Get your hands up, Rip!" Nelson barked; his gun drawn. He was on edge. He remembered Rip as the fastest and most accurate draw he had ever seen.

"You can see my hands, Nelson. I don't need to raise them." Rip was casual and unfazed.

Nelson wasn't. He motioned again with his gun for Rip to raise his hands. "Get 'em up, Rip. I'm afraid you'll make my boys nervous. I would hate to see someone get shot."

Rip smiled slowly. "In that case, I am afraid you're going to be very disappointed in about a minute or two."

"Now, why is that?" Nelson asked, trying to sound casual, even though he was extremely wary of Rip. He cautiously observed Rip's every move, as did the members of Nelson's gang, who had heard many stories about Rip Gatlin's uncanny fluency with a handgun. They kept their eyes locked on his shooting hand, indicated by the string of Cherokee corn beads that dangled down from Rip's right wrist.

The Hunt for Frederick Douglass
Terry Balagia

"I am afraid one of your boys is going to make the mistake of thinking they can steal our captive and claim the reward for themselves," Rip said.

"Well, we did have that discussion," Nelson responded.

"Oh yeah? How did it end up?" Rip asked.

"Not very good for you, I'm afraid," Nelson said.

"Enough talk!" one of Nelson's gang members spat. His horse whinnied, tossing its head as it spun around, reflecting its rider's anxiety.

Nelson interjected, "Rip, I don't believe you ever met my little brother, Hank. He wasn't around way back when you first came up here. But he rides with me now that he is all grown up. The only problem is...Hank can get excited at times." Nelson smiled as he said it.

At that, Hank nudged his horse closer to Rip.

"I can see that," Rip said.

By now, Hank was right in front of Rip. He took out his revolver and pointed it directly at Rip's face. "Hand over your wagon!" Hank snarled with such intensity that spittle sprayed from his mouth onto Rip's face. Rip didn't flinch. He looked over at Nelson, then he slowly reached up with his shooting hand and wiped his face.

By now, Hank was all worked up. He grabbed a rope, looped with a noose tied at one end, and waved it around. "We could just string up your captive right here and now, and that way, no one gets the reward. Would that make you happy, Rip?" Rip did not respond.

Hank turned and directed his angry spew at Jonas. "How 'bout you, Runaway? Do you want to hang from that tree over yonder? Well, do you?" Jonas was terrified. He knew what evil white men were capable of. Throughout his entire life, he had seen them commit unspeakable acts on his people.

The Hunt for Frederick Douglass
Terry Balagia

Hank rode up to the cage and stuck the noose between the bars in an attempt to frighten Jonas. It worked. Jonas pushed himself into the back corner of the small cage, shaking and whimpering. Nelson and his gang members laughed and egged Hank on. Hank spurred his horse, causing it to bump into Rip's mare.

Rip had about enough of Hank. Having wiped the man's spittle from his brow, Rip brought his shooting hand back down to his side. He slid the same hand around to the back of his saddle along the cantle, where he had stashed the derringer. No one in Nelson's gang noticed. They were too busy laughing at Hank's antics. But Cadence saw it all and was prepared.

The last thing anyone heard Hank say was, "Who's to keep us from lynching this runaway right here and now?"

Rip answered in Spanish, as a Texas Ranger was apt to do. "*Ese sería yo.*" Then he repeated it in English. "That would be me."

They all stopped laughing and looked at Rip.

Quicker than the mind can form a thought, Rip's hand found the derringer behind his saddle, and as Blade took one step sideways and twisted her body. From behind his back, Rip fired the derringer. He shot the noose out of Hank's grasp, exploding the rope into pieces, and putting a small hole in Hank's hand. The bullet came to rest in Hank's right ribs with a punch that knocked him off his horse onto the ground.

Cadence didn't hesitate. In an instant, he slid the 8-gauge scattergun from under the bench seat of the wagon, pulled the hammer back, and pointed it at Nelson and his boys. Rip dropped the derringer onto his crotch and drew and cocked both of his Colt .44 revolvers. Nelson's gang froze. It took a total of three seconds.

The Hunt for Frederick Douglass
Terry Balagia

CHAPTER 2

"**DAMMIT, NOW, JUST** hold on, Rip!"

Nelson holstered his revolver and hopped to the ground to care for his younger brother, who was whimpering from the pain. Several of the gang members got down from their horses to help. Hank was rolling around on the ground like he was on fire. The group tied a neckerchief tight around the small hole in Hank's hand to stop the bleeding, while someone else grabbed their Barlow pocketknife and plucked the bullet from Hank's side.

"Nobody is hanging nobody," Rip said. "Is that clear?" Rip and Cadence still had their guns drawn, locked, and loaded. Everyone seemed very clear.

"You need to calm down now, Rip."

"Oh, I'm plenty calm, Nelson, unless your brother starts talking again about coming between me and my sworn duty to bring this man in. Nothing and no one comes between me and my duty. You know that about me." Nelson didn't respond. He was too busy scrambling around with his men, getting Hank back into the saddle so they could get him to a doctor in Richmond.

"Hell, it was just a derringer." Cadence laughed at their fastidiousness as he looked over at Rip, who did not smile. Cadence stopped mid-laugh and returned his full attention to the gang, his scattergun pointed at them.

"Now, we are going to go our way," Rip said, "and I suggest you men do the same."

The Hunt for Frederick Douglass
Terry Balagia

Rip nudged Blade with his thigh, and she gently moved forward. The three other members of Nelson's gang were Comancheros. And though all three were known to be very bad hombres, they each slowly holstered their guns and opened a path for the wagon to pass. Rip and Cadence relaxed their guard and rode through.

No one was more relieved than Jonas. He looked down at the puddle of piss beneath the rip in the crotch of his leather pants.

Nelson's guys wrapped up Hank's hand and side as best they could. "You didn't have to shoot him, Rip! We could have worked something out!" Nelson shouted after him.

"I think things worked out just fine," Rip shouted back. Cadence laughed at Rip's comment.

Nelson and his gang saddled Hank up and rushed past Rip and Cadence at full gallop on their way to Doc Brandt's office in town. Rip let them pass without a word. Nelson shouted something as they rode off, but Rip didn't respond.

Rip wasn't one to ruminate on how someone had done him wrong. That wasn't his way. He didn't hold on to things as most people did, instead, he practiced his Cherokee teachings for the art of maintaining a silent, balanced mind. It involved suppressing the fearful chatter in his head into absolute silence. A stillness he controlled. Then within that silence, he learned to use all his senses: integrating sight, sound, smell, and taste into one transcendent sense of knowing. Only a silent mind could be fully aware and connect to the natural world or cultivate the ability to see the unseeable and to hear the unhearable.

In a silent mind, there was no room for thoughts of revenge or hate. The moment Rip might ruminate on his hate for someone may be the same moment the Spirits were letting him know there was danger ahead, or an ambush lying in wait. Rip knew, as the

Cherokee knew, that if his mind was clouded over with angry thoughts, he was certain to miss something. And out here, the something your missed could be the something that killed you.

Cadence found *Moby Dick* and with one hand put it back in the sack with his remaining books under the wagon seat while holding the reins in the other. As Nelson's gang got a little farther away, Cadence chuckled.

"That was a great shot back there, Rip," Cadence said, trying to loosen him up. Rip was his usual mum self. "They took their eye off of your shooting hand," Cadence called out above the creaking wagon and the horses. "You let Hank's spit get on you so you could start moving your hand without them taking notice. And like you always taught me, if you can get your hand moving, you can get the drop on anyone."

Rip did not respond but smiled ever so slightly to himself.

"Who was a better shot, Rip? You or my pa?" Cadence asked. Rip knew where this was going.

"I'm not in the mood, Cadence." Rip deflected his query.

"Come on Rip, you have so many great stories about my pa. You know I love to hear you talk about him," Cadence begged.

"He was a great shot, your pa," Rip acquiesced. "Let's leave it at that for now."

I bet he was the best there ever was, Cadence thought to himself. He reached under the buckboard bench and grabbed the book. Cadence often read aloud. At first, Rip had resented it, but over time, had grown to enjoy it. It amazed Rip how someone could write a book ten years before, or a thousand years even, and he could still hear the writers' words like they were sitting there next to him, telling him how they thought about things back when.

The Hunt for Frederick Douglass
Terry Balagia

Cadence opened it to the bookmark and read. "'I came here to hunt whales, not my commander's vengeance on a dumb brute!' cried Starbuck, 'that simply smote thee from blind instinct! Madness! To be enraged with a dumb thing, Captain Ahab, seems blasphemous.'"

Rip and Cadence were heading up a slight incline in the road when they heard galloping hoofbeats coming toward them. A courier flag appeared over the rise, and shortly after, a single rider wearing a Virginia Militia uniform crested the hill. He recognized Rip and rode right up to him, stopping abruptly and performing a hurried salute.

"Captain Gatlin?"

Rip did not return the salute.

The militiaman identified himself as a courier from the president's office in Richmond with an urgent message from President Jefferson Davis. Whereupon he opened his courier pouch and handed Rip a folded piece of Crane stationery with the newly formed CSA seal.

"They told me you would take this road, Sir." Rip looked at him thoughtfully then handed the message to Cadence.

"Read it, Little Cade."

Cadence took the message, opened it, and read.

"The Confederate States of America hereby requests the presence of Captain Rip Gatlin immediately upon his return to Richmond, to attend a meeting with President Jefferson Davis at the temporary headquarters at the Spotswood Hotel." Cadence turned the note over, looking for more words.

"That's it." Cadence handed the message back to Rip, who gave it back to the courier.

The Hunt for Frederick Douglass
Terry Balagia

"Lead the way, Soldier," Rip said, as the courier turned his horse and led them back to Richmond and to Jefferson Davis.

For the rest of the ride back Cadence read aloud from his books and got to know the young courier who was about his age. Rip could not help but wonder why the president of the Confederacy wanted to meet with him. *Whatever it is, I know it can't be good.*

Rip instinctively leaned into his early Cherokee training and once again quickly silenced his mind. He concluded it didn't matter. The war was coming and that would change everything. Like when summer was about to turn into fall, he could smell it in the air

The travelers made their way to Richmond by early afternoon. Immediately upon arriving, the courier took his leave as he saluted Rip.

"Pleasure riding with you, Captain Gatlin. Good riding with you too, Cadence. You read really good, by the way."

"Thanks, Ricky! Keep out of harm's way and all that."

The young courier veered off down Main Street to the dispatch office. Rip, Cadence, and the wagon continued straight down Broad Street to Potomac Avenue, and finally toward the marshal's office.

The Hunt for Frederick Douglass
Terry Balagia

CHAPTER 3

MARSHAL JIM MADDOX had walked back a little too briskly from Doc Brandt's office. He stopped now to rest in the shade of the plankwood boardwalk that wrapped around the front of his office in downtown Richmond.

As he stood there catching his breath, Maddox surveyed the streets around him. *This is my town*, he thought as he turned his aging eyes to look first down one direction of the street and then the other.

That's when he spotted them.

About a hundred yards down Potomac Avenue, he saw two figures riding in the middle of the street, heading directly toward him. One was on horseback, while the other was handling a buckboard wagon with a cage mounted in the back. Marshal Maddox recognized instantly who it was. He had been expecting them.

"Looks like he did it again," the marshal mumbled to himself.

Richmond's Marshal Maddox was no fan of the famed Texas Ranger, Rip Gatlin.

They had first encountered each other fifteen years ago when Rip tracked an escaped fugitive from Texas to Virginia. Maddox did not appreciate a Texas Ranger encroaching on his territory, but as a lawman, he was obliged to help. Things ended in a bloody mess, which Maddox had always blamed on Rip.

Marshal Maddox reached into his inside coat pocket and brought out a large leather pouch full of chewing tobacco. He took a generous handful and stuffed it into his mouth as if it were stick candy. Deputy Hale came out of the office and stood on the plank walkway next to the marshal. He could see Rip and Cadence coming down Potomac Avenue toward them.

"Looks like they captured another one, Marshal. That makes them five out of five," Deputy Hale said in disbelief. "They are making the rest of us look like incompetent fools."

"Yes, they are." Maddox leaned out over the railing and spit fresh tobacco juice into the street. It made a big brown splat as it hit the ground.

As they drew closer, the marshal could see the thin, shirtless man chained to the bottom of the cage. As they slowly walked their horses up to the front of the marshal's office, Cadence reached in his saddlebag for the reward poster. He unfolded it and began to read.

"Two hundred dollars reward offered by the subscriber. A dark, black-skinned slave, about thirty years old, six feet and an inch tall, stout-made, and active. He is well-spoken and goes by the name Jonas. He will make for Detroit through the states Kentucky or Virginia, or the upper part of Tennessee." Cadence finished, then folded up the post and slipped it into his saddlebag.

Marshal Maddox nodded as he slowly stepped down to the cobblestone street and walked around the wagon, examining the man locked in the cage. The goods seemed intact. The marshal motioned for his deputies to take the runaway slave, then he took Rip into his office to count out the reward money.

Marshal Maddox's office was nothing more than a large room with a jail cell in one corner, a big black iron safe in the other, and the marshal's desk in the middle. The safe door was wide open, and a lockbox sat on the marshal's desk. Maddox reached into the lockbox, took out the reward money, and counted it onto the desk. Deputy Hale stood right beside him.

"Looks like it's the last time we will do this," Marshal Maddox announced.

Rip slapped his hat on his thigh, knocking the trail dust off. "It's good riddance if you ask me. I was not sent here to hunt runaways."

"Oh, then you don't want the reward money either, I reckon?" Maddox stopped counting and looked up at Rip. There was no response.

The marshal looked back down and continued counting out the gold coins. "You were sent here to render help in addressing local law enforcement issues," the marshal said. "And currently our biggest law enforcement issue is whatever I tell you it is."

Deputy Hale found that amusing and chuckled, causing Maddox to smile at his own witticism. He stopped counting and looked at Rip again.

"But it don't matter, anyhow, Rip. Your month here is over. And frankly, I'm thrilled. All you've done is cause me trouble. I just left Foster Nelson and his brother at Doc Brandt's office," Maddox said. "They wanted to file a complaint and have me arrest you. This ain't Texas, Rip. You just can't go 'round shooting people you disagree with."

"They were trying to commandeer my capture, Marshal." Rip protested.

"That's not what they say," Deputy Hale stepped in.

"Then why don't you arrest me?" Rip looked the deputy square in the eye, and then glanced back at Maddox, Maddox was thinking how he would love to arrest Rip Gatlin. But he knew Rip was right, so he dropped his stare.

The Hunt for Frederick Douglass
Terry Balagia

Cadence came into the marshal's office as Maddox finished counting out the reward money. He stacked the gold coins on his desk. There were three octagonal fifty-dollar gold slugs in one stack, and a twenty-dollar, a ten-dollar, and four five-dollar gold coins in the stack alongside it. Marshal Maddox reached over and took one of the fifty-dollar coins sitting on top of the first stack, leaving a hundred-and-fifty dollars remaining.

"The poster said two hundred," Rip said.

"Oh, didn't you hear? It came down fifty dollars recently," the marshal said as he slipped the fifty-dollar gold coin into his pocket. He looked at Rip and said, "Marshal has to get paid somehow."

Rip shook his head. He gathered up what was left of the reward money and slid three five-dollar gold coins across the desk to Cadence. They fell to the ground. One rolled over and stopped at Deputy Hale's boot. Unabashed, Cadence dropped to his knees to pick them up.

Their business concluded, Maddox closed the lockbox and slid it over to Hale, who carried it over to the safe.

Marshal Maddox turned to Rip. "Now, I was told to escort you over to the Spotswood Hotel. From what I hear you have some highly confidential meeting with President Davis. So, we better get you there." His voice suddenly lowered in a threatening manner. "Before they come looking for you."

CHAPTER 4

MARSHAL MADDOX WALKED Rip outside and down Potomac Avenue toward the Spotswood Hotel. Cadence followed behind in the street with their horses. He held the reins in one hand, and in the other, he studied a two-week-old edition of *The Richmond Dispatch* he'd found in the marshal's office. He read it aloud as they walked.

"March first through seventh, 1861, *The Richmond Dispatch* reports on the arrival of his excellency, the Honorable Jefferson Davis, president and commander-in-chief of the Army and Navy of the Confederate States of America," Cadence proudly resounded as they made their way to the Spotswood Hotel. "President Davis was escorted to a carriage in waiting by Thomas W. Hoeninger, of the Spotswood Hotel, and was drawn toward that elegant 'traveler's rest' by four splendid bays." Cadence looked up, amused. "Hey, that's where we're going," he said.

The walk from the marshal's office to the hotel was on a concrete walkway. Every street had concrete walkways on both sides in all directions, except when you crossed the mostly cobblestone streets. But Rip's favorite amenity in Richmond was the icehouses. He could order an ice-cold beer in the middle of summer. They even put ice in the drinks. Certainly, the Spotswood Hotel bar would have one as well. But Rip wasn't going there for a drink.

"I don't know if you can feel it, Rip. But everyone here is on edge of late," Marshal Maddox explained as they walked. "It's like the North and the South are sitting on a keg of powder, and every one of us is a match." Maddox leaned off the sidewalk and spit tobacco juice in the dirt for emphasis. "You start to get a feeling that everything is about to explode."

Rip nodded. He responded to every bit of the tension that was building and listened as the marshal continued.

"In spite of that, the thing folks here fear the most, more than a war, is a slave uprising. Why? Did you know that there are counties here in Virginia where the slaves outnumber the Whites? Can you imagine what that thought does to people? Some have taken turns standing watch at night for fear of there being some kind of organized slave rebellion. Folks don't feel like they can trust their local slave patrols anymore. They're afraid that if the slaves were to rise up in one state, they would rise all over the South at the same time. Imagine that, Rip. Why, I hear in Louisiana they recently killed forty slaves in an uprising on the German Coast outside New Orleans. Stuck their heads on fence posts all along the road for a hundred miles."

Maddox leaned toward the street and again spat tobacco juice onto the dirt street. He wiped his chin with his sleeve. "Can you imagine desecrating a body like that, chopping off their heads? It's unchristian if you ask me. But they say that's how you keep them in line, down there," the marshal explained.

"I reckon," Rip responded.

———————— • ————————

THEY WERE ON Main Street, about to cross Seventh Street, when Rip and Cadence got their first look at the spectacular Spotswood Hotel rising in front of them. It had opened two months previously and was a magnificent sight. It sat on the southeast corner of Eighth and Main streets, just blocks away from the state capitol building, and served as the de facto headquarters for the newly formed Confederate States of America.

Cadence tied the horses to the hitching rail in front of the grand building as Rip and Maddox walked up to the magnificent front doors. Cadence watched as Rip and Marshal Maddox walked through the elegant entrance of the hotel. And suddenly were gone.

Cadence knew he had time to kill and looked around at all the interesting city people who made their way to and fro in such a hurry. Everyone in the city was dressed so nicely. Cadence noticed two young women in large silk, dress hats and satin-and-lace hoop skirts, the latest fashions from Felicite Apparel. They smiled at him. Cadence tried to smile back, but it seemed more of a snarl than a smile. He tried to lean back against a pillar in the front of the Spotswood, but the pillars were round, and Cadence almost fell over backward on his butt.

When he next looked up, the women were laughing and walking in the opposite direction down the sidewalk. He shrugged. *So much for city life,* he thought.

The interior and lobby of the Spotswood Hotel were stunning. The Richmond Dispatch called it *the talk of the town*. It was a vast circular room, with a ceiling two stories tall and a majestic chandelier made with over 10,000 dangling pieces of cut crystal. There were gas lights everywhere, it seemed. Marshal Maddox looked bothered.

"This place is richer than possum gravy. If you liken to that sort of thing," the marshal said. He certainly didn't. He not only seemed impervious to the elegant surroundings of the lavish lobby. He seemed downright annoyed by the place.

Maddox had a concerned look on his face. He was all business.

The Hunt for Frederick Douglass
Terry Balagia

"I don't know why they want to meet with you, Rip. But from what I hear, it is serious business. Which means you can't be pulling your normal antics with these men," he said. Rip nodded, not sure which antics of his to which Maddox was referring.

The men headed across the open lobby toward the expansive double stairway that took up the entire opposite side of the grand room. Rip followed the marshal as he started up the stairs.

———————— • ————————

THE IMMENSE STAIRWAY was covered with deep green, padded carpet, and thick, dark wood railings, which Rip held onto with a tight grasp. He did not like being indoors. He especially did not like being indoors on the second floor.

There was a growing rumble of murmuring voices, noise, and shouts coming from above as they climbed the stairs to the floor above. Once there, it was a flurry of movement and chaos—at least in Rip's eyes.

There were security details, congressional aides, and groups of congressmen either walking briskly down the hallway or hunkered together in intense gatherings. Rip followed Marshal Maddox through the crowded hallway. A US Marshal and a Texas Ranger usually made for an imposing visual, but not so much to this crowd.

They walked by one room where there was no bed, or sitting area, nor any furniture, as such. There was only a long table with four telegraph machines lined up alongside each other, with teams of two, sitting across from each other on either side of the long table, operating each station. The four sets of telegraph wires snaked up the wall and out a second-floor window. All the wires and glass insulators looked recently installed. The four teams pounded out messages and jotted down notes at a dizzying rate.

When they came to a fork in the hallway, Maddox nodded toward the double doors where two Virginia militiamen stood guard.

"That's the Presidential Suite. That's where you are meeting with President Davis." He turned to face Rip and cautioned him one more time. "Remember to watch yourself, Rip. Those boys in there are not very forgiving—if you know what I mean."

Rip squinted his eyes. "Marshal, I don't reckon I do know what you mean."

"What I mean is you and I have our differences. I make no secret of that, Rip. But we're both lawmen, and as one lawman to another, I have to warn you, those men in there are different. They expect results instantly. And if'n they don't get them, they are off chasing the next thing, with even more urgency. So, no matter what they promise you, no matter how much they may think they mean it, they don't. Not a lick of it. And in a pinch, these guys will drop you like a hot rock, and never look back." The marshal took his hat off and wiped his forehead with his handkerchief and then swiped it around the inside brim of his hat. "I don't know if what I'm saying is making a bit of sense to you, or not. It's just one man's opinion. You can take it for what it's worth."

Marshal Maddox put his cowboy hat back on his massive head, turned around, and headed back through the corridor and down the stairs, leaving Rip standing there thinking he had not felt this alone since he was twelve years old and White Elk initiated him into Cherokee manhood by leaving him with his ankle tied to a stake in front of a wolf's cave, blindfolded, in the middle of winter. But at least then he had a knife.

———— • ————

The Hunt for Frederick Douglass
Terry Balagia

The old warrior says to the young one,

'There is a battle between two wolves inside us all.

One is evil. It is anger, jealousy, greed, resentment,

inferiority, lies, and ego.

The other is good. It is joy, peace, love hope,

humility, kindness, empathy, and truth.'

The young one grows concerned.
'Which wolf wins?' he asks.

The old warrior answers,
'The one you feed.'

~ Cherokee proverb.

CHAPTER 5

As Rip noticed the similarities between those two situations, an impressive-looking younger man wearing a waistcoat and bowtie interrupted his thoughts. He extended his hand and introduced himself as Joseph R. Davis, nephew of President Jefferson Davis. He then walked Rip to the door of the President's suite, where he knocked on the door and then quickly opened it, let Rip go inside, then closed it behind him.

Rip stood there as his eyes adjusted to the dim lights. He could see the suite was quite large, with a big open sitting room and two corridors leading off to private bed chambers. It was a corner suite with two windows along one side and one window on the other, each covered in thick, heavy curtains and drapery from ceiling to floor. Because the gaslights were turned low, the room was dark and made eerie by shadows.

Jeff Davis looked over and jumped to his feet, welcoming Rip the minute he realized he had entered the suite. The thin, wiry Davis had a nervous energy about him, along with a tendency to control or dominate the room. He introduced Rip to Vice President Alexander Stephens, the architect of the Confederate constitution, who was much smaller than Rip had imagined. In fact, he was downright tiny. *He can't weigh over a hundred pounds*, Rip thought to himself as he shook Stephens' hand.

Rip also shook hands with the Scotsman, Allan Pinkerton, the founder, and owner of the famous private detective agency from Chicago. Pinkerton provided security to President Lincoln and was trying to build a business relationship with the new Confederate government as well.

The Hunt for Frederick Douglass
Terry Balagia

"Now gentlemen, I will have you know we are in the presence of a Texas Ranger." President Davis spoke as he glanced at a small notecard in his hand. "One of Stephen F. Austin's founding members from when he reformed the Texas Rangers after winning their independence from Mexico at the Alamo."

"From what I have read, Captain Thomas 'Rip' Gatlin served at the Alamo under Colonel Crockett and fought with great honor I was told at San Jacinto with Governor Houston—who speaks highly of you, I might add," President Davis continued speaking as he walked Rip over to the big chair Davis had previously occupied. The President motioned for Rip to have a seat and continued his oration.

"We first want to thank Governor Houston for his generous support. I refer of course to the convoy of supplies he had you escort here, all the way from Texas, Captain." President Davis held up his glass for a toast. "And also, for the use of Captain Gatlin's services for the past month." President Davis suddenly realized the glass he was holding was empty.

"I would toast you with a drink, Sir, but I see I do not have one." Davis motioned to a steward holding a silver tray of freshly poured bourbons. He stepped forward from out of the shadows. Rip had not realized the steward was there.

"Can I get you a drink, Captain? Gentlemen? Because I'm going to have one," President Davis proclaimed. The two other men nodded as the steward took their empty glasses and replaced them with full ones. Rip waved the steward off, as President Davis, newly armed with a full glass, continued talking to the room.

"Now, gentlemen, not only did Captain Gatlin arrive here bearing gifts but his stay here over the past month has proven an invaluable gift as well. Why, from what I hear, in the four weeks Captain Gatlin has been leading our slave patrol efforts here in

Richmond, he has caught every one of the runaways he has pursued. Five assignments. Five captures."

President Davis held his glass up toward Rip, a tributary gesture that Vice President Stephens and Pinkerton enjoined. "Now that we have fresh drinks, we can do this properly," Davis extolled. "Let us toast our thanks to Governor Houston for the financial and military aid he sent, and for loaning us his best Texas Ranger in our time of need."

"Hear, hear," someone said. All three took a drink. Rip saw these were not their first drinks of the day. Nor, he supposed, would they be the last.

"They say that when you go after a man, Captain, you never fail," President Davis said as he slurped a big gulp of bourbon, to both reward and encourage his mouth simultaneously.

"What's your secret?"

"I never quit, Sir," Rip answered. "You can't fail if you never give up."

President Davis nodded. Without further pleasantries, he walked over and stood in front of Rip and stared down at him quietly for a moment.

"Captain, I realize your assignment here in Richmond was temporary. And that your time with us is over. But before you return to Texas, we were hoping we could entice you to take just one more assignment. If you don't mind giving us a few more minutes of your time, we can explain." Davis looked around at the others and then back at Rip.

"Simply put, Captain, we want to avoid a war by bringing the new President Lincoln to the negotiating table and agreeing to a peaceful separation of the states. And if Lincoln will enter the talks in good faith," Davis leaned in, "then, as a demonstration of our sincerity, the South will agree to set Frederick Douglass free. How does that sound?"

Rip was stunned. "Pardon me, Mr. President?" Rip looked perplexed. "Frederick Douglass?"

Alex Stephens stood up. "He's that ex-slave who's traveling around the North getting folks all riled up with his speeches and editorials. Northerners treat him like he is some kind of damn saint sent from Heaven above. Like he is their African baby Jesus, for God's sakes. Why, I hear they are packing them in at a dollar a head just to hear him speak."

Davis interrupted Stephens, and said, "He's a damn book-reading, troublemaking, Negro is what he is. At one point he started an anti-slavery newspaper up North—until we were able to shut that down." Davis took a sip and chuckled to himself. "We hired some local boys to go up there and get his printing press and toss it into Lake Erie! But from what we now hear he is printing his paper again. The rest of the time Douglass is traveling around the North giving speeches and secretly supports local Underground Railroad activities."

Rip knew about Frederick Douglass from newspaper articles Cadence had read to him of the well-spoken ex-slave abolitionist. "I am very aware of who Frederick Douglass is, Sir. I was not aware that the South had captured him," Rip said. "Being out on the trail, sometimes for weeks at a time, we rarely hear about events until well after they occur."

Jeff Davis smiled and folded his arms across his chest and stared intently at Rip. "We haven't captured Frederick Douglass, Captain Gatlin. Not yet at least. You see, that's where you come in."

President Davis smiled in a way that made Rip remember what Sam Houston told Rip before he sent him up here: "Be wary of Jeff

Davis. I know him well, served with him in the Senate. He is as ambitious as Lucifer and as cold as a lizard."

President Davis looked around the room, and the other two men nodded at him as if they had just made a silent agreement. President Davis looked back at Rip. Rip had no idea what was about to come. Nor did he realize that after this moment, his life would never be the same.

———— ◈ ————

The Texas Ranger's duty is not a blind duty.

It's the best attempt at justice that can be done at the time.

It's doing the right thing because it is the right thing to do.

But you best do it quickly.

The Hunt for Frederick Douglass
Terry Balagia

CHAPTER 6

PRESIDENT DAVIS STARED down at Rip and announced didactically: "Captain Gatlin, your assignment is to go up North, capture Frederick Douglass, and bring him back here to us, where we can begin the trial that will either end in Frederick Douglass being hanged or in President Lincoln coming to the negotiation table. As it is, Lincoln refuses to negotiate with us because he refuses to acknowledge the Southern states' right to succeed. But, if we were to capture Frederick Douglass, the uproar in the North would demand their president negotiate for his release."

He leaned in closer to Rip. "Allowing us to secure a final and peaceful resolution with the North and preserve slavery in the South, forever." At this, President Davis rocked back on his heels, stood tall, and took a big sip of whiskey.

"To that end, we have engaged the overpriced services of the Pinkerton Agency," President Davis said sarcastically as he turned to face Pinkerton, "to help organize and execute the plan. Explain the plan to this gentleman if you would please." President Davis stepped to the side as Pinkerton got up and took over. He was a short, middle-aged man with a thick Scottish brogue, red waxed hair combed back off his forehead, and a big red mustache.

"Your cover will be as an official courier from the Confederate States of America, on behalf of President Jefferson Davis," Pinkerton said to Rip in his thick Scottish burr. "Once in Washington, you will deliver a letter to the White House from President Davis proposing that negotiations begin. You will then await Lincoln's response." At this, Pinkerton broke into an irrepressibly impish smile.

The Hunt for Frederick Douglass
Terry Balagia

"But that is all just a ruse, Laddy. For on this same day, Frederick Douglass is scheduled to give a speech to the Abolitionist Society there in Washington, and that is the real reason for the charade."

President Davis pulled a chair right up in front of Rip and sat down. "There have been a lot of efforts by many people in the North and in the South to avoid a war. All their efforts have failed. At this very moment, former president, John Tyler, is in Washington at the Willard Hotel convening what they've been promoting as the Peace Convention. Which, from what we hear in the latest telegram, has failed drastically."

Vice President Alexander Stephens leaned between the two with a stern look on his face. "Frankly, Captain, we were counting on that Peace Convention being successful."

"But it's not!" President Davis said angrily. He turned back to face Rip. "Which is why this plan is so important. This plan is the very last chance to prevent a war between the North and the South. Don't you want to help us do that, Captain?" President Davis was on the verge of begging. He interrupted his own all-important plea to pour the last of the bourbon from his glass into his mouth. He let it swish around, then as he swallowed it, his eyes rested on Rip.

"We want you to arrest Frederick Douglass and bring him back, Captain. All of which is perfectly legal under the Fugitive Slave Act. You can hunt and arrest runaway slaves anywhere, in the North or in the South."

Stephens interrupted with a sense of urgency, "However, for the record, Frederick Douglass bought his freedom over ten years ago. But we no longer recognize that purchase as legitimate. In fact, we put a reward on him back then that is still standing. So legally, we will be within our rights to arrest him. But of course, he is within his rights to resist. And keep in mind that he is a big, strong man."

The Hunt for Frederick Douglass
Terry Balagia

The Vice President smiled at Rip and crossed his legs as he leaned back in his chair.

President Davis interceded impatiently. "The point is that you can arrest Frederick Douglass wherever you find him. In the North or in the South. Or in the middle of the damn Mississippi River. All of which is perfectly legal." President Davis stood up and rubbed his hands together. "So, what do you say, Captain? Do we have a deal?"

Davis stood in front of Rip, looking down at him sitting in the chair. Rip looked down at his boots. He hated being indoors. It always made him feel trapped. He felt trapped now.

Rip looked up at President Davis. "With all due respect, Sir, I could use a little more clarity. You see, I'm not from the North or the South. I'm from Texas. And as far as Texas is concerned, we don't have a dog in this fight."

"You damn sure do!" Davis screamed in Rip's face. He had no patience for this kind of response. "You may be from Texas now, but you will be part of the Confederacy very soon, Captain! I can assure you of that." President Davis turned in a huff and walked around the room taking deep breaths. He picked up his empty glass and motioned to the steward to bring him another one.

"Who do you think you are, talking to me like that?" Jeff Davis looked sideways at Rip as he walked over to his desk and picked up a crisp piece of stationery. "I was hoping you would do this of your own volition, Captain. You would have been rewarded handsomely if you had! But of course, I knew better." He held up a letter signed by Sam Houston. "I took the liberty of asking your good friend, and your governor, to agree in writing that you fulfill this one last assignment before you leave for Texas."

He tossed Houston's letter to Rip. It fell to the floor. Rip picked it up and looked at it. He saw Sam Houston's signature. The rest could be a foreign language for all Rip knew. He did not know how to read much more than the letters in his own name. He didn't even realize he was holding the letter upside-down.

"So now instead of doing it for reward money, you will be doing it because you are ordered to. So much for your obstinance, Sir."

Pinkerton leaned over and diplomatically took the letter from Rip with a polite smile. "For the benefit of the room" Pinkerton said and began reading the letter from Governor Houston.

"'Thomas, if they are reading this letter to you then I can assume you refused President Davis' request. But I need you to do this last mission for me, as an old friend. As far-fetched as this plan might sound, it may be the very last chance to avoid a war between the states. Isn't that worth taking the chance? I certainly think it is. I also think you would probably agree.'"

"He closes by saying that he will write a letter to the White House in advance of your trip, giving President Lincoln a respectful nudge, and introducing you, properly. And this final sentiment to you, 'Captain, I know you won't let me down, old friend.' Signed, Governor Sam Houston, Texas.'"

Jeff Davis glared at the Texas Ranger. "Is that enough clarity for you, Captain?" he mocked. Pinkerton slipped the letter for Lincoln, along with Rip's secret orders outlining the plan, the courier medallion, and a letter of passage into a leather diplomatic courier shoulder pouch. Rip reluctantly took hold of the courier pouch, and in doing so, accepted the assignment. President Davis smiled as he saw Rip acquiesce—unable to further demur.

As they all stood, Pinkerton looked at Rip and cautioned him, "The tricky thing is that you must get to Washington in four days. That is when Frederick Douglass is speaking. Which means you need to leave now."

"We will get there," Rip responded dismissively.

The Hunt for Frederick Douglass
Terry Balagia

"I expect good news, Captain. And only good news. And I expect it quickly. We need to know if we are making war or peace." Davis stared squarely at Rip, who nodded in response. "In the meantime, we will prepare for both."

Jeff Davis held up his glass one last time and said to the room, "If capturing Frederick Douglass and putting him on trial does not bring the North to their knees, then we'll just hang the book-reading bastard and start this war ourselves. Good day, gentlemen."

The Hunt for Frederick Douglass
Terry Balagia

CHAPTER 7

THE MEETING ENDED, the men left the suite, and Rip headed downstairs. He had never wanted to get out of a room so fast in his life. Being indoors always made him feel closed in. It was like being in a cave. Or perhaps he felt trapped because of the next-to-impossible duty on which he and Cadence were about to embark.

President Davis and Pinkerton made it sound so simple. But there was nothing simple about this assignment. Added to that was the fact that Frederick Douglass would not go with them peacefully. And like Stephens had gleefully pointed out, Frederick Douglass was a tall and robust man.

Rip needed a plan, but he had a four-day journey to come up with one. He headed to the downstairs bar. Pinkerton followed hurriedly down the stairs after him. He saw Rip disappear into the darkened doorway at the far side of the grand lobby. Pinkerton entered and saw Rip at the bar. He walked up next to him.

"May I buy you a drink, Captain?"

"No. But you could go outside and wait for Cadence to return with the horses. And tell him I will be right there." Rip leaned in at the bar and ordered two double-shots of whiskey with shaved ice. Pinkerton handled the put-off well and went out to the front of the hotel. He didn't mind because Cadence was the one he wanted to talk to anyway.

Pinkerton knew what Cadence looked like. He had spied on Cadence, Rip, and Maddox from the second-floor window before their meeting. He had seen them sauntering down the street together.

The Hunt for Frederick Douglass
Terry Balagia

But even without that peek he would have easily spotted Cadence in the middle of the high society individuals and business elite surrounding and flocking to the Spotswood Hotel these days. They were all dressed in the most formal daily attire. But not Cadence. Pinkerton instantly spotted him in his dust-covered trail clothes amongst the street crowd outside the hotel. Cadence was hard to miss. He had the defiant look of a rebel—with the guns to match.

Pinkerton walked up to him. "You must be Cadence," he said as he stuck out his hand. "I'm Allan Pinkerton." Cadence didn't take it. He barely looked up.

"Big news, Laddy," he said, trying to make small talk. "Looks like you boys will be heading to Washington in the morning."

Cadence was unresponsive as he unwrapped the reins from around the rail and waited for Rip. Pinkerton kept at it. He noticed Rip's horse, Blade, and all of Rip's gear. Especially the larger-than-life knife dangling from Rip's saddle.

"Now I read somewhere that Jim Bowie actually gave his knife to Rip. Is that true?"

"He never talks about that stuff to me. But I have heard him tell folks he was bringing Colonel Bowie his whiskey ration from Colonel Crockett on one of the final nights of the siege and when he handed Colonel Bowie his jug, Bowie gave Rip his knife in return. He was already bedridden with two loaded muskets. One on each side. He told Rip he didn't want them using his own knife on him."

Pinkerton pulled himself close to Cadence, disregarding his feigned interest in the knife altogether. In a half-whisper, he said, "If you ask me, seems like Rip is getting a little soft in his old age, wouldn't you agree?" Cadence made a face like he had just stepped in some horse shit.

He looked down at the snotty Scotsman. "He ain't in his old age. And Rip damn sure ain't getting soft."

Just then, Rip came sauntering out of the Spotswood looking all around as if he were feeling two whiskeys better. "Let's go, Little Cade." Rip undid the reins and mounted Blade.

Cadence had started to mount up, when Pinkerton grabbed his arm and whispered, "Just let me know when you are ready to go on your own. I am sure it can be arranged. You will finally get the money you deserve. You will never get that with Rip."

"Go fuck a pig," Cadence told him as he got on his horse. Pinkerton headed back into the hotel feeling like he had just delivered an important message to Cadence. But Cadence had no desire to work on his own, not as long as Rip was around. But he was mindful of the coins jingling in his pants pocket, the crumbs that Rip tossed him as his share of the reward money. He took as much risk as Rip. Yet he got paid a fraction of what Rip kept for himself. But Cadence was not about to discuss that with Pinkerton. *This is between me and Rip*, he thought as they rode down the street together. Rip could sense that something was not right with Cadence.

"What's eating at your craw?"

"That Pinkerton fellow. He thinks he's too smart for his britches."

Rip chuckled and shook his head. "Pay him no mind. He don't know donkey dung from wild honey."

Rip and Cadence headed back to the marshal's office to prep and load the wagon. Helped by Deputy Hale and the other deputies, they dismantled the iron cage from the buckboard and set it aside. No sense in posing as diplomatic couriers with an iron cage on their wagon. An assortment of chains and manacles were tossed in the back of the buckboard and covered with a large Indian blanket.

The faint remnant flavor of bourbon lingered in Rip's mouth. He could still taste the burn of the whiskey and the cold of the ice. Now, it was off to Washington D.C., to go on a little hunting trip.

The hunt for Frederick Douglass.

CHAPTER 8

CHARLES SWELLGOOD WAITED nervously in the lobby of the Willard Hotel in downtown Washington, D.C. This was not where Frederick Douglass was staying, but Charles had arranged to conduct the interview there. He looked at his pocket watch. Twenty minutes late, but then Frederick Douglass had warned Charles he had a previous engagement that may run long.

World leaders, diplomats, ambassadors, and well-known speakers were always coming to Washington. So, having Frederick Douglass in town to speak at the Georgetown Ladies' Speaker Series was certainly big news. For Charles Swellgood, interviewing these big names and political giants was the best part of the job. He had recently become political staff editor of *The Washington Star* and was especially eager to make his mark. How could he not jump at the opportunity to interview the well-spoken and renowned abolitionist?

Admittedly, Swellgood did not know the number of meetings Frederick had lined up while on this trip to the floundering nation's capital. Besides the speaking engagement, Frederick had scheduled countless sit-downs and one-on-ones with congressmen, judges, and noted constitutionalists. And those were just the publicly known meetings.

There were also a series of meetings that authorities would not find acceptable—including meeting with his old childhood friend, Harriet Tubman, who was expected in Washington around the same time. Word came through the grapevine just that morning confirming her arrival via the underground railroad. The message was hidden in the morning slave song that was sung before sunrise as the workers made their way to the fields for a full day of labor. They sang,

> *Moses is bringing a load of potatoes to Heaven. Seven parcels large.*

> *Let the station master know and the stockholder, too, that the gospel train has departed, loaded with baggage and a milk bag that's coming through.*

This was a code meant for the so-called station master. Seven families would arrive that evening needing a place to hide and sleep for the night. The station master would know that the only place around big enough for a group that size was the large livery barn near Ford's Theater, which they often used when coming through D.C.

More formally, Frederick Douglass had come to Washington at the request of William Lloyd Garrison, a former mentor and a regular on the speaker circuit. The Georgetown Ladies' Anti-Slavery Society was sponsoring a speaking tour and asked Garrison to invite Frederick Douglass to come speak. The event would be held at Ford's Theater and Frederick graciously accepted the invitation. The Georgetown Ladies' Board of Directors responded by sending him a two-way passage by boat and by rail.

Before leaving Rochester, and in anticipation of the trip Frederick, penned a new editorial entitled, "The Union and How to Save It." He gave explicit instructions to put it on the front page of the March 1861 issue of the *Douglass' Monthly.*

It was mid-morning when the tall and statuesque Douglass entered the luxurious lobby of the Willard Hotel with an air about him like that of royalty. He was a spectacle to behold. Physically, he was large-framed and strikingly handsome. His very comport appeared exceedingly elegant...as if he were born into money, which of course he was not. Yet he appeared eerily comfortable in such lavish surroundings. He was dressed impeccably in a black suit, a knee-length overcoat, and his customary black bowtie, his beaver-skin top hat in hand. There were only a few people in the lobby at the time and those who were there instantly recognized him.

He was greeted immediately by Charles.

"Good to see you, Mr. Douglass, Sir." Charles extended his hand, which Frederick was quick to grasp. He sized up Charles instantly.

"You are the gentleman from *The Washington Star*, I presume."

"Yessir, Charles Swellgood. Such a privilege to make your acquaintance, Mr. Douglass." Charles heard the shakiness in his own voice and took a deep breath. "This is quite an honor, Sir."

"The honor is all mine, good man." Frederick's smiling face and warm baritone voice reassured Charles in a comforting way. "I realize you must have a host of questions. Unfortunately, my time is rather pressed."

They moved briskly to the corner of the lobby, sat on one of the plush green velvet sofas, and began a twenty-minute interview. Charles had deliberately chosen the Willard Hotel, where recently the delegates from twenty-one states stayed and attended what was billed as the Peace Conference. It had only recently disbanded. It was hosted by former president, John Tyler, and held next to the Willard Hotel in the Willard Convention Hall. The conference had started on February 4th and lasted the entire month. Thirteen states refused to participate altogether, the same thirteen that would soon make up the totality of the newly formed Confederate States of America.

Charles Swellgood was coming down from a full month of reporting on the heated debates. He was full of questions for his dignified guest. Most of which regarded the possibility of hostilities between the states. But that's not where he started.

The Hunt for Frederick Douglass
Terry Balagia

"My first question is regarding the relationship between you and Mrs. Harriet Tubman. How did it begin, and has it continued to this day?"

"Well, that first part of your question is easy." He smiled. "Our connection began at birth." Then he stopped and looked across at Swellgood. "You said take it from the beginning, "Frederick said as he let go with one of his trademark booming laughs, the suddenness and volume of which took Charles by surprise.

"I was actually born and raised in Maryland in Talbott County. Araminta, or Minty, as Harriet's family called her then, was born and grew up in Dorchester County, which is the county next to Talbot. She is one of my biggest supporters and dearest friends, as I am one of hers."

"Though you may find no record it of it, we were a close-knit community. All the plantations were connected with one another. There was a rare ability to make everyone aware of things almost in an instant. We knew all that was happening on all the plantations in that county and the counties next to those as well. So, Harriet's family and my family were all awfully close back in the day. But that was a long time ago."

Frederick paused. "Now, Mr. Swellgood, if you have specific questions, please feel free to fire away, but I am not comfortable commenting further on Mrs. Tubman nor her activities and what I may or may not know in that regard."

"Most certainly, Mr. Douglass. I have a question regarding comments on Christianity that appeared in your autobiography years ago that some considered offensive."

Frederick was quick to respond.

"What I have said, respecting and against religion, I mean strictly to apply to the slaveholders who call themselves Christians. What I was pointing out was that the distance between Christianity as lived by Christ and Christianity as lived by the slaveholder are miles apart. The slave auctioneer's bell and the church bell chime in with each other. If you can understand what I mean." Frederick intertwined his long fingers together as if demonstrating his point. "Let me try another way. Do you think Christ would own slaves?"

Charles did not respond.

Frederick smiled broadly. "The slave prison and the church stand near each other, and they mutually help each other. The dealer gives his blood-stained gold to support the pulpit, and the pulpit, in return, covers his infernal business with the garb of Christianity. It is all the truth. It is only offensive because it is true. I am considered offensive because I see it as it is, and I call it."

"You understand, I see the widest of difference between the Christianity of Christ and the religion called Christianity in this land. If you love the one, you must then naturally abhor the corrupt, slaveholding, women-whipping, cradle-plundering, hypocritical Christianity of the other. Indeed, I can see no reason for calling the religion of this land Christianity."

Charles scribbled his notes as he went on to his next question.

"Regarding the possibility of a war. Where are you on the question of war, Sir? Do you feel, as many others do, that a war between the northern states and the newly formed Confederacy is inevitable?"

"I am not one to want for war, Mr. Swellgood. Nothing can come of war but death. But as I have said many times before: power concedes nothing without a demand. Never has and never will. So, we will see. I am hopeful, though, that this young republic has reached a level of maturity where the judgment of good people is what guides us, not the evil machinations of a war-mongering populace."

The Hunt for Frederick Douglass
Terry Balagia

Charles wrote hurriedly into his notebook, eager to capture every word Frederick Douglass said.

"May I say, on a more upbeat note," Swellgood added, "It appears that your presence here in D.C. is causing quite a stir. I think we heard that the Ford's Theater is sold out on the night of your speech scheduled a few days from today."

"Now, that is some good news, Mr. Swellgood. Good news to hear, indeed." Frederick took a quick glance at his pocket watch. "Seeing how it is Washington D.C. and I am sure you have interviews with people much more important than myself, I feel like I have taken up enough of your valuable time. So, if you do not mind, I will take my leave of you now, Sir."

Frederick stood tall with his hand out to shake as Charles rose with his pencil still in his hand.

"One more question before you go, Mr. Douglass. You will give a speech entitled, 'What to the Slave Is the Fourth of July?' You first gave that speech over nine years ago." Charles looked down quickly at his notes. "Back in 1852...why bring it back out now?"

"Why? Because slavery still exists, my good man. That is why. That speech is all about how slavery violates our Constitution. It poses the question of why any slave should honor the birth of this nation. It has meant nothing to slaves other than having a more colorful oppressor. It is an outrage that the role of government would be to suppress a portion of the population, especially a government based on the precept that all men are created equal."

Frederick stepped back and nodded his head to the rather irksome Swellgood. "I feel I have a right to speak and speak strongly. And until we build the consensus needed in the legislature to revisit the slavery issue and abolish it once and for all, I will continue to give that speech. If I must, I will give it every day, over and over again until slavery is gone from this land. I hope that answers your question. Good day, Sir."

Charles was still jotting it down as the great man left.

The Hunt for Frederick Douglass
Terry Balagia

CHAPTER 9

RIP AND CADENCE were up early the next morning.

They started before sunrise on the main road from Richmond to Arlington. Rip rode Blade, with Cadence following in the buckboard pulled by Paint, now considerably lighter without the weight of the heavy iron cage.

"I picked up some reading material at the Richmond library." Cadence had several new books stacked under the bench seat in the wagon alongside his law books. "I told the nice lady I may have checked them out forever since we don't know when we are coming back. She said she trusts me. She said I have an honest face. Do you think I have an honest face, Rip?" As he reached for one of the books he had borrowed, Cadence waited for a response, which he knew would never come.

"I found this here book written by Frederick Douglass, himself. I figured we might want to read about him before we capture him." Cadence opened the book to the portrait of Frederick Douglass across from the book's title page. "He looks rather stern, if not downright ornery in this portrait. I wouldn't want to run into him in some dark alley. On second thought, we do want to run into him in some dark alley." Cadence smiled at his own cleverness.

"Near our horses," Rip added, always mindful of teaching the boy.

"Near our horses," Cadence repeated studiously. He scanned the pages, reading different passages. "Listen to this, Rip. He's got this one quote, 'One Man and God make a majority.' Sounds like

53

something you would say about a Texas Ranger. 'One Texas Ranger and God make a majority.'" Cadence looked over at Rip.

Rip repeated the phrase to himself, *One man and God make a majority. That does sound like Texas Ranger thinking.*

The first two days of the trip were uneventful, though the farther north they traveled, the more they sensed runaway slave activity. They heard bloodhounds howling on each of the first two nights, although they encountered no trouble. But on their final night on the road to Washington, with Rip handling the buckboard and Cadence out in front on horseback, that changed.

It was dark and windy as if a storm might come. Rip pulled down the brim of his hat to help shield himself from the wind as he held the reins on Blade, who was pulling the wagon. The slave patrols were out in force that night. Rip and Cadence could hear the bloodhounds howling in the distance, but closer than they had been the nights before.

At first, the howls were random and sporadic. It sounded like the dogs were all around them but off in the distance. Then, the direction of the howls changed, indicating that an escape had occurred at a nearby plantation. The sound of the dogs now came from a single point just west of them and approaching fast.

Cadence was getting riled up as the bloodhounds got nearer to them. But Rip remained unperturbed. He reminded himself that their job was no longer to hunt runaway slaves. Their job was to get to Washington D.C. by tomorrow early afternoon.

Suddenly, the flash of a body shot across the pale dirt road. It came on a diagonal from behind them, cutting across the road right in front of their wagon and into the tall dark grass on the other side. The lead pack of howling bloodhounds was right on the heels of the runaway, coming from the left. Out of reflex, Cadence took off after the runway. His cow pony was at full gallop in an instant.

The Hunt for Frederick Douglass
Terry Balagia

Rip screamed out after him, "Cadence, what are you doing! We are not slave-hunting!" But Cadence didn't hear him. He was already long gone. Rip rumbled down the road after him, pushing Blade as fast as she could go with the rickety buckboard.

Cadence caught up to the runaway in no time. He was a thin young boy, maybe twelve years old. Right then, the first two bloodhounds jumped the tall grass with their jaws wide open and tongues drooling.

The handcuffs on the runaway had an unusually long leash of lighter chain that trailed behind him as he ran for his life. Cadence reached down and grabbed the chain and pulled the young boy up onto his saddle as the lead dog arrived on the scene and leapt at him.

Cadence rode away quickly, the boy across his saddle. They were long gone by the time the rest of the hounds and the local slave patrol arrived.

Cadence knew how to shake trailing bloodhounds, or anyone for that matter. He learned and mastered the art from Rip, like Rip had learned it from the Cherokee. First, he traversed the creek several times in different places, confusing the dogs and confounding their scent. Then he rode along the middle of the creek for nearly a quarter mile. And as he came up onto the bank, he ripped a small patch off the young boy's britches and tossed it in the brush on the other side. Then, cutting his pony back across the road, did not stop riding until the sounds of the dogs grew faint and distant. Cadence could tell from the direction of howls that the slave patrol went the other way and was now lost. He circled back around and came to the same road farther down a ways.

He stopped on the side of the road and tossed the runaway onto the ground. He looked around to get his bearings and to figure out where Rip was. Cadence stuck a couple of fingers in his mouth and let out a piercing, loud shrill of a whistle that could be heard for miles. A sound Rip recognized.

"Rip, Bring the buckboard! I caught a runaway!"

Cadence dismounted and grabbed the irons on the young boy's wrists, securing him until Rip arrived. The boy shook violently, his system shocked with adrenaline and fear. Cadence pushed him to the ground and stood above him, putting his boot on the long leader of the chain extending from the manacles on the bloody wrists of the terrified little boy.

Suddenly a small, but proud woman stepped out from the shadows of the woods and walked brazenly up to Cadence. Cadence looked up. Seeing the small woman, he thought he had caught another runaway. He reached toward her.

"Are you with him?" he asked. The short, defiant woman stood there as determined as stone. She did not answer. Cadence tried again, grabbing her by the wrist and asking, "Who is your master?"

He barely finished the question. In one move, the small-framed woman reached down and grabbed the chain Cadence was standing on and pulled it up with such sudden force it knocked Cadence off his feet. She had the chain wrapped around his neck before he knew what was happening.

"My Master is Jesus Christ...and I don't see no sandals on your feet, cracker-boy!" she said through clenched teeth as she choked Cadence with the chain.

At that moment Rip arrived, frantically handling the wagon along the road while screaming curse words at Cadence for riding off on his own like that. He saw the small woman with the chain wrapped around Cadence's neck. Other traveling souls came out from the woods into the moonlight. There was a large group of them, all heading north.

The Hunt for Frederick Douglass
Terry Balagia

Rip heard someone call her Moses. At that, Rip turned to face her. He looked at her long and hard. He now realized who this woman. She was more legend than real. The runaways knew her as Moses because she was always leading her people to the promised land. But Rip knew of her by the name she took when she claimed her freedom—Mrs. Harriet Tubman. He also knew she was not someone to be messing with.

"Please accept our apologies, Mrs. Tubman. Cadence here meant no harm." Rip called out as he struggled to bring the wagon to a halt and simultaneously reached under the buckboard seat into the supply box. He brought out a 2-pound jute bag half-full of roasted coffee beans and offered it up. "I would appreciate it if you let up on the chain, Mrs. Tubman."

Harriet looked up at Rip, evaluating his sincerity. Satisfied, she nodded as one of her ladies cautiously accepted the coffee.

Harriet let go of the chain around Cadence's neck. He dropped to the ground and coughed until he got his breath back. Rip jumped off the wagon and tended to Cadence as he apologized and then thanked her. "I truly appreciate it, ma'am." As he helped Cadence to his feet he whispered sternly, "You messed up big time, Little Cade."

Cadence was still gathering his wits about him. "I would have gladly apologized if I wasn't busy being choked so hard," he mumbled back. Cadence looked over at Mrs. Tubman. "I apologize, Ma'am."

From the shadows, Rip could see nearly three dozen runaways she was leading through the woods to the northern states, then on to Canada.

A half dozen or so of her strong-armed men came over and stood menacingly around her.

The Hunt for Frederick Douglass
Terry Balagia

She stared fiercely at Rip. It was one of those moments that could have gone either way.

Then Rip noticed the manacles on the young runaway.

"If you give me one moment, I think I may have a key that might fit those wrist manacles." Rip walked to the back of the wagon and grabbed the ring of skeleton keys off his saddle.

Harriet did not respond. She showed an expressionless face on the outside, but inside she was praying one of Rip's keys would work. Rip returned with the keys. The young boy could only stare up at him. He was still terrified, but a huge wave of spirit flowed over him with the thought that the heavy irons may soon be gone. He had prayed for an angel to come and free him from the heavy iron cuffs and chain. He looked up at Rip and thought, *he does not look like what I expected an angel would look like.* He stared, confused as Rip tried one key after another, until one released the heavy iron cuffs. The little boy could not believe his eyes as they fell to the ground.

Harriet leaned over and rubbed the boy's bloody wrists. "He has been wearing those chains since we found him. Right neighborly for you to come along and to have a key to free him."

Rip grabbed the chains and tossed them into the back of the wagon, then lifted the young boy to his feet. Harriet's ladies immediately applied medicinal aid to the young boy's swollen wrists, wiping away the blood, applying aloe dressing, and wrapping them in eucalyptus leaves.

All the while Harriet looked long and hard at Rip. She saw his Texas Ranger badge and realized she knew of him. As they finished and prepared to leave, she looked at Rip one last time. "We will be keeping an eye on you, Ranger man," she warned him prophetically.

He nodded, acknowledging her comment. Then he looked over at her men. She waited a moment then casually instructed her men to stand aside, allowing Rip and Cadence to pass. The young boy, now wrapped in a blanket, took a long last look at Rip.

Rip and Cadence got the wagon back on the road, then sat and watched the desperate souls crossing in front on their unforgiving trek to the next stop along the Underground Railroad.

"They look so tired, don't they, Rip?"

Rip didn't respond. The two continued riding all night.

O' Great Spirit

Who made all races, look kindly upon the whole human family, and take away the arrogance and hatred which separates us from our brothers.

~ Cherokee Prayer

The Hunt for Frederick Douglass
Terry Balagia

CHAPTER 10

IT WAS ALMOST noon on the fourth day when Rip and Cadence arrived at the Long Bridge in Arlington, which crossed the Potomac River and connected Virginia to the District of Columbia. The midday sun heated the top of the lazy Potomac, causing a shroud of fog to rise up and engulf the massively long bridge as Rip and Cadence approached the guard gates on the Virginia side.

Rip handled the reins. He and Cadence sat on the bench seat with both horses hitched to the wagon as they rode up to the guards. Rip undid his diplomatic pouch and presented the transit voucher and letter of appointment at the White House along with the assorted other required items. As this was going on there was a small group of Virginia soldiers off to one side, one of whom heard Rip's name and came walking over. He told them he was from Tennessee.

"Limestone to be exact. The same town where Davy Crockett was born. I was wondering if I could shake hands with you, Captain Gatlin? If you don't mind." Rip obliged. As they shook hands, the Tennessean went on. "I can't believe I am meeting Rip Gatlin, the youngest soldier at the Alamo. Why, growing up all we ever heard were about the heroics of Davy Crockett and all the men around him, including yourself. Us young'uns dreamed of growing up and being like young Captain Gatlin. I never thought you was a real person." He stopped gushing long enough to turn to the other young soldiers as the handshake ended.

"From the time we was babies we were told how Rip Gatlin fought until the fall of the Alamo, when Colonel Crockett sent him out on a final perimeter patrol. Rip was from San Antone and knew

61

The Hunt for Frederick Douglass
Terry Balagia

all the alleyways, secret tunnels, and passages, to get in and out of the mission. So, Davy would send him out on reconnaissance. By the time Rip returned that last time, Santa Anna's men had already surrounded the mission and the final siege had begun." The young Tennessean turned to face Rip. "You was just a kid, we was told. Eighteen or so, right? Same age as us now. Anyway, I hear you sat there on your horse and watched in horror as the Alamo and all who occupied it were murdered."

They were all looking at him. "Just to clarify," Rip said to their eager faces, "I wasn't a captain back then. That came later. And Davy, I mean Colonel, Crockett's idea of reconnaissance was actually sending me out for whiskey and smoking tobacco." Rip could not repress the smile that came to his lips as he continued. "Turns out I was sweet on this little Mexican girl that coerced me into staying the night. If not for her and her sweet delights, I would have been barricaded in the Alamo the next morning with all the others." Rip looked at the young soldiers around him. He smiled at the twist of fate that saved his life. The young faces stared up at him.

It always made Rip uncomfortable remembering the Alamo and all those men and friends he had lost. "The siege had gone on for thirteen days," he went on. "It was a Saturday night. The next day would be the last day, Sunday. Truth be known, I think Colonel Crockett knew it was going to be the last night of the siege and that the next morning they would make the final attack.

"When he sent me out, he still had a full jug of corn mash. So, I asked him, 'But what if they attack in the morning?'

Crockett said, 'Then I guess you will miss it. In which case, do something bigger than yourself someday to make ol' Davy proud. Live your life like it is a story people will tell around a campfire. And tell it big.' That was the last thing Davy Crockett said to me. He laughed like he was making a joke, which he was always doing. But

62

that's what he said. I was convinced Colonel Crockett sent me out that night knowing I would come back too late and miss the final siege."

Rip wiped his eyes, something Cadence had never seen him do before. "I wish that I never met that little Mexican girl," he mumbled after a long pause. "I wish I had been there that morning and died with the rest of them." They were all struck silent.

The Tennessean continued his tale. The other soldiers turned back to him. They hung on his every word. "The way I heard was after that you rode off to join Sam Houston's army and took revenge at the battle of San Jacinto. I heard it said that Sam Houston credits Rip Gatlin with providing the scouting information that led to their victory that day." The young soldier turned back to look at Rip. "Yessir, Captain Rip Gatlin, the only man to survive the Alamo. At least that's how I heard it told."

When the young soldier from Tennessee was done, they all looked at Rip for a response.

But Rip did not comment on the fact or the myth of it all. "Well, that and a cup of coffee will get you a cup of coffee," Rip mumbled to their collected disappointment.

The guards raised the gate onto the Long Bridge and watched Rip and Cadence cross, leaving the South behind them.

As they rode across the Long Bridge, Cadence glanced up at Rip. He always knew Rip was someone people had heard about. When he was a boy, the nuns at the orphanage in San Antonio said many things about Rip to Cadence, but Cadence never thought to ask Rip himself.

"Was that all true about you and Governor Houston?"

"You mean, General Houston," Rip corrected. "Or at least that's how he is known to me. Mostly true, I suppose."

The Hunt for Frederick Douglass
Terry Balagia

"But why do you call him General Houston? He's governor, right?" Cadence was confused.

"Because when I first met Sam Houston," Rip explained, "it was at San Jacinto, just like that soldier back there said. And Sam was the general of the Army of the Republic of Texas. I was eighteen, or close to it. Like he said, I had just arrived from escaping that slaughter at the Alamo. As you can imagine, I was hungry, hurt, and scared." Rip looked at Cadence then back at the road. He continued.

"After the slaughter at the Alamo, I escaped up to the Brazos River and hid out from Santa Anna and his men for a week or so. Then I hightailed it to the Red River and stayed with the Cherokee for a dozen days or maybe twice that. I was lost after the massacre at the Alamo. Word got out that General Houston and the Texas Army were going to make a stand in the bayous around San Jacinto Bay. I rode nonstop from the Red River to San Jacinto in less than two days. I was still pretty shaken up over escaping the Alamo, and so turned around by the time I arrived at San Jacinto that I ended up riding right through the middle of Santa Anna's army's camp." Rip chortled. "And that's a fact." Rip laughed to himself as he handled the reins and watched to keep his horses steady on the swaying bridge.

"Now don't ask me why, but Santa Anna had his fifteen-hundred-man army camp on a field with a slight high ground in the middle of it that kept them from seeing over to the other side. It didn't matter they thought, because on the other side it was marsh, swamp, and thicket trees. Santa Anna figured no one in their right mind would camp in that." Halfway across the Long Bridge Rip looked over at Cadence. "No one except for General Houston and his eight hundred-man Texas army," Rip said, smiling proudly.

Cadence was suddenly all ears. "So, what did you do then?"

The Hunt for Frederick Douglass
Terry Balagia

"Well, when I finally made it to the Texas camp, they took me immediately to see General Houston. I told General Houston that the entire Mexican army was in siesta. I had heard the soldiers complaining that they had marched all night. And that they were so over-confident they hadn't even posted sentries. When I commented I had just walked my horse right through the middle of their encampment, the other commanders didn't believe me. 'It can't be true,' one of them said. I learned later that was Juan Seguin. One bad hombre. But you couldn't blame them. They had no idea who I was. Sam did not know me either. But Sam Houston and Colonel Crocket both had their roots in Tennessee and Sam Houston knew Davy Crockett very well, and he knew I had served directly under Colonel Crockett at the Alamo. And he knew Davy could read the quality of a man the way others could read a book.

"Anyway," Rip continued, "as General Houston listened to all of his commanders, he didn't once take his eyes off me. He told me later that I looked like I had just ridden back from Hell. I was trying to act tough on the outside, but Sam Houston could see how frightening it all had been for the eighteen-year-old me. He also recognized the Cherokee corn-beads I wore. Same as he had always worn. So he knew I had been initiated, just like him. When his commanders had finished arguing against me, General Houston turned and grabbed me by the shoulders and spoke to me in the Cherokee tongue, *"U-na-dv-ne-lv-di*," he said. I understood he meant *show me.*

"Together he and I went back the way I had come, right down a natural drainage ditch—a ravine—a real deep one, about ten feet deep that cut across the elevated field where Santa Anna's main army was camped. He could not believe it, but that ditch went right down the middle of Santa Anna's sleeping army. I was about to walk him all the way up the bloody thing. But he did not want to risk going any further."

The Hunt for Frederick Douglass
Terry Balagia

"'I've seen enough young man,' General Houston said to me. No one saw us or seemed to notice. Before we headed back to the men, General Houston grabbed me and asked me, 'What was your name again, soldier?'"

"I told him, 'Tommy Gatlin, General.' He told me, 'It's Captain Gatlin, from now on and as of this damn moment!' He threw me a hurried salute, to make it official." Rip looked at Cadence and grinned, remembering the fear of that day.

Cadence wondered why he never asked about the Alamo before. It was an amazing story, and he could not believe he had never heard Rip tell it. They were halfway across the Long Bridge, and Cadence hoped it would not end. He wanted to hear more.

"So, what happened next?" he asked.

"General Houston and I hustled back to the troops hidden in the woods and the swamp. Houston told them to mount up and prepare to make a surprise attack. He yelled out to Juan Seguin to take his men around to the east and get in position. He ordered Tommy Rusk to take his men around to the other side. He told Eddie Burleson to get his men and take them right up the middle position. And for the rest to follow Captain Gatlin—me—up the ditch."

Rip's eyes widened. "Well, I shit and froze at the same time when I heard him call my name. General Houston must have known how scared I was because I heard him call me again.

"'Captain Gatlin,' I heard him say. 'You will remember this day for the rest of your life!' he said. 'As will all of you. As I will remember the men slaughtered at Goliad. And at the Alamo. Those men were my friends. And I remember them all. I remember how they were treated by these soldiers laying in siesta right over that ridge. So, if any of you get scared out there today, just remember the men, our friends, at the Alamo and you will do just fine!'"

The Hunt for Frederick Douglass
Terry Balagia

"The men were so ginned up they were about to explode. The minute General Houston finished saying that someone yelled out, 'Remember the Alamo!' Someone else yelled, 'Remember Goliad!' Then we were all yelling as we poured over those sleeping troops. Some of them never knew what hit them." Rip looked over at Cadence. He grew suddenly serious and gloomy.

"Santa Anna killed all the Texans who surrendered at Goliad. Butchered them. Same as at the Alamo. If it had not been for General Houston, we would have done the same to them at San Jacinto. But he said, 'Remember boys, we are Texans, and we will hold Texans to a higher standard.'"

"As it was, we killed more than half of those men. We killed men in their sleep. Putting on their boots. Running for their guns. Running for their lives. Even swimming across the San Jacinto River. Like we were shooting turtles." Rip took a deep breath and looked away as he said the last part as if turning his head would move the image out of his mind's eye. "I don't think I have ever seen so much killing in all my life, Little Cade."

Rip took a breath, and his eyes and his attention returned to the bridge road they were crossing. He looked back at Cadence.

"Keep in mind, we were out-numbered over two to one. We didn't know how it would turn out. We were scared to death and had no idea we would completely overrun the Mexican troops. But we did. And that was the Battle of San Jacinto, where the Republic of Texas was born. Imagine that." Rip rubbed his chin, his eyes lost in the memory. He looked back at Cadence and then at the road ahead.

"After the battle, the General had a bad leg wound and they laid him out as comfortable as they could make him, under this giant oak tree. He called me over and had me bend down so he could say it in my ear, 'Thomas, an angel sent you to me this morning. Do you realize that son? You done mighty good out there today. Mighty good.' Since then, Houston has been a president, a senator, and a governor—twice. Throughout it all, I keep calling him General. It always seems to fit. And to this day he keeps calling me Thomas."

By the time Rip finished telling his story, the two men had arrived on the other side of the Long Bridge. They were now in the North, where at any minute they could be arrested and shot as spies for what they were about to attempt. Now they had to figure out how to arrest Frederick Douglass and get back across that bridge before the night's end—and before anyone found out.

CHAPTER 11

ON THE NORTHERN side of the Long Bridge, Rip and Cadence were greeted by a solitary Union soldier. They showed their credentials, and he let them pass. The next stop would be the White House at the end of Pennsylvania Avenue.

The Capitol building was in clear view, showing off the gigantic steel skeleton where the dome would eventually sit when it was finished. Cadence had never seen a building so big. Off to the south toward the Potomac, he and Rip could see sticking up from the ground, the first 150 feet or so of what would become the monument to George Washington. Cadence could only imagine how tall it would be when it was finished. The buildings were grand sights to behold. Cadence's eyes were as big as saucers. *Who thinks of these things?* he wondered.

"It certainly has grown since I was here last." Rip looked around, trying to remember his way to the Willard Hotel. He remembered there was a stable nearby. Rip guided Cadence farther up Pennsylvania Avenue toward the White House and eventually found the Willard Hotel and the stables.

Rip brought the wagon into the Cavender Livery Stable and Saddle Company. He barked orders before he even pulled and latched the hand brake.

"Tighten the hound braces and grease the wheels and the undercarriage." Two stable hands immediately began unlatching Blade and separating her from the buckboard. They unsaddled the horses and gave both animals a quick combing, as Rip hopped out and walked a complete circle around the wagon, checking each wheel housing along the way.

"Check the grease reservoir in the wheel boxing. I could hear a chuckle in the axles, sliding back and forth when we were on the road," Rip told the master blacksmith. He nodded and put a second team on their wagon.

Rip turned to Cadence. "Stay here with the wagon. And make sure my girl gets some good attention. It'll be another hard few days on her when we leave."

Rip had them saddle a fresh livery horse, took the courier pouch, headed back out to Pennsylvania Avenue, turned right, and rode the two blocks to the White House.

The guards at the gate checked Rip's courier credentials. They took Rip's guns, held his horse, and asked him to wait there. Two minutes later, a Senate page came out and escorted Rip to the side entrance under the White House portico. There was a small desk inside the door with a US marshal sitting behind it. A Marine stood guard at perfect, unflinching attention beside the desk. The marshal asked Rip for his credentials. As Rip presented his courier pouch and medallion, he looked around at the spectacular surroundings.

It looks like a nice place to visit, but I wouldn't want to be the guy who lives here, Rip surmised.

A US Marshal gave Rip's credentials back and handed him a letter. "This came from the Office of the Governor of Texas for you, Captain Gatlin. We were told to hold it for your arrival." He handed an envelope to Rip. Rip looked at it, then slid it into his coat pocket, making a mental note to have Cadence read it to him later.

"Much obliged," he said to the marshal.

The marshal nodded. "They are sending someone for you," he said. Minutes later, a second White House page approached Rip and said, "Follow me."

Rip followed as the page took him back outside through the kitchen exit. They walked along a path through the grass to the Department of War building behind the White House. The page walked him down to the dark, damp basement. "This is where President Lincoln spends most of his time," the page told him as they wound down the stairwell. Rip could see the cement floor of the basement below them.

The page explained that the White House telegraph office was not located in the White House. "It is here in the basement of the Department of War building." The intern looked up and behind himself as he spoke to Rip.

"Since the inauguration, President Lincoln has been spending almost all his time here." The intern shrugged his shoulders. "He reads every one of the telegraphs from his generals." All the Union generals were busy preparing for war in all parts of the Union, the young man explained, a war that was looking more and more inevitable. "The President is especially eager to hear any word from Major Robert Anderson, the general in charge of Fort Sumter off the coast of Charleston," the page concluded. Rip nodded that he understood.

The page left Rip on a wooden bench down in the basement and told him someone would be right with him. He took Rip's credentials and walked halfway down the hall to another young man standing outside the door to the telegraph room. *He must be one of Lincoln's secretaries*, Rip thought. The page handed Rip's credentials to him then continued down the hallway toward the other end of the building and left. Lincoln's secretary looked through the papers, glanced down the hall at Rip sitting on the bench, and disappeared abruptly into the telegraph room.

The Hunt for Frederick Douglass
Terry Balagia

Chapter 12

Rip's instructions were to hand the letter from Davis directly to Lincoln, so he continued to wait. After a short time, Lincoln came out of the telegraph room. Rip saw his tall, erect figure down the hallway. The President's secretary, John Hay, stood next to him. Lincoln looked at his secretary and said something. John Hay nodded, then handed Rip's credentials to the President. Lincoln looked at them, then came walking down the hallway toward Rip, who stood up as Lincoln approached and gave him a soft handshake.

"What was it like, the Alamo?" Lincoln, the history buff, asked Rip right off as he handed Rip's credentials back to him.

"The truth, Sir?" Rip wanted to be careful with his words.

"Yes, please—the truth," Lincoln urged.

"It was terrifying," Rip confided, "I was scared shitless most of the time."

Lincoln looked Rip up and down as he nodded.

"Yes. I imagine you were." Lincoln motioned to the bench and said, "Please." He waited for Rip to sit, then he sat down on the bench alongside him.

"I understand Sam Houston is a mentor of sorts of yours. Good man, Sam. He made a great senator while he was here. He wrote me a note saying to expect you and he spoke very highly of you."

Rip looked up at the erect posture and imposing presence of President Lincoln and tried his best at smiling back. Then he asked,

"Now if you don't mind me asking, sir, what's it like being President?"

Lincoln looked at him as if he were about to say something profound. His look of sternness slowly morphed into a big smile that took over his entire face. "Why, I'm scared shitless, too!" he said as he let out a loud laugh that echoed down the mostly deserted hallway.

Rip took the envelope containing the letter from President Davis out of the courier pouch and handed it to President Lincoln. Lincoln wrestled with opening the envelope, then slowly read aloud the letter President Davis had written to him. When he finished, President Lincoln held the letter to his chest, then leaned way back on the bench and closed his eyes for a minute or two.

Then Lincoln sat up and turned the letter over. He wrote something on the back of it and said to Rip, "Take this back to Jeff Davis. Let's see what he decides to do." Lincoln finished writing the short note and handed it to Rip. "What do you think?" Lincoln asked him.

Rip looked at it. It was one sentence. He stared at it as if he were reading. Then he looked up at President Lincoln. "It's good, Mr. President." Lincoln looked askance at Rip and nodded.

Good, Rip thought to himself, pleased that the president could not tell he did not know how to read.

Rip slipped the note into the courier pouch and was escorted back outside to where his horse was waiting. He buckled his gun belt and mounted his horse. The ruse part of the mission was complete.

They had succeeded so far...they had maintained their cover as couriers and completed the first part of the job. But the real purpose of the mission would start now. It was the night Frederick Douglass was speaking. Rip still did not have a plan. He and Cadence would

74

have to figure it out as they went. They had to find some way to arrest Frederick Douglass and get back across the Potomac before the night's end.

The Hunt for Frederick Douglass
Terry Balagia

CHAPTER 13

WHEN HE ARRIVED back at the Cavender Livery Stable and Saddle Company, the wagon was not yet ready. He told Cadence to saddle up Paint and Blade and they both rode the five blocks to Ford's Theater.

They went down to 10th Street and saw a large crowd moving up the sidewalks toward the theater's entrance. It was just before sunset, and a crowd gathered in the street in front of the theater. The day's closing speeches planned for later in the evening would conclude with that of Frederick Douglass.

On their way to the theater, Rip and Cadence slow-walked their horses down the wide street, through the lavishly dressed and lively foot traffic. A big banner draped down from the roof covered the entire front of the building. Cadence looked up and read the banner aloud.

"Georgetown Ladies' Anti-Slavery Society Speaker Series sponsored by the Liberator Weekly Journal Presents Frederick Douglass' What to The Slave Is The Fourth of July?'"

They rode past Ford's Theater to the alleyway that ran alongside it. They headed down the alley past the side door to the theater and proceeded to the huge livery stable and barn behind it. The entire time, Rip looked around the street and the large and growing crowd. He was trying to think of a plan to capture Frederick Douglass. The tricky thing would be getting him alone somewhere, out of the public's view. Rip had hoped that the crowd for tonight would be a lot smaller, but the sidewalks and streets were packed.

The Hunt for Frederick Douglass
Terry Balagia

People flowed down the sidewalks from all directions. The crowd was mixed—some affluent and professional Black freemen, but mostly White townsfolk, socialites, politicians, and their staff.

The speeches had been going on all day, with the biggest names coming on at the end.

Frederick Douglass was a celebrity of significance among the White intelligentsia in Washington. He was the unanimous choice to headline the event and give the final speech. People who would not dream of coming during the day were now out on the town in their fanciest clothes for the chance to be seen with or near the famous Frederick Douglass.

Rip and Cadence tied their mounts up inside of the livery stable right down the alleyway from the Ford Theater. They walked back up the alley along the side of the theater toward 10th Street and the theater's front entrance.

There were autograph seekers near the side door of the theater; an entire group of them. Rip and Cadence had seen nothing like it before. Grown women and some men who had purchased his book or copies of Douglass' newspaper were holding them out and waving them, hoping to get Frederick Douglass to sign his name on whatever it was. They came with pencils, ink pens and portable inkwells. Some even had those new-fangled fountain pens. Rip had no reference for people asking for a signature.

"I think I read somewhere they call them autographs," Cadence shook his head, then chortled. "It makes no sense to me." He looked over at Rip. He was smiling, too. Cadence laughed. "City-folk are strange aren't they, Rip?"

There were abolitionists out in front of Ford's Theater, dressed in traditional Quaker clothing. The men in their large black hats, big bow ties, and heavily starched collars, and the women in their simple skirts of black cotton and wool, with silk collar trim and black Quaker bonnets. There was another group in front of the Ford made up mostly of women. They were holding signs and protesting with chants and songs and blocking most of the street traffic. A pair of constables came and broke them up. Rip could not read what was written on the signs. He couldn't tell whether they were celebrating the fact Frederick Douglass was speaking here tonight or protesting against it. Or if they *were* protesting, whether they were protesting on a matter altogether different.

The Hunt for Frederick Douglass
Terry Balagia

CHAPTER 14

RIP AND CADENCE went inside the theater to get away from the more raucous street crowd, though inside it was noisy, too. It was smoky, as well. There was a circus-like atmosphere in the lobby where booze and food were available for sale. A man near the front door holding tickets called out, "Get your good seats right here!" Another man who looked a lot like him at the base of the stairs called out, "Balcony, front row seats, right here!" The din was deafening.

The crowd inside the theater was more elegant in appearance and general decorum, though every bit as loud. It was made up equally of men and women—some as couples, some grouped by gender. The way they were dressed was so elegant. Cadence had seen nothing like it before. He thought, *the way they are dressed makes them different from myself, as if there are better versions of people than me.*

A guy stood behind a small table near the main door to the theater with a giant stack of *Douglass' Monthly newspapers.* Cadence walked over and picked one up, considered it momentarily, then bought it. He looked over at Rip, who was across the crowded lobby. Cadence held the *Monthly* up and grabbed a pencil from the clerk, mocking the autograph seekers they had seen out in front of the theater. It made Rip smile, which was not an easy thing to do. Cadence laughed as he handed the pencil back to the clerk and thanked him.

Before the speeches began, Cadence followed Rip back outside Ford's Theater for some air. He used the opportunity to quickly run down the alley to the livery stable where their horses were tied and stuff the monthly newspaper into his saddlebag. Then he stopped and stood still and quiet. He heard voices in the huge dark enclosed barn-like structure. He looked back into the shadows but could see nothing. He thought he had heard children's voices. Cadence grew quiet and still and listened again but heard nothing. He assumed it was his imagination. He turned and left.

Rip was waiting for Cadence in the alley. He stood near the steps to the side door of the Ford Theater, looking around and trying to find an advantage in the location. Rip had hoped for a road nearby for a fast getaway, but there wasn't one. His brow furrowed as he reached for the tobacco pouch in his vest. Cadence came back from the barn to join him.

Rip looked down at him.

"There may be a big war coming soon, compadre. That's why I am so eager to be done with Virginia and get back to Texas. Do you agree?"

"Sure, Rip. I'm with you. I'm all for getting back to Texas, pronto," Cadence responded with a nod.

"I don't want us to be anywhere near here when it starts. I figure Texas is so big, we can go out to West Texas or up in the panhandle where this war will never reach."

"But ain't that all Cherokee country? Isn't that where you and Sam Houston went to live?"

"It is Cherokee country, but I would much prefer living with Cherokee than living with White men, Cadence. Cherokees make sense when they talk. And they keep their word. You can trust a Cherokee. White men lie." Rip smiled as if to himself. "White Elk explained the discrepancy between the Cherokee and the White man is the White man believes he has privileges, while the Cherokee assumes he has duties. Big difference, kid."

Cadence stared up at him. "I think you live that way, Rip. To me you exemplify that view of life."

"I appreciate that, Kid. Though I must disagree with your conclusion. We can discuss that another time along with your future...oh shit, that reminds me...I almost forgot.

Rip suddenly stopped himself mid-sentence and patted his vest pockets, careful not to spill any tobacco from his pouch, as he felt around. He reached inside his vest and took out the letter the US Marshal handed him at the White House earlier.

"This came from General Houston's office. Read it for me will you, Son?" Rip handed an envelope to Cadence. "They were holding it for me at the White House and I pert near forgot about it."

Cadence opened it, took out a letter with a short note attached to it, and proceeded to read aloud to Rip. "I told you I would get it done, Thomas!—Sam."

"If it's what I think it is," Rip told him, "the letter is for you. It's from..."

Cadence looked at the letter, finishing Rip's sentence. "...the office of the commandant at West Point. 'Dear sir, you have been recommended by the governor of Texas for a seat in this coming fall semester entering class of 1861.'" Silence filled the space around him as Cadence read the rest of the letter to himself.

"It was part of my deal with General Houston to escort the convoy up here. He was pleased to do it, too. He said you will do very well at the Point," Rip explained.

Cadence was speechless. He read the letter a second time. He stood still as it sunk in. "I didn't know you had asked the general for this, Rip. I don't know what to say."

"I think you say 'yes,'" Rip offered.

"I'm accepted to West Point?" Cadence slapped the side of his head. "This is more than I could have ever asked for." He looked at Rip with tears in his eyes. "But what about you? What will you do

83

without me around?" Cadence asked, chewing on his lower lip. Rip looked down at him.

"I'll be back in Austin, and you can come back when you graduate. Assuming a war don't start," Rip said as he took off his hat. He reached his fingers behind the inner hatband and took out a small stack of rolling papers. He peeled one sheet off the stack, then put them back in his hatband. He grabbed a pinch of tobacco and gingerly measured it with his eyes as he spread it across the tiny sheet of rolling paper with his nimble-fingered hands.

Holding the letter, Cadence asked, "Would that make you proud of me, Rip? If I were to go to West Point?"

Rip looked at him with his face contorted in a foul expression. "Now what kind of huckleberry question is that? This has got nothing to do with me, Cadence. This is all about you. I wish it were about me."

"I would love to have the kind of education and future you are going to have, Cade. This is going to open worlds for you. Why, Son, with an education like that, you can go on to do anything you can dream of. It will change everything for you. At one time, it would have changed everything for me."

"How do you figure?" Cadence looked over at him.

Rip did not have to think twice. The words came right out of his mouth, but in a soft voice, as if he were saying them to himself. "I would have been a better man."

"What do you mean, Rip? You are a great man."

"No, Son. I'm not a great man. Why, there is very little that's even good about me. Great men don't do the things I have done in my life, Cadence."

"You're a Texas Ranger."

"No matter. I'm not a great man. Now, I have been around some great men. Sam Houston, he's a great man. He could inspire men to ride their horses into bullets. Colonel Davy Crockett was a living legend. I swear if I had seen him fly through the air, it would not have surprised me. I will add Jim Bowie to any man's list of great men because he gave his life on that final day at the mission. He also gave me his knife." Rip reminiscently fondled the hilt of the Bowie knife on his belt.

"I met another great man just today," Rip was talking more than he usually would. "President Lincoln. That man has greatness in him, as sure as a rattlesnake's got venom."

"But me? I am not a great man. But I sure know greatness in men when I see it." Rip looked away down the pedestrian-filled streets of downtown Washington, D.C, then turned back to Cadence and continued.

"Now, Jeff Davis is not my cup of tea, but some consider him to be of great intellect. But having a great intellect does not make you a great man. You have to do great things with it. But none of that is me. I don't have any of that." Rip finished and looked down, emoting a certain melancholy.

"Now your pa, he was a great man." Rip looked over at Cadence and saw his eyes grow wide and happy.

"Really, Rip?" Cadence lit up from the inside like someone pulled the tarp off of the lantern in his belly and suddenly his eyes exploded with light. This was not missed by Rip.

"Yessir. Big Cade had it all," Rip continued.

"Do you think my pa would be proud of me?" Cadence was hanging on Rip's every word.

The Hunt for Frederick Douglass
Terry Balagia

"Well, of course. He gave you his name, didn't he? He called you Little Cade. He called himself Big Cade. I'd say he was immensely proud of you, Kid."

"Tell me how he was great, Rip. Would you put him on the same list as Lincoln?" Cadence inquired.

"Definitely. Big Cade would be right up there with President Lincoln and Sam Houston. That's what I would say." Rip brought his attention back to the cigarette he was rolling.

"You *know* what my words would be." Cadence lifted his chin as he spoke. "I would say you are at the very top of my list of great men I have met, Rip."

Rip smiled. "I appreciate that, Little Cade. Though you are not so little anymore, are you?" Rip reached into his hat behind the inside hatband and took out a match.

"Do you think my pa would have been a better man if he had gone to West Point, Rip?" Cadence looked up at him with eager eyes.

"He didn't need it, kid. Like I said, your father, Big Cade, he had it all." Rip reached over to strike the match on the red brick wall of Ford's theater. His hand stopped midair.

CHAPTER 15

SUDDENLY, THE SIDE door of the Ford Theater burst open. Some of Washington, DC's most prominent White—and Negro—civic and political leaders stepped out of the smoke-filled theater into the side alley to congregate in the fresh air.

Rip and Cadence unexpectedly found themselves in the middle of this high-brow, high-society world. They wore their dusty trail clothes while the other men were dressed in evening clothes. Some were drinking. They milled around, all talking simultaneously.

The door opened a second time and more of Washington's most influential men stepped out to partake in the pleasant night air and the stimulating discussion and politicking. There was the abolitionist William Lloyd Garrison, who was here to speak, as was Secretary of State William Seward. With him was Senator Stephen Douglas, the man who had just recently lost the election to Abraham Lincoln. The exclusive grouping continued to spill out the side door of the theater, pushing the previous conglomeration further into the darkness of the alley.

Rip was oblivious to the elite crowd surrounding him. All except for one of them. Caught up in this mass of great minds Rip recognized the one he was here to see, looking like the picture in the book Cadence had shown him. Cadence noticed him, too.

The crowd jostled Rip and he dropped his match. He was about to grab another one when Cadence nudged him. Rip looked up to see Frederick Douglass walking toward them. He stopped about six feet from them and noticed Rip and Cadence in their dusty, worn trail gear.

The Hunt for Frederick Douglass
Terry Balagia

Frederick acknowledged Cadence with a nod of his head. Cadence nodded back. He saw Rip about to light a match for his cigarette and took another step or two toward him. As Rip was trying to think up a way to approach this man, he suddenly found the man advancing toward him. Here he was, face to face with Frederick Douglass. When he looked into his eyes, he could see into the man, as the man could see into him.

"Excuse me, Friend, would you be so kind as to allow me to use the light from your match?" Frederick asked him. Rip was caught off guard. He took the hand-rolled from between his lips and offered it to the man, thinking he was asking for a smoke.

"No, just the light," Frederick clarified. "So, I can see my notes."

Rip looked down and saw the man was holding his speech and a pencil in his large hands. He then looked into the face of Frederick Douglass. Frederick stared back. He stood several inches taller than Rip, with shoulders every bit as broad.

Just then the side door reopened, and the group filed back into the theater.

As they moved back inside, Rip stepped in closer to Frederick and lit a match for him. The men continued to file back inside as Douglass made last-minute pencil marks on his notes from the light cast by Rip's match. Cadence noticed this interaction between Rip and Douglass, and he moved in a little closer. By now the men were mostly all back inside and the three of them were left outside, alone.

Rip looked up and down the side alley. There was a moment when everything suddenly went silent. For only a brief instant it seemed like the world was suddenly deserted. Cadence felt it too. There was no one around. He slowly reached down and silently pulled back the hammer back on his Colt revolver.

The Hunt for Frederick Douglass
Terry Balagia

Rip sized up Frederick Douglass. He was a tall and imposing man. He would be hard to bring down. The horses were all the way down the alley. If they could just get him to head in that direction, it would improve their prospects of pulling this off.

Both Rip and Cadence moved in closer. The match in Rip's hand grew dim. Rip moved in further as Douglass made the final tweaks to his speech. The match threw off its last spark of light, then went out.

With a quick nod, Frederick Douglass folded his notes, stuffed them in his coat pocket, thanked Rip, turned up the stairs, entered through the side door of Ford's Theater...and was gone.

The Hunt for Frederick Douglass
Terry Balagia

CHAPTER 16

"**DAMMIT, RIP, THAT** was it! We could have had him!" Cadence complained in a hushed, but urgent tone the minute Frederick was gone. "Hell, Rip, it seemed like the perfect time. You should have made a move. You should have pulled your gun out and arrested him. Right then and there."

"Are you crazy, kid?" But Rip was already thinking about each moment that had transpired. No, it was not the right moment. Their horses were at the livery at the other end of the alley. Had Frederick Douglass struggled, and they had to assume he would, they could never drag him the length of the alley without attracting a crowd. They had to be near the horses.

They had not even picked up the wagon yet. It was across town at Cavender's Livery Stable. Rip knew they needed the wagon with them. That way, they could secure him and get him across the Long Bridge into Virginia before anyone realized what was going on. This was not the right time, nor the place. But it would come. Rip looked around as Cadence continued to second-guess their move. Or lack of a move.

"It just seemed like the perfect moment." Cadence showed his frustration. "It was suddenly so quiet, and no one was around. Didn't you feel it, Rip? You are always telling me how you can sense things that others don't. Well, that's how I feel now about what just happened to you. It's like you lost your nerve or went soft or something."

The Hunt for Frederick Douglass
Terry Balagia

But Rip was busy wondering what they would do for the hour or so before Frederick Douglass went on stage to speak. Rip looked at Cadence and realized how off-balance the young man was. Then looking around he noticed the activity in front of the Senator Hotel across the way. The lobby bar at the Senator Hotel was the finest tavern in all of DC.

"Come with me." Rip grabbed Cadence by the arm and led him across the way to the type of establishment Cadence had never had the nerve, nor the opportunity to enter. Once there, Rip planned to order a steak dinner for himself and exposing Cadence to some female company—his first ever.

They went across the street and down half a block to the Tavern at the Senator Hotel. Cadence's eyes widened as they went through the swinging doors and entered the loud, smoky, exclusive saloon. Full of Washington's finest. Rip dragged him across the crowded floor and immediately took a table near the bar.

Cadence could not stop his eyes from growing. He was mesmerized by the atmosphere, by the women, by the way they were dressed...the way they acted. They were aggressive, approaching the men with a confidence he had never seen before. And the smell of flowers and perfumes filled the air around them, exciting his senses. Admittedly, Cadence's experience being around women was mostly limited to the nuns who raised him at the orphanage. The women here seemed nothing like the nuns. He was uneasy. But he loved the excitement of it.

"You can eat afterward." Rip had to shout in Cadence's ear to be heard above the noise. "Believe me, you will have a big appetite when you are finished."

Cadence was not sure what Rip was referring to nor what would happen to him. Their table was near the corner, with the entire bar in front of them. The women working there were a combination of waitresses, attendants, or hostesses who would dance and sing for pay, or simply entertain you with their exuberance. There were also some of Washington, DC's most prominent high-end sex workers walking the room. Their combined presence intended to sell more drinks to the upscale DC lawyers, businessmen, government contractors and the numerous hope-to-be's, plus congressional staffers and clerks—and it often worked. Together it made for a hormone-charged atmosphere for Cadence. He was as scared as he was excited. And as excited as he was scared.

Rip wasted little time. He saw a more mature woman standing near the bar and motioned for her to come over. He wanted someone with experience, knowing Cadence was new at this and may need some added instruction or special attention. She saw Rip wave and immediately sashayed over to him. Rip stood up and slapped Cadence in the back of the head to do the same. He flinched from the slap and slowly stood.

"Good evening, ma'am, my name is Rip Gatlin, and this is my young friend, Cadence."

The attractive, heavy-set woman gave Rip a controlling smile and shook his hand. "So nice to make your acquaintance, Rip Gatlin." She smiled at Cadence. "My name is April St. Germaine. I run this place. Please make yourselves at home and let me know what your pleasure is this evening. And please sit down." The two men sat back down.

"I know what I want," Rip did not hesitate. "My pleasure will be the thickest steak you got and a couple of whiskeys. As for Cadence here, his pleasure is going to be of a somewhat different ilk, if you know what I mean. And he may require a more experienced hand, if you will."

April smiled in approval and eyed Cadence up and down like he was a stick of dried meat while chewing on one of her fingernails. Rip took out a couple of silver dollars from his belt pocket.

The Hunt for Frederick Douglass
Terry Balagia

Cadence stopped him. "Rip, what are you doing?" he said nervously. "What are you talking about?" Cadence turned to the woman standing by their table. "No, ma'am, I'm sorry. I am not interested. Thank you for your time, though." Cadence pulled on Rip's arm. Rip laughed loudly and slapped Cadence on the back. Cadence was finding all this incredibly humiliating. Rip turned to address April.

"He does not realize what he is missing, Miss April." Rip politely extended his hand out to her again. She clasped his hand with hers and smiled lovingly at Rip.

As Rip was making a friend, Cadence looked around and spotted a girl that looked younger than he was. She had yellow-blonde hair done up in ringlets with a red ribbon that matched her fancy red velvet gown and her stunning crimson lips. She was talking with two gentlemen at the bar. Cadenced noticed their expensive tailcoats and top hats, typical *Washington, DC types*, he thought. He knew he couldn't compete with those kinds of folks. But he couldn't help imagining as he stared at her. He could not stop himself. As she talked, Cadence stared a hole right through her. *She's so beautiful*, he thought. *Perhaps the most beautiful girl I've ever seen.*

She noticed and smiled back.

Cadence looked away nervously. Then he looked back. The next minute, she left the conversation at the bar with the two lobbyists and made a beeline for the table where Cadence and Rip were sitting. Cadence saw her coming, and his eyeballs grew so wide he felt like they might pop out of his head and roll across the sawdust-covered floor.

"Lydia Lee," she said, extending her hand practically into Cadence's face. He could barely react; he was frightened to death. She picked up his hand for him and shook it, grinning broadly.

The Hunt for Frederick Douglass
Terry Balagia

"You gentlemen mind me disturbin' you?" She combined this with the most incredible smile Cadence had ever seen. *The word disturbin' seems too unpleasant a word to be coming out of such a beautiful mouth*, he thought. Cadence was gobsmacked. Staring at her was as blinding as staring directly into the Texas sun in the middle of summer at twelve noon.

Rip did not notice. He was too busy watching April as she commandeered the next steak dinner coming out of the kitchen and directed it toward their table. When it got there, Rip moved over to the empty table adjacent to theirs, leaving Cadence and Lydia alone.

"You are on your own now," he whispered to Cadence as he slid his seat, "Be sure to tell her you got accepted to West Point," Rip said with a smile. "Women love a man with a plan," he said as he devoured the steak in front of him.

Cadence was numb. He could not form a word. His jaw dropped, and he could only sit there and stare at this gorgeous blonde, smiling girl...with sky-blue eyes and red lips that matched a red ribbon, which hung down between her powdered-white breasts. He was frozen. *The world just stopped. So has my heart*, he thought. At least it seemed that way. Cadence thought he might pass out. But he couldn't—he didn't want to miss a single second of being with Lydia.

Lydia was in her element when men stared at her. *She even talks beautifully*, Cadence thought as he listened. Her hands flitted and flirted in harmony with her sing-song voice. It went up high and then it ran back down lyrically as if the words she spoke were notes on a musical scale.

She smiled and suddenly Cadence believed his heart had stopped beating. Lydia flashed another smile and his heart started up again. It was a form of teasing, like one might flash a black ace of spades in a game of five-card stud.

The Hunt for Frederick Douglass
Terry Balagia

"Just so you know, I'm not one of those *Shady Ladies;* if that's what your fancy is, you got the wrong girl. So feel free to pick another. I'm just here to dazzle you with my charms." Lydia smiled and posed for a second as if she were on a stage. And in Cadence's eyes she was. "I make a percentage off what you spend. So spend up, Mister!" She leaned over and nudged him with her elbow, grinning playfully like a guy might do. But she was so girlie and feminine at the same time. Cade quickly ordered a beer.

"Plus, Miss April gives me a room to live in upstairs. I'm also the house seamstress. Not officially or anything, but that's what I do. That and trying to get men like you to order more drinks." She shot him that smile again. "I'm a little new at this but I'm getting better. So, what do you think of me so far?" She teased him as she smiled and held that pose.

Cadence was in a trance. He did not know what to make of the most enchanting girl he had ever laid eyes on. She was talking and smiling and touching him in ways he had never imagined. But to a knowing eye, she was a cat toying with a baby mouse. Her paws were her smiles, her eyes were her swats. Her touches assaulted his shoulder, brushed against his leg, and made him feel all at once excited, scared, and exhausted. Meanwhile, the look in her eyes said she would swallow him whole.

"So, aren't you going to tell me your name?" Lydia Lee asked.

Cadence had to think for a second, and responded, "It's Cadence," though he could barely remember himself.

"Do you mean like in music? The rhythm? You see. I took piano as a kid." She smiled and he was sure his pulse skipped a beat. "There are the notes, then there is the rhythm, or the tempo."

The Hunt for Frederick Douglass
Terry Balagia

Cadence did not know what she was talking about and was too entranced to figure it out. "I don't know much about musical things; I just know it as my name."

"All right, then. Nice to meet you, Cadence." They shook hands again. Only this time as she said his name there was something familiar about the way it rolled around her mouth. As if she had said his name a million times before. Though she had never even heard of it before this night.

At the same time Cadence looked into her eyes and seemed to lose his train of thought, but then recovered enough to ask her, "What should I call you, Lydia Lee?"

How about you call me yours? Lydia thought, and the feeling surprised her. In her six-months of working the floor she had never experienced a connection with the men who frequented the place. Admittedly, Cadence appeared different from the usual clientele. He was dressed differently, having just come off the trail. And smelled different. And sitting with him in this moment somehow made her feel different. But she wouldn't dare say it. One beer led to another and another yet, again.

Rip looked over at Cadence enraptured with Lydia and felt confident that he would be pre-occupied for the evening. Rip smiled and ordered two double whiskeys with shaved ice, which was his version of dessert. These he downed with sheer indulgence. Gatlin paid the waitress for the meal, plus added a five-dollar gold piece for Miss April and for Cadence's new friend. Rip wiped his mouth and his teeth and finally headed back over to Ford's Theater, just as Frederick Douglass was about to come on stage to speak.

Cadence saw Rip stand up and head for the door and thought, *it seems like a good time for me to do the same. I best be leaving now.*

The Hunt for Frederick Douglass
Terry Balagia

Though he did not want to. Though he had no place to go for now. But he was in an unknown territory without Rip being around. So, Cade reluctantly stood up and reached over to grab his hat off the table next to Lydia. As he did, it brought his face close to hers. He turned toward her. His face inches away. It seemed like she moved in even closer, and then he heard her whisper so softly he thought perhaps he imagined it.

"Aren't you going to kiss me goodnight?"

He was acutely aware of the soft presence of her breath in his face, and the spider thin blonde hairs that tickled and beguiled his cheeks, pulling him closer to her. He had never kissed a girl before. He had barely ever even seen it done. Cadence was terrified. But it was the kind of terror he suffered jumping off the cliff into the water at Hamilton's pool. Or the first time he rode a bull at a rodeo.

He did not know where it came from, nor what to do with it, nor what to make of the giant feeling that swelled up inside his chest, shortening his breath and causing him to lean into her further, yet ever so slightly. When he felt her hot breath in the inside of his mouth and their lips touched, Cadence left this world in a way that he could never have imagined. He was sure he'd gotten sucked up in a giant twister or maybe caught in a mud slide on the banks of the Colorado. It was wet and slippery and thrilling all at once and grew in velocity at a great and growing rate until he spun out of control into her welcoming arms.

On that first night it was true that the inexperienced youth knew nothing about what they were doing. Lydia knew everything. But she had never known a kiss to disarm her the way she felt with Cadence. She may have done it all before. But she realized in that moment she had never been alive to it all before. Nor felt it at all.

For Cadence, it was like someone lit a bonfire in his heart, and there was so much kindlin' and dry wood it torched him inside and out. He thought his heart would explode several times that first time they found themselves in bed together. It was like riding a wild feral mustang bareback through a West Texas thunderstorm.

Meanwhile, Rip spent his time in a different pursuit...one named Frederick Douglass. But by the time he crossed back over the street to the Ford Theater it looked like Rip was too late.

The Hunt for Frederick Douglass
Terry Balagia

CHAPTER 17

THE DOORS OF Ford's theater were about to close. The front of the theater was mobbed by others also hoping to get in. Rip got through the outer doors and into the lobby, but not much further.

The place was thick with the gathering of people. Half of them were looking over the shoulders of those in front of them, trying to get a peek at the orators on the stage. Rip, with his presence and his Texas Ranger badge, loosened the crowd enough to move through the lobby and into the theater, albeit crammed up in the back. There were chairs against the wall, and Rip slumped into one of them. He was drained and uneasy and was a bit disturbed but did not know why.

Rip felt wobbly inside, but not from the two double whiskeys. No, it came from a disturbance at a deeper level. Something was not right. He wondered if perhaps he'd stepped into a different world. Everything was familiar and yet simultaneously different. He had spent the last month getting paid to catch Black men with no shirts, no shoes, and no freedom. Yet, there was Frederick Douglass, sitting on stage in a chair next to other distinguished speakers. Rip thought, *all I've done is cross the Potomac River and suddenly I'm in a different world.*

Rip had heard him speak earlier when Frederick Douglass had asked him to light a match. His manner and his voice sounded so sophisticated and confident. Rip remembered staring at Douglass and watching as he wrote the thoughts from his head as they came to him. It was evident that this man's intellect was abundant and imposing. He was far superior to Rip.

101

The Hunt for Frederick Douglass
Terry Balagia

Now this man was about to speak to a distinguished crowd. Standing there in awe, awaiting his words, Douglass did not seem to Rip like merely an escaped slave dolled up in a suit of fine clothes. Rather, this was a human like Rip—only with the voice of God.

The applause began as the emcee approached the podium to introduce the final speaker of the evening. The air was full of excitement and bubbling expectation.

"Please be aware," the emcee began, "that by special request, Mr. Douglass has been asked to give a repeat performance of the Fourth of July speech he first gave here, in the nation's capital, some nine years ago, which we all remember so profoundly, and which is ever so much more relevant today. So, without further ado, it is my pleasure to present the honorable writer and orator extraordinaire, Mister Frederick Douglass."

The roar of appreciation exploded from those standing in the room and the shouting was deafening. Frederick Douglass sat on stage and after being introduced, then stood and approached the podium, where he stood...seemingly flawless. Then, a glorious stream of words came from his mouth. The words he spoke that night were like none Rip had ever heard.

"Fellow citizens, pardon me. Allow me to ask, 'why am I called upon to speak about the Fourth of July?' What exactly have I, or those I represent, to do with *your* day of national independence? Why would I honor the Fourth of July and Independence Day for America? I would question whether the great principles of political freedom and of natural justice, embodied in that Declaration of Independence, are extended to us."

"Your high Independence Day celebrations only reveal the immeasurable distance between us. The blessings in which you, on that day, rejoice, are not enjoyed in common. The rich inheritance of justice, liberty, prosperity, and independence, bequeathed by your fathers, is shared by you, not by me. The sunlight that brought life and healing to you, has brought stripes and death to me. The Fourth of July celebration is yours, not mine. You may rejoice, I must mourn."

"Fellow citizens; above your national, tumultuous joy, I hear the mournful wail of millions! Whose chains, heavy and grievous yesterday, are today rendered more intolerable by the jubilee shouts that reach them."

"I declare, with all my soul, that the character and conduct of this nation never looked blacker to me than on the Fourth of July! Whether we turn to the declarations of the past, or to the professions of the present, the conduct of the nation seems equally hideous and revolting."

"I will stand with God and the crushed and bleeding slave on this occasion. I will, on behalf of humanity, for which I am outraged, on behalf of liberty, which is oppressed in the name of the Constitution and the Bible, and are ignored and violated, dare to question and condemn, with all the force I can muster, everything that maintains slavery—the great sin and disgrace of America!"

"I will not equivocate; I will not excuse; I will use the severest language I can command; for there is not a man beneath the canopy of heaven, who does not know that slavery is wrong."

Rip closed his eyes. He listened as Frederick Douglass spoke on. In his mind, he saw the faces of each slave he had captured. They pleaded with him as he locked the heavy chains on them. He blocked out their voices. All those cries and pleas. Rip thought he had never heard them... he had shut them out, completely ignored them.

But they were coming back, his celebrated string of five for five haunting him, their pleas for him to let them go. He thought he had not heard them, but he had. They had gathered together and were locked deep inside his conscience. The cries of desperate pain had stored up inside Rip like a giant hot-air balloon that now exploded and released every one of those moments. The father they found hiding in the swamps. The mother with her two kids who were considered property and had to be captured and returned. The screaming men, pleading women, and horrified children—all looking at Rip like they were looking at a monster.

The preaching voice of Frederick Douglass continued to pound away at the hard outer shell covering Rip's heart.

"Would you have me argue that man is entitled to liberty? Must I argue the wrongfulness of slavery? Am I to argue that it is wrong to make men brutes, to rob them of their liberty, to work them without wages, to keep them ignorant of their relations to their fellow men, to beat them with sticks, to flay their flesh with the lash, to load their limbs with irons, to hunt them with dogs, to sell them at auction, to sunder their families, to knock out their teeth, to burn their flesh, to starve them into obedience and submission to their masters? Must I argue that a system thus marked with blood, and stained with pollution, is wrong? No! I will not. I have better employment for my time and strength than such arguments would imply. "

"At a time like this, scorching iron, not convincing argument, is needed...it is not the gentle shower, but thunder. We need the storm, the whirlwind, and the earthquake...it is not light that is needed but scorching iron and the fire!"

With this final utterance, his speech ended. The crowd erupted in an avalanche of applause. Everyone stood on their feet, clapping, and calling out in support for Douglass.

CHAPTER 18

WHILE RIP WAS in the back row of the theater imagining glimpses of a new awareness, Cadence was learning of the opposite sex for the first time in his young life He was experiencing things he did not realize were possible. He liked it. He liked it a lot. And he loved Lydia.

When his time was up, he said his goodbyes to Lydia, but not until she made him promise he would come back later, whatever that meant. He was quick to agree and headed back over to Ford's Theater right as it was emptying.

Inside the theater, Rip opened his eyes, feeling disoriented, as if he had fallen asleep during the speech. Or perhaps they had added a slice of peyote button to his drink, as some bars in the West featured. Whatever it was, his imagination was spinning. He realized how unexpectedly mesmerized and moved he was. He had met great men before. Frederick Douglass was yet another.

Yet as powerful as it was hearing Frederick Douglass speak, it did not make Rip doubt his mission. Whether something shifted inside him somewhere deep, or his perspective ached from the pain that sudden growth can cause, Rip still had a job to do. If anything, hearing Frederick Douglass' speech made Rip want to capture him even more, driven by a wish to dominate a man who scared him, and the urge to spend more time with him.

Rip stayed seated until the theater cleared out. From his seat along the back wall of the theater, he saw Douglass shaking hands with other men on the dais, gathering his notes from the podium and exiting the stage toward the side door that led out to the alley.

The Hunt for Frederick Douglass
Terry Balagia

Rip got up, still wobbly, and headed out the theater's front doors. Most of the people had left or were leaving. There were stragglers in the street in front of the theater, but soon the *elegant* crowd dispersed and seemed to evaporate into the ether. Rip walked out onto 10th Street and turned right, into the alley. He saw Frederick walking up ahead, alone. Rip stopped and let him get farther ahead as a cushion; Cadence came running over, having just left Lydia at the Senator Hotel.

"Is that him, yonder?" Cadence caught his breath and could see the imposing figure heading away from them toward 11th street.

"Yeah. Just walk with me." With Cadence alongside him, Rip walked casually, like a theatergoer, toward the sidewalk,. "Be very calm." They patiently followed from about fifty feet behind Douglass. "Let's give him more room. Let's get back far enough that he doesn't see us. But not so far that we lose him. Let's see where he is going."

The two followed Frederick as he purposefully walked across town. They were careful not to let him see them, making sure to not talk too loudly. But Cadence was talkative that night. Even more than usual.

"Her name is Lydia. Isn't that the most beautiful name? I think it is the most beautiful name I have ever heard. What do you think, Rip? You saw her. Wasn't she beautiful? Like an angel. And the way she smiled at me, Rip. Could you feel inside your chest like I could when she smiled? I feel like I am suddenly rich! Like someone gave me a bunch of money or something. Thanks for doing that, Rip. It is something I would have loved to have shared with my real father. But you and he were like brothers, right Rip? You and my pa were like brothers, right?"

The Hunt for Frederick Douglass
Terry Balagia

Rip was not in the mood for Cadence's endless questions about his father. Instead, Rip was trying to reconcile the feelings that arose in him when Frederick Douglass spoke, with the task at hand.

Besides, he still had not thought of any plan for how they would arrest the man, and time was running out.

"Tell me again how it happened, Rip?" Cadence was excited and wanted to talk.

"How what happened, kid?" Rip looked around.

"When the fugitive shot my pa," Cadence prodded Rip.

"Why, Cadence? It always ends the same. It ain't ever going to end any differently. No matter how many times I tell it to you. I don't know why you keep asking. Besides, we got work right here. Here and now. So, let's keep our wits about us. Keep our minds active and balanced."

"Come on, Rip. Just one more time. It's just that this is my first time being out of Texas, and up near where you and my pa were when my pa was shot. It makes me think about him more. Besides, we have been walking for a long time."

"Then why do you need to hear it again?"

"It feels good when you tell it. I wish I remembered him, Rip, but I don't. Hearing you talk about him the way you do, makes it sound like he is still alive."

"Dammit, Kid." Rip finally gave in. "One more time, and that is it. Is that clear?" Rip feigned anger and looked sternly at Cadence. Cadence smiled with anticipation, though he had heard Rip tell the story a million times before.

"We were stationed out of San Marcos and got word that some convicted murderer awaiting execution had escaped from Tarrant County Jail. He was a dangerous fellow. He strangled one of the guards with his chains, grabbed his gun, and shot two more. Me and your pa, Big Cade, picked up his trail just north of Waco and followed that good-for-nothing all the way up through Texarkana, through Arkansas, across Tennessee, and into Virginia—the first time either of us had ever even been outside of Texas.

"When we got to Richmond, we had heard from an eyewitness that this convict was headed to the shack where his wife and kids were, in the valley north of Richmond. So, we headed that direction. Now Cade and I were thinking that sounded about right. If you were him, you would probably want to see your wife and your family. But this monster was not going there to see them. He was going to kill them."

Cadence could not take his eyes off Rip, totally mesmerized by the story.

"We deputized Maddox and Hale and borrowed Nelson from the local slave patrol to form a posse and show us where the shack was. As Cade and I approached, I heard the wife shrieking and then the gunshot that silenced her. We heard him shooting his kids one at a time, and Big Cade, out of instinct, jumped off his horse and ran in that shack with his guns blazing and shot the fugitive, but not before the fugitive had gotten a shot off that hit your pa in the gut. By the time I ran in there, I saw your pa was shot and lay dying. So, I came back to San Antonio to the nun's foster school and orphanage where you stayed when Cade and I had to leave, and I told them I would look out for you. But I left you there so they could teach you.

"That is where you learned about how to be an honorable person and where you learned how to read. As a kid, I spent those years living with the Cherokee and never spent enough time in the schoolroom long enough to learn how to read, which I regret. So, I made them teach you everything about reading, writing, and arithmetic. The next thing you know, fifteen years went by. Now, look at you, Cadence." Rip looked back at Cadence. "Your pa wanted me to see to it that you grew up to be a good person. He would be enormously proud of the job you have done, Cadence."

"Thanks to you, Rip. You sure were a good friend to my pa to have done that," Cadence acknowledged.

"Well, that and a cup of coffee will get you a cup of coffee," was all Rip had to say.

Cadence waited a bit before he asked, "You left out the part where you shot the fugitive and killed him."

"Well, of course, I shot and killed him," Rip responded.

Cadence looked confused. "It's just you seem like you never tell it quite the same."

"What is that supposed to mean?" Rip was defensive. Cadence didn't answer. They kept walking along in silence. Then Cadence asked him,

"What about you, Rip?"

"What about me, what?" Rip feigned interest.

"You said my pa would be proud of me. Are you proud of me?" Cadence looked up at Rip wondering. Rip was not in the mood.

"Now what kind of huckleberry question is that?"

They walked in silence for a bit. But something was eating at Cadence about the events in the story as Rip always told it.

"Something I've always wondered," Cadence continued. "I mean, when you and my pa rode up, why did he jump off his horse and run in without waiting for you?"

Rip was in no mood to oblige him any longer. "Cadence, quit asking so damn many questions. I don't know why your pa went and did what he did, but he got shot and it's too late now to change it. Now stop talking."

The Hunt for Frederick Douglass
Terry Balagia

CHAPTER 19

THEY FOLLOWED FREDERICK Douglass to the most prominent Negro hotel in Washington. Instead of going through the front, he went around to the back where there was a large storage room surrounded by windows. He knocked on a door and disappeared inside when it opened.

Rip and Cadence walked quietly along the outside of the room and looked for a window to peer through without being seen themselves. They spotted Douglass sitting at a table next to a large lantern that lit up the entire room. Another man with a massive ledger sat next to him...taking notes. Much to Rip's surprise, Harriet Tubman was at the table, too. Off to her side was a small entourage, and a much larger group in the back. Standing beside Frederick they could see one young man who looked a lot like him. He was clearly one of Frederick's sons. Behind him were seven other young Black men their age. They each had on their mother's best version at sewing together a Union army uniform and beamed with pride. Their smiles were so big and full of love they formed a beam of shining light that pointed to Heaven.

The rest of the vast storehouse was alive with families of runaway slaves waiting to be added to the great ledger. They signed up and then waited for arrangements to be made so they could continue on the underground railroad up to Canada.

"Look behind her. Behind Miss Moses," Cadence whispered to Rip. "There's that boy runaway I caught the other night." Rip looked behind Mrs. Tubman and saw, standing in the shadows, the twelve-year-old runaway slave boy Cadence had captured the night before.

he Hunt for Frederick Douglass
Terry Balagia

The purpose of the meeting was announced by the man at the ledger, who called out that the executive committee meeting was now in session.

"The sole order of business this evening is the soldier issue and the ongoing efforts to create the first Negro battalion in the Union Army." The man turned and looked at Frederick.

Frederick explained, "As we discussed several meetings ago, President Lincoln wrote me asking if I thought that, in the event there is a war between the North and the South, would the Negroes consider fighting for the Union if it were in fact ever allowed? He said it would take some time before he can get it through Congress, but before he gets the wheels in motion, did I think it was a good idea?"

"I told him the Negro will consider it our patriotic duty to fight for the Union and for the end of slavery. We just need the training and the chance, to which he responded, 'You find me the men. I will get them the training.'"

"Tonight, we will walk our boys to the riverboats to bid them farewell. They have been invited to go through preliminary training down the river at Fort Briggs. And after that, these fine young men will be heading to Massachusetts, where Mr. Lincoln assures me, he will use his legislative power to make the Massachusetts 54th Regiment the first all-Negro regiment in the Union Army if war does break out.

"Now these things take time, so these boys cannot officially enlist yet. But when it becomes official, our boys, my eldest son included, will be there, already trained, and ready to go. For it is said that you are not judged by the height you have risen, but by the depth you have climbed. Lord knows these boys of ours have climbed mountains."

Frederick's eldest son stood there, tall, and proud. Behind him were seven other strong young men with eager smiles on their faces, thinking of what lie in front of them. Little did they yet know of the horrors of war. They were still very caught up in the romance of it all. That would soon change. Everyone clapped with approval and with great pride and hope.

Frederick smiled broadly. "So enough now of these business matters, let's go and celebrate our sons, with a loving trek to the pier to see them off."

The meeting ended, and the group escorted their aspiring young soldiers to the harbor to watch them board the river steamboat and to say goodbye. They made the short walk to the pier at the water's edge. A huge, fancy riverboat sat waiting. The young men stared at the big showy steamboat where an entire brigade of new White recruits were boarding. All their families and friends were crying, waving, and kissing one last time. There was a band on the upper deck of the steamboat, playing marching music that inspired everyone, especially the young Black men, hopeful for when they could enlist like their White counterparts. Their adrenaline pumped as the boys waited their turn to load onto the giant colorful riverboat.

As the last brigade of new recruits boarded, the gate suddenly came down before the group of young Black men could set foot on the ramp. They could only stand and stare at the impressive steamboat as it moved away from the shore without them.

As the large vessel left, it revealed the muddy shore and the wobbly wooden planks that led through the mud to the flatboat awaiting the Negro soon-to-be soldiers. They stepped gingerly across the mud-covered plankway to the flatboat and boarded. There were a lot of tears—of joy and of sadness—as family

113

members hugged and said their goodbyes to their formerly enslaved sons. They were off to train and someday become soldiers fighting for the freedom of their brethren and their progeny, and to a future America where to enslave your fellow man would no longer be tolerated.

Rip and Cadence continued to stalk Frederick Douglass from the shadows, watching him say goodbye to his son. Then, after he bade goodnight to the larger group at the muddy boat launch, they followed him further as he headed back up River Road to Tenth Street toward Ford's theater and the livery barn.

They didn't realize that Harriet Tubman, ever watchful over her cherished friend, Frederick, had left the meeting late and had spotted Rip and Cadence following him. Nor did they realize she recognized them from their encounter on the road the night before. *Something about those two strangers doesn't sit right*, Harriet had thought, so she silently followed them.

She watched as Frederick gave the two men the slip, only to circle back and confront them. She saw him as he walked with them to the livery barn, chatting amicably as they went. Frederick was thinking they were in awe of his notoriety; Harriet knew something else was brewing.

She slipped into the barn, silently watching as her suspicions were verified. They jumped Frederick. The younger one left in a hurry as Frederick struggled with the other, a burlap feed sack over his head.

It was as the older one, the Ranger man, stood his ground and drew his six-shooter that Harriet saw her chance. She stepped from the shadows, grabbed the red-hot iron tongs, and thrust them into the face of Frederick's attacker, burning the Ranger man's face half off as she recited from scripture, before being overcome by a seizure and falling to the ground alongside him.

PART TWO

IT IS ALWAYS better to kill fast and be wrong—than to be right but take too long to decide.

Often a Texas Ranger finds himself beyond the reach of the legal system, where there is no judge and no jury. But there is still a need for justice.

Should someone be killed? If so, who does he kill first? What if he is wrong?

Or worse, what if he doesn't decide quickly enough, and they kill him instead?

It is a split-second world. No courtroom. No jury. And no second chances.

he Hunt for Frederick Douglass
Terry Balagia

It is always better to kill fast than to be right but take too long to decide.

CHAPTER 20

RIP LET OUT a scream of pain that sent chills up the spine of any human who heard it. In that moment Harriet dropped the poker and fell into a convulsive fit on the hay-covered floor of the large barn. Harriet suffered from a form of epilepsy caused by a wound to her forehead in childhood. The brain seizures came without warning. The convulsions would suddenly take hold of her and knock her to the ground and twist her small frame with muscle spasms until she lost consciousness. Over time, Her ladies had grown accustomed to the fits.

Harriet fell to the ground right alongside Rip as he writhed in pain. Many gathered around her as the others helped Frederick get to his feet. As they helped him out of the grain sack, he looked down at Harriet and Rip on the hard sod floor.

Harriet was unconscious.

Frederick motioned for them to help him, and they picked her up and placed her on the back of one of the wagons. Then Frederick moved to where Rip lay and had some men roll him over so he could examine Rip. Old Alice was by his side, as was Ethel, both assisting as they picked away at the hay stuck to the bloody mess that was Rip's face. With the straw all gone, they could see the severity of the wound. Rip's cheek was burned through on one side, and the skin over his right eye looked as if it had melted away. His entire face was swollen so badly that his mouth had sealed shut, as had both of his eyes. They were shocked at the damage Harriet had done with the hot tongs. Alice recoiled and covered her eyes out of reflex.

"What exactly *were* you thinking Mrs. Tubman?" Frederick said, though he knew she couldn't hear him. But the others understood his shock at the wound she had imparted on this man.

"She was only trying to protect you, Mr. Douglass. She meant well," Alice said in Harriet's defense.

"Enough." Frederick interrupted her. "Put him up there too. We cannot in God's name leave him here like that. He needs some tending to, Miss Alice."

She nodded and turned to Ethel. "Quickly, bring around the second wagon. Lord knows we don't want Mrs. Tubman and him sharing the same wagon." Ethel scurried around, encouraging them to carry Rip to her wagon, which was tied up outside the barn.

"Get him moved up there before the sheriff comes," Frederick instructed. They carefully laid Rip on some bedding and covered him in supplies and burlap sacks of cotton.

"Now hurry and get these folks out of here before the authorities show up." Frederick's words worked magic on the traveling runaways. Within minutes they had packed what few things they had and were gone into the night.

Just then, Cadence returned with the wagon. He was expecting to find Rip with Frederick Douglass tied and ready for travel. Instead, he discovered a considerable commotion brewing in and around the front of the barn.

Cadence quickly pulled the buckboard to the side of the road and into the shadows. He looked through the trees and could see that Rip was severely wounded. He watched, as under the personal care of Frederick Douglass, they carefully lifted Rip onto the wagon. Cadence heard horses coming up behind him, so he quickly pulled the wagon away from the path and into an open lot behind the barn. He got off the wagon to get a better look as the local marshal showed up with a couple of deputies and the local constable.

Cadence saw that Blade had gotten loose and was in the shadows behind the barn. He let out a soft whistle and Blade came trotting over. Cadence slipped her some stale dried carrot bits from his vest pocket and rubbed her nose. He could see that Rip's saddle was intact. Cadence tied the reins of Rip's horse to the back of the buckboard and snuck in closer to see what he could hear. The marshal was asking all kinds of questions, mostly about the welfare of Frederick Douglass.

Frederick assured them he was all right, except for a good size bump to the head. They cleaned it up and someone brought a bucket of ice, which they fashioned into a cold compress to apply to his head. A newspaper reporter from the *Evening Star* showed up and interviewed anyone who would speak to him...especially keen to wrangle a quote from Frederick, who was eager to oblige.

"Thank goodness for my trademark head of hair. It protected me from the blow," Douglass was quoted as smiling and saying. The paper's sketch artist showed up and made a quick rendering of the scene to appear in the next day's paper.

Cadence then heard someone say, "There were two of them!" And someone else suggested forming a posse to look for the other person. Cadence hid in the shadows, and upon hearing this, headed back to the buckboard and quietly rode away.

No one noticed the leather courier pouch that had fallen off Rip during the struggle. It was kicked across the stable into the barn. If found, the pouch containing the orders that revealed Rip's mission would get him shot instantly as a spy. The pouch would have laid there and not been found for several days. Even then, its contents probably would have been discarded by the illiterate stable boys who would have discovered it and scrambled to sell the leather pouch for a generous sum.

But someone did notice it.

The same twelve-year-old runaway Cadence had tried to capture the night before was hiding in the shadows and spotted the pouch after everyone left. After the commotion and the barn had emptied out, the young boy walked over. He picked up the pouch, looked it over, brushed it off, tucked it under his ragged shirt, and left.

CHAPTER 21

EVERYONE CLEARED OUT of the barn and stable area and moved back into the night. Locals gathered to form a posse. They had no clue that moments before, over thirty runaway slaves had been in that very spot.

The local sheriff and constable were mostly concerned with Frederick and his well-being. They were responsible for safety and security in a city that was host to many celebrated speakers and politicians. To have one of its most prominent visitors assaulted would bring great shame upon their reputations. Nearby reporters caught wind and were drawn to the large barn behind Ford's Theater.

Meanwhile, Frederick Douglass regaled the crowd with tales of his speaking tours, past and present, of all the cities he had traveled to, and the many people he'd had the privilege to meet. He was stalling, providing the right amount of distraction while the ladies led the community, and Rip, into the night, invisible and unseen in the darkness.

With great deliberation, Frederick spoke long enough to give the community a significant head start on their way to the next stop. Most of the group was splitting off and heading on up to Canada. A smaller group, including Harriet, her ladies, and her protectors, were turning around and heading back west on the C&O Canal Road. They were going to a secluded hidden encampment on the northern bank of the Potomac, where the next load of runaways would cross, and where Rip could get medical attention.

The minute the authorities and reporters were satisfied, Frederick smiled and bade them all a good night. His plan now was to hightail it over to the road Harriet and the rest of them were on, hoping to catch up with them. He took off with his long strides, trying to make up time.

Once on the road, it seemed everyone Douglass walked past recognized him. Even at this late hour, people were still out on the town enjoying the night. They either waved from across the road or crossed over to greet him. Groups gathered around Frederick, and it was hard for him to resist an audience. Besides, Frederick was too nice to say no. But it had been an exhausting evening, and he had a long way to go to catch up with Harriet and her gathering. Frederick walked on the road for over an hour when an elegant carriage pulled up alongside him.

"Pardon us. You are Frederick Douglass?" a man inside asked.

Frederick struck a pose. "Well, that depends on who is asking."

The response was ladies giggling. "We were at your talk at Ford's theater," one lady exclaimed.

"Fantastic! And how was I?" he charmed.

"Delightful!" she proclaimed.

"May we give you a ride?" the man queried.

"I would be ever so hard-pressed to deny your offer." Frederick reached up as his foot found the step and pulled himself up and into the carriage. They immediately slid over to make room as he eagerly joined them.

The energetic and excited horses pulling the carriage broke into a trot. They took Frederick on the C&O Canal Road going west until they made it to part of the entourage trailing Ms. Tubman's wagon. It took the better part of an hour. Frederick thanked them for the ride, then hopped out to join Harriet, who had regained consciousness soon after her group had started down the road. She heard the excitement behind her as her famous friend rejoined the much smaller community.

"He came in a carriage, no less," one woman joshed him. Frederick smiled. Harriet did not turn around.

"He needs the carriage to carry that big head he has to lug around with him," Harriet said, making the women laugh. Frederick joined them good-naturedly.

"There was room for you, Minty. I was helping you get away. That's all." Frederick looked at Harriet and then gave her a hug. "I am glad you are okay. You scare me when you have those fits of yours. I'm afraid you are going to fall someday and hurt yourself," Frederick said affectionately.

Harriet shrugged his arm off her. "Let go of me, you giant toad." They all laughed loudly and did not hear Rip moaning until Harriet shut them up.

"He must be hurting," Ethel reported to Harriet, "although he's been unconscious most of the way."

"Stop the wagon," Harriet ordered.

She had Ethel crawl on top of the wagon and drip some morphine through Rip's nostrils and into the small opening that had been his mouth, now sealed shut from the swelling caused by the burn. After a minute or two, he was out again.

"We should dump him on the side of the road and let the coyotes eat him if you ask me," Harriet said.

"We are not asking you, Minty," Frederick corrected her.

The Hunt for Frederick Douglass
Terry Balagia

CHAPTER 22

CADENCE WAS ON his own and scared.

He thought Rip was still alive, but he couldn't be sure, and that scared him more. He could only imagine the severity of the wound Rip had suffered. Cadence knew he had to follow them. That was Cadence's duty right now to make sure Rip didn't die—if he wasn't dead already.

Cadence tried to remember what Rip always said, "Duty is the closest thing we have to family. When you have a duty, you have responsibilities. You have people who need you, who depend on you, and who put their lives in your hands. You learn right from wrong. And just like family, they push you to be better. And you believe in the same things."

Cadence slowly made his way in the buckboard wagon along the C&O Canal Road, trying to stay on the side and in the shadows as he went. The canal itself was well guarded, but the service road that ran alongside it was old and forgotten. Traveling at night was usually a safe route for travelers on the Underground Railroad. The community was up ahead of him by an hour or so. They split apart and the larger group headed north toward Ohio and on to Canada.

The smaller group followed Harriet to the hidden encampment where they had previously been. It was mostly Harriet and her favorites: Ethel and Alice, her band of six stout bodyguards, the twelve-year-old boy, and a handful of others.

Cadence was determined to find them and Rip.

The community walked long into the night. At some point, Harriet took them off the main road, and they found themselves on a road even more narrow than the one before. They followed this road as it slowly became a trail. It became so tight that the wagon wouldn't fit through. To go any farther, they had to proceed in a single file.

Harriet told them to unload the wagon and leave it and instructed everyone to grab something to carry. She had four of her big men lift Rip onto a makeshift stretcher. Once the wagon was emptied and covered with brush, their *Moses* continued leading them down the narrow trail.

Finally, the trail twisted around until it led into a dense forest of tall river cane bamboo. It was like walking through a tunnel with tall green walls as everyone continued to follow Harriet. The trail finally came to an abrupt stop at the base of a rock cliff. They all looked around. On either side was the tallest and most dense cane grove they had ever seen. Harriet was standing in the front of the line, with Frederick next to her. They seemed unperturbed by what looked like a dead-end into a cliff side.

Harriet turned to the side to face the forest of the thick growing cane. Each person watched as she took a breath and then stepped right into the thicket and disappeared. The rest of them turned to face the forest and followed.

At thirty feet wide, the forest of river cane was a hidden door of sorts, thick enough to keep whatever was on the other side of it out of sight, yet the individual stalks were spaced just wide enough to allow someone to step around them without disturbance.

The group wove their way through the tall cane, the big men struggling to carry Rip through without dropping him. Soon the wall of bamboo gave way to a large open greenbelt leading to and revealing a vast, unexpected city of tents, campfires, and floating rafts. Everything was nestled quietly in a shallow cove on the southern bank of a large tributary where it fed into the Potomac

River. Those who had faithfully followed Harried stared in awe and relief.

Cadence left the horses and wagon on the side of the road and ran to catch up with them. He got there in time to see them disappear into the tall stalks but waited a bit then followed them through.

What unfolded before Cade's eyes was a main stop on the underground railroad; a sizable hidden community of runaway slaves shielded from view from the road and from the waterway. They were protected by the coincidence of nature and awaited their turn to make their way along the invisible railroad. Last stop, Canada.

Tents went all the way to the water's edge, where the flatboats began. There were over fifty boats that, when tied together, could create a flatboat bridge between the banks of the Potomac. Here in the cove, the boats created a seemingly endless floating city. It was hard to identify where the ground ended, and the flatboats began. There were lit candles, lanterns, and small stove fires on every flatboat, creating a scene that looked like fireflies floating on the water.

The sentries standing watch eagerly waited to greet Harriet and her bodyguards with shared enthusiasm. But Harriet knew they didn't have the time...as she quickly instructed her men to carry Rip into the hospital tent.

The hospital tent was a small space, with only two beds and barely room for Harriet and her ladies to assist. It was the place where the needy were cared for with ancient medicines passed down from African healers over the ages. The assumption was that nature provided all the medicines man would ever need in the roots, tree bark, plants, crushed insects, dried snake and lizard skins, and countless dozens of other ingredients in the world around him.

Along the back wall of the tent was a large bookshelf, but in place of books were rows upon rows of seemingly every variety of dried plants, barks, roots, fungi, or seeds known to man...and then some. Each contained in tiny jars, vessels, and vases—mayapple, red pepper, comfrey, snakeroot, pokeweed, and red oak bark—all cures for different ills. Dozens of clay pots and mortar bowls took up every remaining inch of the tent, neatly stacked along shelves on all sides. They each contained a different herbal remedy, treatment, or cure. There was jimsonweed for rheumatism and cow manure and mint tea for consumption. Chestnut leaf for asthma and sassafras root tea for blood circulation were also visible.

The assistants were ready for Harriet who, against her better judgment, arrived and immediately got to work on Rip. The ladies gave Rip's wounded face a thorough cleaning and fresh, clean bandages.

Harriet leaned over Rip as he regained consciousness. He squirmed and contorted his body as the pain came to him. The severe burn on Rip's face and mouth caused him to moan with agonizing intensity. The anguish was too much for him, and he began to kick around and fight those trying to assist him.

"Hold him, ladies. Men, get in here. Get some morphine." She dripped a few drops into his nose. Rip's muscles immediately relaxed. After a moment he was out.

"That seems to work, Miss Moses."

"Well, I hope so. I gave him enough to put an elephant to sleep."

CHAPTER 23

HOURS PASSED. CADENCE spotted Harriet's entourage of ladies leaving the hospital tent. He waited a while longer and watched Harriet leave as well. He waited for her to get further away, then quietly made his way over to the hospital tent and slipped inside. He found Rip lying on a cot. He was unconscious, but he was alive, his entire head wrapped in bandages. There was a small hole for his nose and another one under it for his mouth. He looked so messed up and mangled that practically all Cadence recognized about him was his boots.

"Rip? Rip? Oh, thank God you are still alive. Quick, Rip, tell me what to do, Rip? What about the mission? What happens now? Rip, help me. Wake up. Okay? Okay? I'm going to get you out of here. Let me get you up, Rip. Just see if you can sit up." In a frenzy, Cadence reached under Rip's back and legs to pick him up.

Harriet returned to the tent in time to stop him.

"You again. Put him flat! And get away before you hurt him. Do you want to save your friend? Don't move him." Cadence let go of Rip and backed away. Harriet straightened Rip out then grabbed the large Bowie knife that hung from Rip's belt and spun around pressing the steel blade against Cadence's throat.

"Are you here to do more damage to Frederick Douglass? Because if you are, I will cut you to pieces where you stand."

Cadence froze. "No ma'am, I don't care about that. I just want Rip to be okay," he told her.

The Hunt for Frederick Douglass
Terry Balagia

"You swear!" Harriet pushed harder on the blade causing a red line of blood to appear on his throat.

"I swear," Cadence carefully whispered, having no doubt this woman was very capable of cutting his throat wide open.

Satisfied with his word, Harriet let him go. "Who is he to you? Is he your father?"

"He is the closest thing to a pa I have. My pa was his partner."

"Are you Cadence? Well, he was doing his best to say your name. Though his mouth is so burnt up he was hard to understand. It sounded like he was saying your name. 'Cadence. Who's going to take care of Cadence?'"

"Rip said that? He's right. I don't know what I would do without him," Cadence cried. "Tell me he's going to be better."

"I can't tell you that. But I can tell you if it were up to me, I would have let him die in that barn." Harriet saw Cadence as if she were looking at him for the first time. He looked exhausted, half-starved. "You need to go. Now. You know the way back."

Harriet looked at Cadence sternly. "You tell anyone where this hidden campground is, your soul will own what happens to those who suffer. Do you understand me?" Cadence nodded his head furiously. He had no desire to continue the mission at this point. He just wanted to make sure Rip would live. He looked up at Harriet.

"But what can I do to help Rip?" he asked her.

"Do you know how to pray, Boy?" Harriet asked him.

"Yes, Ma'am," Cadence answered earnestly.

"Then you should pray for your pa's friend."

At that moment, Frederick walked into the hospital tent, joined by three or four other stout men, all with dinner plates piled high with food. The aroma alone was enough to make Cadence realize how famished he was. He could not remember the last time he had eaten. Cadence looked up and saw Frederick amongst the other men. He quickly stood, stepped back, drew his gun, and said, "Frederick Douglass, I'm taking you in."

At first, they stiffened up, looking scared. Then they looked at Cadence standing there, shivering, and hungry as a feral dog. Frederick was the first to respond. He looked down at Cadence.

"Something about me just makes you want to draw your gun, don't it?" As Frederick said this, they all laughed hard. "No, you are not taking me in," Frederick told him emphatically. "I'm eating dinner. And I suggest you put that gun down and do the same." The others shrugged their shoulders, grabbed their forks, and ate, unthreatened by Cadence standing there, gun drawn.

Cadence was humiliated, but he was too tired, hungry, and just plain exhausted to know what to do next. Harriet nudged him with a plate of freshly cooked food: black-eyed peas, cornbread, steamed kale, a pile of stewed potatoes, and a big chunk of ginger cake.

"Put that gun away and take this instead. Here." She handed him the plate. Cadence was mesmerized by the food. He had seen nothing that looked as mouthwatering. He shoveled the food into his mouth. Harriet looked over at Rip. Then motioned to the men.

"His throat and nasal passage were blistered by the heat. Those blisters may seep fluid. You men give me a hand and turn him over. Otherwise, his lungs will choke." The big men put down their plates and got on both sides of Rip to turn him over, with teamwork and precision that showed the quality of the care Rip was getting

Harriet turned from directing the men to look again at Cadence, who continued to shovel food into his mouth. She grabbed him a second plate of food.

The Hunt for Frederick Douglass
Terry Balagia

"Take this with you and go," Harriet told him. "I will get word to you when Rip is healed. But for now, you best go."

"How will you know where I'll be?" Cadence asked.

"We will know." Harriet nodded. "We have our ways. Now you go."

Cadence listened to her, took the plate of food, and left.

He started his long walk back to where he had tied the horses and stashed the wagon earlier. Once there, he hitched the horses to the wagon and made it back to DC before sunrise.

Cadence took the horses and the wagon and left them at Cavender Livery and made sure that they were taken care of.

He had no idea what to do next.

He thought again about Lydia. He knew nothing about love nor about women in general. But he knew in that moment he wanted more of whatever she had stirred inside him.

CHAPTER 24

LYDIA WOKE UP early that morning.

The sunlight was coming through the opened curtain of her second-floor bedroom at the Senator Hotel right above the tavern, and directly into her eyes. *How on earth could I have left the window open?* she wondered. She was having a lot of quiet days lately, in terms of her work and her clientele, which resulted in her not having to stay up as late and getting up earlier in the mornings. It was a new habit she was beginning to like.

The morning light streamed through the window from the sunrise, illuminating her pretty face as Lydia, slightly annoyed, struggled to get out of bed, closed the window, and pulled down the shade. She turned around to get back into bed and saw a fully clothed man lying in her bed next to the spot where she woke up.

Lydia let out a yelp. April knocked on her door.

"Honey, you alright in there?"

"Yes, Missus, I just stubbed my little toe. I'm fine. Thank you!"

She recognized his dusty trail clothes and jumped back on the bed, turning his head to see his handsome face. She screamed with joy when she saw her hunch was right—it was Cadence! Her enthusiastic response, plus the fact that she instantly straddled his body and bounced up and down excitedly, woke him. He looked up at her sleepy-eyed and dreamy.

"Could I stay here a couple of days?" Cadence asked her.

"April will make you pay for all my time. I don't think you can afford that," she told him.

"I have a little saved up. I don't care about the money," he said.

She smiled. "Neither do I."

She leaned down and hugged him hard, then she rolled over, pulling him on top of her with her legs wrapped around him in an embrace that answered his main question, and a slew of other unasked questions, with an affirming, "yes." Cadence and Lydia spent the rest of that day and night in bed. He spent some of the time sleeping. But the rest of the time...not. Every second was spent enjoying Lydia. They ate, they bathed, they shopped, they played. Cadence stayed the entire next day as well and through the following night. Every moment for Cadence was filled with bliss.

On day three they lay in bed all morning, completely naked.

"Don't you have an interest in knowing about me?" Lydia asked him. "You never ask me anything."

"Like what?" Cadence could only stare at her.

"Anything. Don't you want to know about me? I'd like to learn more about you."

"There's not much to learn about me," Cadence demurred.

But Lydia persisted. "I bet there is. Come on. Tell me about you."

"No." Cadence protested. He could not imagine talking to someone about his simple life. Even though he had been accepted into West Point, he thought that probably would mean nothing to her. He was afraid that the more she knew about him, the more she would not like him. "I promise you there is nothing worth telling you. I'd rather hear about you."

Lydia beamed her glorious smile. She was enjoying how this was going. "You do? Okay. So, what exactly do you want to know?" She crawled closer to him under the sheets.

The Hunt for Frederick Douglass
Terry Balagia

"Whatever you want to tell me." Cadence was disarmed and distracted by her physical proximity.

"Okay, well I was born on a small farm in the Oklahoma Territory. We were headed to Texas, but we never made it. I had one older sister and a younger brother. When I was nine, my mother was at her sister's helping her back from the fever. Father came in one night to my bed and hurt me. I knew what he had done was evil. I knew he had ruined me. I am fairly certain he had been doing the same to my older sister as well. My mama left him. She remarried when I was fourteen. Until my step daddy tried to do the same. So, one night I ran away. I got married at sixteen and then I miscarried a baby, and my husband left me on my own. I was a seamstress apprentice for a while. I was very good at it. But then I left there and came east here to Washington to be President. But I ended up working in a saloon instead." She slowly beamed her powerful smile at him.

Cadence smiled back at her as he crawled toward her. Lydia became suddenly serious. "That's my story. That's who I am. Do you hate me now? Do you hate my story? Some men think it is sexy, to be raped by my father. I loved him so much. I think he loved me too. I miss him sometimes." She was looking up at him. "Do you think I'm dirty, Cadence?"

Cadence didn't, and he told her so. Her past did not affect how he felt about her. Not one bit. He loved life when he was with her. He suddenly looked at everything differently. He now started each day with pure happiness. He had never been happy first thing in the morning in his lonely, deprived life—until he met Lydia. Now he also knew what it was to be in love. Lydia changed all that was inside of Cadence in those three days. She didn't want him to leave and used all her charm to get him to stay. It worked.

The Hunt for Frederick Douglass
Terry Balagia

One morning she turned to him in bed and asked, "Do you think we are compatible? I think we are. I would make you so happy, Cadence."

He knew she was right. "You already do, Lydia."

Three days turned into seven.

CHAPTER 25

IT WAS THREE days and nights of Rip not seeing, nor to eat or drink anything. He was in a constant state of morphine-enhanced semi-consciousness. He had little to no recollection of anything he did or said during that period.

After three days, Rip could finally open his remaining eye and saw Alice washing his wounds with warm water. Behind her, Rip could see the blurry shapes of Ethel and Harriet, who were in the tent as well. Ethel gathered the old bandages into a ball and added them to a larger pile that needed to be cleaned or burned. She saw Rip's eye trying to open. She wiped the crust away, allowing him to see better. She was smiling at him.

"Welcome back to the land of the living, Mr. Ranger," Ethel announced to the tent.

Harriet and the other attendant, Alice, turned to look at the bounty hunter who had tried to capture Frederick Douglass. When Rip made eye contact with Harriet, she shook her head in disapproval of the very sight of him. She looked long and hard as the Ranger laid there while the women re-wrapped his head and half of his face in bandages.

"If it were up to me, we would have left you for dead." Harriet turned and left the tent.

It was later in the morning when Rip opened his eye again. The harsh midday sun caused him to squint. It had been three days of nothing but darkness. He rubbed his eye briskly, wiping out the sleep and crust. It took Rip's brain several minutes to adjust. When he regained his focus, he saw two little boys and one little girl staring at him from behind the tent drape. The little girl and one of the boys looked to be about three years old, and the other boy looked to be no older than five. The little girl was wearing a tattered, but immaculate boy's cotton pullover shirt with a piece of rope around her waist as a belt. The boys were wearing very worn, homemade hemp overalls and no shirts. The overalls had been patched and re-patched many times often with whatever cloth was available, making them very colorful. Both pairs were clean and pressed flat.

All three were staring at Rip, mystified. He saw them and struggled to remember where he was and what had happened over the last three days. Rip carefully ran a hand over his face and remembered the severe wound he received four nights ago. *To these kids I must look horrific*, he thought. *I must look scary to them, like a monster.*

Rip lifted his head suddenly and did his best to make a growling sound as he made claws with his hands. The children ran away. He smiled and chuckled, which turned into a cough, and then he fell back asleep.

It was evening again when two of Harriet's women came carrying a large pot of steaming water. They took it into the hospital tent, where Ethel and Alice attended to Rip. They poured it into a larger tub already half-full of water, stripped him nude, and helped him into the giant tub. There was a stack of washed and folded rags of many colors. After Rip was bathed and his face shaved clean, including his mustache, they helped him back to the stretcher. One lady took a pitcher with a small spout made from a river cane stalk and slowly poured warm soup broth into Rip's barely open mouth. It was the first food he had swallowed in three days. She told him they had been dribbling small amounts of water into his mouth the past few days...that his mouth was healing.

The Hunt for Frederick Douglass
Terry Balagia

Another one of the gentle ladies told Rip they had been bathing his face several times a day and lathering him in neem tree oil and fresh aloe vera and wrapping his face in witch hazel leaves.

"That is why you is doing so well," Ethel told Rip. "Now that you can really swallow, we can sit you up and feed you. Here, drink this. It will build up your strength."

Ethel and Alice helped Rip sit up and poured a thick, syrupy green drink that smelled like bacon grease and chicken fat broth; it was chock full of various roots, plants, fruits, leaves, and different tree barks. "This will have you strong and healthy in no time."

Rip winced as they poured the concoction down his throat in spurts. "Where am I?" Rip managed to whisper between gulps. Before either lady could respond, Harriet appeared at the tent entrance.

"You are in God's hands, that's where you are," Harriet answered him. "Time to change your evil ways, snake." Ethel and Alice were startled by her voice and turned to see Harriet at the tent entrance. Harriet walked over to Rip's side. She pulled back the bandage far enough to reveal the monstrous wound. "I suppose you're going to make it, Mr. Ranger," Harriet told him.

"I remember nothing." Rip groaned and attempted to stand, but the hurt caused him to fall back onto the stretcher. Ethel came over to help him straighten out flat on his back. "My face is hurting." He tried to get up again.

"It has to be feeling better than it did three days ago," Harriet said as the other two ladies held Rip down to keep him from trying to sit up again. Rip finally gave in and laid back down. He reached up and touched his face and was sensitive to the giant bandage of salve and leaves covering one side of his face and head.

The Hunt for Frederick Douglass
Terry Balagia

"What happened to me?" Rip had no recollection of that night in the barn.

"You got in a tussle with someone who seems to have beat your ass," Harriet responded before the other ladies had a chance. She handed him a lady's hand-held mirror. He could only see with one eye, which made him feel oddly off balance and dizzy. Rip looked into the mirror and saw half of his face and one of his eyes covered in bandages. "Who did this to me?" he asked the ladies. They were silent.

Harriet looked up at him. "It was me." She left the hospital tent.

Rip slept the rest of the day.

CHAPTER 26

THE DAYS OF sleeping helped Rip recover. As his mouth healed, he ate and drank buckets of water, making him better, still.

That afternoon Ethel and Alice came in and woke Rip to clean his wounds and change his bandages again. When they finished, the women helped him sit up and for the first time in days, Rip stayed sitting up on his own. He opened his only good eye and turned to face the changes in the coming night sky. It was a glorious evening.

A twilight world descended over the camp as the sun set, and the evening fires burned low. Firepots hung from the trees up to the water's edge. From there, the pots hung at the bow of each square flatboat, candles at each corner. The boats were lashed to each other and covered the hidden cove in the wide and peaceful marshland on the banks of the Potomac.

The sky had the soft and fading light of sunset. Frederick came by and nodded to the two ladies, who left the two men alone. Frederick gave Rip a big smile and gazed across the sprawling camp.

"Welcome to station number nine."

"Where are we?" Rip asked him.

"I can't tell you that, other than that we're on the northern side of the Potomac. When our brethren come to the southern side, we put out our flatboat bridge for them to walk across. Once they cross, this is their first stop in Freedom's Land. Once here they have a much safer trek crossing the northern states on the way to Canada," Frederick explained. "Harriet and her crew go back and forth bringing new communities of runaways each time." Frederick looked out over all the sleeping souls. "It is their first taste of freedom. I love giving them that gift."

He looked back at Rip. "Freedom, for the first time in their lives." Frederick stared back into his eyes, wondering if Rip understood a word of the journey he was revealing to him.

"Come, walk with me." Frederick helped Rip stand as he rose from the cot, and they walked toward the tent opening and down the main path.

Rip looked at the world unfolding around him. He saw as many as sixty flatboats, with their small fire pots and hanging lanterns. They were gathered near the banks on either side of the Potomac. But whenever a new group of runaways gathered on the southern bank, they would line the flatboats alongside each other and lash them together to make a footbridge to bring runaways across. They did this only in the early morning hours when it was dark and safe to do so. Most of the time the flatboats were docked in the coves, predominantly on the upper side and well concealed by dense vegetation that flourished on each bank of the river.

Most evenings the people in the camp would congregate at the northern edge of the water for their evening supper. Sometimes, there would be upwards of two hundred people passing through on the northern bank of the river, although the numbers always changed as various groups of freedom-seekers flowed through. This was the first taste of freedom for many who were lucky enough to find their way here. It was a collection of different families, reflecting myriad countries of origin. Each culture was reflected in the different foods and music styles emanating from different parts of the camp. Everything was going on all at once.

There were two men out on the water playing a jug and a mouth-harp. Near the water's edge, there was one guy on a kora lute and another on a stringed instrument that looked like a cross between a banjo and an akonting. Two younger men accompanied them on talking drums and tambourines. While simultaneously, up near the kitchen tent, a large group of women stood around a giant iron kettle of steaming creole jambalaya, singing spirituals with powerful voices...while tossing handfuls of healing herbs and spices into a broth that filled the air with fragrant and unexpected aromas. Across from the meeting tent was a group made up of a bass, a cello, and two violins, playing Bach and Mozart...wafting and mixing perfectly with the smells of rice and red beans. The unlikely congregation had no money in the bank and no permanent roof over their heads, but they were the happiest gathering of people Rip had ever seen. Everyone participated in perfect harmony—no drama, no victims—just a shared and unifying quest to continue north.

It was a vast camp with a large kitchen tent where people came out with plates stacked high with freshly cooked food. On one flatboat, Rip saw a group of very young kids sitting in a circle with their teacher taking turns reading aloud from a book. On the flatboat next to them was another group of youngsters gathered around a woman writing the alphabet in big, bold letters on a handheld slate.

Over near the trail leading out of the protected area, Rip saw a wagon with a large lit lantern carrying used clothing and rags, shirts, pants, and other items being dispersed in the dark of night by some local Quakers, who were all dressed in their customary somber and plain clothes as they distributed the goods. There were mismatched used shoes, boots, and such being given away.

Rip watched one of the underground leaders he discovered were called conductors, parcel out items to a small family. A little girl was staring down at the new pair of shoes on her feet. Her smile glowed so brightly it put the nearby firepots to shame. Frederick smiled as broadly. He was proud of everything that had been established here. He turned to Rip saying, "I don't know what appeals to me the most, the music made by these wonderful musicians, or the music made by giggling, happy children."

Frederick turned around and helped Rip make his way back toward the hospital tent. He nodded toward the Quackers as if acknowledging their efforts. "We get occasional support from some in the area. Little good it does, I might add. That man you see standing over there is Reverend Buckley, who brings supplies whenever he can." Frederick nodded toward the wagon. The wagon driver was a big, burly man in regular clothing. He looked piercingly over at Rip, as if he were memorizing every detail.

The two made it back to the tent and Frederick helped Rip duck under the flap and return to his cot, continuing his narration as he went. "The White lady is his wife. She is also one of our regular teachers." When Frederick said "teacher," it made Rip think about the orphanage. Then it hit him.

"Where is Cadence? Is he all right? Does he know that I'm here? I completely forgot to ask about him, and Blade, my horse. He was there. We were at the barn." Only now did Rip gradually begin to remember the events that led him to this, and to his wounds.

"Cadence is fine," Frederick reassured him. "He came looking for you in quite a state. We will send for him soon. But we need to get your health back first." Frederick turned to Ethel, and she took Rip's arm and walked him to his bed.

"I will leave you now, so she can medicate you for sleep." Frederick nodded and Ethel helped lay him on his cot and administered some morphine.

He soon fell asleep.

CHAPTER 27

THE NEXT TIME Rip awoke, he couldn't tell whether it was the middle of the night or the early morning hours. The large tarp on the side of the hospital tent was wide open, and before Rip was a sky full of stars. He was not used to having only one working eye. He saw the moon was a crescent up in the sky above him. As he turned his head further around, he saw Frederick sitting in front of him on the tent's dirt floor. He was looking out over the river, writing in his notebook. He spoke the words softly as he wrote, scratched out, and rewrote them. Rip heard Douglass' deep, resonant baritone voice, which sounded like a preacher, reading his own words of freedom and liberation. Rip was hearing words that would live for hundreds of years, being written down for the first time.

"Why, there is not a man beneath the canopy of heaven who does not know that slavery is wrong for him. The soul that is within me, no man can degrade. For the White man's happiness cannot be purchased by the Black man's misery."

Rip was barely conscious. He looked at Frederick with his half-opened good eye. Frederick saw Rip staring at him.

"You know I have been a slave hunter. Why would you want to save me?" Rip mumbled.

Frederick looked thoughtful. "I just see a man in need, Brother. You were blind, and now you can see. Use the sight wisely, which the Lord returned to you."

"But after all I have done, I'm not worth saving." Rip answered, barely coherent.

145

The Hunt for Frederick Douglass
Terry Balagia

"I've got a secret for you." Frederick walked over and looked Rip squarely in the eye. "Neither am I." Frederick went back to his spot on the floor. "But that is not for me or you to judge, now, is it?"

That was the last thing Rip remembered before he fell back into a deep, healing sleep.

Rip awoke the next morning and again, he was cleansed and fed. When he finished eating, Ethel took Rip outside. "You need to walk around and get your blood flowing." She walked with him, and they saw how the community worked because of the support of surrounding farmers and religious leaders.

There were church services and lectures and school for the kids, with Bible study and crafts. One old man who helped drive one of the Quaker wagons looked familiar to Rip. He was the only one not dressed in Quaker garb. It was as if they had seen each other in Richmond. He looked at Rip, too.

During the first week at the camp, Rip's health and strength improved dramatically—partly from all the sleep, partly from the medicines they applied, and partly from the healing foods he was fed. The changing of his dressing; the cleaning; the air-drying, and homeopathic salves made of tree bark, maple sap, and witch hazel; the constant attention. And the stream of love that emanated and flowed from tent to tent and from flatboat to flatboat also bolstered his strength.

Rip got the best medical care from Alice and Ethel, who stayed with him almost every minute. The hospital tent was in the middle of the camp; it offered some of the most attentive care possible, especially considering it all had to be packed up and moved at a moment's notice if word came that raiders were approaching.

The Hunt for Frederick Douglass
Terry Balagia

SINCE THE BEGINNING of the year, events had been leading the North and the South toward a confrontation over the Union forces at Ft. Sumter. In January, after South Carolina seceded from the Union, their governor, Francis Pickens, petitioned then-president, Buchanan, to surrender the fort. They had been going back and forth for several months. Meanwhile, the troops holding the fort needed supplies.

In January, President Buchanan tried a resupply effort in a non-military steamboat only to have it fired upon by cadets from the nearby Citadel military academy. It was not much of an exchange, but it was enough to turn the Union vessel around, preventing the Union from resupplying Major Robert Anderson and his small band of men who occupied the fort.

It was now the beginning of April, and newly elected President Lincoln knew he needed to resupply the men stationed there. He recognized the need on his first day in office when he received a telegraph from Major Anderson warning that provisions were desperately low, and the Confederates demanding they surrender Fort Sumter. Anderson reported he would rather, "abandon Ft. Sumter rather than have the war start over it."

Lincoln agreed with Anderson's assessment, but he had won the presidency based on his promise that the federal government would not recognize secession and that Lincoln would preserve all Union property, including forts and military installations.

President Lincoln knew he was obligated to maintain the men at Ft. Sumter, and that they needed to be resupplied. But the act of honoring this commitment might give the South no other choice but to blow the ship clear out of the water...thus starting the war. It was Lincoln's call, and he was quickly running out of time.

Before he made such a serious decision, Lincoln consulted with his cabinet. John Hay, who had led Lincoln's campaign and became one of his private secretaries in the White House, assembled the cabinet members in his office, which was next to the President's office. It was the place in which they were gathering so frequently it was quickly dubbed the Cabinet Room. In it was a large table surround with big leather chairs. On the table was an elegant platter of pastries, breakfast meats and assorted fruits and cheeses.

The cabinet members filed in precisely on time. Assembled were Secretary of State William H. Seward, Secretary of the Treasury Salmon P. Chase, Attorney General Edward Bates, Secretary of the Navy Gideon Welles, Postmaster General Montgomery Blair, Secretary of the Interior Caleb B. Smith, and Secretary of War Edwin Stanton. Each arrived...with tremendous baggage and ego, which made teamwork a challenge to orchestrate.

Lincoln believed he could trust them all as a group because he knew he could trust none of them individually. He hoped that all their distrust would cancel itself out, leaving him a range of impassioned points of view. Secretary of State Seward started by stating the obvious—as if he owned it.

"Mr. President, the world is hanging in the balance. We need to proceed thoughtfully. The wrong action may be misinterpreted." But it was a good caution. Many slave-owning states were still part of the Union: North Carolina, Virginia, Tennessee, Kentucky, Missouri, and Arkansas. But they were all teetering. The debates, on whether to leave the Union or to stay, raged in each of those state houses, and others, including Texas,

After a long session of discovering exactly how much they all disagreed on about everything, Lincoln realized what he had thought all along—it came down to him. It ultimately was his call.

"We can always turn the ship around if it gets fired upon. Isn't that correct, Commander?" Lincoln turned to Gideon Welles, his

Secretary of the Navy, who was seated at the far end of the large table.

"Well, I mean, I certainly think we would know if it seemed safe to proceed or not," Welles replied, not making much sense. Chase gave him a sideways gaze.

Lincoln shook his head. "We have men who are starving to death as we speak, no breakfast meats or fancy pastries like we have here. These men are hunting rats. Do you know what hunger feels like, gentlemen? Those are our men! This is our fort!"

The Hunt for Frederick Douglass
Terry Balagia

CHAPTER 28

TIME WAS RUNNING out for Jeff Davis, as well.

From what they had gleaned from well-placed spies in DC, the attempt to capture Frederick Douglass did not reap results. It was their last chance at avoiding war and it had now gone asunder. Jeff Davis realized it was time to focus on the inevitability of the coming conflict.

The drapes in the Presidential Suite at the Spotswood Hotel in Richmond were open, and the sunlight poured in as President Davis studied a large map of Charleston Bay that covered the large conference room table. His nephew was in the room, along with a few other aides. Davis called for the Vice President, who immediately entered the conference room, making Davis wonder if he had been waiting at the door like a puppy.

"Take me through all this," Davis motioned at the map as Alexander Stephens entered the room. "Where are we with Fort Sumter?"

"Latest report is that the men holed up inside ran out of supplies twenty-three days ago. I can't imagine them holding on much longer."

"That's old news. You told me that this morning. Someone! Get me some recent damn information!" Stephens scrambled through the most recent reports and telegrams, looking for something to satiate the President.

"Excuse me, Uncle Jeff, I mean Mr. President, sir?"

The Hunt for Frederick Douglass
Terry Balagia

Davis looked up and saw his nephew, Joseph Davis, standing in the doorway with a stack of telegrams for his uncle.

"What is it, Joseph?"

"Sir, we have a report that the Union is planning to send a ship to resupply Fort Sumter again, just as they tried in January." Joseph referred to the paper in his hand and read the report.

"A convoy of three unarmed merchant ships were spotted by our spies as it left New York harbor yesterday to resupply General Anderson and his men at Fort Sumter before they starve to death."

President Davis stiffened up. "This may bring things to a head quicker than we may have thought."

"It could start the war." Stephens forewarned.

"Or it could avoid it. Maybe what the North needs is another failed resupply effort to get them to realize they could lose a war with us—that they are better off avoiding it at all costs." Davis walked around the room. "Where are we with capturing Frederick Douglass? Where is Pinkerton? I want a report on the status of that mission before it becomes irrelevant!"

"We have spies in the underground railroad," Stephens said, reading from the reports, telegrams, and papers in his hands. "One, the drivers for the Quakers. Though there is certain information they will not tell us."

Davis spun around to face him. "You mean information like the secret location of that underground railroad hideaway?" he snapped. That missing piece of information had been a burr in Jefferson Davis' saddle for a while now.

"We are working on that, Mr. President," Stephens said. "But from what we have gleaned from our sources that help supply the camp, Rip Gatlin attempted to arrest Frederick Douglass ten days ago and suffered severe wounds in the attempt."

"Who was wounded? Frederick Douglass was wounded?"

"No, sir, Rip Gatlin, the Texas Ranger, was wounded. Quite severely."

President Davis came over and stood face to face with Stephens. "I don't give jack-rabbit shit about Rip-Damn-Gatlin! I care about capturing Frederick Douglass! Now tell me, when is that going to happen?" Davis called for his nephew. "Joseph! Get me Pinkerton. I want some progress. Nothing is happening." Davis turned back to Stephens. "Where is this Underground Railroad camp? Will your spies tell you that?"

"No. We have not been able to ascertain the location where they are hiding. But we are getting close to finding out. We just can't find anyone who will cooperate."

Allan Pinkerton entered the conference room. Davis saw him and continued his rant.

"Goddammit, Pinkerton, it has been ten days, and yet we have no word from Rip Gatlin?"

"No word from him, Mr. President, but our spies tell us Rip did try but failed to capture Frederick Douglass and that he suffered severe wounds in the attempt."

"Dammit. I know that already!" Jefferson reacted. "I do not want to hear about the Texas Ranger. I knew his heart wasn't in it from the beginning. Damn that Rip Gatlin!"

"From what we have ascertained, the Ranger made a valiant effort, Mr. President."

"I don't want valiant efforts, Mr. Pinkerton. I want some damn results." He turned to Alex Stephens. "I thought I told you to tell

Pinkerton to hire that other gang of slave hunters. What's their name?"

"Foster Nelson's gang."

"That's them. Bring in Nelson's gang. Time is running out to prevent this war, gentlemen!" Jeff Davis turned to face Pinkerton. "Now go hire Nelson's gang and give them the same mission. Tell Nelson he can kill Rip Gatlin as far as I'm concerned." Pinkerton smiled in agreement. "Tell them I want someone to bring me Frederick Douglass, now. Or this war is going to start without him! Is that clear?"

Davis did not wait for an answer. "In the meantime, gentlemen, we have a war to prepare for."

CHAPTER 29

THAT NIGHT, RIP opened his one good eye in a sleepy mist and saw Frederick sitting at the edge of the tent's floor staring out over the poor souls sound asleep all around them.

"Look at them," Frederick said, looking lovingly at the bodies that lay in cots and blankets, in tents, on flatboats, and in hammocks swinging between trees. "They are so peaceful."

Rip looked around and saw people with rags as clothes, no socks, and worn-out shoes.

"But they are so poor."

Frederick stared at Rip with a look in his eyes that revealed that though his body was here, his thoughts were somewhere else.

"In this world, they appear very poor. But in their souls, they are very rich. It is all in how you see things," Frederick said to Rip quietly, and with great patience. "There is freedom in not owning anything."

Frederick set his notebook and pencil down and walked over and sat on the cot across from Rip.

"Have you ever heard the story of the frog in the rain barrel? His entire view of the world was a round circle of sky. Then one day, a bird comes from out of the sky, lands on the rim of the rain barrel, and starts describing the world—that it has trees, mountains, flowers, people, and cities. The frog cannot believe this, so he works hard, building up his legs. He gets stronger and stronger, and one day he jumps clear out of the barrel."

Rip looked at him.

The Hunt for Frederick Douglass
Terry Balagia

"What happened to the frog?"

Frederick turned to Rip, and a certain softness appeared to cover his face.

"Why, he ends up sitting here talking to you." Frederick smiled. "Now ask yourself, what world do you come from? The rain barrel? Or the big blue sky?"

Rip stared at him. The words Frederick spoke weighed heavily on him; the injured man was once again feeling very sleepy. Frederick got up and returned to his spot at the edge of the tent. The best time to write was at night when the rest of the community was asleep. He took out his notebook and went back to tweaking the commentary he was writing. He had an old pencil and a small moleskin notebook. Frederick studied his words thoughtfully as he wrote them down. "I call this *It Takes A Great Man To Be A Slave,*" he said, as he cleared his throat and recited:

It takes a great man to be a slave.

It takes a great man to look like a weak man when he endures abuse.

It takes a great man or woman to hold their tongue when their tongue is the most righteous thing about them.

It takes a great man and a great woman to endure their children being sold and taken away from them and to survive its pain.

It takes greatness to endure the long, hard days.

It takes greatness to know that what you do today plows the field for future generations. Black and White generations will look back on you and see the greatness you embodied to have survived the scourge of slavery.

Oh, it is a scourge and, oh, it is but temporary. These hundreds of years will be, but a brief section of history taught in school to our children and nothing more. As is all history. As perhaps it should be.

The Hunt for Frederick Douglass
Terry Balagia

But the strength required of our race to endure this section of our American history will radiate through our veins for generations to come, because of the great men and women who were born into, endured, and transcended during the time of slavery.

For whom else could bear the pain of a slave's life, save a people full of greatness.

The Hunt for Frederick Douglass
Terry Balagia

CHAPTER 30

CADENCE LOVED BEING with Lydia, but it had been ten days since Rip was wounded, and he was getting anxious. He thought he would have heard from the community by now regarding Rip's well-being. He decided he would wait no longer for Harriet to send him a message.

"I need to go check on Rip," Cadence said that night.

"I thought you said that lady would send for you?" Lydia pouted.

"I can't wait for her. I need to go see for myself."

"Will I see you again?" Lydia looked up at him. He took her face in his hands and looked her right in the eye.

"Only if you want me. It will be up to you. Because you can bet that I will always want to see more of you for the rest of my life." Cadence kissed her, and they fell back into bed.

From that day on Lydia had no other clients.

Cadence was up early the next morning and got ready to leave to go check on Rip. As he and Lydia kissed goodbye at the door, Eduardo Arenas, one of Nelson's Comancheros was watching Having heard Rip and Cadence had frequented the establishment days before, Nelson's gang had arrived earlier that morning and staked out the Senator Hotel from down the street. Arenas nodded to Hank Nelson. "Mira...over there." Hank Nelson looked across the broad avenue at Cadence and Lydia, who were unaware of their presence, as he rubbed his sore ribs with his good hand and smiled. "It looks like it's time to bait the trap."

The Hunt for Frederick Douglass
Terry Balagia

Later that morning, Cadence hitched both horses to the wagon and took it up the road he had taken the night of Rip's wounding. He took the wagon to where the trail got too narrow, and the road ended. Once there, he tethered the two horses, then sat there until it got dark.

He patiently waited as long after sunset as he could, and then he continued on the trail. He got to the dead-end at the base of the cliff with the river cane forest on each side. He turned to the left and then gently weaved his way through the bamboo stalks to the hidden camp. He easily avoided the sentries and found his way to the hospital tent where Rip was staying. He looked in, but Rip was not there.

Candles were burning in many tents and on most of the flatboats in the water. Cadence knew they stayed hidden during the day and traveled and went to school during the night. Cadence peeked into several tents and found one full of children and candlelight, with a large blackboard on one side. In front of the class, Ethel taught the alphabet to a bunch of young children. But here he saw something different.

It looked familiar and odd at the same time. Cadence rubbed his eyes and looked again. In the back of the classroom, all bandaged up, but sitting in a small chair, with a small piece of chalk and a writing slate in his lap, sat Rip.

Cadence quickly backed away from the tent flap before anyone saw him. He could not believe what he had seen. He backed into the shadows and waited for the class to finish.

Then Cadence followed Ethel and Rip as she walked him back to his tent.

"We need to wash those wounds, please," Cadence heard as he approached the tent. He peeked in, and Rip reacted immediately.

The Hunt for Frederick Douglass
Terry Balagia

"Cadence!"

"Rip!"

Rip grabbed Cadence in a bear hug. "Hey, Son, I have been so worried about you. Are you okay? Where are you staying?" Rip looked him up and down with his unbandaged eye.

"Calm down, Rip. You are the one who is injured. I thought you were maybe dead until I saw how these good people have been taking such good care of you. Look at you, Rip. You look so much better. I mean, you still look horrible, but much better."

Rip smiled and Cadence laughed, more from the relief of knowing the other was okay than anything else.

"It is great to see you, Kid. I was so worried. I am so glad you are alright," Rip said.

Cadence looked around to make sure they were alone. "Are you okay, Rip? You haven't gone soft on me now, have you?"

"Gone soft? What are you talking about, kid?" He frowned.

"Is the mission still on?" Cadence was unsure. "Or have you given up?"

"There is no giving up," he snapped back. "The mission is still on. This injury was a turn into a box canyon. We turn around, go back out of the canyon, and we are back on track. I am going to need a couple of more days before I can travel. But I am glad you're alright."

Cadence sighed a deep breath. "That's such a relief," he said. "I've wanted to talk with you. I was so scared without you being around at first. Then it got to be alright."

"I'm glad, Kid," Rip reassured him. "You're growing up. That's good."

"I'm thinking about maybe sticking around Washington," Cadence mumbled softly. "Maybe try to find work there."

"What?" Rip looked at him like he had a monkey sitting on his head. Then it dawned on him. "It's that girl, isn't it? That one from the tavern the other night. Lydia? Right? Goodness, Cadence. I told you, don't be messing with women. They can be quite dangerous."

Cadence got instantly excited. "I think I'm in love with her, Rip. I want to marry her."

"You can't love her, Cadence. You just met her," he said, half pleading and half commanding. "Love takes time before you know what's right or wrong. Especially, when it comes to choosing a wife."

Cadence shook his head. "I know what I feel in my heart. What I feel is love. No doubt in my mind."

"Just hold your damn horses. We have a duty to complete. Besides, I met her already. Or have you forgotten? I am the one who took you there in the first place. We can deal with your friend, Lydia, after we've completed our mission. Shit, this is all I need. You're going to be thinking with that bull's cock you keep swinging, and if you don't watch out, you are going to get one of us killed."

Rip got suddenly serious. "Now listen to me. I don't know what's going to happen. But I'm getting Spirit whisperings telling me that things may go to hell, and I may need to make a fast retreat. So, just in case, I want you to stash that buckboard with our supplies at the old Conrad Ferry. No one uses that crossing anymore so it will be safe and unguarded. Once I cross that's where I will camp out. I'll send for you to bring the horses and we will head back to Texas from there. *Comprende, amigo?*"

"*Comprende*, Rip," Cadence responded obediently.

The Hunt for Frederick Douglass
Terry Balagia

"We are not giving up. I still plan on capturing Frederick or arresting him and bringing him in somehow. I just haven't figured it out yet. Come back in a few more days. Let me finish healing up. By then, I will have come up with a plan. And give my regards to Lydia." Rip smiled, then Cadence smiled back at him and left.

The Hunt for Frederick Douglass
Terry Balagia

CHAPTER 31

CADENCE MADE HIS way out of the camp carefully eluding the sentries, through the cane forest, and back up the path to the horses and wagon. He was smiling at Rip saying to give his regards to Lydia. He couldn't wait to tell her more about Rip. It was late into the night, so he expected to get back by dawn.

Cadence rode into Washington as the sun was rising. The first thing he did was take the horses to the livery stables. He got them fed and washed, then he washed in the water trough.

"These horses will need to rest awhile if you're planning on taking them back out," the blacksmith told him.

"I already figured as much. I've got to take this wagon out this afternoon, so I'll just use one of yours. But I've got someplace to be, just now."

He was eager to see Lydia. Fully resolved, Cadence headed across the street to the Senator Hotel to propose marriage to Lydia. He walked in and Sam, the day manager, was cleaning up from the night before. April was sitting at a table doing the books and looked tense and startled to see him. He thought that was strange since he had been there for the past ten days.

"Lydia is not here," April said before he could ask.

"Where'd she go?" Cadence looked chagrined.

"She got up early to do some errands." April looked up at him. "I can give her a message." Cadence was at a loss. He did not know what to do.

"Well, do you know when she is coming back?" he asked defeatedly. "It's going to be awhile, I'm afraid." April felt bad as she said it.

Cadence was confused. "Will you please tell her Cadence came by?"

"I certainly will, young fellow." April tried not to make eye contact, which made Cadence put off by her behavior. She had previously been so warm and welcoming to him. Now she acted like she did not know who he was. Hurt, dejected, and confused he slowly turned and walked out the door.

Once outside on Broad Street, he looked up at Lydia's bedroom window. He thought he saw someone in there. He was wondering if she had someone else in her room with her. He knew that seeing other men was how she made a living, but he wanted to believe what they had was different. He felt like they were headed on a different path, a trail that would take them far away from the Tavern at the Senator Hotel. *But maybe that's just my imagination. Maybe to Lydia I am just another cowboy.* That thought alone was enough to make him sad and jealous. He suffered the emptiness rising inside his body, engulfing him. He tried not to think about her, but he couldn't help it.

Thinking about Lydia all day long had quickly become Cade's favorite thing to do. The way she smiled, the sound of her laugh, the sound of her voice. That funny thing she did with her lips when she smiled and joked with him about something. The clothes she selected, the perfumes she wore. Together, this list made him feel like no one had ever made him feel inside. Whenever he closed his eyes and thought of her, everything about her—everything that surrounded her, everything she attracted into her orbit—was shiny like gold.

The Hunt for Frederick Douglass
Terry Balagia

He had hoped that she felt the same way about him. He thought that even though she spent time with other men, it differed from when she spent time with Cadence. *But maybe I'm wrong, maybe it is me she is faking it with, the way she fakes it with all the others.* Cadence suddenly stopped in the middle of the wide street. He turned back to face the Senator Hotel.

He felt like he was splitting in two. He needed to find out where he stood with her.

Cadence walked back, went back inside the Senator Hotel, and headed directly across the lobby, past the tavern bar, and to the staircase in the corner. April jumped up from her table.

"Cadence, I told you she is not here."

He walked past her. "I saw someone in her room from the street."

April crossed the room to the stairs, but Cadence was already halfway up. "Do not go up there, young man! Only escorted men are allowed up those stairs!" Cadence stopped obediently in the middle of the stairway.

What Cadence could not see was that up in Lydia's room, she had someone with her. It was the entire Foster Nelson gang. Their guns were drawn and cocked, and they hoped Cadence would come up to visit.

"Is he coming up?" Hank whispered to the man near the door.

"I don't know. I can't hear," the man whispered back.

"Well, get out there and listen," Hank said in a hushed but stern tone. "And don't let him see you!" Hank's man started into the hallway. He peered down the stairs and saw April approach Cadence on the stairs but couldn't hear what she said.

The Hunt for Frederick Douglass
Terry Balagia

April grabbed Cadence by the arm. "One of the other girls is using Lydia's room. She's not here." Her voice softened as she whispered, "I will let her know you came by when she gets back, Cadence. But now, you need to leave."

There were two other girls in Lydia's room. Hank and his men covered their mouths and pointed guns at their heads. They heard the front doors swinging. Nelson was by the window and saw Cadence heading across the street back to the livery.

"There he is. He's leaving." Nelson watched Cadence cross the street. Cadence was halfway across when he suddenly stopped and turned around, looking up at Lydia's window. "Get back. He's looking up here." Nelson pulled away from view and pushed the man across from him to move back as well.

Hank was pissed. He could see their opportunity slipping away. He grabbed Lydia by her arm and shook her violently.

"Stand up and wave to him. Call him up here. Tell him you want to give him something to think about."

"No."

"Call to him before he walks away. Get him to come up here."

"Lydia, please! Don't mess with these monsters," one of the other girls pleaded. "Do what they're telling you. Call to him!"

"Why, so they can hurt him? I won't do it." She looked up at Hank. "I won't let you hurt him," Lydia said defiantly.

Nelson was at the window and watched as Cadence went into the livery and never looked back.

"He's gone." Nelson turned away from the window.

Hank was still holding Lydia's arm and saw it was too late. Hank took his pistol, reared back, and brought it down on her angelic face with great force. He knocked the consciousness out of her, her blood spilling all over the white bedspread.

The girls screamed and ran to her.

"Let's get out of here," Nelson said as he and his boys left.

When he got to Cavender Livery, Cadence had them hitch one of their horses to the wagon. He arranged for Paint and Blade to stay for the next few days and headed out of town on the road to Conrad's Ferry.

Cadence rode along the ferry road, which took a good part of the day. He was getting more and more depressed thinking about Lydia, wondering if he meant nothing to her. After a while, his stomach acted queasy, and Cadence realized he had not eaten since leaving the camp. He reached into the grub sack and found some old, moldy jerky. He wolfed it down, only to feel it come right back up.

He pulled over and vomited profusely.

The Hunt for Frederick Douglass
Terry Balagia

CHAPTER 32

CADENCE SLEPT IN the wagon that night. The next morning, he was feeling better, probably because he woke up to vomit again during the night. Whatever upset his stomach was now gone, but he still felt sick when he thought about Lydia not loving him, which was every waking moment. Regardless, Cadence got to Conrad's Ferry and stashed the wagon. Then he saddled up and started back for town.

As he slow-walked the livery horse along the ferry road back to Washington, Cadence could only think of Lydia. With every thought of her, his chest hurt, and the pain in his stomach returned. Rip had told him time and again, "Women are very dangerous creatures, and not to be handled lightly. You better think long and hard before you tangle with one of them because she will prevail. Of that, you can be sure." Cadence realized Rip was right.

Cadence decided he would go back to the Senator Hotel and ask about her romantic intentions, if any. It was that last thought, which caused Cadence to drop his head and his guard. He did not notice a tree limb covering half the road, forcing his horse and Cadence to pass under a tree branch that hung out over the other side of the road. As Cadence came through sullenly, Hank Nelson was waiting above with a lariat, crouched and patient. Mindless and unaware that Nelson and his gang had set a trap, Cadence walked right into it.

The next thing Cadence knew, he was dangling by his feet, choking from his body weight. He couldn't find his guns with either hand, and he tried to grab the rope choking him. He could see Hank in the tree above, smiling and laughing. Lacking oxygen, Cadence quickly passed out. When he woke up on the ground, Cade could hear Nelson yelling at his younger brother.

"You better hope he comes to, you stupid jackass! You didn't have to yank him so hard. You could have broken his neck!" Nelson screamed.

"I had to so he wouldn't be aware enough to grab his guns," Hank defended. "I'm sure Rip has taught him a thing or two about handling a gun."

"He's waking up," one of Nelson's gang members said.

"You are goddamn lucky, Hank." Nelson reprimanded. "You better hope he is okay."

Hank gently shook their captive. "Hey, Cadence, are you alright?" Cadence heard someone asking him. They tied his hands as he was waking up. Through a foggy gaze, he could see Nelson.

"Get him up on his horse. Keep his hands tied. Get him some water too." Nelson barked orders. Cadence was coming around. He quickly sized up the odds against him. As they got him back up on his horse Nelson rode up alongside him and took the reins of Cadence's horse and looked him square in the eyes.

"Cadence, we just have some very important people in Richmond who want to talk with you. Now you just be cooperative. We have several long days ahead of us to get you there. I expect you to behave and you will be just fine." After they put him on his horse, tied his hands to the saddle horn, and took all his guns, Cadence thought it best to head back with them.

Besides, he was still mostly upset about Lydia.

Nelson and his gang were bringing Cadence back to Richmond for questioning. Going from DC to Richmond was a lot faster on horseback than when pulling a buckboard wagon, but it would still take a couple of days of hard riding.

When the riders arrived at Long Bridge, Nelson reached into his saddlebag and brought out his papers of transit. Cadence could see the papers gave Nelson diplomatic immunity, naming the man as a Deputy of the Confederate States of America, hunting runaway slaves with the authority of the Fugitive Slave Act of 1850. Otherwise, a criminal person like Nelson would himself be wanted here in Maryland, and with an impressive reward, Cadence was sure.

There were three guards on the Washington side. Only one was perusing Nelson's papers. Cadence leaned over to the main guard.

"These men have no authority to be bringing me back forcibly," Cadence protested in his thick Texas drawl.

The one border guard who was looking at the papers glanced up at Cadence. He saw his hands were tied. He shrugged his shoulders.

"We don't care, Tex. You are all a bunch of stupid southern hicks as far as we're concerned." He handed the papers back to Nelson, who smiled over at Cadence.

"Let them pass," the border guard hollered. They raised the gate.

The riders spent the next day and a half pushing the horses hard and covering a lot of ground. Cadence was not talking much. Although there were five of them riding in Nelson's gang, his chances of riding off and escaping were not good, yet his hands were tied, and were kept so the entire time they traveled.

Along the way, Cadence was nervous that Nelson stared at him in a funny way. They had been riding so hard that there was little time to talk. But early on the second morning, they had made such good time, they could ease up. The horses needed the break in pace. The men did, too and knew they could now be in Richmond by nightfall. Nelson walked his horse alongside Cadence's, where they walked in silence for a while, and glanced at Cadence every now and then, but Cadence tried not to notice. He was still in a sulk over Lydia, only now he was also worrying about Rip again.

CHAPTER 33

"YOU DON'T REMEMBER me, do you?" Nelson asked Cadence.

"Of course, I remember," Cadence responded in disbelief. "You guys jumped Rip, and me and tried to steal our captive."

"Not from the other day," Nelson snapped. "I mean, do you remember me back when you and your family lived here? Or were you too young back then to remember?"

"My family?" Cadence looked at him confused. "What are you talking about? I don't have a family."

Nelson did not answer. He turned away. Cadence thought Nelson was playing games with him. He wondered how Nelson could say something as ridiculous as what he had said, and then not say anything else about it. They rode further along; finally, Cadence could not hold back.

"What the hell are you talking about, Nelson?" he asked him.

Nelson looked at Cadence and said something else that sounded every bit as hard to believe. "I knew you when you were really little," he announced. "You really don't remember, do you?"

Cadence could not respond. He could only stare back at Nelson.

"It was fifteen years ago, so you must have been around five years old. That was when Rip came all the way from Texas tracking your father from the Tarrant County Jail. They hired me and some other local boys to help out. They said to expect the Texas Rangers. But then only one Ranger shows up. Turns out, it was Rip Gatlin. But as the saying goes, one Texas Ranger is all you need. And in this case, the saying was right."

175

"That is not true! My pa and Rip were partners. They were always together."

"Together? Partners? What are you talking about? Rip Gatlin rode alone. Everybody knows that. Until you come along, Rip Gatlin was a real lone wolf. No one could ever partner with him. His partners kept getting killed, so no one would ride with him. Rip is too damn reckless to put up with for most folks. And his partners never lasted long enough to prove themselves to him. Except for you."

Cadence was convinced that Nelson was mistaken. "That's not right. My pa was Big Cadence. He and Rip were Texas Rangers together from when the Republic was first formed. How could you not know my pa, if you knew Rip?"

Nelson rubbed his chin. "I'm telling you; I knew your pa. Rip came up here tracking him. He wasn't no Texas Ranger named Big Cade, either. He was Johnny McDaniel, Crazy Johnny, we called him. He broke out of prison down in Texas and came up here to kill your momma because he thought she had some kids with someone else, which was nonsense. But like I said, he was Crazy Johnny. So, he escaped and hightailed up here with Rip Gatlin in pursuit. We cornered him in a shed at your family's place. He was threatening to kill you all, starting with your momma. Then Rip Gatlin comes riding up and puts a hole in his forehead from about thirty yards away. Never seen anything like that shot in my life. It was simply impossible. But he killed him dead. Just in time, too, cuz Crazy Johnny was about to blow your cute little blond head off." Nelson looked at Cadence.

"That was your father. Not Big Cade or whatever Rip told you." Nelson lifted his eyebrows to add emphasis to what he was saying.

"That is a fucking lie. That's not how it happened!" Cadence was dumbfounded. "I'm from Texas, bred, born, and raised. My father was called Big Cade. He and Rip were partners forever until a fugitive killed him up here. Rip came back to Texas and took me to the Mission Orphanage, and the sisters raised me just like they raised Rip."

"Well, I will tell you right now, you were not born in Texas. You lived outside of Richmond with your ma, brother, and sister. I knew them because I buried them." Nelson turned to the side and spat as if to add emphasis.

"I don't know about that other yarn Rip has fed you because I was there. I saw it. Rip killed Johnny, your father. He had just killed your mother and your older brother and twin sister and was about to kill you when Rip made that shot. I should know, I was riding right beside him when he did it. Put a hole dead-center in the middle of Crazy Johnny's head. Best shot I have ever seen in my life. He took the shot from his horse as we rode up. The mud was gone, so there were spaces between the logs. He placed his shot through one of those spaces in between two logs. One shot. Bang! And the whole thing was over. I hadn't even gotten my gun out of my holster," Nelson chortled.

He looked at Cadence and said with the confidence that only comes from having been there. "Honest as I sit here, your father was not a Texas Ranger. He was a cold-blooded murderer. And Rip killed him dead."

Cadence refused to believe Nelson. He vigorously shook his head, saying "No, no, no." But he was heartbroken by Nelson's claim. He could remember none of it, yet somewhere inside him, it resonated as true. It made sense. Rip's stories about his dad always seemed to have holes in them. He never told them quite the same way twice. He was always leaving something out or changing bits of information.

The Hunt for Frederick Douglass
Terry Balagia

Suddenly, Cadence experienced a swell of emotion. It hit him hard, and he started crying. Softly at first, then sobbing so hard he choked on his own breath. Cadence's sobs grew deep and heart-wrenching as he rode alongside Nelson. The men in Nelson's gang didn't know what to make of it. Seeing him crying was funny to them. They laughed and mocked him, especially Hank.

Yet, Nelson connected with it. This was the crying of a man looking back at the madness and violence in his life while he was still young enough for it to hurt him. It was a sorrow that ignited the latent grief in every man's heart from the violence they received at an early age, and the violence they freely administered to others.

"Shut the fuck up, Hank," Nelson reprimanded his younger brother. Hank stopped, then the others calmed down.

Later on, Nelson looked over at Cadence, who was still deep in his own thoughts. Through Nelson's eyes at that moment was the same hurt little boy he remembered seeing fifteen years ago. He remembered Rip reaching down and lifting Cadence up to his saddle and slowly riding off, headed back to Texas.

Nelson rode up next to Cadence. He reached over and untied his wrists.

"Ask Rip about it when you see him next," Nelson mumbled.

"I plan on it." Cadence surprised himself with the hurt and anger he felt suddenly growing inside of him for Rip. Before that moment he could never imagine having anything but great affection for Rip. So, this sudden urge to hate him was new and unexpected. But it was starting to grow with a ferocious rage.

In silence, the men continued onward to Richmond.

CHAPTER 34

THAT SAME MORNING in the community, Rip was feeling better and healing well. He had lost his right eye but was getting accustomed to not having any sight on that side. He noticed that his very sense of perception seemed to have grown duller on that side. Ethel came into his tent and washed him up and took the bandages off. Harriet came in and joined her. She came over to Rip with a clear purpose in mind.

"He is healing nicely don't you think, Miss Harriet?" But Harriet was oblivious to Ethel's question. She stared intently into Rip's torn face.

"I have something to show you," she said to him and then turned and walked out of the tent. He looked at Ethel then got up and followed Harriet. She led him down the path, across the campground to the summer kitchen, where everyone was cooking, cleaning, serving, and eating. Past the slop pile and the chickens and pigs. She took Rip down near the water line. The sound of laughter and giggling children screaming in joy played in the background. For Harriet, children's laughter sounded like free spirits running around in the afterlife.

She took him out on the farthest flatboat, and they stood by the water. She turned to face him.

"I don't like you," Harriet told him. "In fact, I hate you. I more than hate you. You are all the evil men I have known in my life. I wish I had killed you that night in the stable." She stared at Rip defiantly. "But Frederick thinks you are special. That you were sent here by God for a reason."

179

The Hunt for Frederick Douglass
Terry Balagia

Harriet stood about an inch from Rip's bandaged face. "I think Frederick is crazy. So, I am here to protect him from himself by warning you that if you do anything to harm Frederick, I will have my men tie you up and skin you alive and serve you to the chickens and the pigs. Do you hear me, Mr. Ranger?" Rip was speechless, motionless. She stepped back and looked around at the beauty of the morning light on the river. She could hear the flowing river and the sound of children playing outside of the food tent.

"Do you hear that laughter? I never heard laughter until I ran north to freedom. But I hear it here when I take new souls on this journey, from captivity to freedom. I do it so I get to hear the children's laughter. The first time in their lives when they can laugh and really feel joy throughout their bodies. The joy of laughing in Freedom's Land. When I hear it, I want to bottle it up and take it to show people what real laughter sounds like. The sound makes me want to shout to the world!"

Harriet stood and untied her dress. She turned around and dropped her covering. Rip looked up at her scarred back, her skin so deformed with scars it did not look like a person's back. It looked more like an armadillo hide. Completely covered with jagged welts, it did not even look human.

"You are looking at the back one gets from a lifetime in slavery and captivity, where they insist on breaking your spirit. Or your body." She looked back over her shoulder, making sure he could see the scars left from a childhood in slavery. "I was born a slave and now I am not." She gave him a stern look. "I will never forget that feeling, the first time I crossed the river and found myself in the North. I could not believe that I was no longer someone's property," Harriet said rubbing her wrists and looking at her hands. "I looked at my hands to see if I was the same person now that I was free. There was such a glory over everything...and I felt like I was in heaven."

The Hunt for Frederick Douglass
Terry Balagia

Harriet pulled her dress back up and tied the front as she turned to face Rip. She turned her attention back to the sound of the children outside the food tent laughing in their first playtime of the day. She looked back at Rip with pity this time. "You will never know the feeling of laughing like them."

Rip was silent.

Harriet looked into Rip's eyes. "Have you ever heard the saying, 'It is the God I see in you I love?' Well, I see no God in you. I see pure evil. But Frederick is stupid in the head. He says he sees a great phoenix in you. I say he is nuts."

Rip nodded in agreement as he slowly sat down on the deck of the flatboat. "To be honest with you, Ms. Harriet, I don't know if there is any God left in me," Rip confided. "Or maybe there never was any God in me. I can't remember when I went from being a good person to the man I am now. I was lost all my life. Like a stray without a herd."

Harriet looked at him and struggled to see him clearly. "The old women used to say, *Kupata waliopotea ni kujifunza njia.*" She sat down on the flatboat, next to Rip wondering whether he had any inkling of what she had said. She leaned in close and whispered. "To get lost is to learn the way." He became very aware of her physical presence near him. Her proximity was healing. Rip could feel it. Harriet leaned in further and smelled his skin. She looked up at him.

"You were once married, weren't you?" Harriet asked.

"How do you know I was married?" Rip became suspicious.

She demurred. "A woman can tell things about a man. Did you have a family?" she pried hard without hesitation.

Rip stiffened in preparation of telling his story. "It was after the Alamo. After they made being a Texas Ranger a real job. I reckoned it was time to settle down. I found the girl of my dreams. She gave me a son while I was away on duty. But I never got to meet him. Before I could get home, the Typhoid came and took them both from me. He was my son, but I never got the chance to see him or hold him. Cadence was what she named him. He was ten months old." Rip stopped for a second. He took a calming breath and looked his most earnest.

"Life is not always fair." Rip looked at Harriet. "Some people are born with means, and some are not. Some are born smart. Some ignorant. Some are born to be leaders. Some are born to be followers. Some die early. Way too early. Some are born slaves. Some are born to be slave catchers. We all have our duty in life to fulfill."

"Bullshit!" Harriet pulled back from him. "There is good, and there is evil. And if you are not one, then you are the other. It ain't no more complicated than that." Harriet stood up abruptly as though to make her point. "Great leaders—men or women—stand their tallest in the darkest of times."

Harriet walked away, leaving him on the gently swaying boats with the beautiful sun and the sound of children laughing in the background.

———— ✦ ————

O' Great Spirit

Help me always to speak the truth quietly,
to listen with an open mind when others
speak, and to remember the peace that
may be found in silence.
~Cherokee Prayer

CHAPTER 35

WHEN NELSON'S GANG kidnapped Cadence and started the trip back to Richmond, all Cadence could think about was finding a way to escape and get back to DC to ask Lydia to marry him. But by the time they got to Richmond, his preoccupation with Lydia had been overcome by his growing hatred for Rip. This didn't minimize the significance of his feelings for Lydia, but instead, his thoughts of her were replaced by an intense and building rage for the lies Rip told him about a pa who never existed. Big Cade, a father whom Cadence had grown to look up to and admire over the years, and had loved as his Pa. Now he understood why the nuns had never told Cadence about his father. He had only heard those stories from Rip.

Cadence memorized everything about his fictitious pa that Rip ever told him. Over the years he heard countless stories of this heroic man who Rip described in the most incredible ways. There were so many variations in the way he would tell them sometimes...as though he forgot how he told it the last time. He would leave something out that was important, and other times he would randomly add things that had not been in the story before.

But now Cadence knew the truth. Rip never had a partner. There was no Big Cade. Instead, Cadence's father was a murdering, escaped convict who killed his wife and children. Not the famous, brave, sharpshooting, gunslinging heroic Texas Ranger Cadence had always believed he was. Those stories were all made-up by Rip. Everything Rip ever told Cadence about having a father, and who that father was, had been lies.

The Hunt for Frederick Douglass
Terry Balagia

Cadence couldn't wrap his brain around it. It got all bundled with his depression over Lydia and morphed into an intense, violent rage directed toward Rip.

Before they got to Richmond, Nelson instructed Hank to give Cadence his guns. As Cadence grabbed his revolvers and his rifle, he remembered the rope burn on his neck from Hank choking him with the lariat. He was half-tempted to flip his revolvers around and blow Hank's brains out.

But he didn't. Instead, Cadence saved his anger for Rip.

They rode that last day in silence. All Cadence could think about were all the lies Rip had told him over the years about a father who never existed. By the time Cadence, Nelson, and his gang reached the outskirts of Richmond, Cadence was more than motivated to make things square between him and Rip.

The biggest question was why Rip would have done that. It seemed cruel and unfair to him. He hated Rip for the lifetime of deception. There would be no forgiving him and Cadence could barely contain his anticipation to see Rip again.

NELSON AND HIS gang, along with Cadence, entered town on Main Street and rode directly to the Spotswood Hotel. They met with Pinkerton, Marshal Maddox, and Joseph Davis immediately upon their arrival in a room on the second floor.

The room was a spacious suite converted into a conference area with no furniture other than a large, round, formal dining table of polished redwood. On top of the table was a gigantic map with all the markings of the terrain and the scale.

The Hunt for Frederick Douglass
Terry Balagia

Cadence took a pencil and stood looking down as he oriented himself with the map. He sketched out exactly where the hidden road was that led to the community of tents and flatboats of the vast hidden slave camp.

Cadence indicated a point on the map on the northern side of the Potomac. "The majority of the camp is here, on the northern bank. So we are going to cross the river at the shallows and then come back down and approach the camp from the northern side." Cadence marked the map as he explained. "The cut-off from the road is hard to see, and then the road continues to narrow starting here." Cadence showed where they needed to leave any wagons. "You have to ditch anything wider than a man. So, no wagons or caissons. After the road thins out, it goes another half a mile, and then it dead ends into the base of a cliff."

Cadence looked around to see if they had all been able to keep up.

"At this point, the trail is surrounded by a thirty-foot high forest of river cane. But if you weave through it about thirty feet or so, it opens up on a hidden lagoon with the most amazing encampment you have ever seen. There must be anywhere from thirty to a hundred-and-thirty or more runaways there at any one time. They have a fleet of maybe thirty flatboats they line up to form a bridge to move people across from the southern side. They have tent schools and classrooms, and even a doctor's tent where they take great care of the injured or the sick. They have a large open summer kitchen over in this area where at all times they are making the most fabulous foods."

Maddox looked around the room. "Hell, Cade, sounds like you are selling homesteads there, you love it so much." They all got a good laugh out of his comment. All except Pinkerton, who was busy sizing up Cadence. He had been impressed with Cadence from the start.

"I want you to lead the group, Cadence," Pinkerton proclaimed.

Maddox jumped in. "But he's Rip's buddy."

Pinkerton looked directly at Cadence. "I'm not sure about that. Not anymore." But Maddox was not convinced.

"Are you willing to bet your life on it?" Maddox demanded. "Because I'm not."

Cadence turned to face the marshal.

"I'm the only one who knows where this turnoff from the road to the hidden valley is located. No one else. Only me. So, if you want to go there, then you will listen to me. Regarding Rip and me, that is something I plan on handling when I get there. But that is between him and me."

Marshal Maddox looked Cadence in the eye defiantly for a long second. Then backed away. "Very well. If it's good enough for you men, I suppose it's good by me."

Joseph Davis stepped forward. He had a message for the room from his uncle. "If I may just read his words directly so as not to incur any possibility of misinterpretation on my part. The president's order is: 'Catch Frederick Douglass now, even if it means killing Rip Gatlin, or we pull the plug on the mission. Gentlemen, the clock is ticking! Jeff Davis.'"

Pinkerton stood in the middle of the room and addressed them.

"Let me make things crystal clear. I want this mission completed. As far as we are concerned, if Rip Gatlin works with us, great. But if he gets in the way, we'll kill him. Does anyone have a problem with that?" Pinkerton looked at Cadence.

The Hunt for Frederick Douglass
Terry Balagia

Works for me, Cadence muttered under his breath. The group went outside and saddled up, taking some Virginia militia soldiers with them. As he mounted up, Cadence noticed the telegraph post next to the hitch rail. He considered sending a telegram to Lydia back in Washington but decided against it.

As he was about to mount up, Nelson walked his horse right up next to Cadence. He looked sternly down at him.

"I've got no quarrel with you, Cadence. But when we find your buddy, Rip, I will demand my justice."

Cadence looked down as if considering Nelson's words. He leaned over and tied the holster straps around his thighs, securing his two Colt revolvers tightly around each of his legs. He looked up at Nelson. "Not if I get to him first."

The Hunt for Frederick Douglass
Terry Balagia

CHAPTER 36

THAT NIGHT AFTER dinner, all the children gathered at the two learning tents for their nightly school sessions.

Rip was getting around on his own now. His wounds were healing nicely. The bandage was off his face except for a single strip wrapped around his head to cover the eye that looked like it had melted shut. He was feeling satiated after another great meal of grits with goat milk cheese and greens, steamed potato, and river trout. Rip could not remember the last time he had eaten so well for so many days in a row.

After dinner, Rip walked over to the two tents where school classes were held most nights. Tonight, they would focus on reading and writing. He saw the runaway Cadence had caught that night on the trail up here. They called him Hannibal. He had a small slate given to him by the Quakers and some chalk. The boy was enthusiastic about learning to read. He seemed to bounce along like he was dancing to music only he could hear. Staring at the kid made Rip wonder if he was too old to learn how to read. He recognized the faint tingling of the excitement he had as a little kid learning from the nuns. Rip had not known that feeling for a long time.

He watched as Hannibal skipped his way to the learning tent, his arms swinging and the shoulder strap of his pouch, which looked strangely familiar to Rip, dangling alongside him. Miss Ethel was holding the tent flap as Hannibal came bounding up.

"I think I am going to impress you in class this evening," he told her.

"And how do you intend to accomplish that, might I ask?"

189

The Hunt for Frederick Douglass
Terry Balagia

"I have in my hands my completion of the homework."

"You wrote out the entire alphabet?"

"That's right, all twenty-four letters."

"There are twenty-six letters in the alphabet, Hannibal."

"Are you sure?" Hannibal looked quizzically at Miss Ethel, not sure if she was serious or joking. She brushed him on the top of his head as he walked in. "I will give you a chance to count them before we start class and you can see for yourself," Miss Ethel told him. Just as Hannibal got inside the learning tent, Miss Ethel closed the flap. That's when they all heard the first scream.

A woman's voice pierced the river sounds of a March evening with a mournful wail that could only mean one thing. A death. Rip heard other women screaming outside in the center garden, then the sounds of general commotion. He followed the sounds and came to the sentry post that guarded the community from the road.

A sentry had come running into the campground announcing there had been a skirmish between Baltimore citizens trying to prevent some Negro recruits from boarding with the Yankee troops bound for Massachusetts. The Negro soldiers had to run for their lives. White mobs poured through the streets attacking them. The boys fought their way out and had to leave much of their gear. Two citizens were killed, and one recruit was fatally wounded. It was Frederick Douglass' eldest son, Freddie. He was dead.

Frederick's knees buckled when he heard the news. His shoulders shuddered with his internalized sobs. Within seconds, his rage could not contain itself in his body any longer. Frederick let out an impassioned scream.

"Why, God? Why involve his innocence in a war you rage on me?"

The Hunt for Frederick Douglass
Terry Balagia

Harriet wrapped herself around him and cried as well. Rip walked up and wanted to embrace them but was unsure how. He slowly backed away.

———— • ————

THEY KEPT THE children in the classroom while the adults tried to make sense of what had happened. Frederick was escorted to his tent and given some hot brandy and laid on his cot. When that did not work, they gave him morphine. Harriet had everyone leave. He even told Harriet to leave him, that he preferred to be alone. It allowed him to continue his argument with God.

Frederick was devastated and impossible to console. He holed up in his tent and cried through the night. He felt responsible. He prayed to God in a loud voice and then screamed out scripture from the book of Job. "How could you do this to me? What did I do to deserve your unrighteous wrath? You jealous, intemperate God!"

Harriet respected Frederick's request and came away from the tent, from his wailing…impossible not to hear from the outside. One of her ladies came running up.

"Miss Harriet, what do we tell the young ones?"

"We say nothing. We go about our business. Everyone back to class. Let's go. Everyone, I say!" Harriet clapped her hands, and everyone dispersed.

She turned to her two ladies. "I'm so afraid for Frederick. I have known him all my life. That boy, his eldest, was his world. This has broken him so. I don't think he will ever be the same after this." Harriet wiped her face, now feeling more resolved than ever. She insisted to Ethel and Alice that everyone should go back to the learning tents.

"School must go on." She left them both.

———— • ————

HANNIBAL CREEK WAS the name given to the twelve-year-old runaway. The young boy had run off from one of the working farms down south and made it to Virginia before he came across the community and was taken in by Harriet. She asked him his name and where he was from. He said no one had ever bothered to give him a name, but that he was from the farming community located around Hannibal Creek, Louisiana. Upon hearing this, Harriet took to calling him Hannibal Creek, and the name stuck.

Hannibal was so excited this traveling community held school classes. The curriculum was structured so that by the time he crossed the northern states and continued into Canada, Hannibal would know how to read and write. The young runaway slave worked hard at his schoolwork every day and daydreamed of what it would be like in Canada, where freedom was the promise. He wondered, *What will freedom feel like? Will I have a new name? Will I really know how to read and write? Imagine, I might finally be somebody!*

He was excited about tonight's classwork. The assignment was to find a book or a newspaper or any printed document, then to copy the letters on your slate in the same order and the same spacing as the printed thing you have found. Most of the kids could find no published papers, except for some old newspapers. Except for a few poster advertisements and someone's letters, there were slim pickings.

The Hunt for Frederick Douglass
Terry Balagia

That was why Hannibal was excited about tonight's class. He had found the pouch in the barn the other night with all those examples of printed words and type. Big letters. Small letters. A lot of words on the pages. He realized how lucky he was to have found the leather pouch. It was beautifully made, plus the papers inside were perfect for school and for learning how to read and write. Hannibal did not consider it stealing. The pouch was just lying there in that stable and would probably still be there if Hannibal had not acquired it for himself. Which means it was his—fair and square.

Everyone went back to their tents for school. Harriet made sure of that. Though she was in a state of shock from the news, she went back into the class, where Hannibal was the first to raise his hand. Instead of calling on him, Miss Ethel saw Harriet enter the tent and went up to her.

"You need to go rest, Child. I know what that boy meant to you. We need you healthy to lead us. Go mourn, Mother. Go mourn his sweet young soul."

Harriet nodded and turned to leave the school tent as the sadness struggled to engulf her. She fended it off as she walked out into the night air.

It was a beautiful night. The water was as still as glass, not a ripple anywhere. All the flatboats had small fire pots hanging from a pole or sitting in a pile of sand looking like fireflies across the hidden waterway. She walked toward the water's edge, thinking about sweet Freddie and the painful hole in Frederick's life that would be there from this day forward.

The Hunt for Frederick Douglass
Terry Balagia

CHAPTER 37

IN THE CLASS tent, Ethel walked by each student, looking down at their slates to see that they copied each letter meticulously, along with any punctuation. When Ethel got to Hannibal, he proudly showed her his fine penmanship and punctuation. She smiled as she read it but stopped smiling before she finished.

Ethel looked down at Hannibal, who was smiling, thinking she was impressed. She looked back at the slate where Hannibal had transposed the printed document he found. It read: "Your mission is to enter the North as a courier and to capture Frederick Douglass and bring him back to Richmond to stand trial."

"Aren't you going to read mine to the class, Miss Ethel?" Hannibal asked. But Ethel was not there. She ran to Harriet's tent. Harriet was turned around with her back to the tent entrance, about to unbutton her dress when she felt a tugging from behind her. She turned to see Ethel's frightened face.

"What is it?" Harriet asked as Ethel grabbed her arm.

"You have to see this."

Harriet followed her to the reading tent and was surprised to find all the children gone except for Hannibal. Several stout sentry guards stood near him. Hannibal sat on a cot, smiling up at Harriet.

"What's this about, Ethel?" Harriet was getting impatient.

Hannibal cleared his throat and sounded out each word as he read aloud to Harriet from his slate. "Captain Gatlin, your mission is to enter the North as a courier and to capture Frederick Douglass and bring him back to Richmond to stand trial."

The Hunt for Frederick Douglass
Terry Balagia

Ethel jumped in. "It's everything Miss Harriet. Travel papers, diplomatic privileges, and the details of their secret mission to capture Frederick and take him down south."

"Where did this come from?" Harriet was burning with rage.

One sentry said to another teacher, "You better take the boy."

"Come along, Hannibal." He was led out of the tent.

Ethel tossed the courier pouch onto the cot where Hannibal had been sitting only moments before. She turned it over, and the contents spilled out. The courier medallion, the letters of transit, the correspondence from President Davis to President Lincoln, the quote Lincoln wrote on the back as his response along with Rip's explicit mission description to capture Frederick Douglass at all costs. His life was considered expendable.

"The boy found it in the stall that night after they tried to arrest Frederick, and everyone had gone. This was not a random, one-time attempt at arresting Frederick, Miss Harriet! This was a mission ordered by President Davis himself. Rip is not going to heal and then leave, never to be seen again. He will try over and over to capture Frederick. And if this bounty hunter doesn't get him, the next one they send will." Ethel was now convinced Harriet's instincts regarding Rip were right. "He is the evil you first thought he was. You was right, Miss Harriet. Alice and I were wrong."

Harriet did not know how to read, had never taken time to learn when she could help others escape to freedom. But she held each document one at a time, looking hard at each as if she could read them.

"I want everyone to please leave me now." The ladies and teachers left but as the group of strong sentries started to file out, she stopped them.

"Not you, gentlemen. I would like for all of you to stay."

196

The Hunt for Frederick Douglass
Terry Balagia

RIP WAS LYING on his cot thinking about his wife, Cassandra.

When he lost his young wife and infant, Rip gave his life to the Rangers. He knew the unmistakable pain of his loss would never go away. The natural instinct was to find something more powerful to overcome the sadness in his heart. Rip found the only way to make the pain go away was to numb it. He numbed it with duty and living with his life always at risk. He never knew when the next gunfight would be with someone who was younger or faster or just lucky enough to release Rip from the pain of this life. He had been plenty lucky through the years...chasing murderers and thieves. But he knew that luck was like the small water barrel on the side of his wagon. It only contained a certain amount. Though it saved him many times. Often, just when he needed it most, sooner or later, it will run out. It is the same thing with luck.

He was on his side with his back to the front flap when he heard a rustle. Harriet's men entered the tent and jumped on Rip, each hoping to give him at least one good punch. They beat Rip badly enough to bring him to the verge of unconsciousness. They dragged him out and strung him up by the arms between two large trees. Harriet stood, orchestrating it all. She had the leather pouch in one hand and all of the letters in the other as one man prepared the leather lash. Two of them secured the ropes to his wrists while the other two got ready to start whipping.

Once he was secured, the men looked over at Harriet for her final word. Harriet walked over to Rip and stuck the documents in his face, and screamed at him, "Do you recognize these letters?" she said in a rage. "Are these your letters? Is this your pouch?"

"Yes," he said.

197

The Hunt for Frederick Douglass
Terry Balagia

Harriet turned away and nodded at the two men to begin. Rip tried to breathe and hold on without screaming. He was about four lashes in when he started to squirm. After that, he could not hold back any longer.

Rip's screams cut through the dense shroud of grief holding solitary court in Frederick's tent. He noticed the sound and then recognized the voice.

Frederick came running out of his tent and was taken aback by what he saw.

"What in God's good name is going on here?" Frederick roared so loud the trees shook. "Stop whipping that man!"

They ignored Frederick's demands.

"We don't work for you. We answer to Miss Harriet," one of them said.

Frederick turned to face Harriet. "Harriet! I command you to stop this insanity!"

She would not budge. "You cannot command me, Freddie!" she responded.

"Stop beating this man!" Frederick screamed again.

Harriet gave her men a look and nodded, and the whipping stopped. Frederick ran over to hold Rip.

"Let him down!" he commanded. Again, the men looked to Harriet for her word, ignoring Frederick.

"Let him down!" he repeated forcefully.

"Keep him tied!" Harriet ordered her men. Freddie looked hard at her.

"I'm doing this for you. To protect you from the line of slave hunters they will send up here to arrest you! That is what we are doing." Harriet was as every bit enraged as he was.

"By violating everything I stand for? By beating an innocent man?" Frederick responded as if out of reflex.

Harriet scoffed. "He is not innocent! He came to arrest you!" She held up the pouch and all the papers to Frederick. He ignored them.

"So now, you are judge and jury?" Frederick challenged her. "This is how a lynching happens, you understand, with the same blind fervor. Regardless of how justified you feel it is, I will not allow it!" He was livid at Harriet's continued refusal to listen to him. "You and I, Harriet, having experienced the whip, having experienced unjust punishment, we have even more of a responsibility to make sure that is not done to others."

She looked up at her tall, lifelong friend.

"Then you tell me what we do with this?" Harriet stuffed the papers into the pouch and held it up to Frederick's face. "You be the judge and jury, Freddie." Harriet tossed the courier pouch and all the contents on the ground and kicked it towards him. She nodded to her men, and they released the ropes on Rip, dropping him to the ground. But keeping him tied to the trees.

Frederick quickly tried to break Rip's fall. Harriet walked over to them. Frederick looked up at her.

"Shame on all of you. Especially you, Mrs. Tubman."

Harriet did not respond. She kicked the pouch again. Frederick let go of Rip and leaned over and picked up the diplomatic pouch and all its contents.

The Hunt for Frederick Douglass
Terry Balagia

"I will give you my decision in the morning." Frederick stood up and returned to his tent.

"Let him stay out here all night," Harriet said, then she retired to her tent as well.

CHAPTER 38

LATER THAT NIGHT when everyone had fallen asleep, Rip heard something in his ear.

"Pssst!" Hannibal whispered. "Wake up, bounty hunter." But Rip was out cold. Hannibal set down the plate of grub so he could shake Rip's shoulder, but the wounds on Rip's back looked too painful for Hannibal to touch. He saw Rip's shirt on the ground beside him and picked it up to drape it over Rip's bloodied back when his silver Texas Ranger badge fell out of the shirt pocket and landed on the ground in front of him. He looked down at it.

Hannibal had never seen a Texas Ranger badge up close. The silver badge in the moonlight was mesmerizing. He heard they were fashioned from a silver Mexican *cinco peso* coin, hammered smooth on one side with a cut out single star shape for the Lone Star State; the words, Texas Ranger, etched on its face.

He made sure Rip was still asleep, then he reached down and gently picked up the badge and slowly turned it over. It was true, the back side still showed the markings of the Mexican coin. *Estados Mexicanos*, Hannibal sounded it out slowly and in a whisper. He smiled at the speed with which he took to learning to read. He put the badge back into the shirt pocket and laid it across Rip's back. None of which seemed to disturb Rip in the slightest.

Rip was dreaming of food and was envisioning a West Texas nighttime bonfire barbeque and a side of beef with a six-foot iron skewer going all the way through it. In Rip's dream, it was being hand-cranked and rotated slowly with bubbling meat fat running down the huge rib-bones and dripping into the fire, making it snap and crackle. The smell was intoxicating.

"Pssst!" Hannibal shook his shoulder. This time the sound woke him.

Rip opened his good eye and saw the kid, Hannibal. He had a tin plate of food he slid under Rip's nose. Rip breathed in the aroma of the hot tin plate filled with steaming stew with a giant chunk of cornbread.

"Help yourself. I got it all for you. I ate my fill already."

Hannibal shoved the plate at Rip again. But Rip was looking around trying to get his bearings. He realized he was lying on the ground. He remembered the ropes around his wrists and saw the two trees where hours ago they had whipped him. It was as if the thought triggered the pain because suddenly an overwhelming burning feeling brought Rip around with a great jolt.

Rip winced as he struggled to sit up while his back burned as if it were on fire.

"You feelin' so much pain is my fault," Hannibal said. He took out a small tin of ointment he had retrieved from the hospital tent and applied it to Rip's back. Rip winced but allowed him to put a coat of salve on his wounds.

"I'll leave this tin so you can put some on in the morning." The boy set the tin on the ground between them, as Rip reached out and grabbed the plate and wooden spoon. Nodding appreciatively, Rip said, "Much obliged," as he devoured the food.

"My name is Hannibal Creek. 'Least that's the name Miss Harriet gave me. Whatever name my momma gave me was lost after she died. The others just called me 'boy' or little'un' or young'un.' I was on the Harrington Plantation. My momma died giving birth when I was really little, and I was sent to stay with a group that slept under the outside stairwell. It was a man and a woman and there was five or eight of us young'uns, depending on different times. The Master's family had them feed us once a day, but I wouldn't call it a meal. It was more like a tray full of scraps and bits from the kitchen staff. They would place the tray piled high with scraps on this old tree stump out back, and we would crowd around and reach in and eat whatever we could grab. When all was said and done, sometimes all I got was the juice from the tray."

Rip barely looked up at Hannibal. He was too consumed with his tin plate of food.

"Until I was big enough to work, I mostly played in the creek, catching crawdads and small perch. Avoiding cottonmouths, mostly. I played with the Master's kids some. Then they started lessons, and I was put to work in the fields. I didn't like that much. I did it until not long ago. One day I thought, *well maybe I don't go to the fields today. Maybe I want to go down to the creek and hunt crawdads and perch. Maybe the Harrington kids will be down there, too.* I walked off down the creek and never came back. I found a church there up the way and a preacher man let me into a back room where I slept with a group of runaways that he let sleep there. They got up and left the next morning. I went with them. We made it into Virginia but was caught by some bounty hunters. They put iron cuffs on each of us. I escaped that first night but still had them cuffs on me. Then I was lucky enough to run into Miss Harriet's group.

"They was on the road to freedom, and I heard them make their calling sound one night. I knew that was not a bird. I started walking toward it. Miss Harriet's men would sometimes do a birdcall at night to notify whatever runaways might be in the area. I was lucky enough to hear it that night and I walked toward it. They kept whistling, and I kept moving toward it until I found them. They did not have the tools to remove my cuffs but promised me they would have them at one of their stops.

"You see, I was praying the entire time that God would reach down and remove those iron cuffs. They hurt so bad. Then came the day, or rather the night, when the good Lord brought me your boy, Cadence, who scared me halfway to death when he chased me down and pulled me up by the cuffs. But then you rode up in the wagon and you had the key to set me free. I prayed so hard for you to come along, Sir, and you did...and you freed me."

Hannibal looked at Rip and sighed.

"Now, I realize I have done you harm on two counts. One is I took your pouch but not completely knowing it was yours. I just thought I found it. Then, I go and get you beat like this when I showed it to the teachers. So, I was hoping I could bring you food and you would accept it and my apologies and my gratitude for having that key."

Rip was so busy eating he had barely heard a word Hannibal said. Having mostly finished the plateful, he now sat back and took his first real look at the kid. Rip forgot what he looked like that first night. But now he was dressed in proper, albeit very worn clothes.

He even had a pair of old shoes that seemed to fit him well.

"No one ever told me my real name or where I came from," Rip told Hannibal. "The nuns made up Thomas Gatlin. It turned into Rip at some point. As a name, it don't mean anything. Like your name, Hannibal Creek. They could have named you anything. Same with me. We would still be who we are, regardless." Rip slid the tin plate back over to Hannibal.

"I am glad I came along with that skeleton key," Rip mumbled to Hannibal. He actually meant it. He looked at Hannibal sitting there. It made Rip sad for the young boy. "I feel sorry for you kid, I truly do."

Hannibal squeezed his eyebrows together in disbelief at what Rip had said and stood up.

"What are you saying? Don't you feel sorry for me old man. I am going to be a famous lawyer someday. My life is going to be great!" Hannibal was defiant. "Mr. Douglass told me that once you learn to read you will be free forever. He said when I learn to read that I can read the law. Did you know there are jobs where men sit around and discuss words all day long? Mr. Douglass said they are called lawyers and that a good lawyer can argue about a word and get paid and work indoors and they live in fine homes. That is what I am going to be. Not some one-eyed bounty hunter like you."

Hannibal leaned over and looked at Rip.

"Funny thing is, right before you said that I was just sitting here thinking and feeling sorry for you." Hannibal grinned. "I feel sorry for you more because whenever I see you, you always look unhappy." He could not stop staring at Rip's melted eyelid. "And your eye looks horrible, Mr. Bounty Hunter. You should cover it up. Or you are going to scare people even more than you already do." Then, Hannibal was gone.

The Hunt for Frederick Douglass
Terry Balagia

CHAPTER 39

RIP WAS SORE and hurt when he woke up the next morning.

It was soon after sunrise and he could feel the crunchy scabs from the lashing on his back. He faintly remembered Hannibal waking him up. The instant he stirred, Alice and Ethel appeared and untied the ropes. They said Frederick told them to come care for him.

"When we told him Harriet had them leave you out here all night, he got very upset. Had us come right out and clean you off. He is so distraught and full of grief over losing Freddie," Alice said, gathering up the rope as Ethel helped Rip stand and walk to the tent area.

Harriet could see them from her tent entrance. He had taken quite a beating. It made no difference to her. Harriet was still angry at Rip for being exactly who she thought he was. As Ethel walked Rip past her tent on the way to the hospital tent, Harriet groaned at them both.

"I hope you let him die, Ethel," Harriet said as they walked by.

"That will be enough out of you, Miss Harriet," Ethel answered right back.

They cleaned Rip up, lathered his back with a cooling salve, put him to bed with some morphine, and he slept through the day.

When Rip woke up it was night. He was lying on his stomach on the bed in his tent. With his good eye, Rip could see Frederick Douglass sitting on the floor near one of the large side flaps. A single candle cast its light on the papers before him. The flap was up, and the sunset sent glistening highlights and diffused colors across the tranquil river setting.

Frederick had the diplomatic pass, Rip's orders, and the papers of transit, sans the diplomatic pouch, spread out in front of him. He looked like he had gotten no sleep the night before. His eyes were red and swollen from releasing all those tears. He was calmer now, a quiet born out of exhaustion. The death of his firstborn and the grief it brought tortured Frederick more than any whipping he had ever received as a slave. It was as if the loss had whipped his heart.

Frederick saw Rip was awake. He got up and took a ladle of water from the small water barrel and handed it to Rip. He gulped it down and gave the ladle back. Frederick set it on the table and picked up the papers detailing Rip's orders.

"All this time, I thought you were one of those run-of-the-mill bounty hunters who just randomly happened upon me and wanted to make a quick buck. I did not realize it was part of a secret mission from Jeff Davis himself. Is this all true?" Frederick looked at the papers and then at Rip.

"I have never said I was anything other than what I am," Rip mumbled, barely audible. He lifted his head and looked hard at Frederick and cleared his throat. "I am a lawman. And I am here on a mission, which it is my sworn duty to complete. No matter how I may feel personally. There is nothing else that comes into it."

Frederick turned to face him. "You put a lot of value on duty, don't you?"

"Duty is all I have. I never had a family. I found serving with other men who I could depend on, and who could depend on me, was the closest thing to family I could find. And its duty that holds us together. So, yes, I hold duty in great value. More than I do my life." He sat up slowly and carefully as he spoke.

"More than your sense of justice? Or your sense of right and wrong?" Frederick stared at him skeptically. "I bet your obligation to duty flies in the face of some of those Cherokee teachings you've told me about. 'Hearing the un-hearable.' 'Seeing the un-seeable.' Those seem to transcend duty to me."

"Sometimes, maybe." Rip considered Frederick's words. "But that does not diminish the value of duty. Nor my commitment to it."

"I hear you, my friend. And I believe you believe. And I want to believe, too. The only flaw in that thinking is that men determine duty, and sometimes those men are wrong or perhaps ill-intended." Frederick got up off the floor and walked over and sat on the bed next to Rip.

"Imagine that," Frederick said sarcastically. "Men being ill-intended and giving orders to men like you and like me—who are well-intended—but whose duty it is to enforce those orders. Who gives men that degree of power over other men? It is not men who are corrupt. It is the structure that puts power into men's hands that is corrupt." He paused. "I'm a believer, too, Rip. And I instilled that in my sons. And I am afraid my eldest son suffered the duty that I forced on him. Shame on me for cultivating that desire for him to enlist."

Frederick took out the large handkerchief he carried with him everywhere and wiped his face briskly all over. "The result of bad leadership is when good men go following their duty, and it is wrong. Or right." Frederick looked down at the pouch and wondered, "If you lose your son, what does it matter whether the cause was right or wrong? You were doing it to make the world a better place for him. But what if he gets killed in the process, what is the point of duty then? The world is no longer a better place. You lost your son. How can it be?" Frederick's eyes were pleading for some kind of response.

The Hunt for Frederick Douglass
Terry Balagia

Rip considered his point and had no way to answer it. Neither did Frederick.

"What if that man or group of men are wrong about what they order you to do? What do you do, then, when you have sworn your duty to complete your mission?" Frederick asked.

Rip stared at him blankly, again unable to answer.

"I don't know either, my friend," Frederick said. "I wrestle with the same questions in my eternal soul."

Frederick brought his attention back to the diplomatic papers in his hand. "So, are you telling me that these are authentic? And that they are yours, not just in your possession?"

"Yes. They are authentic," He nodded. "And they are my orders. That is all true."

"Am I correct in believing that Jefferson Davis just wants to use me as a pawn? That he intends on setting me free?"

"That's his plan," Rip responded.

"Do you trust Jefferson Davis?" Frederick asked.

"Not for a second," Rip retorted. "But I trust Sam Houston as I would my father. And...Sam Houston said, 'as crazy as this sounds if it can prevent a civil war, then it is a good plan.'" Rip looked at Frederick. "He would also say the only problem is that we will never know if it is the right decision until way after it's over."

Rip sat up very slowly and reached for his shirt. His wounds were still tender. He could barely move. Frederick observed him.

"You are still on this mission as far as you are concerned, aren't you?" Frederick smiled. "Look at you with your burned face and whip lashes on your back. You should see what I see sitting here looking at you. You look more like a runaway slave than you do a Texas Ranger. We become the thing we hate the most."

Rip gingerly put on his shirt. "I still plan on capturing you when I heal," he said.

"You may not have to." Frederick Douglass looked back at the documents. Rip assumed he did not hear him correctly.

"You are like this country. I think you are split in two, my friend. Someday that civil war inside of you will explode. Your heart versus your head. What will Rip Gatlin do then?" Frederick looked at him. "When that time comes, and trust me, it *will* come, remember this old proverb: *When God pushes you to the edge of a cliff, be not afraid. For either He will catch you when you fall, or He will teach you to fly.*"

Frederick dropped his stare back to the documents, looking for the letter to Lincoln from Jeff Davis. "It says here you were required to hand-deliver it to the President, personally. Tell me, what did you think of Lincoln?"

Rip thought back to his brief meeting with President Lincoln and struggled to think of a way to describe his impression of the new president.

"He seemed to be a rather unusual man. Very different from what I expected," he told Frederick.

Frederick shook his head, perplexed. "Lincoln doesn't grasp it. I would have preferred an anti-slavery activist like Salmon Chase as President. Lincoln's problem is that he sees both sides so well he sees nothing. He is taint when it comes to slavery. He t'aint for it and he t'aint against it," Frederick smiled. "And he agrees with neither. He is a great disappointment if you ask me. But we will see. I am willing to be convinced otherwise." Frederick rubbed his chin and smiled.

"I certainly would not want any man to tar and feather me because I was once ignorant when I was younger. So, I should not judge Lincoln too quickly. As for me, I used to view the Constitution as supportive of slavery. I once famously said that the original intent and meaning of the Constitution were as a pro-slavery instrument, But now, many years later, as I consider it and talk to other learned friends, I feel just the opposite. Nowhere is slavery referenced in that great document. Don't you think our forefathers knew what they were doing by excluding it?"

Frederick continued, "I have come to believe that they knew it would someday be abolished. In fact, I believe we can use the Constitution to have slavery declared unconstitutional and abolish slavery peacefully, without a great war. I feel Congress is slowly moving in that direction. To bring slavery to the Supreme Court. To abolish it once and for all. So, let us refrain from casting judgment on President Lincoln for now. Let's see if he can grow into the job he has undertaken."

Rip watched Douglass look again at Davis' letter, then turn it over and read Lincoln's response. He smiled and nodded his head. "I love Lincoln's response, though. You see, just when you think you know someone, they go and surprise you."

Frederick held up the response written on the back of President Davis' letter.

"It is a quote from Jalaluddin Rumi. He was a very wise man, Rip. A Persian mystic poet who, three hundred years ago, wrote this quote. 'Out beyond your way and my way there is a field. I will meet you there.'"

Frederick looked up at Rip and smiled. "One of my favorite quotes. Lincoln chose to use that as his response. It sounds to me like he wants to meet. Or at least is very willing."

Suddenly, Frederick looked at Rip and said the last thing Rip would ever have expected to hear come from his mouth.

"Arrest me and take me back, Slave-Hunter. Maybe we can avert this war after all."

CHAPTER 40

RIP LOOKED AT Frederick in disbelief. "Are you delirious?"

Frederick shook his head. "No. I am very serious."

Rip could see Frederick's eyes were bloodshot and swollen from crying and staying up all night grieving his son. "I think you are very distraught over the loss of your son, which you have every right to be, but you are not in your right frame of mind, *amigo*."

Frederick stood and grabbed Rip's shoulders. "Yes, I am distraught. I will always be torn up from this day on. But I thought soundly about this decision all night long." Frederick looked determined, resolved in some way. "You are an angel to me, Rip. Sent down from God to capture me and take me back to play a small role in bringing the North and the South together to solve their differences peacefully. It occurred to me amid my grief: this is why we met. This is why you have been sent here. It took time for me to see it, but I know it is the right thing to do."

Rip shook his head. He looked into Frederick's deep, soulful eyes. "You better think about this long and hard," he said. "I must tell you, there are no guarantees. If I put those chains on you and load you into that wagon, you become my prisoner. And when I hand you over to Jefferson Davis and Pinkerton, they will have you and can do whatever they want, and there is nothing I can do to stop them. They could grab you and hang you if they wanted to. Or they may do as they say, which is to release you once Lincoln agrees on sitting down and having talks with the South. Either way, I don't trust these men that I work for—not one bit. I don't think you should either. Because it could go either way."

The Hunt for Frederick Douglass
Terry Balagia

Rip turned and walked around the small tent. He stopped himself and turned back to face Frederick. "But if you are willing to take that risk, I will be happy to bring you in." He smiled. "I planned on bringing you in any way. Your willing surrender just makes it a lot easier."

Frederick returned his good humor. "I don't know about that. You failed pretty miserably the last time you tried. And there were two of you." Frederick looked at him and slowly smiled. He then reached down and took the travel documents and handed them to Rip.

"Before I forget. Here are all your papers. I don't know what happened to the leather pouch, I seemed to have misplaced it. But I'm sure it will turn up." Rip thought instantly of Hannibal. Just then, Harriet entered the tent in a huff.

"Frederick, I have been searching all over for you." She stopped when she saw Rip was up and seemingly recovered. "Oh, I was rather hoping you would be dead," Harriet said to him.

Rip stepped closer to her. "I never lied to you. I never once tried to make you think I am anything other than what I am."

Frederick cleared his throat, commanding Harriet's attention.

"Harriet, I have decided. I am going back with Rip. He will turn me over to Jefferson Davis; they can follow their plan and use me to start negotiations to avoid an outbreak of war. And then they will release me."

Harriet looked at him like he had gotten into the corn mash. "And just what fairytale land are you living in, Freddie?"

"It's no fairytale, Woman. I surrender and Lincoln agrees to meet, and I am released. It is that simple." Frederick stared at her. Harriet stared right back at him.

"Says who?" she demanded.

"Says, Rip. Tell her, Rip." Frederick turned to him, but Harriet was quick to react.

"Oh, you believe this snake?" Harriet looked aggressively at Rip. "I believe nothing that comes out of his lying mouth." She glared at him. "Look at him. He is a snake. if you take in an injured snake and heal him, don't be surprised when he bites you. A snake is a snake and always will be," Harriet insisted.

Frederick would have none of it. "I would unite with anybody to do right, and with nobody to do wrong," her old friend firmly announced as he looked at Harriet. "And I cannot disagree more, Madam. For me, this man's role in getting me involved gives purpose and meaning for losing my son. Rip is our catalyst to help us shift the winds of war and the future of our people."

Frederick's eyes searched Harriet's face for some sign of a supportive gesture but found none. "As for me, there is nothing else I am good for. There is nothing else I will ever do after losing my boy. I want to turn myself in and trust the rest to God. Besides, we read their orders. They very much intend to release me as an incentive for negotiations to begin. We read Lincoln's response, which is very positive and open to meeting. So, once they can announce they have captured me, then Lincoln is motivated to publicly agree to meet, at which time I will get released. I may be back in a matter of weeks."

Harriet was still skeptical. "And what? We avert a war?"

"Precisely, Madam!" Frederick proclaimed. "What else do you think we have been discussing?"

Harriet walked over to Frederick and drew her short body up against his tall one and shouted in his face.

The Hunt for Frederick Douglass
Terry Balagia

"And then what happens, Frederick? Do we keep slavery? Probably. That is the whole idea of negotiating and avoiding war, it really means negotiating to preserve slavery. Is that what you want to accomplish?" She looked condescendingly at him. "Don't you realize the trap? You help prevent the war, and at the same time, Frederick, you institutionalize slavery in the South forever! Their idea of negotiating means the North agrees to let slavery continue as opposed to fighting a war."

"Fighting that war and killing countless other sons!" Frederick protested.

"Yes!" Harriet screamed back. "While it is indeed a vile thought to consider, it may be exactly what it takes to rid the land of slavery once and for all! Maybe it will take paying that high of a price—along with destroying the very economic and cultural foundation of the South—to end the scourge of slavery."

Harriet paused. "*The thing worse than rebellion is the thing that causes rebellion.* Remember those words, Freddie? Those were your words. You said them yourself. You also said, *If there is no struggle there is no progress.*"

"Yes, I said those words. I meant them, too, but that was before I lost my son. Now I know the price those words reference."

She looked up at her most valued friend, and as if resigning herself said, "If war is the price we must pay to rid this country of slavery, then best we pay it now!"

"Like I said," Rip interjected. "I don't trust President Davis, but I heard him say that Frederick would be released once Lincoln agrees to start negotiations. I may not trust him, but it sounds like the last hope to avert the war to me."

Harriet spun around and burned a hole through Rip with her eyes. "We don't care what you think, Bounty Hunter. Your words

216

mean nothing. Only your actions. And your actions show me you are a snake in the grass waiting to strike."

"Now, Minty, please," Frederick entreated, causing her to spin around to face her wrath on him.

"And you, with your pumped-up hairdo, and your pumped-up head are willing to throw yourself on the bonfire and be burned to ash to go along with it," Harriet attacked. "So suddenly you think you are going to be the missing piece to bring the North and the South together. That your very presence will stop the great war before it starts. Just like a powerful god. Why Freddie, I had no idea you were so almighty and powerful. Why, I have been praying to the wrong god all along. It's been you the whole time I should have been praying to, not the Almighty. From what you are telling me, you are the Almighty. Is that right?"

"Hush now, woman! Stop talking your foolishness!" Frederick deflected.

"You are the fool, Sir! Not me! You let the evil Jeff Davis and the two-faced Rip Gatlin lure you into the devil's lair!" Harriet pointed at Rip.

"And don't ever hush me again, Freddie! I will bend you over and whip your skinny ass myself!"

Frederick looked at the woman and shook his head. He took a deep, clearing breath, looked at her again, and lowering the temperature in the room, took another deep breath before asking, "Isn't it worth a try? Isn't everything worth a try? Anything is better than losing a son. A War Between the States could cost thousands of sons. I cannot imagine a country with parents filled with the pain I now feel." He slowly shook his head in acceptance. "Perhaps it is part hopefulness, perhaps it is part suicide. I cannot say, Harriet. But either way, I know God will be there to catch me if I fall."

The Hunt for Frederick Douglass
Terry Balagia

"Look at me, Freddie." Harriet reached up and grabbed ahold of the tall man's shirt. "The thought of losing that many sons is crippling. But if that is what it costs, then that is the price to be paid. Otherwise, slavery will become an established institution for generations to come." She pulled at him until he heard her stare. "What happens if you avoid a war but enshrine the enslavement of your brothers and sisters forever? What will you say to them then, Freddie?"

The great man looked down at her. "I will say to them that we will persevere, and we will not stop our battle until slavery is abolished—but by civil discourse, not by civil war."

CHAPTER 41

FOR THE NEXT two days, Cadence led Nelson and a larger gang on the road from Richmond to the hidden slave community on the banks of the Potomac River. In their gang were a dozen of some of the roughest hired gunslingers, bounty hunters, Comancheros, Indian trackers, cattle-rustlers and part-time lawmen and militiamen that Confederate money could buy. Each of them was wanted in most of the surrounding states for various crimes and were worth several thousand dollars in reward money apiece. Nelson knew them all. It was a tough bunch of men to handle.

After the second day of hard riding, they crossed the Potomac and made it to just before the trail cut off from the road. They stopped well short of the hidden cove. Cadence did not want them to get too close and risk being spotted. They set up camp and bedded down for some sleep, with the plan being to attack at sunrise.

Nelson came up next to Cadence as they dismounted.

"You know, Cadence, we could just ride up there now and get it done and head back home tonight."

"No." Cadence shook his head. "They do most of their traveling at night. The time to get them is early morning."

Nelson nodded. "Makes sense." He realized they had pushed themselves hard getting there from Richmond. The men were exhausted, as were the horses. Each of the men knew they were getting up before the sunrise, so were eager to lay out their bedrolls and call it a night right after grub.

The Hunt for Frederick Douglass
Terry Balagia

Once the men bedded down, it was not long before everyone was asleep. Everyone except Cadence. He waited until they were all in full repose and then quietly got out of his bedroll, saddled his pony, and snuck back to the road that led to the slave camp. Having a score to settle with Rip, Cadence had decided he would give Rip one last chance to tell the truth about killing his father.

Cadence pressed his horse hard, making it quickly to the trail that led to the hidden lagoon. Tethering the horse to a cedar tree and heading down the trail on foot, he arrived at the base of the cliff, where the trail dead-ended and the bamboo forest began. He wove through the bamboo cane and came out onto the hidden lagoon and the vast camp of flatboats and tents. Cadence was careful to avoid the sentries as he made his way to the hospital tent looking for Rip, but Rip was not there. Most of the classroom tents were dark, and all the kids were asleep. He searched around, looking for which tent Rip could be in, while continuing to dodge the sentries.

He needed to find Rip's tent. But he could not go around and stick his nose into each tent or flatboat and not expect to get caught. Though he was not sure what else he could do. So, Cadence did what he always did in situations like this, he wondered, *what Rip would do. Rip would tell me to fall back on our Cherokee spirit training.*

Cadence calmed himself. He stopped and found a spot in the bushes right near a row of tents, sat down, crossed his legs, and became as quiet as he could, both inside and out. Closing his eyes and taking deep breaths in a syncopated rhythm, he found the necessary balance of breath and no breath. Cadence invoked the Sacred Grandmother, which lit the Sacred Fire inside him, and then he let his breath flow and become effortless. The air of life flew in and out and through him as he listened to the sounds of the Sacred Mother Earth, but with his feelings—not with his ears. He listened with his heart and with a subtle sense that often goes before the sense of hearing. He continued breathing deeply, and soon he was in a canyon of sound while he listened to every animal, every insect, and every plant stretch and breathe in the web of life that connected them.

Cadence checked in with each part of his feelings, and what they heard between his breaths, and his heart—beating more calmly now.

Then out of nowhere, he heard it. It was way back there in the auditory spectrum of his consciousness, but he recognized it. It stood apart, emerging from all the hundreds of thousands of insects, animals, and creatures of the night and the sounds they made. Even with all that audio distraction, Cadence could hear it, the unmistakable sound of Rip snoring.

He positioned his head toward where the sound was coming from and opened his eyes. He saw it was coming from the direction of a small group of tents right near the river's edge. Cadence got up and wove and stopped and hid his way until he got closer and could easily hear Rip's snores.

He circled in on the tent at the source of the sound. Cadence peeked in to make sure no one else was there. He saw Rip on a bedroll consisting of an Indian woven mat on top of a feather-stuffed blanket. He was sleeping on his face. Cadence saw the scabs and whip marks on Rip's back. They looked deep and painful. A thick coat of healing salve covered his wounds.

One of Harriet's lady caretakers was in the other corner near the opening of the tent, asleep. Cadence wanted to haul back and hit Rip while he was dead asleep, but he looked around and grabbed a small pillow. He gripped it in both hands and put it over Rip's face to smother him.

Losing his nerve, he threw the pillow down and took out his six-shooter and put it into Rip's face. He cocked the trigger and Rips' one good eye immediately opened. Cadence was almost in tears, and his hands were shaking as he whispered, "Rip, I am going to give you one chance to answer this question: did you shoot my father?"

"Cadence, what kind of stupid, huckleberry question is that." Rip fanned Cadence's gun out of his face. "Did you remember to stash that buckboard near Conrad's Ferry like I told you?"

At that, Cadence grabbed Rip, wounds and all, and dragged him out of his covers. He pulled him outside the tent, so as not to disturb the caretaker and have sentries descend on him. Rip was wounded and could barely move. Cade tossed Rip onto the ground, stood back, and pointed the gun at him again.

"I am going to ask you one more time, Rip. Was the fugitive my pa, and did you kill him?" he hissed.

"Cadence, you cannot threaten someone to do something, and then when they don't do it, give them another chance. You lose your credibility, and the other person knows you will not shoot them," Rip coached somewhat sarcastically.

"Darn it, Rip! Nelson told me the whole story. He told me he was there, and that you had no partner named Cadence. And that the fugitive was my father and that you killed him. You killed him!" Cadence was shaking with rage.

Rip looked at him in disbelief. "Cadence, you believe, Nelson? The guy that tried to bushwhack us and steal our runaway at gunpoint just a fortnight ago? He was willing to kill you that day. Now you think he is suddenly your friend and telling you the truth?"

Cadence looked down. He stopped momentarily. Rip made a good point. But he still didn't believe him. "Answer the question."

Rip stayed firm. "I will not honor such a stupid question with an answer."

But Cadence was not convinced. "Maybe that's because you know it's true and you never lie. I know that about you, Rip. Or at least I thought I knew that about you. But now I realize you have lied to me my whole life. Everything you have told me about my pa was a lie that I have been living all my life."

Rip was unfazed "So, what did Nelson want in return? I am sure he asked you for something. It's not his style not to. What was it, Cade? What did Nelson make you give them?" Cadence looked down and away, which he always did when he lied. Rip knew this. "I don't know what you're talking about."

"Oh, sure you do, Kid. Let me guess, don't tell me. It was the location of this place. Was it, Cadence? It was, wasn't it? Shame on you, little Cade. Big mistake, Kid."

Cadence couldn't form the words to answer. He waved his gun in Rip's face instead.

Rip swatted it away. "Cadence, you get that gun out of my face. You do that one more time, and I swear I am going to spank your fanny."

"I hate you, Rip! You lying, good for nothing, pile of cowshit!" Cadence continued to wave his gun in Rip's face.

Rip slapped it away the first couple of times, and then, as he slapped at the gun he came back with the same hand and slapped Cadence's face, hard.

Rip was injured and not very agile, nor could he throw much of a punch, but when he slapped Cadence, he knocked Cadence's gun to the ground. They both jumped for it but quickly wrestled around while Cadence got in an occasional punch. Rip could not move well, and Cade was getting the best of him until Rip got on top and held Cadence's arms down so he couldn't punch anymore. The young man was crying out of frustration—the older man was just plain pissed.

Ethel woke up and went to get the sentries. They arrived quickly and held Cadence back. After he caught his breath, Rip instructed them to let Cadence go. The sentries walked Cadence out through the front of the camp.

As he left, Cadence cried and screamed out, "I'm going to kill you, Rip Gatlin!"

"You just make sure that wagon is at Conrad's Ferry like I told you!" Rip yelled back.

CHAPTER 42

CADENCE SCRAMBLED THROUGH the thick bamboo stalks fuming with rage, and a little beat up and hurt from his fight with Rip. He got back to Nelson's camp as fast as he could, pushing his already spent pony to a fast gallop the entire way. Tears were streaming down his face the whole ride.

Rip would regret what he did. Cadence relished the thought. He could imagine the look on Rip's face when he saw Cadence leading the posse into the hidden camp to arrest Frederick. Maybe Rip as well. Or maybe Rip would get roughed up a bit. Whatever transpired, Cadence could not wait to be there when it happened, which would be as soon as he could get back and get Nelson and the gang saddled up and riding.

Cadence rode up to the campsite. It was an hour before sunrise, but a hint of light was rimming the eastern edge of the cloudless horizon. Nelson was up but most of the men were still asleep. Their expanded gang included a grub master, who was already up and stoking the morning campfire, heating his griddle pan, and boiling water for coffee. The Comanchero Indian trackers were up and ready to move out. As was their Comanche companion.

As Cadence rode up, he made a commotion and woke up the rest of the gang.

"Let's go, you men." He walked his pony up to each sleeping bag, stirring the dirt around them. "Let's go. Get up!" Cadence barked at them.

Nelson was already up and believed he had them on schedule.

The Hunt for Frederick Douglass
Terry Balagia

"Now hold on there, Cadence. These men need to get their morning grub."

Cadence disagreed. "We can eat when we get back. We have a forty-five-minute ride ahead of us before we even get there."

"All the more reason to let these men get some food in their bellies. Now come on, Cadence. You should switch horses as well. That pony is looking done."

The horse is beat, and the frying bacon smells good, and we do have the time. Cadence paid attention to his thoughts, got off and allowed someone to get him a fresh mount as he wolfed down some food and coffee and the rest of the men prepared. As they ate, Cadence scraped the ground with the bottom of his foot smoothing it out. Then he took his rifle and used it to carve a line into the dirt to show the trail they would follow. "It gets too narrow the last quarter of a mile. We are going to leave our horses and go on foot in this last section."

Cadence looked around, making sure everyone was giving him their attention. He marked a full circle showing where the hidden valley was. "We will end up on the high ground in a bamboo grove that will provide good cover for our advance."

They loaded up their guns, doused the fire, and mounted their horses. Cadence led them up the road as far as it went until it got narrow and turned into a trail. He dismounted, and the two Comanchero trackers, Garza, Arenas, and the Apache, joined him at the lead. The rest of the men followed. They were all well-armed and experienced lawmen and bounty hunters. It was a mean, dirty bunch as far as Cadence was concerned.

They proceeded on foot.

They headed down the trail, with Cadence leading the way. The farther the bounty hunters went down the narrow path, the more the twelve other men looked around at each other, wondering if this twenty-year-old kid actually knew where he was going. It was nighttime both times Cadence had gone there, so now maybe he was confused in the light of day.

It was early morning, and the sun was barely up as they moved silently and stealthily down the trail. To the man, each gun was cocked as the troop stepped through the thirty feet of bamboo and charged.

In the rush down the hill into the slave camp, the unthinkable was discovered. The entire campsite was empty. All the inhabitants were gone. The hidden lagoon looked untouched. The tents and campsites had vanished. All the flatbed boats had disappeared. The entire place looked pristine and empty.

Cadence looked around in disbelief. He was just here, not two or three hours ago. How did they pack up and empty this hidden valley in so short a time without so much as a leaf left disturbed? Cadence wiped his eyes several times and then looked around to make sure he was seeing what was in front of him. Dumbstruck, he was questioning himself and whether he imagined the community of runaway slaves was ever here in the first place.

Cadence continued to look around. He was sure this was the right place.

Nelson broke out through the bamboo and strolled around, looking bewildered.

"Well, where in the hell are they, Cadence?" Nelson asked.

"They must have caught wind that we were coming," one of the other gang members said to Cadence. Cadence looked up to see it was the Comanchero's leader, Garza.

"Perhaps there is a spy in our mist," he said, looking at Cadence.

The Hunt for Frederick Douglass
Terry Balagia

Nelson turned to face Cadence. "Speaking of which, where were you last night for your horse to be so lathered this morning? Did you come to warn your buddies that we were about to arrest them?" The other gang members were equally curious.

"I was out scouting this place," Cadence insisted. "Besides, why would I warn them, Nelson? I'm the one who showed you the way here in the first place."

"I don't know why you would want to warn them, Cadence," Nelson pressed. "Why don't you tell us?"

PART THREE

A TEXAS RANGER would rather wound a man than kill him.

He'd rather not shoot him at all if he can.

But you can't ever tell what's on a man's mind especially when he's pointing a gun at you.

Chances are he's meaning to kill you first.

The Hunt for Frederick Douglass
Terry Balagia

CHAPTER 43

THE HUNT FOR Frederick Douglass was now over, thanks to his decision to turn himself in to Rip. The next part of the mission was for Rip to get him back to Richmond safely and in one piece.

From the minute the sentries dragged Cadence away bloody, screaming, and frustrated, Rip and Frederick went immediately to work. They needed everyone to pick up and move out fast. There was no time to waste. Rip knew Cadence would return with an overpowering and indiscriminate force, so they had to move quickly. First, they dispersed the flatboats to hidden coves up and down river from there. The community would continue on their way north to Canada. Before they left the hidden lagoon, Rip and Frederick and a small group of sentries made one last walk-through making sure the campsite showed no evidence they had been there.

After that Rip and Frederick gathered their things and loaded them into one of the Quaker's wagons for their trip down south. He and Frederick fastened the two Quaker horses to the harness as the rest of the community walked on foot in the other direction, north, to freedom. Many were silently waving their goodbyes and sweet wishes and prayers to Frederick. Some even to Rip.

Rip waved back at some, then reached inside his coat pocket to make sure he had the travel documents, the diplomatic medallion, and the assorted papers he would need for the bridge and border crossing. They were there, although he wished he had the pouch to keep them in. Gatlin climbed up onto the bench seat. Frederick was quick to join him.

They sat and watched the constant flow of souls parading silently past them along the other side of the road. Hannibal came walking up from across the road. He broke away from the long and seemingly endless line of community folks. This was the kid who had brought him the food, he remembered. Rip had not seen him since the other night. Hannibal had a big grin on his face, and he was carrying something in a turnip sack in his hands. The young boy jumped up on the side of the wagon next to Rip.

"I am smiling because I have two gifts for you. One is this." He handed the sack to Rip, who reached in and pulled out his diplomatic pouch. "I told you I would return the pouch I took."

Rip noticed that a strip of leather was missing from the shoulder strap. "What happened here?" Rip asked him.

Hannibal smiled even more broadly. "That's the second gift." He revealed a leather eyepatch and head strap he had crafted from a portion of the shoulder strap. Hannibal eagerly wrapped the newly crafted leather band around Rip's head, right beneath his cowboy hat.

He tied it in the back then centered the patch, so it covered his atrocious looking eye. "There you are," he said. "Big improvement."

Rip stuffed the travel papers into the pouch, which he stuck underneath the bench seat. He sat up and adjusted his new eye patch without resistance. He figured it would take some getting used to but gave Hannibal a nod and a tug on the brow of his cowboy hat and gathered the reins.

Hannibal gave him a wink of approval. "Travel safe. Remember me when I am a famous lawyer." Hannibal jumped off the wagon as Harriet came walking by. Surrounding Harriet was Ethel and Alice and the rest of her ladies. They were all moving north in complete silence.

Harriet separated herself from the group and crossed the road and walked up to their wagon to address Frederick one more time.

She looked up at him as he settled himself on the wooden bench next to Rip.

"I can see you refused to see things my way, Freddie," Harriet started off. "And that you are determined to commit suicide out of grief for losing your firstborn. I understand all that. The problem is you don't understand all that. You don't understand what you, yourself, are going through. But we all see it. And future generations will see it, too. They will know you did it while in a state of grief over your son's death." Harriet looked at him and continued, "Our cause is not served by losing our leader. Don't you see that?"

Harriet looked over and scowled at Rip. "Even the snake sitting beside you will admit to that, won't you, Snake?" Rip did not respond. He refused to engage. "You can't even look at me, can you?" She prodded him. "Tell me, can you look him in the eye and promise him that they won't hang his Black ass the minute they get their evil White hands on him? Can you assure us that won't happen, famous Texas Ranger? You can't, can you?"

Rip looked at her confidently. Then he recited a quote from Frederick Douglass himself. "Those who profess to favor freedom and yet depreciate agitation are men who want crops without plowing up the ground."

Frederick smiled and applauded lightly. "Well said, Sir."

Rip looked at Harriet with a stern expression. "There is some risk involved, yes."

"Some risk?" Harriet was aghast. "Are you calling them hanging him *some risk*? I don't think you can risk any more than that. There is not just *some* risk on going through with this fool-hearted plan. There is a significant risk that they will hang him. Am I right?"

At this, Frederick interceded.

The Hunt for Frederick Douglass
Terry Balagia

"Woman, listen to me. I know you mean well. With all your heart, you mean well. But dammit, so do I. I mean well, too. I mean to take a chance, even if it is just a small chance with great risks, to save the lives of America's sons, husbands, slaves, and freemen."

Then he spoke low, almost a whisper. "It will be carnage, Minty. A tragedy of human destruction rarely occurring in history, and never before seen on America's shores in the short time since its inception upon this earth. I don't need a guarantee. I only need a slight chance. Because if there is even a sliver of a chance, I will take it. It is worth it a million times over."

Frederick gave her a minute to absorb his thoughts. "Don't you think, Minty, that if the devil ever comes to you and offers up one life, where you will have a chance to save a hundred thousand, or more, human beings, you will take it? Wouldn't you, Girl? This may be my calling of a lifetime. Maybe my entire life has brought me to this time in history for me to make a difference. What if this is the moment God has spent my life preparing me for. Do I want it said that when faced with the opportunity to do something great, Frederick Douglass was too selfish, or too much of a coward? That he pulled away from his confrontation with history? I am not asking Rip to promise me this will work, Minty. I just need Rip to be the platform that gives me a shot at saving America from splitting in two."

Harriet waited until he was finished and gave herself a moment to understand his viewpoint. "Then maybe you are right, Frederick. In which case, then maybe, I am selfish. But I am determined to stay selfish then. Because I don't want to see you hurt, not to a hair on your big, hairy head. Does that make me selfish, Frederick?" she pleaded.

Frederick understood. "I do believe men are tired of this talk of war. There have been many attempts to avoid this war. I think that means none of these men, North or South, want a war. They are looking for an excuse to avoid it permanently. Maybe using me gives them that excuse. As Sam Houston said, 'it may sound crazy, but it is the last best chance at avoiding the war.' That has to be a chance worth taking. How can we not?"

Harriet shook her head in exasperation. "Maybe so, Freddie. Maybe so. But regardless, have no fear. I will be watching over you." Harriet Tubman turned with the rest of her community and continued north in the other direction on Reservoir Road. Rip held the reins in his hands and looked at the road with his one good eye. He gave Frederick a nod, and they headed south.

After a short distance, Harriet grabbed a small group and doubled back to secretly follow Rip and Frederick as they headed to Richmond. Hannibal went with them. As she had said, she planned to watch over them. She knew in her heart that Rip and Frederick would need someone to watch out for them.

The Hunt for Frederick Douglass
Terry Balagia

CHAPTER 44

BACK IN RICHMOND, the anticipation of the North preparing to resupply Fort Sumter created significant excitement. The entire second floor spilling down to the lobby was amassed by lobbyists, congressional members, cabinet members, executive advisors, and bankers. The cigar smoke billowing willy-nilly extended from the bar in the lobby, along with the roar of discussion, argument, and persuasion at an ear-splitting volume. There was also plenty of bourbon flowing to help lubricate and animate the discussions.

President Davis called an emergency meeting of his cabinet. They immediately drafted articles of war against the northern states. He appointed his vice president, Alex Stephens, to oversee and write the first draft.

One of the office staff came and grabbed Pinkerton and escorted him out of his spacious office into the telegraph room where he found a tiny desk wedged against the wall amidst the noise of four incessantly typing telegraph machines. Pinkerton's belongings were in piles atop the small desk. This was his new office. The move was a true reflection of how suddenly unimportant Pinkerton's mission was.

He was aware of the fact that he was about to lose his fee for not completing the capture of Frederick Douglass. The mission was fast becoming a giant waste of time and a significant financial loss. Plus, it meant he would have little chance of getting any more assignments from President Davis and the CSA in the future. Pinkerton needed to think of something, and he needed to think fast.

The Hunt for Frederick Douglass
Terry Balagia

Back in the war suite, President Davis gave the command to authorize the formation of the Confederate Army. Next, he gave his staff approval to draft the attack plan on Ft. Sumter. They had been preparing for this eventuality, so everyone was excited to finally put their plans to paper.

"Someone needs to get a solid confirmation from Bobby Lee," President Davis barked, "that when push comes to shove, he is going to fight for the Confederacy and his home state of Virginia over leadership of the Union forces. By God, with General Lee whipping up on the North, this war will be over in three months at the most." Jeff Davis took a big puff on the fat cigar in his mouth. He leaned way back in his chair as he blew out the smoke.

LeRoy Pope Walker, Secretary of War, heard his president. "I cannot confirm anything, but we hear-tell that General Lee is going to the White House to give President Lincoln his final decision any day now." He looked around the room at the other cabinet officials.

Vice President Stephens nodded his head in agreement. "I know for a fact Bobby Lee owns slaves. He inherited around two hundred from his father-in-law some years back. You know he's going to risk his life defending that much property."

"He won't be fighting for slavery," President Jeff Davis said. "He will be fighting for Virginia. How can a man turn on his own home?" he asked.

"Well, with all due respect, Mr. President, if you are fighting for Virginia, you are fighting for slavery. No state in the South has more slaves than Virginia. Why, without slavery, Virginia would have no economy!"

President Davis continued, "Now what are we to do? Change our entire way of life? You can't ask that of a people. It makes no sense." Davis looked around the room, now silent. Then he shook his head as if he had gone through this line of thinking a million times before.

He returned from his thoughts to the group in the room. "Our attack on Fort Sumter will be both the start and the instant end of the war, I believe. For I am convinced that once we show our might by crushing that Union fort, and once they surrender it to the new Confederate States of America, we will then use our victory to impose our military prowess on all the northern capitals, beginning with Washington, DC! And to that, I believe the Union forces are neither ready, nor equipped to respond. Thus, they will capitulate. Along with the anti-secessionists."

Clearly, there was no longer any interest in—nor discussion of—the plan to capture Frederick Douglass.

The Hunt for Frederick Douglass
Terry Balagia

CHAPTER 45

RIP AND FREDERICK Douglass arrived at the Long Bridge border crossing, which Rip had come through only three weeks before with Cadence. Back then there was only one guard on the northern side of the Long Bridge crossing. But now it was dramatically more militarized. They had constructed a guard post on each side of the road and Rip counted seven guards on duty at the gate. Plus, there were newly constructed soldier barracks alongside the crossing gate guardhouse where at least two dozen Union soldiers were unpacking their gear and getting settled.

The guards were dumbfounded at the sight of Rip Gatlin approaching them in his wagon with his prisoner, Frederick Douglass. The Northern guards were even more amazed that Frederick Douglass was not in chains but heading south all of his own free will. The Northern border guards did not want to let them pass, but the Fugitive Slave Act required them to.

As they awaited permission, the guards asked Frederick if he wanted them to intervene, to which he thanked them politely but made it clear that he was headed south to meet with President Davis to help prevent a war. He left it at that.

Finally, the guard in charge allowed them to pass. They raised the crossing gate, and Rip and Frederick Douglass started across the Long Bridge on the buckboard wagon. As they got closer to the southern side of the Potomac River, Rip could see the other side was built up and well-fortified. It was nothing like it had been a matter of weeks ago. Rip observed there was a newly built shelter around the guard booth with a small scattergun cannon manned by two young Virginia Militiamen. Some of the Confederate Army were also Virginia Militiamen. Some had already received their new uniforms. For most, the uniform was the first pair of new clothes they had ever owned in their entire lives.

It was clear, both sides were preparing for war.

Rip remembered when he and Cadence had crossed this bridge a few weeks before, thinking, *It was such a short time ago, yet it seems like a lifetime.*

Rip remembered telling the young guards on the Virginia side stories about his experience at the Alamo and the battle of San Jacinto. Their young eyes had been as big as goose eggs. *Now, look at them—armed, scared, and eager to fight, but they have no idea how ugly war is or how much it will affect them for the rest of their lives. Assuming they even survive.*

The feeling of concern for the young soldiers reminded him of Cadence, and he wondered where he was in all of this. He had not heard hide nor hair from Cadence since their fight, the thought of which made him sick to his stomach as nothing else could. He worried about the kid's safety and his health. If he was riding with Nelson and his expanded gang, then he was with a vile bunch.

Cadence would not stomach them for long. Nor would they put up with him. What concerned Rip at the moment—more than his own safety—was how Nelson's gang would kill Cadence and ditch his body off the trail somewhere, and no one would ever know.

Gatlin and Douglass crossed the Long Bridge and approached the crossing gate on the Southern side of the Potomac River. The word that Rip Gatlin was coming in with Frederick Douglass had beaten them across the river. A dozen or more Confederate soldiers were guarding the gate crossing, eager to get a peek at the famous anti-slavery orator and the Texas Ranger bringing him in.

The Hunt for Frederick Douglass
Terry Balagia

Perched on the wagon bench seat alongside Rip, Frederick rested in his authenticity as a great man, proud and self-respecting. He sat tall and erect, holding himself with great dignity as always. The Virginia soldiers at the guard posts stared awestruck as Rip and Frederick's wagon approached.

They arrived at the checkpoint, and as expected, the guards on the Southern side held them and checked their papers. Following the new rules of protocol, guards at the checkpoint telegraphed the Spotswood Hotel to ask permission to allow the prisoner, Frederick Douglass, to cross through Virginia and into the South.

The group of Virginia militia at the crossing gate were rather chatty regarding the capture of Frederick Douglass. The young Tennessean was in the crowd of soldiers. He could not believe what he was witnessing.

"Bringing in Frederick Douglass. What a great ribbon-bow at the top of an already legendary career, Captain!" He looked as if he were memorizing this moment so he could tell folks about it for the rest of his life.

The other soldiers looked on.

"It's about time someone shut that educated mouth of his," Rip heard. Many of the other comments were simply the vilest and most reprehensible things these young soldiers could think of saying to Frederick Douglass.

"Have some respect for me and my prisoner, soldier!" Rip reprimanded the young men sternly. They looked up at him and froze. "Act like soldiers. Soldiers don't heckle prisoners. Show some respect for the right to dignity."

The commanding officer of the guards came over to reprimand them.

The Hunt for Frederick Douglass
Terry Balagia

"Knock it off, men! You heard him! Shut your holes! That's an order!"

Under his breath, Rip started to apologize to his traveling companion. Sensing it, Frederick smiled and repeated one of his own lines, "If there is no struggle, there is no progress."

It took about fifteen minutes, but the word came back. Not from the Spotswood Hotel, but from the Richmond telegraph office, "The CSA welcomes them!" The response was marked as received and approved by Allan Pinkerton.

CHAPTER 46

EARLIER, PINKERTON HAD found himself at a crossroads. He had been in Richmond for three months, forging a new business relationship with the Confederate States of America. But this morning, he was heading down to the lobby of the Spotswood Hotel to see the hotel manager after receiving a message under his room door.

When he got to the front desk, they informed him that the CSA was no longer covering his bill. He was now on his own dime. Pinkerton thanked them and stood in the lobby for a moment. The potential for landing this account was not looking good, he thought. Yesterday they had taken away Pinkerton's large office suite and stuck him on a tiny desk in the telegraph room. Now they were no longer covering his room and board. If Pinkerton did not think of something soon, he would lose this opportunity to charge the client and any possibility of ever working with the Confederate States again. Plus, he could not invoice for three months of billing for the company's most expensive executive—himself. He was now under the gun to capture and deliver Frederick Douglass for the mission to be billable, and that was not looking even remotely possible.

Pinkerton headed back upstairs to his tiny corner of the telegraph room. It comprised a small bedside table as a desk, his travel-size writing and stationery set, and a small clerk's chair to sit on. Allan Pinkerton no longer felt very important.

Pinkerton was sitting in his little corner, feeling sorry for himself when he heard, in the din of four constantly ticking and tapping telegraph stations, one of the soldiers reading out his message. It captured Pinkerton's ear.

The Hunt for Frederick Douglass
Terry Balagia

Outpost 12 Potomac River crossing Long Bridge. Commander Report: Urgent!

Rip Gatlin asking permission to cross. In his custody is Frederick Douglass. Allow entrance?

Pinkerton's eyebrow twitched intuitively.

He looked over as the soldier put the message onto the stack for President Davis. It was placed in a stack designated as not marked urgent nor essential. Pinkerton looked around to see that all the soldiers in the room were distracted, doing their jobs. He casually reached over and slipped the telegram into his coat pocket.

He headed outside for a little fresh air and to determine whether what he thought he had heard was true. The minute he got outside Pinkerton took the telegram out of his pocket. He reminded himself that stealing from the President's pile broke a ton of laws. He acknowledged the fact, but it did not stop him as he opened the note. Rip Gatlin was asking permission to cross, along with his prisoner, Frederick Douglass. He read it again and again. He could not believe it. Rip Gatlin had done it!

Suddenly, Pinkerton's hopes of getting paid were still alive. If Rip made the four-day trip down to Richmond safely, Pinkerton's mission would be complete, and the agency would get their fees covered for the last three months plus an ongoing contract for service. But Pinkerton was not one to sit and wait and hope. He was a doer.

He headed to the telegraph office and on no one's authority but his own, Pinkerton wired permission to let Rip and his prisoner pass through the crossing gate at the Long Bridge. That done, and having broken even more laws, he headed toward Marshal Maddox's office.

The Hunt for Frederick Douglass
Terry Balagia

The marshal was being appointed a colonel in the Virginia Militia to prepare for Virginia seceding and the militia becoming part of the CSA Army. Likewise, his office was now half marshal's office and half Army headquarters. It looked the same on the inside, but outside the marshal's office, there was a crowd of young new soldiers spilling out into the street. All of them were in new grey and gold trimmed Virginia Militia uniforms, soon to be the Army of the Confederate States of America.

Pinkerton met briefly with Marshal Maddox, now Colonel Maddox, and told him he needed Maddox to assemble a platoon of soldiers to accompany them to meet Rip and retrieve Frederick Douglass. Maddox was happy to oblige and quickly picked twenty-four soldiers from the new recruits to form the detail.

Pinkerton headed back to his office in the telegraph room, closed all his ledgers and work, and packed his briefcase. In all his shuffling around, he effortlessly slipped the telegram out of his coat pocket and into its previous stack. Pinkerton looked around at the busy little bodies transcribing and sending out telegrams. No one noticed him doing a thing.

Satisfied, Pinkerton headed back to his hotel room, stowed his briefcase, changed into his riding clothes, and headed back downstairs. Maddox had already assembled the platoon of soldiers. In their new uniforms, they all looked the part. In sad reality, the troop was disorganized, awkwardly uncomfortable, untrained, and inexperienced.

Pinkerton mounted up. He and Colonel Maddox led the platoon of green, new soldiers. They headed out of Richmond on their way to take custody of Frederick Douglass.

The Hunt for Frederick Douglass
Terry Balagia

CHAPTER 47

BACK AT THE Long Bridge, crossing permission was received to lift the gate.

The gate at the bridge closed behind Rip and Frederick. They were now in the South. The tension was palpable. Frederick never imagined he would voluntarily return south of the Mason-Dixon line, but here he was.

They rode along the rest of the afternoon without saying much—each man mostly lost in his own thoughts.

"I have a friend back in England. A Black man from Africa, from the lower Niger. He says back in the Kongo and the Kasanje Kingdom, they say that the lucky ones are the ones who got caught and thrown onto the slave boats," Frederick said after a long stretch of silence.

"Can you imagine that? This is an African man telling me, 'the ones who got caught and sold into slavery were lucky because their lineage will now grow up in America while my children and grandchildren will grow up in the Kongo. Now, which legacy would you rather have given your lineage?' he asked me incredulously."

"But I answered him, asking how my children can be thought of as lucky, when here they are born into slavery. How is that lucky? I said his descendants are the lucky ones, not the poor slave who gets captured and sold into ownership. But he disagreed fervently with me, saying that my lineage will grow up in the greatest democracy man has ever created, where all are created equal. That we will survive our life enduring slavery, and in exchange, someday slavery will be gone, and my descendants will live in freedom," Frederick said.

"His point was to remind me that to our grandchildren and great-grandchildren our days in bondage will only be stories. They will read about the horrors of slavery, but they will not live them. But those of us born into slavery in America are offered a gateway of freedom to those who follow us into this world. We are paying the price for the freedom for our sons and our daughters. A great man and woman can take pride in a perspective like that. That is something we own that is of great value to our souls."

Frederick grew quiet again as the wagon continued to plod along down the road.

———— • ————

At that same moment back in Richmond, Jeff Davis gave the order to start cannon fire on Fort Sumter. Behind them, the Long Bridge guards received the news via telegraph that the war had begun, and they quickly shut down the border crossing. Not knowing what else to do, each side aimed their long rifles at the guards on the opposite end of the bridge.

Meanwhile, having long since crossed the bridge and cleared the checkpoints, Rip and Frederick continued to Richmond having no inkling that the war they were on this mission to prevent had started. They would not hear. There was no telegraph until Richmond. There were few travelers along their route and when they saw others, they avoided contact.

After half a day of traveling, the fear of getting caught or being spotted and recognized slowly gave way. They both eased back into the clickity-clack of the horses on the dirt road and the tug and pull of the metal-rimmed, wooden wheel of the wagon. During that first day, Frederick talked about planning for the future but then drifted into talking about the past.

"The first time I had my own newspaper," Frederick began. "it grew into an impressive size and circulation. I named it *The North Star*. We had our own printing press, an editorial board, and a roster of regular advertisers. I had such big plans."

Rip was listening. "*The North Star?*"

"Yes." Frederick got excited. "It is what all runaways are told when they start out. To follow the North Star. If you go north long enough, you will cross into Freedom's Land."

Rip nodded his head in understanding.

"We spread the word throughout all the plantations. You tell your young ones who want to run away to follow the North Star all night and day for however long it takes until you start seeing White men working the fields. Then you know you are in the North. Harriet inspired it."

"That makes sense. Even a dimwit like me can understand its meaning," Rip said. "The North Star. It is like a guiding light."

"Exactly." Frederick smiled.

"So, what happened to it?" Rip was watching the road and handling the reins.

"Someone paid a gang of ruffians to come in one night and smash the printing press. So that was that. But we were able to raise the money for a new one. So, this time I began a monthly edition called *Douglass' Monthly*. It's been two—or has it been closer to three—years, now?"

The Hunt for Frederick Douglass
Terry Balagia

CHAPTER 48

"I ENVISION A newspaper that teaches you how to read. That is what I want to do with my monthly. In the back each month we have lesson plans for beginners. It will teach the alphabet. Then it will teach new words, and then sentences and then paragraphs and then stories that change the world. You would keep issues around forever. Start your own small library, even. It would free our people with reading and learning and exploring new thoughts and ideas." Frederick grew more and more excited as he spoke.

"That is freedom, my friend, the freedom of the mind. The freedom of the imagination. The freedom to have hope. The freedom to believe in something better. The freedom to try. To strive. To ultimately achieve. That is the promise of freedom. That is the promise of America. The *North Star* started to spread that vision. Now I am going to bring all of that into my *Douglass' Monthly*. Bit by bit. I want it to be an instrument whereby adults and children alike will learn to read, which will transport them into an entirely new world. They will grow up seeing themselves differently than we were able to see ourselves when we were young. In my *Douglass Monthly*, we print thoughtful opinions and points of view. It is a platform for honest debate. We can ask our readers thoughtful questions and print their answers. "Is Slavery Against God's Laws?" Or "The Economics of Slavery." Or something like "Justifying Slavery."

Frederick gestured with his hands as he spoke...as if he were speaking to a grand audience instead of just Rip and the horses. "Slavery is a learned institution. It is passed down from generation to generation, like a momma's cornbread recipe. Some say, 'well, you can't unlearn things.' I say you don't have to unlearn it, just stop teaching it." He laughed at his own frankness.

"That's the problem. Slave owners teach hate for the Negro to help them justify slavery. We need to stop teaching it. To stop passing hate down to the young ones. The *Douglass Monthly* is going to help our people unlearn their limitations by learning how to read. That is one thing I do like about President Lincoln. That is how he escaped the poverty he was born into by learning how to read. And then reading everything he could get his hands on. We are the same in that way." Frederick looked at Rip after having talked his ear off.

"What do you have to say about that?"

Rip paused for a second. "I make it a rule to never talk to my captives."

Rip and Frederick looked at each other, expressionless, then slowly smiled and broke into laughter.

That night around the campfire, Rip cleaned up the pans and threw a few more logs on the fire and crawled into his bedroll. Frederick was sitting around the fire using the light as he wrote and read his words aloud.

"You, mister White man, say the Negro is dumb—but you are the ones who make them dumb. You complain 'they don't know how to read' but it is because you do not let them learn how to read. Knowledge makes a man unfit to be a slave. So, you keep them dumb. Not being able to read is the invisible chain of slavery.

"You see slaves living in hovels like animals because you force them to live that way. You perpetuate the limitations to our standards of living because you taught us to believe that we have limitations. You built an image of how we think or don't think of ourselves. The Negro's life is determined by the limitations placed around him by the White man. Plus, the limitations the Negro race places on ourselves." Frederick stopped reading and looked over at Rip as he tapped the side of his head. "It is easier to enslave the body when you first condition their minds."

Rip had never been around a man of words. He was spellbound by Frederick's ability to think a profound thought and then write it down to make a rational argument that made you want to get up and do something.

"You speak and write so powerfully," Rip told him when he finished.

"Thank you, my friend," Frederick said as he scribbled changes. "Oftentimes, after people hear me give a speech and they come to me and ask about my education. 'Where did you go to college? Did you go to this school or to that school,' they will ask. And I laugh and say I was not afforded the opportunity to go to college. I was born into a more enlightened education. I attended the university of slavery, where I earned degrees in patience and forbearance, with additional studies in cruelty. While attending said school I studied the horrors that White men are capable of. Lucifer wrote the textbook himself. I wrote my thesis on the shame of raping twelve-year-old slave girls. I got my degrees in law, both sets of laws, the laws that apply to White men and the laws that apply to Black men. Why I have many diplomas, I tell them. I wear them as whip scars on my back." Frederick looked at him and slowly formed a smile. "Most people don't like that answer very much." Then Frederick let out one of his customary laughs. Rip looked at him. Still thinking about the words Frederick was writing in his notebook.

"What are you working on? Is that what would be in your newspaper?" Rip asked. "Or is that a speech? Or is that what you plan on saying to Jefferson Davis when you meet him?"

Frederick smiled and looked up at Rip.

The Hunt for Frederick Douglass
Terry Balagia

"That is a very provocative question, my friend. Truth be told, it's probably a little of all three." Frederick smiled as he imagined his opportunity to meet face to face with President Jefferson Davis.

"What will you say to him, do you think?" Rip probed.

Frederick became removed and thoughtful. "I imagine I will try to appeal to his human side, at first. Try to convince him that what he refers to as slaves are people. Failing that, then perhaps talk to his economic side. Assuming all of that fails, or perhaps in the course of speaking of all that, I will certainly pour out my heart and my mind to him. I will ask now, 'do you believe in God the Father? And if you do, do you believe the Almighty loves human beings with darker skin any less?'"

Rip could not wait for that meeting. He planned on getting a front row center seat.

"Have you ever seen slavery, Rip? I mean, truly seen it. The poverty. The pain. The heavy weight of oppression pushing down on your chest. On your soul. Families separated. You ever have a kid, Rip?"

Rip stared back silently.

Frederick continued, "Can you imagine someone selling you to another plantation, hundreds of miles away from your wife and children? Tearing your family apart as you would cattle or horses? People with hearts and feelings and hopes and dreams. Or imagine another man having his way with your wife, Rip. Whenever the master felt like it. Could you endure that? I couldn't."

"I don't know that much about slavery," Rip said. "We never saw much slavery where I was. The Mexican government, to their credit, outlawed slavery in Texas. Sam Houston tried to keep it that way. But when we became part of the United States, slavery became legal. I know in East Texas some of those large cotton farms in

The Hunt for Frederick Douglass
Terry Balagia

Louisiana bleed over into East Texas and they have slavery there. But as you go west, the availability of Mexican laborers makes it cheaper to hire them than to provide room and board for a bunch of slave families. So, slavery never took much hold in other places in Texas because it didn't make financial sense."

Frederick Douglass looked at Rip as if a light went on inside his head.

"Why Rip, that makes a lot of sense," Frederick said.

Rip nodded in agreement with himself and with what he had said. "I mean you can talk till you are blue in the face about what's right and what's wrong. But you show a slave owner a way to cut labor cost, and he will do away with slavery in a mosquito second. And believe me, that is fast." Rip smiled at his phrasing.

Frederick sat and stared at the one-eyed man.

"You are more than you let on to be, Rip Gatlin. I must admit you do surprise me, especially for a lawman."

The Hunt for Frederick Douglass
Terry Balagia

CHAPTER 49

PRESIDENT DAVIS HAD been planning an attack on Fort Sumter for several months. The assault was designed using the cannon fire from the three military installations surrounding it in the Charleston Harbor, Fort Moultrie, and Fort Johnson with their Whitworth guns and the Cummings Batteries. It was expected to be a brief engagement.

They ran everything from the second floor at the Spotswood and the four telegraph operators there. President Davis' suite was transformed into the war room. Maps and charts of Charleston Harbor were spread out all over the giant table.

Davis leaned over the table and smoked his cigar. His glass of bourbon formed a water ring in the middle of the Charleston Harbor as he pointed out the details of the attack to the room.

At four-thirty in the morning on April 12th, the first cannon fired from Fort Johnson on James Island at Fort Sumter. The shot was aimed to sail clear over the fort, which had two purposes: to demonstrate the power of the big guns and to give a distance by which to start graduated marking. The next missile was fired short of the target. Between those two points, the metrics took over as the cannoneers gradually pulled one in and let the other one out until they determined the range line squarely on target.

Fort Sumter, surrounded by two other forts and three additional Confederate batteries totaling over forty-eight cannons and howitzers, was pummeled with over three-thousand shells in thirty-three hours.

The Hunt for Frederick Douglass
Terry Balagia

In the thirty-fourth hour of the bombardment, a large fire started within Fort Sumter. General Anderson and his men could no longer maintain the battle against the surrounding three Southern Batteries. Without further battering, at two o'clock in the afternoon, they surrendered Fort Sumter.

Jeff Davis and his suite were ecstatic at the news that General Anderson had surrendered Fort Sumter. They ordered champagne and the entire lobby broke out into a jubilee, feeling like they had won the war and confident that the North would now capitulate.

Joseph Davis, the President's nephew, came in with telegraph messages for President Davis. An extravagant dinner was being prepared at the hotel. The atmosphere was one of utter triumph.

In a rather large voice, Joseph called out, "Uncle Jeff, listen to this." Then he corrected himself. "I'm sorry, I mean, uh Mr. President, sir?"

"Joseph, my boy, bring those over here." Davis waved for him to come closer. "Let's see if we can tear through those quickly."

"I prioritized this stack, Mr. President. May I read it?"

"But yes, of course." President Davis approved. "As long as it is good news. Only good news tonight, Joseph." There was a murmur of agreement. "A telegram from the Long Bridge," Joseph said, scanning the cable. "Rip Gatlin was asking to cross the Long Bridge with his prisoner, Frederick Douglass!"

"Well Damn! How do you like that? Rip Gatlin captured Frederick Douglass! Hells Bells! What do you know!" Davis took a big gulp from his glass of bourbon and read the telegram again to himself.

"It's a little late to avoid the war, Joseph. I don't know if you can call that good news. It's like walking in with yesterday's fish. It rather stinks," Davis laughed. "I assume we'll soon have Douglass in our hands. Looks like we will have to give him a fair trial. And then promptly hang him."

The Hunt for Frederick Douglass
Terry Balagia

CHAPTER 50

CADENCE COULD NOT get back to Richmond fast enough. They left the deserted hidden lagoon within minutes after arriving. Everyone in Nelson's gang assumed Cadence had tipped them off.

"Why would I lead you there and then slip the word that we were coming?" Cadence protested. "That makes no sense. I don't give a shit if you guys don't believe me."

They crossed the Potomac and headed south on the road back to Richmond.

They traveled the rest of the way in complete silence. Cadence rode out in front at a pace his pony could maintain all day long. Nelson and his men followed behind him. Cadence cringed both nights when they stopped to make camp. He could feel their suspicious eyes behind his back. They didn't buy his story and were all furious with him. He wanted to get back to Richmond as fast as they could and give his side of the story to Marshal Maddox himself to make sure they didn't blame him. Cadence knew he would pass through these parts again. He wanted to keep his name clean.

The other thing Cadence had been thinking about was Lydia and getting her back. Every time he thought of Lydia he felt an ache inside himself. Cadence ached for her so badly and resolved himself to the fact that he was over his puppy love. *I know what I want! To go back to Washington, marry Lydia, and be with her for the rest of my life. To hell with Rip and all his lies.* Cadence would start a life with Lydia. He was thinking he would take her down to Texas and find some open acreage out in West Texas somewhere, maybe in the panhandle, where no one wanted to live but Longhorn cattle, peyote cactus, horned frogs, and what was left of the Cherokee. He and Lydia would move there, start ranching, and raise a whole bunch of cattle and kids.

Nelson, Cadence, and the gang wasted no time. They managed the three-day horseback ride in two and a half days. As the group approached the city, they were exhausted and depressed. Nelson rode up alongside Cadence.

"First thing though, let's go check in with Marshal Maddox. You can tell your side of the story. Hell, I don't give a shit anymore. You can ask him about Rip, too. You never got around to doing that before. He knew your ma and her family pretty well, if I recall. He will corroborate what I said about Rip killing your pa. You can ask Deputy Hale, too. He was there."

It was late in the day when they got into town in the midst of what appeared to be a commotion. People were running out into the streets and celebrating. As they continued riding through downtown Richmond, Nelson's group could see that Spotswood was the center of the excitement.

People were crowding in front of the hotel whooping and hollering. A jubilant man ran up to them in the middle of the street.

"Did you guys hear? Fort Sumter has fallen!"

All kinds of town folks were coming into the streets, shaking hands, and congratulating each other over the war that had finally started. People were overjoyed, like it was the beginning of the end. They all hoped and assumed it would be a short war and peace would be made quickly. Perhaps with few, if any killings. After all, no one had been killed during the attack on Fort Sumter.

As Nelson and the posse proceeded toward the marshal's office, four of the local guys that rode with them waved to Nelson and took their leave.

The Hunt for Frederick Douglass
Terry Balagia

As two others rode off. Then another still, Nelson called out after them, "To each his own!"

That left Nelson's original gang which now included himself, his brother Hank and the three Comancheros: Garza, Arenas, and the one they called the Apache, although he was clearly Comanche from what Cadence could tell. He had Comanche wampum woven into his buckskin tunic and into the handiwork on his moccasins. He *was* Comanche, and as Rip had so often reminded Cadence, the Comanche were the sworn enemy to the Cherokee People. Cadence knew that Rip would not like these three. So, Cadence decided he didn't like them, either.

As they rode up to the marshal's office and dismounted Deputy Hale came walking through the door. He had Marshal Maddox's personal tobacco stash and was helping himself to a chaw.

"Marshal Maddox is not here." Deputy Hale told them as he put a fresh handful of chewing tobacco into his wet mouth. "In fact, he ain't a marshal anymore—it's Colonel Maddox." Deputy Hale flashed his tobacco-stained grin. They stared back blankly. "Ain't you boys heard the big news? The war done started. We already captured Fort Sumter." Deputy Hale spit again.

"We heard. Just now. Riding into town." Nelson said as he tied his horse to the rail post over the water trough so his horse could drink. The others followed.

"Do you want to hear some even bigger news?" Deputy Hale went on, "Rip Gatlin is on his way back and he's bringing Frederick Douglass with him."

"What?" Nelson and Cadence reacted in perfect unison.

"That be the truth. You can scalp me if I'm lying." Deputy Hale spat a brown glop of tobacco spit into the street gutter. "That's where Marshal Mad . . . Shit! Colonel Maddox is. Pinkerton came by, and he and Colonel Maddox left here with a platoon of new recruits to meet them halfway and take custody of Frederick Douglass. Pinkerton does not want to risk anything going wrong between the Long Bridge and here. They left earlier this morning; should be back in a day or two."

Deputy Hale spat again. "Ya know, I hate seeing a reward go uncollected. That's what happens the minute Rip hands him over. There is a huge reward that no one is going to collect. Now a smart man would head on out there and see if he could somehow get to Rip before Pinkerton and Maddox do. Or better yet, wait for the Marshal...shit! I mean the Colonel, outside of town tomorrow or the next day and find a way to finagle a portion of that reward money. I'm sure the Marshal, I mean the Colonel, would be willing to work something out.

"How much reward are we talking about, Deputy?"

"Last I checked it was upwards of twenty-thousand dollars. In gold, too. Not printed money."

"Holy Jesus..." another mumbled.

"As I said, Rip can't claim it. But you men would be paid handsomely for bringing in Frederick Douglass. Or shooting him dead." Deputy Hale leaned over the hitch rail and slowly coaxed more saliva from the wad of tobacco from his mouth and into the street. "I'm just saying, a smart group of men could make some big money." He looked them square in the eye. "But you didn't hear any of that from me, though I expect to be rewarded if something of that sort were to transpire. If you know what I mean."

"Oh, I know exactly what you mean, Hale." Nelson grinned. "We can work something out if that were to transpire." Nelson looked around at the gang and then at Hank, who was smiling like a prairie dog. Hank slid his Springfield hunting rifle from the rifle sleeve hanging off his saddle.

"I would love to be the one who shoots Frederick Douglass. It would be an honor. My name would go down in the history books."

"Too bad you never learnt how to read them books," one of the Comancheros joked, and they all laughed at Hank.

"Well, the lot of you best stop jawing and start riding if you hope to bushwhack Rip before Pinkerton and Maddox meet up with them," Deputy Hale reminded them.

"I think we liked your second idea better. To let the Marshal bring him most of the way back, and we can intercept them outside of town and work some kind of deal." Nelson slapped his thigh enthusiastically. "Besides, I love the thought of Rip having done all the hard work, and us getting the reward." Nelson looked around at all the celebration going on around them.

"And...my ass is too raw to get back into the saddle just yet. I say we get some grub, and some shut eye and re-group in the morning. Then we can take a little ride outside of town and wait for Marshal...I mean Colonel Maddox, and see if'n he will let us take Frederick Douglass off his hands for a tidy sum. You boys want to ride with me, let me know. It's up to you. I plan on getting some good food and then partake in some of this celebrating that's going on. Maybe indulge myself a bit."

"Let's meet up right here tomorrow. That is assuming you boys are still interested?"

Garza reassured Nelson. "Don't you worry, *amigo*. We will be here. Of that you can be sure."

Nelson looked over at Cadence. "You're coming with us ain't you, Cade? Oh shit, that reminds me," Nelson suddenly thought of something and turned to face Deputy Hale. "Hey, Hale, speaking of Rip, would you clear something up for us? I was telling Cadence here—"he turned to Cadence with an aside, "by the way your name was not Cadence—that you knew his family. Tell him who he is, and that he was born right here."

"Why, he is right, Cadence. I guess you were too young to remember. I can't recall what all the names were, but we all knew you. You were one of the McDaniel kids who lived outside of town fifteen or so years ago. Rip took you with him back to Texas when no one else wanted to claim you, frankly speaking."

Nelson smiled and nodded his head in an 'I-told-you' sort of way. "And tell him that Rip was the one who killed his pa," Nelson insisted.

Deputy Hale nodded. "Nelson's damn right about that. Rip put one right between his eyes. From about 100 feet away, I'd say. While on his horse. Through a chink in the log wall of that old cabin. Damnedest shot I'd ever seen." The deputy put his index finger on his own forehead as if to show him the spot. "Why, Rip never told you about any of that?"

"Oh, he told him," Nelson interjected. "He just never told him the truth. Rip loaded the kid up with a bunch of horseshit about some imaginary father. Then he takes most all of their reward money, like you would do if you were a guardian."

Deputy Hale nodded his head, remembering that day when Rip tossed the gold coins across the desk to Cadence. "I seen him do it, too. It makes sense. That's probably why Rip told you that. It makes him your legal guardian, so he can get you to do half the work while keeping all the reward money for himself. Meanwhile you could get killed at any time."

268

The Hunt for Frederick Douglass
Terry Balagia

Just hearing Deputy Hale confirm Nelson's story was like dropping a nickel in the bucket of growing resentment Cadence was feeling toward Rip. He had gone from admiring Rip all his life to realizing that Rip had been taking advantage of him all these years. Plus hiding the fact that he filled him full of lies about a make-believe father he never had. While lying about killing Cadence's real father at the same time. Cadence had a growing anger for Rip he was finding difficult to contain.

Deputy Hale spat again. "That's how he got his name, you know, 'RIP.' I had another Texas Ranger tell me that in the early days Rip could never keep a partner. They always seemed to get killed. Each time Rip would have to file a report, but he didn't know how to read or write. But he did know how to sign his name. So, he would have one of the other Rangers write the report, then someone showed him how to write R I P, for Rest In Peace, and he took to writing it and then his name, as his signature. So, on all the official documents it would read R-I-P Gatlin. The other Texas Rangers took to calling him Rip. And it stuck." Deputy Hale looked up.

"That's because he is purely bad luck," Nelson concluded. "If you're riding with Rip, you're as good as snakebit. Hell, Cadence, you're the first partner he's ever had this long. I'd say he owes you a fortune after all these years."

Cadence had turned and walked over to the hitching rail and tended to his horse. He had no desire to hear any more from Deputy Hale or Nelson about how Rip had lied to him all his life. It only made him angrier. And he did not think he could take getting any angrier than he already was. Plus, he had no intention to ride with these men any longer. He thought of what Rip often said, *You ride with thieves, you hang with thieves.*

He then responded to Nelson, "That may be, but what's between Rip and me, stays between Rip and me. I plan on settling up with him when he's headed back to DC. Which is where I'll be waiting for him.

"What makes you think Rip's heading back to Washington?"

"Because that's where he left Blade, and he ain't leaving without that horse. They go back a long way and I reckon there's nothin' on this earth he loves more. But I don't know when. It may be in two days or in two weeks, but whenever it is, I plan on being there to greet him when he arrives. But like I said, that's between me and Rip. It don't concern none of you." I'm done riding with you and your boys, Nelson.

"To each his own, Cadence." Nelson responded. "To each his own."

CHAPTER 51

RIP AND FREDERICK were in northern Virginia, heading south on the Old Richmond Road somewhere between the Long Bridge and Richmond. They had no idea the war had begun...or that Frederick Douglass' heroic attempt to offer himself hoping to avert the war was now simply little more than an act of suicide. Or that Rip was unknowingly delivering Frederick Douglass to be hanged.

The men were two days into what was normally a four-day journey by wagon from Washington, DC. Rip thought it wise to avoid people. Even though he had his diplomatic papers, he was not taking any chances. If local authorities here discovered he had captured Frederick Douglass, they would take him from Rip's custody and lynch the man on the spot, regardless of the courier pouch and the letters contained inside and take his body in for the reward money. They could not afford to be stopped or recognized by anyone. Until he delivered Frederick secretly and successfully to Richmond, his mission was not over.

They saw a noticeable increase in people fleeing the South. Many were poor Whites who were not optimistic about staying. There was also a lot of troop movement. For a full day, Rip and Frederick camped in a hollow to avoid being spotted by the Virginia Militia troops that occupied the roads all around them.

Rip and Frederick did not know that since the war had started, there was no value in capturing Frederick Douglass, other than publicly trying, humiliating, and then murdering him by hanging. While this would still be great fun in Jeff Davis' eyes, it was no longer a mission of urgency and significance nor a great strategic value to get Lincoln to the negotiating table. As far as anyone on either side was concerned, the negotiating table no longer existed—if it ever had.

Like the community of runaways, Rip and Frederick traveled at night most of the way. They had a lit lantern on a long pole extending up and over the horses, lighting the trail for them, and the pages of Frederick's journal. He was always writing with his pencil in his black moleskin notebook and talking. Like he was on this night.

He spent a lot of time talking. He was a natural- born speaker and loved having an audience to practice his powerful speaking voice. For Rip, it was almost like when Cadence would read to him, only better. He learned a lot listening to Frederick, and he enjoyed the sound of Frederick's melodious voice. Tonight, was no different.

"You know I have great respect for our Founding Fathers, though I am sometimes critical. Especially Jefferson, declaring independence from Britain while denying slaves their freedom at the same time—which I find deplorable. But I still respect him and his intellect, and what they did, especially those documents they wrote.

"Though, having said that, in my humble opinion I believe he gets too much credit sometimes for certain things he did not do. For example, Jefferson actually lifted that line in the Declaration of Independence, 'life, liberty, and the pursuit of happiness' from John Locke, the English philosopher who wrote 'life, liberty, and the pursuit of property,' eighty-some-odd years before.

"Though to his credit, Jefferson changed the word *property* to *happiness*. So regardless of what I may think of Thomas Jefferson as history's greatest hypocrite—he had the brilliance of spirit to change the tangible to the esoteric. From *property* to *happiness*. What a beautifully high ideal for man to aspire to. And to say that happiness is more valuable than property. What an outrageous thought or phrase to choose as the goal for its People; for their reason to revolt. So, though I may have some gigantic differences with him on some things, I find that his adding that one word is almost genius. Don't you, Rip?"

But instead of waiting for Rip to answer Frederick continued. This time with an almost impish smile. "Of course, in Plato's, Republic, Socrates ponders 'whether the just man is happy or unhappy.' Implying that happiness is the scale against which the quality of one's life is to be measured. Perhaps this is the 'pursuit of happiness' which inspired Jefferson? Certainly, he read Plato. You know he read Locke, as well. He brought together both men's thoughts and in doing so he created an entirely new one. That's what great minds do, Rip. And Jefferson was most certainly a great mind." Then, scribbling in his notebook, he stayed silent for a good hour, writing the entire time. Only to start talking again hours later about something entirely new.

"Take a listen to this," Frederick said out of the blue, "and tell me if it means anything to you: *It takes a blessed man to forgive. And an even more blessed man to learn how to unhate.* Imagine having no concept of hate in your mind? You may find you no longer hate yourself."

Rip looked puzzled. "I don't know if I know what unhate means. You mean to forgive someone?"

"No." Frederick responded. "You see, unhating is bigger than forgiveness. Unhating is to completely forget your hate. I don't mean to deny it or ignore hate. I am talking about wiping it away from your thoughts of that person, or that thing. You can still have the memory without the anger being there. Imagine that.

"You can't, can you? It's hard to do. For example, I am in the process of unhating Jefferson Davis, a man I truly despise. But I need to embrace him and engulf him with my spirit, or we will never solve the problem at hand. Now how do I do that? How can I change the way I feel about someone I hate with all my being? And rightly so." Frederick looked at Rip as if Rip knew the answer. Rip looked back at him, still puzzled.

"Why are you asking me?" Rip asked. "I don't know much about these things."

Frederick looked at him.

"The process of unhating is calling up everyone you taught yourself how to hate and thinking the opposite of whatever made you hate that person in the first place," Frederick spoke slowly as he explained what he considered a critical understanding.

"Imagine you had been a slave," he continued. "Can you forgive your master for owning you and treating you like cattle? Do you hate him? Of course, you do. Does he deserve to be righteously hated? Hell, yes, he does! Can you forgive a person like that? I doubt it, but maybe, just maybe now can you think of him and have no feeling of hate to forgive him for? I am not talking about ignoring your hate or suppressing it, both of which only make it stronger.

"I am talking about having no hate to forgive, or to forget. Just wiping it away like chalk on a slate. No pain in your heart when you think of him. Hard to do. People say they forgive but they never really do. They may think they do, but they don't. To truly forgive someone you have to forgive yourself. That is where that hate starts. You hate that master for treating you like property, but even more, you hate yourself for accepting that you are property. Human beings are too imperfect to judge themselves. Yet we all do it. Now do you understand?" Frederick asked.

The Hunt for Frederick Douglass
Terry Balagia

Rip looked at Frederick. His hands held the reins as his head struggled to hold the thought. Maybe his heart was struggling. At the same time, it made sense to Rip on some level.

"Can *you* unhate?" Frederick asked him.

Rip looked at him. "I don't know if I know," he said.

Frederick shook his head and tried again. "Practice it on yourself. Take something you did that you hate yourself for. Now think of that same thing without hating yourself for having done it. That is unhate."

Rip thought about something he hated himself for doing and he instantly thought of lying to Cadence about who his father was for all those years. He hated its having bothered Cadence that Rip lied to him. He only knew that all these years later it worked out. Cadence was now grown, resourceful, and on his way to becoming a solid citizen and man.

"Does that make sense?" Frederick asked.

He thought about it for a few minutes. "I am not always good with thinking about things. I'm even worse with saying the things I am thinking. So, when I hear you say, 'learn to unhate,' I know you understand it. So that makes me want to believe it. But it is hard for my mind to unhate something."

Frederick nodded empathetically. "I agree with you Rip. I think it is hard for all of us to understand how to unhate. Because we teach ourselves *to* hate. It sounds funny, but it is true. We practice hating all the time. Do we ever practice unhating? No. But we should. My point is: mastering anything requires time and practice. So, let us practice unhating. Let's make that mastery part of our everyday life. And let's see where it takes us." Frederick looked over at Rip.

The Hunt for Frederick Douglass
Terry Balagia

Rip looked from the horses to Frederick, then back to the horses again. "I think if I knew how to read, I would think of things like that. But for me, it is rather hard to practice something that I don't even understand," Rip told him.

"As it should be," Frederick agreed. "First time you try to do anything it is hard because you have no experience at it. But you know by the end...when you have mastered it and it becomes second nature. Then you can go on to master the next thing and the next thing and the next thing. So, we start by unhating ourselves and then we work on unhating everyone else. By then you realize you were never hating other people. You have always really only been hating yourself the whole time."

Frederick gave Rip a nudge with his elbow. "I wish I had my books with me. There is one I would give you, once you learn to read, that is. It's about the instant transformation of the human soul by an English author named Charles Dickens. It's about an old hate-filled miser named Scrooge who transforms overnight into a generous benefactor. All from having visions that ghosts were visiting him."

Rip looked sideways at Frederick. "I'm glad I don't read."

"No, it is an amazing thought. To think that by changing the way you look at things, you can change yourself. And become an entirely different person, overnight. Wonderful thought, isn't it, Rip?"

Rip had no response; he felt no need. Frederick had a wonderful way of working with words and language and Rip found it relaxing listening to him talk. Sometimes with those words, he even put thoughts in Rip's head.

They continued to make progress on their way to Richmond. Right before midnight they found a stream and stopped for the horses to rest. Rip found a can of sardines in the grub bag and several handfuls of dried beef for their supper. They sat on the buckboard in the moonlight and ate. Frederick used the light from the moon to illuminate his journal as he continued to write.

"The best men, the best people I have known in this life were slaves," Frederick said out of the blue. He had a stick of salted beef in one hand and a pencil in the other. "I think it takes a great man to be a slave." Then he looked at Rip and exploded with one of his booming laughs. "I guess that sounds rather presumptuous or self-serving for me to say." Then he settled himself down. "But I do believe it is true. I truly believe it takes a great man or a great woman for that matter—let us not forget our sisters who suffer through their own perilous war against slavery—it takes a greatness of spirit to survive being a slave. A greatness that not all men nor women possess. A fortitude or spirit deep down inside that others do not have access to. A greatness. You said you think Lincoln is a great man. Do you think Lincoln could allow himself to be treated the way a slave is treated? No, of course he wouldn't. He would resist like many men do and they would kill him. Or whip him continually until they broke his will. And then kill him." Frederick said.

"Think of your Sam Houston. Could he do it? Would he let them take his children away from him and sell them to a farm many miles away? Or take his wife and use her as they want and there was nothing he could do about it except live with it or die from it. What would Sam Houston do? A slave has no choice. A slave must bear it all or die. To endure the life of a slave is to suffer under the heavy weight of slavery. It takes a great man or woman to survive all that. All the while, not hating yourself for allowing another human being to treat you, a child of God, in such a horrific way. Yessir, to endure that life, the life of a slave, you have to have greatness in you." Frederick looked down at his journal and read aloud the words on which he had been working...

The Hunt for Frederick Douglass
Terry Balagia

It takes a man of great discipline to hold his tongue.
To keep his hands from forming into fists.
To avoid the trappings of this worldly experience.
To practice virtue without the mechanism of reward.
To do right by God and by all God's creatures every day, every moment. Every thought. Every breath.
To have injustice burn your heart to ash, yet you more than endure.
You THRIVE.
You stand tall.
You believe in your strength of body, mind, and soul.
You deliver all the elements of having greatness that are required.
Dare you to not fall short on even one if you want to survive.
You want to meet a great man or a great woman? Then meet a slave.
For they have disciplines of self-control and self-mastery that others will never perfect.

CHAPTER 52

CADENCE WALKED AWAY from Deputy Hale and Nelson with his mind made up. He needed two things from Rip. First, Rip had to pay back all the reward money Cadence had been cheated out of all those years. The second was his admission he killed Cadence's father. He needed to hear the truth out of Rip's mouth about why he lied to him all his life.

Nothing short of these two demands would satisfy Cadence.

As he walked his horse over to the livery and arranged for a fresh mount, he remembered the two library books, one on Frederick Douglass, the other written by him that Cadence had borrowed. Taking them out of his saddle bag, he walked them to the library, and slipped the books through the return slot in the side door. Then he headed to the telegraph office, which was situated just opposite the library, to come up with a proposal to Lydia, or at the very least to ask her to mull it over the coming days while he rode up there.

When Cadence arrived at the telegraph office, he was astonished to find an old message for him from April back at the Senator Hotel. Actually, there were three messages from last week to yesterday.

He read them in order from oldest to most recent:

CADENCE STOP COME BACK URGENT STOP LYDIA HURT STOP
SHE ASKS FOR YOU CONSTANTLY STOP PLEASE RESPOND STOP

CADENCE STOP DID YOU GET MY EARLIER TELEGRAM STOP
LYDIA WAS ATTACKED STOP

279

The Hunt for Frederick Douglass
Terry Balagia

HAVE NOT HEARD FROM YOU STOP
WONDERING IF YOU CARE ANYMORE. STOP

Cadence was out the door and on his fresh horse. He was about to dig in his spurs, but then he stopped. He dismounted and rushed back in to send two telegraphs.

One to Lydia saying: I HURT SO BAD INSIDE FOR YOU STOP

The second one to April. Three simple words: ON MY WAY STOP

Cadence was back on his horse in an instant and flying down the Old Richmond Road headed north. He rode as though his life depended on it.

The news of Lydia being attacked made him even more eager to get there. Who would attack her? And why?

The funny thing was, as angry as the news of her injury made him, there was an underlying feeling of intense jubilation. She loved him after all! While he was spending all that time thinking of her, she had also been thinking of him. As he was preparing to write a marriage proposal telegram to her, she had been calling for him.

As his horse raced forward, Cade's thoughts went wild. He had no idea how badly Lydia was hurt. He prayed she was all right— even alive. At this point, he did not know. He thought about when he had gone by to see her at the Senator Hotel, but April wouldn't let him go upstairs and told him to leave.

Cadence remembered how much that hurt him.

But now he realized Lydia was calling out for him when she needed him most. That awareness created a feeling of love inside of him that was so big he could hardly contain it. It was even bigger than Cadence's desire for revenge against Rip—at least for now.

She loved him as much as he loved her! It was his dream come true. His answered prayers.

The Hunt for Frederick Douglass
Terry Balagia

He continued to push the horse faster. His worrying thoughts raced to keep up with them both. Cadence imagined what could have happened to Lydia and how badly she might be hurt.

Cadence knew the main roads and the back roads quite well by now. He made breakneck speed, leaving the main road and cutting across farmlands and pastures to beat a trail to the Long Bridge. By the time he got there it was around noon. There was a long line of wagons and horses and pack mules waiting to go through. Hordes of families were moving up North in anticipation of the war reaching here. Some had papers to pass, some didn't. Some had family present to claim them, while others were turned away and made to go back.

Cadence looked around at all the others. Knowing he did not have the papers to pass between the borders, he got out of the line and rode his horse upriver, where the river flattened out and he crossed it in the shallows.

Cadence took the river road east and quickly arrived in Washington. The clock on the National Bank building said it was nearly two o'clock. Cadence knew he needed a bath and some sleep, and he couldn't remember the last time he ate anything, but he wasn't thinking about any of that now. He was only thinking about Lydia. In the two short weeks he had known her, he had gone from loving her to missing her to hating himself to hating her and back to being madly in love with her all over again. Rip was right when he warned his young partner to stay away from women. Thinking about Lydia confused Cadence in ways that made him wonder if maybe he was going insane.

To that, Cadence could imagine Rip saying something like, "No, you're not insane. You're in love. Not much difference in the two."

The Hunt for Frederick Douglass
Terry Balagia

CHAPTER 53

INSIDE THE SENATOR Hotel lobby the girls were busy setting up the tavern bar for the evening crowd. April was at a table in the back doing the bookkeeping. It was still early, and the bar was not open, but that did not stop Cadence from knocking on the closed and locked double doors from the outside.

"Just a minute," he heard.

One girl opened the curtain; with a gasp she then turned to the others in the room and shrieked, "He came back!"

April opened the door and hugged Cadence, smothering his face in her very generous bosom. "I knew you would come back. I told everyone you were different from the others, and here you are!" April burst into tears.

Cadence was startled but touched.

"Why are you crying?"

"Why you silly man, I am crying because I am overjoyed to see you. More importantly, she will be ecstatic to see you. April turned to Lucinda. "See Lucinda, you stupid bitch. I told you he would come back. By the way, you're fired. Get your shit and get out of here." Lucinda cried but April didn't care. She turned back to Cadence. "You should hurry. The doctor is coming by soon."

"The doctor? For what? Tell me what happened."

"I will tell you, but I don't want you to go flying off the handle. That day you came by Nelson and his guys were waiting to ambush you and Hank got a little rough with Lydia."

The Hunt for Frederick Douglass
Terry Balagia

"Damn him, I will track him down and kill him, so help me God."

"You will not. You will go upstairs to that girl who needs you. And who loves you. She is feeling better, and I don't want you overreacting and making her think it looks bad. Even though it does. Now promise me that, Cadence."

"Fine. But I also promise that Hank Nelson will soon be dead."

"Good enough. Go ahead, Cadence. You can go up—but only for a moment." April smothered him again in an embrace and sent him on his way upstairs.

As Cadence bounded up the stairs, the other girls consoled Lucinda.

"Don't worry, deary, she never means it. She just says stuff like that when she's mad," April heard them say.

"Oh, yes, I did!" April called from the stairs. "Now get your shit and go. I mean it, you unromantic thing, you. You said he would never come back for Lydia, and he did! You were wrong! If you don't believe in romance, then you don't belong here in the Senator Hotel."

Cadence knocked on Lydia's door. He heard her weakly whisper for him to come in.

He opened the door. Lydia was standing next to the bed, dressed in travel clothes. Her hair was in a bun and a bonnet. Alongside her were two packed carpet bags. She was stunningly beautiful, even though half of her face and one of her eyes were covered in bandages. Cadence stopped in his tracks and looked at her. *I had forgotten how beautiful she was!*. He took a second to catch his breath, wanting to ask about her face and what Hank had done to her, but he noticed the luggage and traveling clothes.

"What's all this?"

"Cadence!" Her face lit up when she saw him, but a shadow quickly came over her and she cast her eyes to the floor. "I'm leaving the Senator Hotel."

"But why?"

"Because I have fallen in love with a man, and I am hoping he proposes to me. And I want to be able to tell our children that I was a seamstress, not working in a saloon when their father proposed to me."

All Cadence heard her say was that she had become enamored with a man, and he felt everything inside of him break down. It was as if he had built something out of big pillars of granite, only to now realize they were playing cards. And Lydia bumped into the table. The entire façade came crashing down around him. It all collapsed, along with Cadence's hopes and dreams. He tried to stand tall, but inside he felt submerged in a pool of darkness.

He looked at her and heard himself ask Lydia. "Has this man proposed to you yet?"

"No," she said.

He realized that even though she was in love with someone else, it didn't matter. He still loved her all the same. She could marry another man, but it would never stop him from still loving her.

The reality was that the most time he had spent with her was in his imagination, anyway. In his mind's eye he had created an entire world. In it he would wake up every morning bathed in happiness. They would have three kids and Lydia would look more beautiful after each one.

It had quickly become his favorite pastime. When he rode for hours and days, he would daydream about being with Lydia. In his imagination, she was always by his side. In this outside world, she was not. And though the world in his head was not real, Cadence had spent so much time there thinking about her, that it had become as though it was real. *I think I love being in my imagination because that is where Lydia is. I realize now I'd rather spend the rest of my life daydreaming we are together than stop thinking about her.* Even if she married the other man and he never saw her again for the rest of his life, he would rather imagine he was with her than to be with any other real woman in real life. Cadence knew it sounded crazy. But that was how he loved her.

Cadence stared at Lydia. Her hat and her gloves were in her hand, her carpet bags on the bed. She stared at him with an unhappy expression on her face. It occurred to him she probably couldn't wait for him to leave.

He tried to think of something to say as he turned toward the door.

"I best be leaving before he gets here."

"It's too late, silly," she said. "He's already here."

Cadence was confused. "I don't understand. He's here?" Cadence looked around the room. Lydia walked over to him and took his hand and walked him over to her full-length mirror in the corner and stood next to him.

"Look," she said. "There he is." She pointed to the two of them in the mirror. "It's you, my love. You are the man I have been waiting for all my life."

He looked at her in confusion and disbelief. He realized she was talking about him. He was the man of her dreams. He saw her start to smile. To Cadence, it was the most beautiful, delicious-looking mouth he had ever seen smiling at him. In response, Cadence's face dropped its hard, ugly mask to reveal pure, unrelenting happiness. He reached for Lydia, pulled her close, and gave her the most gentle and romantic kiss he could muster.

In his elation he had neglected to ask her about Hank and her injuries. But it did not matter. That instant they were interrupted by a knock on her door. It was Doc Hanson. He arrived to further examine and question Lydia, and promptly kicked Cadence out of the room so he could meet with her alone.

"I'll talk to you, young man, in a moment," the doctor said.

Cadence went downstairs and collapsed onto a padded chair in the corner of the empty bar, surprised, puzzled, and confiding in April. "What does he want to meet with me for?"

The Hunt for Frederick Douglass
Terry Balagia

CHAPTER 54

AS THEY GOT closer to Richmond, Rip and Frederick continued traveling at night to avoid being seen. It was dark on the road going south that night. Frederick took his turn handling the reins of the buckboard wagon with Rip alongside him, and talked, as had become their routine.

"When I was young, I had no idea I was a slave. They just threw us kids together to play, Negro and White. And then one day the White kids started going to school. Why couldn't I go to school, I wondered?"

Frederick looked at Rip. "I was not aware I was a slave until I realized I couldn't do the things I hoped for. I wanted to go to school, too. But they would not let us."

Frederick smiled at the absurdity of the thought. "Now why was that?" He did not wait for Rip to answer. "Because knowledge makes a man unfit to be a slave, that's why."

Frederick looked straight ahead at the road in front of them. "Yessir, it is going to take more than a giant war to rid this country of its hatred of the Negro. The reason for that is beyond me to see. But God holds the answer. Unfortunately, He ain't telling nobody," Frederick said with a chuckle.

Rip smiled. He never saw anyone enjoy laughing as much as Frederick. His laugh was contagious, too. In minutes he had Rip wanting to laugh along with him. Rip wondered how a man like Frederick Douglass, who had experienced so much misery and struggle, could be so joyful and quick to laugh.

The Hunt for Frederick Douglass
Terry Balagia

Frederick continued. "If there is a war, what will you do? At some point, Texas will join the other Southern states. Will you fight for the Confederacy?"

Rip shook his head. "Me? No. I plan on going back home, heading far enough out into West Texas where a man can ignore the rest of the world. Besides, Sam Houston is no fan of slavery. And as long as Sam Houston is governor, Texas will stay out of the war. If there is one."

Rip turned to Frederick. "Let me ask you. Say there is a war, and the North wins. And there is no more slavery. What happens then? Have you thought about that?"

Frederick looked at him in disbelief. "Have I thought about there being no slavery? We think about it all the time. We even gave it a name. We call that day *The Break*. I have thought of nothing else all my life, but the day when this country rids itself of enslaving its fellow man and letting all my people go free. That day *will* come. It will be a glorious day. I hope it happens without war. I feel strongly about that."

Rip mumbled, "But it may take a war."

Frederick nodded agreeingly. "Yes. It may. But I fear the result of that war will create a resentment of the African in this country, which I fear will last for many generations of Americans. Perhaps slavery will be eradicated," Frederick declared, "But poverty will unfortunately continue. How will the people get fed and earn a living in the meantime? I may be wrong, but I believe there will be even more animosity toward the Negros because of the war. Anger that will keep the former slaves under the heel of the White man's boot, one way or another. At least in the South." He took out his handkerchief and wiped his forehead, then he put the cloth back in his pants pocket and looked over at Rip. "If there is a war, it may get rid of slavery, but it won't get rid of hate. Many things will never change."

"Name one thing that won't change?" Rip queried.

"White people," Frederick responded instantly and then chuckled at himself with his loud booming laugh. Like many of Frederick's humorous comments, it was spontaneous and very funny, but there was also a lot of anger behind his humor.

"And the Negro people as well. It is all people who, in many ways, will not change. The White people will find acceptable ways to hide, or to express their anger at the Negro for making the country go through a war. The Negro will not change either. He will allow himself to always remain in a place of accepting inferiority in ways that will be part of how things work. The Negro himself will falsely mold the Negro self-image as inferior. At the same time, this very behavior will falsely empower White people to feel superior. Unless someone comes along to show them that these patterns can be changed—that everything about slavery *can* be changed—nothing will change, war or no war."

Frederick stopped and calmed himself. He turned and gave Rip a look out of the corner of his eye as he handled the reins. "As I have said in many a speech and many an editorial, the limits of tyrants are prescribed by the endurance of those whom they oppress. And unfortunately, over time the Negro has been *conditioned* to regard themselves as inferior or lesser than the White man. And their ability to endure is endless—even for oppression. You see, Rip, the thing infects the Black man as it does the White man.

"Many things will change. But many things will not. Not when the North wins, nor any time after, for lifetimes. Slavery will be gone, yes. That will be a fact. But the anger and the resentment will still be there, for it runs deep in the hearts of White men. They will teach that anger and resentment to their young as a way to scapegoat their own disappointments, their shortcoming, and the deficiencies in their lives. Especially if there is a war and we force the South to end slavery. And that bitterness we will see pour from every stream. It will be so much better if we can convince the South to change on its own accord. I fear, that if not mitigated, this great war that looms before us will extract such a high price from both the North and the South and generate a reservoir of hate and a resentment toward the Negro that will last as long as the Republic itself."

Frederick stared intently out over the horses, as if looking into a distant future. "You should know, Rip, that the thing worse than rebellion is the thing that causes rebellion. And that thing will grow stronger and stronger. That thing will be in the system, like dumping manure in a water well. It will poison everything— education, banking, policing, ruling, voting. Slavery may be gone, but that thing will still be with us."

CHAPTER 55

CADENCE FELL ASLEEP in the padded chair for what must have been an hour, but it might as well have been for days, it felt so good. He woke up in an aroused state.

He was aware of soft lips landing soft petal-like touches, a blanket of little kisses, she called it, in the most beautiful voice he had ever heard. It was Lydia on top of him, kissing him. Her face was clear of bandages after having met with the Doctor. Regardless, the woman was a living, breathing erotic dream for Cadence.

"Your face. Let me see." Cadence looked where Hank had hit her on her left cheekbone. "I knew something was going on that day. I thought I saw someone up in your room near the window. I'm going to kill him for what he did to you, Lydia!"

"Stop that talk, Cadence. Hank Nelson is a bad man. I don't want you anywhere near him. He will get his soon enough. Besides, I'm not letting you go anywhere." She wrapped her legs around him and kissed his face.

"The doctor said it needs the air to finish healing, so he took the bandages off. I hope it is not too horrible to look at me. It's not so bad now," Lydia said. "It got so much better starting three days ago. That was the day April read me the telegram you sent saying you were coming back. All the love that I had been holding inside of me, and locked up for you, exploded all over my body and healed me."

"Will you marry me?"

"Yes."

The Hunt for Frederick Douglass
Terry Balagia

They kissed again until April loudly cleared her throat. "Doctor Hanson would like to see the both of you together now."

Lydia looked up at Cadence. "That's right. The doctor said there was something about my condition that he needed to talk to the two of us about."

They straightened themselves and walked into one of the side parlors, where Dr. Kevin J. P. Hanson waited. He had a close rapport with most of the girls at the Senator Hotel and served as the unofficial doctor of the establishment, holding his place as one of its most regular customers. He turned to Cadence. But Cadence was too anxious to give the doctor a chance to say anything.

"Doctor, if it is anything serious, I may not have the money to pay you back, but I am willing to sign a promissory note for any amount and give terms to pay it back, and no one will work harder to honor that debt, Sir."

Dr. Hanson was amused. "Well, young fellow, it is very serious, and it certainly is going to cost you a pretty penny over the course of your life. But it is not an illness. It's a baby."

Cadence leaned back as the words came out of Dr. Hanson's mouth, his eyes widening to the size of a silver dollar.

"I know each girl's cycle like the back of my hand, though I could not say for sure until I did a physical examination. And of course, And of course, I needed to ask Lydia about any recent partners to confirm that you are, in fact, the father."

"Father?" Cadence almost swallowed the word.

The doctor took Lydia by the shoulders and stared into her eyes softly and said, "My dear, you are pregnant."

Her mouth hung open.

"What?" Lydia asked.

The Hunt for Frederick Douglass
Terry Balagia

"This has nothing to do with your cheek. It is healing fine. Your other eye is going to be fine as well. I noticed several symptoms during my first examination and time has confirmed my suspicions. It turns out something is growing inside you that will bring you a lifetime of happiness. It appears to be healthy and progressing nicely, I assure you both. Now, if you will excuse me." The good doctor left, leaving the flabbergasted couple alone in the room.

Cadence was beside himself. "Is it really mine?" he asked, not out of doubt but out of pure excitement. "Wait! Don't answer that. Let me say something first," he said. "Tell me the truth. Or lie to me. I don't care. Tell me anything you want. Please tell me that if I am not the real father, you will let me be his pa. Or hers. I just want to be with you for the rest of my life. Tell me whatever you need to tell me, just tell me you will marry me because I am going to love any baby that comes from you. My love for you is that immense."

They spent a beautiful morning together. All of it in bed, where he told her he would be leaving soon. He had to finish something between himself and Rip. But until then, he was all hers.

They got up and dressed, walked out to the top of the stairs, and stopped. He and Lydia looked down at where Sam and his staff, plus April and the ladies, were preparing the hotel lobby and adjoining tavern for another day. Cadence looked at Lydia and then loudly cleared his throat, announcing their presence to everyone below and demanding their attention.

"I'm sorry. I didn't mean to startle ya'll. But we would like all of you to be the first to hear the news—other than Doc Hanson that is—Lydia and I are getting married."

"Plus, we're having a baby!" Lydia screamed as she hurried down the stairs and her friends hurried up them to meet her. It was a spontaneous explosion of excitement. They screamed, laughed, hugged, kissed, and cried all over each other.

The Hunt for Frederick Douglass
Terry Balagia

Sam dropped everything and had his crew dress a table for a romantic breakfast. They brought in cut flowers from the back and arranged them in a vase atop a white linen tablecloth. Sam dug up some old bottles of his finest Champagne and had them prepare poached eggs served on fresh biscuits with cream gravy, a bacon slab, some hot grits, and plenty of black coffee.

Cadence kept on explaining himself between all the hugs and congratulations. "At least we are engaged, for now!" He told them. "As soon as I get back, we plan on going to see the judge and make it all legal. And I will make Lydia my wife."

At that moment, they heard the bell ring at the hotel clerk's desk. April looked up to see Supreme Court Justice Judge Wallace Scott III checking-in while in town during the seasonal sessions. All on the taxpayer's generous tabulation, no doubt.

"Better yet," April said as she slowly stood up from the table. "Why don't we do the ceremony right now!" She walked over and greeted the justice, explained the situation, then grabbed his Honor by the arm and escorted him over to their gathering. She looked at Cadence and smiled every step of the way. "Looks like I found me a judge," April exclaimed, "And I think if we look hard enough, we can find a bible around here somewhere."

Chapter 56

APRIL TOOK OVER immediately. She walked the judge over to the bar and reached down and pulled out the King James Bible she kept beneath it. All the ladies were there, as well as Doc Hanson and Sam. The judge presided. Lydia, with her bruised face, still looked angelic. Cadence was out of his mind with happiness. He was so happy he was concerned he might vomit all over the borrowed suit jacket the judge lent him for the ceremony. They filled out the wedding license, said "I do," and an *Our Father*, and it was done.

Cadence never remembered crying in his life, and now here he was...weeping for the third time in as many weeks. He loved Lydia so much he wondered if something terrible would happen to him. This all felt too good to even imagine, much less experience.

Once the ceremony was finally over, Cadence grabbed his new bride gently around the waist and whisked her outside the Senator Hotel and into the night air. It was a beautiful afternoon, a spectacular day to be wed.

"I need to go get Paint and Blade from the livery and go find Rip," he told her.

"Cadence, I thought we talked about this. Can't we just be happy? Why do you have to go back to all that stuff? Our life is being together and planning our future. Not settling old grudges from the past."

"Now, Lydia, I told you how much this means to me. I have to make things right between Rip and me. He owes me for a lifetime of lies. And for killing my birth father. I can't rest until I get my satisfaction from him."

She looked into his eyes and ran her fingers through his hair. With her right index finger, she made tiny circles around the edge of his ear which hardened him instantly.

"Please don't leave, Cadence. I am afraid you won't make it back this time." She looked down at his pants. "We haven't even had our honeymoon."

"We will honeymoon when I return," he assured her with a kiss before walking away toward the livery. "I promise." He turned and left Lydia on the steps of the Senator Hotel, got both Blade and Paint from the livery near the White House and headed to Conrad's Ferry.

Cadence knew exactly how Rip's thinking would go. He would never leave for Texas without Blade, who was here in Washington, which is why Rip had Cadence stash the wagon at Conrad's Ferry. So, after Rip delivered Douglass, it would be easy for Rip to sneak back over to the north and get Blade.

Conrad's Ferry was the perfect place. It had a dilapidated old rigging that still worked...if the rope wasn't worn bare. Cadence would find out when he got there. But it was the perfect place to cross because no one used it anymore. These days most everyone used the Long Bridge to cross the Potomac.

So that is where Cadence would wait. He planned to ambush Rip and make him apologize for telling all those lies, and to make him beg for his life. If he didn't answer everything precisely right, Cadence figured he was mad enough to shoot Rip on the spot.

With a heart half-filled with love and half-filled with hate, Cadence pushed Paint and Blade along the channel road that led to the northern bank of the Potomac and Conrad's Ferry.

The Hunt for Frederick Douglass
Terry Balagia

FREDERICK AND RIP were still two days out from Richmond; they had been traveling all night but had taken several breaks, so they continued into the sunlit morning along the main road. A single lane dirt road, it cut right through a section of rich farmland. There was a large open field of cotton with hundreds of slaves working on both sides of the road. There were substantial timber forests beyond the fields.

"Did Cadence ever read to you from *The North Star*?"

Rip thought for a second. "He may have."

"It was a weekly newspaper. Our motto was, *Right is of no sex, Truth is of no color, God is the Father of us all, and we are all Brethren*." The memory made Frederick smile. "That paper saved me, Rip. It was the only way to keep my thoughts from turning bitter. When I was young, I had seen so much cruelty and evil. And I would think about what I had seen, and those thoughts would make me so angry I would get sick to my stomach and vomit. That's why I never smile when they take a photograph of me. Then one day, God said to me, 'Why do you put those thoughts in your head? Why choose thoughts that make you feel sick inside? How are you going to change the world if you are always sick?' And it started to make a lot of sense, to make your thoughts about good things and not about bad things."

"What happened?" Rip wanted to know.

"I changed. Overnight." Frederick was sincere. "I made myself change. What God said made perfect sense, how could I ignore it? So, from then on, I would not put those bad thoughts in my head. I still keep them out. I had previously spent the same amount of effort churning thoughts of hate and anger; I now use it to write speeches, reach out to people, or write powerful editorials."

They rode a ways farther in the comfortable kind of quiet that two people share when they enjoy each other's presence. After a while, Rip wondered about what lay before them. Busy handling the reins, he nudged Frederick with his shoulder.

"Have you thought anymore about what you are going to say to President Davis?"

"I have thought about nothing else." Frederick sounded hopeful.

"You are so good with words. You may well convince him." Rip was thinking that maybe it was possible.

Frederick was more realistic. "I don't think I can convince Jefferson Davis of anything. The more I think about it the more I don't know what will work, if anything. I know this much: what I currently preach cannot work." He looked over at Rip.

"Why do you say that?" Rip was surprised.

"Because it has not worked so far," Frederick said with his fantastic laugh. "Sad...but true. My sermons are great for people who already agree with me. But they do nothing to convince those who oppose us. So, what is going to be different about me saying it again, in a different way, to the president of the Confederacy?" Frederick slowly shook his head from side to side.

"How do you convince someone that the way they structure their entire way of life is immoral or wrong and must change completely? That realization is not in them. It is out of reach for them. In fact, I sometimes think my strong moral arguments make the pro-slavery-minded more determined than ever to hold on to their corrupt system. So, I am in the process of finding a new way to convince them, Rip. I have been praying to God to help me find a way. I think it has to be a solution, not an argument. Not convincing Davis with my words but rather convincing him with a solution to the problem."

"What is the solution?" Rip asked him.

"First, you must understand the problem before you can solve it. And the problem, as I see it, is how the South still operates its businesses. Forget that *all men are created equal* bull-manure! I am talking about the big, important question: how can the plantation owners maintain an economy based on a slave workforce if there is no longer slavery? *That* is the problem." Frederick looked over at Rip.

Rip shook his head in bewilderment. "How do you go about doing that?"

"By demonstrating to these large estates it is more economical to pay wages and be free from the expense, both financial and emotional, of owning people. Pay them a modest wage and let them fend for themselves and their families. By doing that, we are not threatening a way of life. But instead, we are augmenting it with a better way of life for all concerned."

Rip nodded. "That sounds convincing."

"It does, doesn't it?" Frederick smiled at Rip. "Actually, it is not my solution. I got the idea from you, my new friend from Texas, who told me that is happening down there. I just applied it to a bigger purpose. I was aware of what the plantation owners were doing in East Texas and assumed that was going on all over the state. In fact, I gave a very impassioned speech regarding the ploys going on in Texas many years ago. I must admit, I was not familiar with the economic dynamics that take place in the rest of that great state of yours. But from what you told me the use of slaves was unnecessary nor economical in the rest of Texas."

"Which demonstrates that a non-slave economy works out better for the ranchers than owning the workers and thus requiring them to provide places to sleep and food to eat and shelter to some degree. It diverts food off their plantation that they could be selling. Why, if you added it all up, the cost to house and provide for the entire families of the slaves one owns, it is not as economical as paying the workers in the family and letting them provide for themselves as they will.

"If you ask me slavery is not free. Slavery is expensive. You pay for guards and security, and you carry around with you the fear and risk of a slave rebellion that could occur at any time." Frederick rubbed his bearded chin.

"That is the common misconception. That slavery is free labor. Ain't nothing free about it, Brother. And our people would rather have cheap wages and freedom than no wages and no freedom. Plus, then the owner is not a sinner in God's eye. Not a minor thing, I assure you.

But if I've learned anything, it is that it no longer makes no sense trying to discuss the immorality of slavery. I say that because that is what I have done all these years, and it has not worked. Besides, I know enough to know that you will not shame these men out of slavery. But you might be able to appeal to their business sense by showing them a more fiscally effective and responsible solution to their labor issue."

He gave Rip a knowing glance. "I knew the only way I would ever get freedom was for me to find a way to purchase myself from my old master. Can you imagine buying yourself from someone, Rip? From someone who believes they own you? No, I bet you can't."

Frederick smiled. "Why, I prayed for freedom for twenty years but received no answer until I prayed with my legs." Freddie laughed again. "That's when I realized I could pray and complain and gripe and get mad and get sad and yell at God, but the system was the system. It would not change for me. Frankly, at that time, I didn't care about changing the system; I just wanted to get myself out of slavery.

"So, I didn't fight them. I no longer opposed the way things were. I worked within their horrid system. I raised the money and bought myself with a group of friends and intellectuals who then set me free. I solved my problem by getting myself free. But this time is different. This time I am coming back to bring justice to others who cannot do it for themselves. This time I *do* want to change the system."

The Hunt for Frederick Douglass
Terry Balagia

CHAPTER 57

AT THE SAME time, much farther down but on the same road, just out of sight, Pinkerton, and a small platoon of twenty-four newly recruited Confederate soldiers marched toward Rip and Frederick. Surrounding them were vast fields that seemed to go on forever. There was a sea of cotton as far as the eye could see, and the fish in that sea were slaves. There were hundreds of them covering the fields.

The road they were on was long and flat, and the air was so clear they could see five miles away. Rip saw the armed escort coming toward them. He immediately pulled the horses to a halt and quickly reached under the wagon bench for his Bardou & Son collapsible telescope.

"Who is it?" Frederick asked as he turned his back and held still as Rip used his shoulder to rest the telescope and help keep it steady. Rip took longer than usual. He wasn't used to having only his left eye. But he could make out Allan Pinkerton and Maddox in front of two dozen soldiers. Pinkerton must have grabbed the troop the minute the permission request telegram came from the Long Bridge.

"It looks like our armed escort is arriving." Rip put the telescope away and let the horses continue their rhythmic gait. He noticed the relief; he could relax now, and no longer needed to worry about getting attacked for the rest of the way back to Richmond. Pinkerton, Maddox, and the soldiers would now take responsibility for Frederick's safety.

Rip planned to continue driving the wagon with Frederick all the way to Richmond, with full military protection. He thought he would stay around Richmond for a week or so or however long it took for Lincoln to agree to meet. At which point he would be there ready to bring Frederick back north when the negotiations began. Assuming Lincoln acquiesced.

Rip assumed it would only take a week or two at the longest. He could see putting off his return to Texas for a couple more weeks. He would send Governor Houston a cable and let him know as soon as they hit Richmond. He would also let him know they completed the mission successfully, and he would return to Austin when Richmond's events were concluded. And of course, he would remember to thank Governor Houston for getting Cadence into West Point. The thought of the boy being a West Point cadet filled Rip with a level of pride he would never admit to Cadence.

———— • ————

HARRIET HAD LOYALLY followed Rip and Frederick since they abandoned the hidden campground three nights before. She left Ethel and Alice to lead the community to the next safe station while she grabbed a couple of her strong men and some of her ladies to travel with her. The lot of them took off after Rip and Frederick minutes after they left. Hannibal had begged to come along and, recognizing that he was determined to go, Harriet allowed him to accompany them, so long as he could keep up.

The *Moses* woman led them across the Potomac at a secluded spot in the shallows that was often used. Then Harriet pushed them until they caught up to Rip and Frederick as they emerged from the check point on the southern side of the Long Bridge.

The Hunt for Frederick Douglass
Terry Balagia

Careful to stay out of Rip and Frederick's sight, they camped out near the two men and traveled parallel to them...watching them yet simultaneously hiding from them. The wagon moved at a crawl, so Harriet and her companions had no problem keeping pace with them on foot. She had already traveled thousands of miles on foot while leading slaves to freedom.

When Rip and Frederick stayed off the road to take cover for half a day to avoid all the recent military movements, Harriet and her group stayed out of sight too. When they broke camp and got back on the road, Harriet's party did as well. So as not to be seen, no fires were made at night. Frederick's loyal follower spent each day continually watching both men.

Harriet had a love-hate relationship with the two men. She loved Frederick, and she hated Rip. Frederick was her soulmate at the cause. Their spirits had been and would be connected through eternity.

In Rip Gatlin, she saw all the evil that men represent. She also saw tremendous raw potential, like a big glob of unmolded clay. It was a potential he had no doubt carried with him through life, and she sensed it. It implied the promise, or perhaps the hope, that no matter what transpired, Rip would be there to make sure events kept a certain balance, that to the best of his ability, some justice would prevail. But that was all unrealized potential. Which is what she hated most about Rip. To have all that potential and not use it was such a waste in her eyes.

Harriet and her entourage of a dozen or more got to the cotton field that Rip and Frederick passed through around the same time. The field seemed to go on forever. The only thing disrupting its enormity was the single-lane road Rip and Frederick were using. Harriet could see Pinkerton and the Virginia Militia troops headed directly at them on the same road—from the opposite direction.

The Hunt for Frederick Douglass
Terry Balagia

She could also see the overseers on horseback. along with the field guards patrolling the workers off in the distance, start to take notice.

Her group came out from the woods that bordered the plantation and infiltrated the working slaves on both sides of the vast cotton field—moving closer and closer toward the road. Harriet whispered to the working slaves as she went from row to row. "It is me, Miss Harriet."

Someone handed Harriet a bag, and she slipped it over her shoulder as she bent over, pretending to pick so she would be overlooked by the guards, who were spread out sparsely through the vast fields.

"It's Moses!" she could hear those around her say. They passed the word like a virus.

"That is Mr. Frederick Douglass on that wagon," Harriet told the laborers as she moved swiftly down the rows. "They are taking our beloved brother to Richmond to put him on trial."

"What?" someone asked.

"Well, that ain't right," another said.

As the word spread that Moses was in the field amongst them, the workers became more aware and increasingly agitated.

Rip and Frederick did not see Harriet, nor her people. They did not know that she was there in that vast field.

Pinkerton was at the front of the Confederate troops alongside Maddox. This was a new unit of cavalry soldiers, but they were already forming an esprit de corps that builds a bond between men about to go into battle.

Rip and Frederick watched the troops coming toward them. "Should I get in the back?" Frederick asked.

"No," Rip said.

The field was wide, and the road went from one end of the horizon to the other. Both the soldiers and Rip and Frederick saw each other from a long way away. They could only stare as the distance between them slowly, steadily shrank. The time blurred. And then, it seemed like suddenly they faced each other from only thirty feet apart. Rip gently pulled back on the reins, bringing the buckboard to a halt.

Colonel Maddox raised his gloved right hand, bringing the twenty-four fresh new soldiers to a full stop.

"Company, halt!" The stop was awkward, but the troop managed to stay in line.

Pinkerton rode up to Rip and Frederick in the wagon. "I must say, Captain Gatlin, I never dreamed you would bring in Frederick Douglass."

"I didn't bring him in. He is coming in on his own accord," Rip responded defiantly. "As you can see."

Pinkerton nodded. "Either way. He is ours now. And you are the man who is responsible. I commend you, Sir." Pinkerton looked over at Colonel Maddox and gave him a nod. "Proceed, Colonel."

Maddox took out an official document and read loudly.

"Frederick Douglass, under the authority of the Confederate States of America, I hereby notify and confirm that you are now considered a prisoner in our official custody: legally, morally, and constitutionally."

Maddox folded the letter and slipped it back in his jacket.

The Hunt for Frederick Douglass
Terry Balagia

CHAPTER 58

"**THE PRISONER HAS** been delivered. This mission is complete," Pinkerton announced.

The surrounding slaves stopped to witness the moment and watched as the Confederate soldiers on their horses wove their way around the wagon, surrounding Rip and Frederick. Colonel Maddox trotted his horse all around, inspecting his young troops' progress from different visual perspectives. He nodded; confident they remained in textbook formation. He directed a small unit of soldiers to advance.

"Unit, dismount!" he barked, as the six soldiers dismounted, and approached the wagon.

"Secure the prisoner!" The soldiers immediately began to manhandle Frederick. They lifted him up from the bench seat in the wagon and ripped away his journal, tossing it beneath the horse.

Rip reached to stop the soldiers. "What are you doing? Take your hands off of him! Put him back here!"

Five soldiers tried to pry Frederick's fingers from around his Bible. Though they couldn't pry the book away, they forced him into the back of the wagon. They tried to fasten iron handcuffs with heavy chains and an iron spiked collar on him.

"He does not belong in chains! Goddammit, Maddox! Get a hold of your men! This man is turning himself in! You have no need, nor cause to chain him!"

311

The Hunt for Frederick Douglass
Terry Balagia

Pinkerton yelled at Rip, "You've completed your duty, Captain Gatlin! Stand down!"

They continued to secure Frederick Douglass. Rip was about to bust loose. For the first time in his adult life, Rip Gatlin did not know what to do next. One of the soldiers tried to slide in on the bench and take the reins, but Rip growled at him.

"I am driving the prisoner. Nobody else but me!" Rip barked at the soldiers surrounding him. Although the one soldier did back away, another was able to slide onto the seat with Rip. Rip elbowed him aggressively, knocking him to the ground.

The slaves stopped working and watched the events unfold as the soldiers wrestled to get Frederick into chains. Rip yelled profanities at them the entire time.

"You worthless-pieces-of-shit, get your hands off that man!" Rip was livid and turned to face the Scotsman. "This is not the deal we made, Pinkerton."

———— • ————

AT THAT MOMENT, a uniformed Virginia militia courier rode up behind the troops coming from Richmond. He rode disturbingly fast and had to pull back full strength on the reins to get the horse to stop, twisting his horse's neck in the process. The exhausted steed then shook its long mane dramatically as it snorted and snickered its protest.

The courier saluted Colonel Maddox as the commanding officer of the small detail, then retrieved a document from his pouch and announced loudly and excitedly as he read off a printed bulletin:

The Hunt for Frederick Douglass
Terry Balagia

"On the twelfth of April, at four o'clock in the morning, the Confederate States of America opened fire on the Union troops at Fort Sumter. Declarations of War have been signed. Fort Sumter has fallen. The war has begun!"

The men whooped and hollered in shared excitement. Finally, they would get to fight! Colonel Maddox cautioned them. "Settle down. Save all that energy for the Yankees, boys." The excitable young men calmed down, even though giddy with anticipation. One of the soldiers said, "It will be great to get bullshit duties like this one over with and get to do some real soldiering."

"And fighting!" another said.

The courier kept reading, "All troops are called upon at this time to report immediately to their commanding officer." When he was done reading the bulletin, he addressed the troops.

"You men are needed back in Richmond. Spread the word!"

He turned to address Pinkerton directly. "Sir, a message for you, as well." The courier handed Pinkerton an envelope with a written note from the Spotswood Hotel. Pinkerton opened and scanned it briefly and smiled.

The courier returned his attention to Colonel Maddox and saluted him. "Now, Sir, if I may have permission to be excused, Sir, I have other messages, some of an urgent nature that need to get back to Richmond." The courier held his salute until Maddox returned it, then promptly rode away. He would make it back to Richmond by morning.

"All right, you heard him, men!" Maddox then promptly announced. "Assemble in formation!" The soldiers turned around and got their horses in the proper place—twenty-four soldiers in three lines of four abreast. Maddox signaled forward with his right arm as the company followed his lead. However, Rip, Frederick, and the wagon did not move. Maddox held his right arm up and stopped the men.

Colonel Maddox turned back and faced Rip. "What's the problem, Gatlin?"

"You heard the courier," Rip answered. "The war has started. There is no need to arrest Frederick Douglass to get Lincoln to negotiate. It is too late for that."

Pinkerton responded, "It was always possible that this mission may not be completed before the war started. We all knew this could happen. Well, guess what? The war began. No one's fault."

"But this is not our deal!" Rip said defiantly.

"It is the mission you agreed to, Gatlin. I suggest you complete your duty." Pinkerton turned to Colonel Maddox. "Colonel?"

"Forward, march!" The Colonel turned his arm forward and down as the entire formation moved. All except for the wagon. Rip sat there with the reins in his hands, not budging an inch.

"Then the deal is off!" Rip called out to Pinkerton. The troops stopped in their tracks. "If the war has already begun, then I am not obligated to hold up my end of the bargain any longer!" Rip announced. "I am turning this wagon around and taking Frederick Douglass back up north, where he belongs."

"Gatlin, Laddy! I am afraid I cannot allow that. Colonel, have your men surround this wagon!"

"You heard him, men!" The two dozen soldiers responded obediently, forming a ring of resistance around Rip and Frederick in the buckboard wagon.

"Damn it, Rip, I told you not to pull your typical shenanigans. But you would not listen to me." Colonel Maddox unsheathed the saber and pointed it at him. He raised his sword and commanded

314

his troops to raise their rifles. Pinkerton drew his pistol. Rip looked to turn around the wagon, but to no avail. The soldiers were blocking his way.

"He belongs to us, Gatlin! We take custody now, Laddy!" Pinkerton called out.

Before Rip could respond Frederick lambasted loudly, "I, Sir, belong to no man!"

Rip smiled. "You heard the man."

Pinkerton looked at Rip and held up the note the courier handed him from the Spotswood Hotel. "Hey Rip, this should interest you. Texas has joined the Confederacy!" Pinkerton called out. At this, Rip stopped.

Pinkerton continued snidely, "It appears the Texas state legislature has done gone and removed Governor Houston and joined the Confederacy. All in one vote. He is no longer your governor, Captain Gatlin. Your orders now come from President Davis. It says here he wants to tell you himself, just as soon as you get back to Richmond." Pinkerton smiled as he spoke. "And that he is looking forward to it with great eagerness."

Rip stopped in his tracks. He could only say faintly, "What?" He swayed, suddenly dizzy. He wondered if it was his eye bothering him. Sam Houston was removed from office as Texas' governor by the legislature. Could that possibly be true?

Chapter 59

"**Your duty is** now to the Confederacy!" Pinkerton chimed. "And to your new president, Jefferson Davis. You have no choice as a lawman. You must obey your new commander-in-chief." The snotty little Irishman's mustache twitched.

"Colonel!" he called out.

Colonel Maddox turned his horse to face Richmond.

"Formation! Attention!" The soldiers turned their horses and fell in formation. They looked ahead of them to the back of Colonel Maddox, who held his gloved hand up at head level, indicating stop and stand.

"Forward, march!" He turned his arm forward and down. When he did, once again the entire formation began to move. Except for the wagon.. Rip sat there with the reins in his hands, not budging an inch.

"No. I don't think we should bring this man in," Rip murmured.

Maddox stopped the soldiers yet again and turned around in his saddle to face Rip.

"What did you say?!" Colonel Maddox screamed at Rip from his spot at the front of the line of troops.

Rip yelled back, "I said we are *not* bringing this man in!"

"Under whose authority?" Pinkerton chimed in to challenge him.

The Hunt for Frederick Douglass
Terry Balagia

Rip responded with a quote he had memorized upon hearing and was hoping for a chance to apply it. "By majority rule: one Texas Ranger and God is a majority!" he yelled back.

Frederick let go a short laugh at Rip's misapplication, though apt, of one of his famous sayings. He looked around, took his Holy Bible, and held it above his head with his long arms, the chains hanging down from them.

"I have a Bible! How's that as an authority?" boomed Frederick across the valley like a cannon volley.

Rip pulled the wagon brake and tied the reins securely to the bench. He reached behind the bench seat and grabbed his rifle, which he always kept loaded. Rip cocked the lever, sliding a bullet into the chamber, and stepped up on the bench seat, standing straight and tall on top of the wagon bench. He looked out over all the mounted soldiers. With his .44-caliber Henry Rimfire rifle in one hand, he drew one of his Colt revolvers with the other. Rip extended both arms and pointed his guns at the soldiers.

"And I have a gun! Or two," Rip announced with a determined, gritty voice that sent a universal shudder through the company of uniformed tenderfoots. The soldiers were not sure what to do with the famous Texas Ranger standing over them...pointing two guns and having a reputation for reckless abandon. The soldiers turned to look at each other. Most had not yet taken their oath to serve.

Frederick saw his chance and threw the still-unlocked chains off himself and climbed onto the bench seat, and sat alongside where Rip was standing, all the while still holding his Bible high in the air.

Pinkerton gave the command. "Take to your arms, men!"

The soldiers obediently slid their long guns from their saddle holsters. Most of the new soldiers were relegated to smooth-bore muskets; none had yet been issued rifle-muskets. However, there were a few Springfields, Smith carbines, and Colt revolving rifles. Regardless, the valley became silent except for the sound of twenty-four guns and rifles being loaded, which reverberated across the fields. The platoon aimed their rifles at Rip.

Rip looked around as he considered the odds. A grin slowly crept across his face. *Twenty-six guns to two guns*, he thought. *To a Texas Ranger, that is what you call a fair fight.* He felt his sense of balance and perception returning in spades.

Harriet watched from the fields. She was too far away to hear them, but when she saw Rip stand up and draw his guns, Harriet fell to her knees and wet herself in the field. "Lord Jesus Christ, the phoenix has risen! How glorious a sight for these eyes to behold!" Harriet shouted.

"Ready!" Pinkerton called out, and all the soldiers responded with the click-clack of rifles, handguns, and muskets being cocked and ready to fire.

In this intense but quiet moment, Rip stood tall, holding his guns on the soldiers as they held theirs on him. He gently leaned toward Frederick and whispered to him.

"Hey Freddie, it would be best if you put down the Bible and pick up a damn gun!"

Frederick looked around, then decided to keep his Bible in one hand but he did reach over and grab Rip's remaining Colt revolver with his other. He pulled back the hammer and held it on the troops.

"I think I'll keep both," Frederick retorted.

"That works for me." Rip uttered as he took his rifle aim off the troops and pointed it at Pinkerton.

"Ladies first..." Rip said as a smile spread across his face.

The Hunt for Frederick Douglass
Terry Balagia

Pinkerton glared back at Rip. "Aim!" Pinkerton roared.

Rip did not want to die. But he realized this time he was going to. He wondered if he would see his deceased wife and his baby boy. As he looked down the barrel of his rifle at Pinkerton, he took solace in the thought he would take Pinkerton with him.

The Hunt for Frederick Douglass
Terry Balagia

CHAPTER 60

HARRIET WAS UP and running, weaving her way through the fields. She motioned for the others to move in closer with her...closer to the stand-off between the troops and the buckboard wagon in the middle of the road.

The overseers patrolling the slaves in the field were taking an interest in the goings-on. Three of them were up on the ridge atop their horses observing the laborers.

Harriet's energy and enthusiasm infected the crowd. The slaves working throughout the two fields had naturally become interested in the happenings and wanted to get closer to see Frederick Douglass. Word continued to spread across the valley full of grass cutters, cotton pickers, and laborers, many with pitchforks, machetes, corn cutters and large scythes in their hands. They quietly moved in closer and closer, surrounding the new recruits.

The overseers and the field guards watched as the slaves encircled and engulfed the soldiers. It looked like trouble. Big trouble. It was clear they would need more men, or they would have a full-scale insurrection on their hands. The field guards turned their horses and galloped toward the plantations. They needed to raise more men, and they needed to do it fast.

The young soldiers, proud to be seen in their brand-new Virginia Militia uniforms, suddenly found themselves surrounded by an overwhelming number of laborers and were not yet trained to know what to do or how to react. Fearful, the young recruits turned and pointed their guns at the slaves, but to no avail. Workers continued to come from all over, unabated, joining the intimidating throng.

"Make ready, men!" Pinkerton drew a deep breath and took one last look around at the green recruits nervously aiming their guns. "Now fire!" Pinkerton screamed.

But none of them did.

Pinkerton turned to Colonel Maddox. "Tell them to fire!"

"On whom?" Maddox responded.

"On everyone, goddammit!" Pinkerton was enraged.

"Fire!" Maddox yelled at the men, but the soldiers still refused the order. They were scared. They aimed at the slaves, but they could not find it in themselves to pull the triggers. One of the slaves standing in front of Pinkerton reached up and pulled Pinkerton's hand down until the pistol pointed to his chest. He looked up at Pinkerton.

"I don't know how many bullets you soldiers have, but you will run out soon." The laborer looked around at the mass of humanity moving in and surrounding Pinkerton, Maddox, and the soldiers. "We will not run out of men."

By this time, Harriet was almost up to the front where the wagon was, and she interjected loudly, "Nor women!"

A second slave took the barrel of one of the soldier's guns and held it up to his chest, and looked the soldier in the eyes. "Shoot me. The sooner you start shooting, the sooner you will run out of bullets."

Another grabbed a soldier's barrel and said, "Shoot me, too."

"And me!" another urged.

The Hunt for Frederick Douglass
Terry Balagia

Then one by one, the strong, unselfish, devoted men and women all grabbed the barrels of the guns near them and held them to their chests, insisting that the soldiers shoot.

"At ease!" Maddox called out. "I said, at ease! Men, holster your weapons!"

But the soldiers couldn't put their guns away. The slaves were taking the weapons from them and passing them along to the slaves behind them, where behind each one, there were many more lined up.

In this milieu of noise, screaming commands, and anxious horses, Hannibal appeared and jumped up on the wagon next to Rip.

"Private Hannibal reporting for duty, Sir!" Rip looked down to see the courageous skinny twelve-year-old saluting up at him. "Give me an order, Captain Gatlin, Sir. Tell me what to do."

"Damn you, Hannibal! Get down before bullets fly!" Rip lifted his boot and pushed Hannibal, gently but forcibly squeezing his little frame behind the wagon sideboard and into safety. *If he stays down,* Rip thought.

Harriet made her way to the wagon. Rip saw her and gave her a nod as he and Frederick sat down on the wagon seat. At which point, Harriet instructed the others to get around the wagon. Without hesitation the men began working together. Rip and Frederick remained on the wagon bench seat, Rip still pointing his guns at Pinkerton, as Harriet's men unhitched the team of horses, lifted the wagon with Rip, Frederick, and Hannibal still in it, and turned it to face the other way. They brought the horses around and re-hitched them to the wagon, which now faced north.

"Rip Gatlin, you are going to be a criminal to the Confederacy!" Pinkerton hollered.

The Hunt for Frederick Douglass
Terry Balagia

Maddox cupped a hand near his mouth and yelled across the cacophony. "He's right, Rip. When the South wins, you will be tried as a war criminal!"

"Which is one of the many reasons I will root for the other side, Marshal!" Rip hollered back. He laughed loudly, joined in short order by Frederick, with his booming baritone cackle.

Rip wasted no time. He set his guns down, grabbed hold of the reins, gave a look around to make sure the way was clear. Making a clicking sound with his tongue as he flicked the reins, they took off, the old buckboard tossing Hannibal around like a sack of feed as the powerful horses found their pace.

"Follow the North Star!" Harriet yelled out to them as they bounced ambitiously down the road in the opposite direction of the soldiers. Then she ran along through the field, calling after them, "I was wrong about you, Rip Gatlin!"

Pinkerton was boiling mad, knowing he was helpless in letting Rip, Frederick, and Hannibal get away. The massive gathering of all the slaves from both fields blocked the road and prevented them from pursuing any farther. Pinkerton, Maddox, and the green militia recruits could only watch as the big horses pranced down the narrow dirt road, the buckboard barely holding together as they headed away from the huge cotton fields back to the edge of the Potomac, to the North, and to safety.

Pinkerton turned to Colonel Maddox, "Exactly what do you propose we do now?"

Maddox shook his head. "We can't do a whole lot. Other than keeping the men calm. I am just thankful none of these boys accidentally fired on anyone. Or we would have had quite a mess on our hands."

"I would say we have quite a mess now, Colonel. We just let Frederick Douglass get away."

"Like I said," Maddox looked at him. "We don't have a lot of choices here now." Maddox smiled to himself as he watched Rip bounce along in the wagon. He sure had a way of surviving that made you wonder. "Looks like he did it again," the Marshal mumbled to himself.

It is not worth it to follow them, Colonel Maddox thought. *It's best to wait for things to die down, and then organize the beleaguered young soldiers the best we can and head them back to Richmond.* Pinkerton continued to protest vehemently, but it did not matter. They couldn't move either way, even if they wanted.

The Hunt for Frederick Douglass
Terry Balagia

CHAPTER 61

AS RIP, FREDERICK, and Hannibal pulled away from confrontation in the field, Harriet made sure the soldiers had no way to go after them. She had the laborers form a human chain of interlocking arms blocking the road and encircling the soldiers.

Harriet kept her men surrounding the soldiers until Rip, Douglass, and the kid were long gone. She continually looked back over her shoulder at the wagon as it grew gradually smaller, and farther away. It was only after they had passed over the horizon that Harriet had her men return all the weapons, after unloading all the bullets, and allowed the soldiers to regroup and head back to Richmond.

It was coming on toward dusk, anyway. The overseers still hadn't returned, and Harriet turned to the slaves and addressed them all.

"Alright my brothers and sisters. Those overseers will be back soon with their rath and anger to punish you for today. So come with me now. We will break into groups and disappear into the night. My men know the way to freedom's land. They know the short-cuts and the roads to use and when to use them. So be quick! The time is now! They can't hurt us if they can't find us. So, let's go, children. No time to waste. Come, run away with us into the night. Into God's grace and freedom's dream."

The Hunt for Frederick Douglass
Terry Balagia

FREDERICK HAD CALMED down. His heart quieted from the fervent pounding it had experienced during the confrontation with the soldiers. Rip looked over at Frederick, wiping the blood from the cuts and slashes meted out by the soldiers and the chains.

"Are you okay?" Rip asked.

"Wound wise, yes. But I'm not okay when it comes to you ruining my chance to meet with Jefferson Davis." Rip was startled by the comment but then saw Frederick smiling. Rip chuckled softly.

"I have news for you. You would have had one brief meeting before they hung you." Rip told him.

"You may be right, but you can be assured that it would have been one hell of a meeting!" Frederick let out his big boom of a laugh only this time it seemed like he would never stop. At some point Rip joined him because it was impossible not to. They laughed so long and hard they disturbed the horses.

It also let Hannibal know it was safe enough to come out of hiding. He tried to climb up onto the bench seat to join Rip and Frederick, but there was no room between the two, so he crawled behind them and sat in the back of the wagon.

Acknowledging Hannibal's presence, Frederick looked at Rip, smiled and said, "Looks like we have ourselves a visitor."

Then Frederick grew more serious. "I am sure we will talk about it later, about what just happened. But for now, let me say what you did back there goes way beyond heroic. I am in awe of your devotion to protecting me, Sir. I swear to God I do not know what you were thinking back there."

Rip smiled. "I wasn't thinking. There was nothing to think about. I just hope we don't regret it later."

The Hunt for Frederick Douglass
Terry Balagia

———— ✦ ————

BACK IN RICHMOND, the excitement started by the fall of Fort Sumter acted as an intoxicant to the entire city. People celebrated like the war was already over, and the South had won. Most people thought it would only last a couple of months, or until the first big battle. They thought whoever won that would win the war. Many young men scrambled to enlist, hoping they could do some fighting before the war ended. Everyone else drank into the wee hours.

What was left of Nelson's gang gathered around the marshal's office the next morning. It was Nelson, his brother Hank, and the three Comancheros.

"Technically, we are still working on President's Davis behalf," Nelson said, thinking aloud. Deputy Hale was sitting in Marshal Maddox's chair with his feet up on the desk, reading.

"I was right about that reward for Frederick Douglass," Deputy Hale said pointing to the list in his hands. "Douglass is worth twenty thousand in gold. You boys should have gone after them. You boys would split a big reward. Instead, you let Pinkerton get the capture and the credit."

Nelson shook his head at Deputy Hale's comment. "That kind of comment does no good now, Hale. That's like milking the cow after she's done been milked. What good is that?"

"Just letting you know what you boys missed out on," Hale said. "I still think you should have gone out there and bushwhacked them before Pinkerton and Maddox got to them."

"What do you mean? You are the one who said we could wait outside of town and strike a deal with Maddox."

"You can, but the split gets smaller. That's all I'm saying."

The Hunt for Frederick Douglass
Terry Balagia

Suddenly, they heard a loud commotion outside. A horse raced through the city streets at a full gallop. It was the returning courier. He was fresh back from delivering the news to Pinkerton and Maddox, having ridden all night.

"The courier is back, Hale!" one of his junior deputies hollered into the office.

They stepped outside and into the shade of the overhang outside the marshal's office as the courier rode up and jumped off his horse. The runner was on the ground before his horse had even come to a stop. He threw a salute. He looked beyond exhausted, like something the hounds dragged home.

"Frederick Douglass and Rip escaped!" he told them hurriedly. Still in a state of shock. "I saw the whole thing myself. It happened right in front of my eyes."

"What?" Deputy Hale was first to address him. "Calm yourself, Soldier." Deputy Hale looked around. "Get this man some water!" Someone handed him a bucket from the water trough and the courier took a long gulp.

"Much obliged," he said, still holding the bucket.

"Now take a breath," Hale calmly instructed, "and tell us what happened."

"They had a big standoff. I was riding hell-bent for leather to get to Richmond. But I looked back a few minutes after I left them; I saw slaves from the fields pouring out from all over and blocking the soldier's way. I don't know why the soldiers didn't shoot, but I saw the slaves turn the wagon completely around. And then Rip and Frederick took off like a twister while the soldiers just stood there surrounded. I took off again after that."

"Where are they now?" Hale asked.

The Hunt for Frederick Douglass
Terry Balagia

"Last I seen they was high tailing it in that rickety buckboard back to the Potomac."

Deputy Hale turned to Nelson. "With that wagon they have to stay on a road. A man could catch up with them before they reach the Potomac."

Nelson didn't have to give it a second thought.

"Let's go boys, saddle up." Nelson got on his horse and looked around, assessing the four men who were still willing to ride with him.

"They won't be able to cross at the Long Bridge this time. They'll have to find another way across the river." Nelson told them.

"We can track him," the Comanchero, Garza, bragged. "The Apache and I can track anything."

Deputy Hale stepped in. "Nelson, if you and your boys don't leave soon your odds are as good as a three-legged bobcat trying to catch up with Rip and Frederick Douglass."

———— ❖ ————

The Hunt for Frederick Douglass
Terry Balagia

Chapter 62

RIP, FREDERICK, AND Hannibal needed to move fast.

Rip knew that as soon as Maddox, Pinkerton and those soldiers got back to Richmond, they would telegraph the Long Bridge and have them arrested if they tried to get across there. They would also have the Virginia Militia scouring the area looking for Rip and his famous prisoner.

He thanked the spirits who whispered to him to have Cadence stash the wagon at Conrad's Ferry. Now he had only to figure out where in the tarnation Conrad Ferry was from here. It would be a race to get to the river and get across it in time.

"Our only chance is to find the road to the old flatboat ferry crossing at Conrad's," he told Frederick as they approached an intersection on Old Richmond Road. "We can't cross at the Long Bridge." Rip looked around at his surroundings trying to get his bearings. He had been pushing the horses hard.

"But, I am afraid I have no idea where we are." Rip said, looking around.

The Old Richmond Road cut through the dense evergreen forest of Northern Virginia, now in full bloom and giving their wagon great cover. They would need it in their race to get to the river and traverse it without getting captured or killed. But Rip knew they had to find a place to cross soon. They were running out of time.

Frederick turned his head this way and that like he recognized where they were. "I grew up in Talbot County just across the way. I know this land like the back of my hand. If you can get us out of this clump of trees, I can get us down to the old ferry crossing at Conrad's."

Rip peered out over the rim of his cowboy hat. "You know how to get to Conrad's Ferry?" he asked.

Frederick grinned broadly. "I do indeed."

———— ◆ ————

IN NO TIME, Nelson and his men were a day's ride outside of Richmond on the main road headed toward the Long Bridge. By noon they ran into Maddox and Pinkerton and the dejected and exhausted new recruits coming back the other way. They had pulled over to rest their horses in a shady grove at a stream under a large oak tree. As they approached them Nelson hollered to Maddox that they were making one last attempt at catching up with Rip and Frederick Douglass.

"You better rest up then, or you will never catch them," Maddox warned. But Nelson waved them off. Maddox tried again. "Pull your horses in the shade for some water and a rest. It is the last good water for ten miles in either direction."

Nelson thought about it, then decided he best heed Maddox's advice. He ordered his men to take a short drink and to fill their canteens and replenish the horses. Pinkerton came staggering over. He saw it as his chance to join them.

"You are never going to catch them from here. They're too far along by now," he warned.

But Maddox waved him off.

"Don't listen to him. Pinkerton's just jealous that he can't ride with you guys."

Pinkerton crossed the road and walked up to Nelson. "He's right, Laddy. I would trade just about anything for a second chance at capturing them both."

"You and your horse will never make it," Maddox hollered from across the way.

Nelson agreed, "Even on a fresh horse you would only slow us down and hold us back, Mr. Pinkerton. In fact, we should not stay here any longer. We are cutting it close at best as it is. Men take your last piss, freshen your water cannisters, and get back on your horses."

Pinkerton watched as they prepared to continue their chase. He still wanted to ride with them, but he knew they were right. He did not have the horse, and he did not have the stamina to keep up with them. However, that did not prevent him from protesting vehemently to Colonel Maddox the entire ride back to Richmond.

Nelson gave Pinkerton and the Colonel a nod, then he and his gang raced after Rip, Frederick, and the boy.

———— ✦ ————

IT TOOK PINKERTON, Maddox, and the group of Confederate troops a full day to get back to Richmond. When they finally arrived, Maddox returned to the marshal's office with the expired troops, and Pinkerton went directly to the Spotswood Hotel.

At the Spotswood, everyone was gathered in President Davis' office suite. After the great success at Ft. Sumter, Davis was now delirious with confidence.

The Hunt for Frederick Douglass
Terry Balagia

"I'll tell you what it is!" Davis was pontificating, his chest puffed out as he strolled across the large lavish room. "We've got those son-of-a-bitches on the run now!" President Davis bragged to everyone in his war room, his bourbon securely in hand.

"It was a gutsy and heroic move, Mr. President," his solicitous vice president chimed in. "My only regret is that we will now go down in history as having started the first aggression in this war. That is what history will record. It would be much better from a historical point of view if it had been the North who were the aggressors."

The Secretary of State for the Confederacy, Robert Toombs, was also present. "I'm afraid I agree. It was a ploy by Lincoln to trick us to fire the first shot. We fell for it. It puts us in the wrong. It is fatal. That's what history will record."

"Goddammit, gentleman, we've been through this! We had no choice. We could not allow Lincoln to resupply the soldiers over at Ft. Sumter. Actually, it was Lincoln's attempt to resupply Ft. Sumter that was an act of war!"

"How does that make sense?" the vice president challenged, though he whispered his question. Davis spun around on him instantly, but it was Stephen Mallory, the Secretary of the Navy, who responded.

"He violated our sovereign waters entering our port harbor!" Mallory extolled. "That is aggression, Sir! Lincoln is the culpable party who started this war."

"Hear, hear!" Davis proclaimed, looking with pride at his secretary of war. "He is more accurate, Mr. Vice President. The attempt to represent us as the aggressors is as unfounded as the complaint made by the wolf against the lamb in the familiar fable.

He who makes the assault is not necessarily he that strikes the first blow or fires the first gun."

Davis took another sip and nodded in Mallory's direction. "This is the man who should chronicle this war on our behalf." Davis continued. "You may want to start taking notes now, Mr. Secretary. This war may be over sooner than we think, and you know, I firmly believe whoever wins the first big battle wins the war." He took a sip of whiskey like it was a doctor's order. "From the looks of it, this war could be over in a month or two."

"Hear, hear." A cabinet official held his glass up. Another one joined him.

"*What history will record?* What history will record, my ass," Davis mocked Vice President Stephenson's earlier comment. "Once we win, we will be the ones writing the history. And we can write it any damn way we want. So much for your history books!" President Davis walked around the room as if warming up his legs for his next significant thought. "Gentlemen, we need another victory. One big, quick win will bring these rascals to their knees. Any suggestions?"

At this point, Jefferson Davis looked over and saw Pinkerton standing at the door, looking somewhat anxious.

"What is it, Pinkerton? You look like you need to piss."

"Mr. President, we went to intercept Rip Gatlin and to take custody of Frederick Douglass, but I am afraid we were overcome by a large group of empowered slaves and were forced to leave there without him."

President Davis was livid. "Did you kill him at least?"

"I'm afraid he got away, Mr. President," Pinkerton mumbled.

"Goddammit, Pinkerton, you keep disappointing us! Whose side are you on, anyway? I told you we were done with that plan.

The Hunt for Frederick Douglass
Terry Balagia

The war has started! There is no longer any need to capture Frederick Douglass!"

His nephew immediately ushered Pinkerton out into the hallway.

"The war has started, Mr. Pinkerton. Your services are no longer needed. The hunt for Frederick Douglass is over. Good day to you, Sir."

CHAPTER 63

RIP, ALONG WITH Frederick and Hannibal, made it to the southern side of the old Conrad Ferry crossing before sunset. The ferry was built on a bend in the river where it narrowed, and both riverbanks were overgrown from nonuse. A forest of high marsh stalks and some tall chestnut oak trees surrounded each side of the bank.

The ferry consisted of a small wooden dock across from an identical dock with a pole on each that had a rope connecting one side to the other. The small platform had a hand-wheel that cranked the rope through to pull the platform across. The wood was long weathered and worn but it had held up. The old rope was tattered from the elements, and the giant wooden hand-crank wheel was missing several spokes, but it still worked. The platform was minimal but big enough for the three of them and the two horses to fit in one crossing. They unhitched the horses and Rip grabbed his gun belt from under the bench of the Quaker's wagon, which they left there. The trio, leading their two horses, made it across the river without incident.

Rip, Frederick, and Hannibal were in the North, safe and sound. They found the wagon where Cadence had stashed it. Rip and Frederick pulled it out of the brush. Rip stuffed his gun belt under the bench seat of the old buckboard and walked the two Quaker horses to the water's edge for a well-deserved drink. These horses had ridden long and hard to get the men safely to the Maryland side. They would need several hours of rest before being hitched back up to another wagon.

The Hunt for Frederick Douglass
Terry Balagia

Frederick walked over and joined Rip and the horses at the edge of the riverbank and watched them drink. Rip was appreciating how much these two horses were enjoying the water when he heard the whinny of a horse that Rip would recognize in his sleep. Rip turned to see Blade moseying toward him, perfectly saddled.

He put his hand up for his Blade to lick. Seeing her made Rip think of Cadence. At that instant, he heard the click of a scattergun being cocked. Rip's sensory perception on his right side had not worked properly since he lost the eye, and he was slow to turn around. When he did, Rip saw a shadow step out from the high marshland weeds onto the small wooden ferry platform with a scatter-gun in his hand pointing at them.

Frederick turned in tandem with Rip and slowly raised his hands. He recognized Cadence, but something looked different. He realized it was the young man's rage. "What's with you pointing guns at me each time we meet?" Frederick asked, trying to be cautious and humorous at the same time.

Cadence's pain was impenetrable. His breathing was heavy and labored. His legs shook fiercely. Tears streamed down his face. He pointed his loaded musket right at Rip, seemingly oblivious to Frederick.

"Rip Gatlin, you are a dirty, rotten rat, and I am going to kill you for lying to me all my life." As Cadence stepped onto the platform it started to slowly drift from the shore. Scatterguns are ineffective if the target is too far away, but for a few feet of distance, it was perfect. Cadence held the gun firmly. "Now I am going to ask you one more time, was what Nelson and Deputy Hale told me true? Did you kill my father?"

The Hunt for Frederick Douglass
Terry Balagia

Rip barely looked up at Cadence. "Hannibal, you get up in that wagon behind the sideboard until I tell you otherwise." Hannibal jumped into the wagon in one bound and laid down flat. He peaked out through the gap in the sideboards.

"And Cadence, I want you to put that gun down. Look at me, Son. I am not even wearing my gun belt." Rip said. He walked over and undid the saddle on Blade and carried it over to the buckboard and tossed it into the back. "You want to shoot an unarmed man?" Rip did not bother looking up at Cadence again but went on with brushing Blade's back and walking her over to the wagon harness. "Furthermore, Cadence, this is not the time nor the place. Now put your gun down and lend a hand."

Cadence pulled the trigger on the scattergun, and it blew a hole through the twelve-foot-high marshland stalks to the right of them. The hole was almost as big as a cannonball would make, or so it seemed to Hannibal. Hannibal had heard nothing so loud in his life. He was glad he was hiding behind the sideboards.

The platform reared up violently from the recoil of the blast. It was all Cadence could do to keep his balance as he quickly but awkwardly reloaded the gun. Rip finished harnessing Blade up to the wagon and turned to face Cadence. He figured the time had come.

"Okay, Cadence, fine. You want to know the truth. I don't blame you. If I were you, I would too. The trouble is that sometimes I have a hard time separating the truth from all the shit I done made up." He stared back at Cadence.

"What Nelson told you was right. Just about every word of it. It was me who shot that son-of-bitch, your father, right between the eyes about one second before he was going blow your brains out. It was me who reached down into a pile of bodies and pulled out a little blood-covered boy. No one else wanted to claim you. So, I put you behind me on my saddle and rode all the way back to Texas and gave you to the same nuns who raised me. I probably should have left you in Virginia. They probably would have found you a good Christian home. I wonder about that sometimes," shrugging his shoulders slightly.

Rip continued. "At the time, all I was thinking was that I didn't want you growing up where everyone knew your father was a murderer who killed your ma and your siblings. I wanted to give you a background that you could be proud of, so I made one up. Because I never had one. No one bothered enough to make up a lie for me about who my parents were. I didn't want it to happen to you. I wanted you to have a story of where you came from. I wanted it to be a good place so you wouldn't end up thinking something was wrong with you, like there was with your real father. So, I made up the perfect father for you to believe in."

Rip took a breath. He walked up closer to the water's edge. Cadence still held the scattergun on him. "I wanted you to think you came from a heroic father," Rip said quietly. "A Texas Ranger who could out-shoot, out-ride, and out-track anyone. I also wanted you to believe that you were bred from that kind of quality stock. Someone of the caliber of the great men I have known, or who helped teach me. So, I made up Big Cade."

Rip looked at Cadence with a sheepish nod. "He never existed. The name Cadence was the name of my ten-month-old son, who died of typhus along with his mother twenty years ago—ending the happiest three years of my life. I guess that makes me an old sentimental huckleberry. I had no buddy or best friend and never any partner who lasted back then. Just like Nelson said. Big Cade wasn't real, but he helped me raise you."

The Hunt for Frederick Douglass
Terry Balagia

"Why didn't you just make it you?" Cadence asked between holding back his sobs. "You could have told me you were my pa. Why did you have to make someone up?"

"Because I wasn't good enough, Cadence. I wanted to get you someone better than me. I was afraid I would not be able to live up to that role of being your pa. But between my bad ways and Big Cade's good ways, I figured it would prepare you for anything life rolled at you," he said.

"Besides, I was always thinking about the fact that as a rule Texas Rangers don't live very long. Chances were highly likely that I would get killed that day or the next day. Or the next. And you were going to be going through life alone. I kept thinking that someday my derringer may misfire, or that I might not see things as well as I used to. Maybe I wouldn't hear their footsteps or anticipate the ambush. Maybe the Cherokee spirits would no longer guide and protect me. Or maybe someday I would just get tired and drop my guard. And I worried about what would happen to you without me there to protect you, or to look out for you, or show you, or just be there. I could not do that if I were dead, and I knew that day was coming sooner than later."

Hannibal slowly raised his head over the top of the sideboard, transfixed by Rip as he continued.

"So, I set out to teach you everything I knew. Every trick, cheat, tool, or weapon you may need, or what you might come up against. I wanted you to be prepared. So, you could live and go on, and then maybe one of us would be of some value to this world after all. Then the darndest thing happened, Cade. I kept *not* getting killed. I figured it was only a matter of time before one of those last-minute things didn't go my way. But it didn't happen. I looked around and wondered how I had survived, and I realized it was because of you, Cadence. You have grown into the best damn Texas Ranger a partner could ever have. Smart, fast, agile, clever, intelligent, charming, and every bit as good with a gun as me. You have it all, Kid. Hell, you are Big Cade now, Cadence."

Though Cadence still held the scatter gun, he was not doing much of a job at holding it on Rip. "You were always a father to me, Rip," Cadence sobbed, clutching the gun tightly.

"I appreciate that, Kid." Rip looked down and blinked a couple of times to hide the wetness surrounding his good eye. "Those stories of Big Cade sure would make your eyes light up. Years later, when I thought of telling you the truth, I was afraid you'd be disappointed. So, I kept it going. I never thought we would come back here to Virginia and have to revisit all those stories and be confronted with what really happened or who your father really was." Rip rubbed his chin and thought for a second.

"I used bad judgment, Cadence. And for that, I am genuinely sorry. And I hope you will someday unhate me for that. You should know that those stories of this heroic father that were so real to you...well, they were real for me, too! Big Cade was the father I imagined or pretended I had when I was a little boy in the orphanage. I would always tell the nuns about my father. I never knew who he was, or my mother, for that matter. But I would tell the other kids that my father was a lawman, and someday he was going to swoop into San Antonio and take me away from the orphanage on adventures with him. He never came. But he was still real to me. Big Cade was very real for me, too. I am going to miss him. I'm going to miss you, too." At that, Cadence slowly let the gun droop down.

"I decided I'm not going to West Point, Rip."

Rip was a bit surprised but very relieved. He nodded. "Good. I don't want you to. Not now that this war has started."

"That's not all, Rip. I married that girl, Lydia. We are having a baby."

At that Rip smiled bigger than Cadence had ever seen him smile in his entire life.

"Well, what do you know! Get in here and give me a hug, Son."

Rip was on the riverbank and Cadence was ten feet away standing on the floating platform. Rip grabbed the rope and pulled him to shore as Frederick climbed up onto the wagon.

The Hunt for Frederick Douglass
Terry Balagia

CHAPTER 64

NELSON, HANK, AND the rest of the gang finally made their way to the crossing at Conrad's Ferry. Nelson was up on Soldier's Hill overlooking the ferry when he heard Cadence fire the scatter gun. He looked out on the river and saw Cadence in the water on the ferry platform barely keeping his balance after firing the big gun. Rip stood on the riverbank in front of the wagon. He could see Frederick Douglass standing next to him and a young Negro boy laying behind the sideboard in the back of the wagon.

"That's them. Let's go." The five of them turned and rode down the hill toward the river's edge. They found a spot in the trees that lined the Potomac on the Virginia side. Hank pulled his horse next to one of the big oaks. He handed his Springfield rifle-musket with its long-range flip-up leaf-sights to his brother to hold and stood up on his saddle. He shimmied up the big tree overlooking the ferry crossing. Nelson reached up and handed Hank his already loaded Springfield. Hank was in a perfect position. He had a direct shooting angle on anyone crossing the river. Hank aimed carefully at the wagon on the edge of the riverbank.

Nelson stood below Hank, cautioning him. "Deputy Hale said the big reward money is for shooting Frederick Douglass. Be sure you aim at him."

"That may be so, big brother, but there would be a lot of satisfaction in shooting Rip Gatlin. And probably reward money as well, from some vile misdeed in his past." Hank was busy adjusting his flip-up leaf sight on the three men and the boy on the river's bank as he spoke.

The Hunt for Frederick Douglass
Terry Balagia

Nelson studied their prey and berated Hank again. "Well, seeing how you may only get one, or maybe two shots off before they take for cover, you better shoot the one that pays reward money we know about. And that is Frederick Douglass. Is that clear, little brother?"

"That's clear," Hank said and continued to focus his Springfield long-range sights in on Frederick who was now sitting on the bench seat of the wagon. The young boy was now standing up in the wagon and prancing around in front of Douglass, unaware of Hank and Nelson in the trees across the river. Nelson took out his Springfield and loaded it as well. He shimmied up the tree to get closer to hand the second rifle to Hank. "At least you can get two shots off, then we jump down to our horses and get the hell out of here. We will come back later to get the bodies."

Rip was at the river's edge pulling on the ferry rope, drawing the platform and Cadence to the shore. Cadence's scattergun hung down at his side. Rip could not see Hank in the trees across the river but Blade, hitched up to the wagon, sensed something in the air and bucked, causing the wagon to shake, and making Hank's target harder to hit.

Rip saw Blade was agitated and sensed something from his right side. It was faint but, it was a disturbance. That's when Rip heard the click of the Springfield rifle being cocked, from a hundred yards away. Hank was having a hard time keeping a bead on Frederick because Blade was causing such a ruckus and shaking the wagon so much. Hank was a little unsure as he slowly squeezed the trigger and fired his first shot.

Rip saw the flash from Hank's gun coming from the trees across the river. There was no sound at first, just the flash of the powder exploding. As he turned to run to the wagon, he heard the sound catch up with the flash.

The Hunt for Frederick Douglass
Terry Balagia

Blade was hitched to the wagon and as she bucked, she put her body in the path of the first shot. Blade twisted her large neck around with an agonizing whinny and slammed to the ground with a loud snort from her powerful nostrils.

Nelson quickly handed his loaded Springfield up to Hank. They switched rifles and Rip heard Nelson reload the first gun as Hank cocked and took aim with the second.

Rip's Cherokee senses were now fully engaged. He saw Blade take the bullet and hit the ground near his feet. He scrambled over Blade as he heard the second Springfield rifle's hammer being cocked.

This time was different for Hank. Without an agitated Blade jumping around and shaking the wagon, Hank held a steady bead on Frederick Douglass. Rip took a giant step up onto the harness shaft of the wagon as Frederick reached to get Hannibal and pull him back down behind the sideboard.

Rip did not see the flash of the second shot but knew it was coming. Diving toward Douglass and Hannibal, Rip heard the second shot fired and, as he flew toward them, yelled for Hannibal to duck down. Rip reached out and pushed Frederick, knocking him into Hannibal...flipping them both into the back of the buckboard wagon.

Rip was mindful of the sudden punch in his lower back and knew at that moment that Hannibal had been spared. The bullet passed through and ricocheted off the bench seat, hitting Frederick in the thigh and barely penetrating the skin. But the red-hot bullet burned so badly Frederick could not help but scream.

Rip returned his attention to Blade. She lay on the ground, still in her harness, the tear in her chest spurting out blood. Rip pushed himself off the wagon bench seat to the ground below, thinking he would comfort his dying horse, but his legs betrayed him, and Rip tumbled to the ground like a marionette without its strings. He landed in a clump right next to Blade, unable to move. There was nothing to do but sit and watch the puddle of dark red blood spread across the dusty ground around him.

CHAPTER 65

AT THE FIRST shot, Cadence still stood on the platform a couple of feet from the river's edge. He dropped the scatter gun and spun around with both Colt revolvers drawn, causing the wooden platform to rock from side to side so badly that he almost fell into the water.

As Hank had prepared to take his second shot, Cadence jumped off the ferry platform trying for the riverbank. He landed near the edge, the water up to the top of his boots. He had his guns still drawn and turned to face the tree across the river. He blanketed them with bullets.

Cade emptied both revolvers, twelve shots in rapid succession, killing Hank and severely wounding Nelson. They both dropped from the tree like dead possums.

But it was too late. Hank had already fired the second shot.

When Nelson hit the ground, he called for help. Garza, his lead Comanchero rode over, drew his gun, and shot Nelson in the head.

"That makes us even, Cadence!" Garza yelled across the river. As if killing Nelson somehow exonerated Garza and the other two Comancheros from Cadence's revenge. Which was not likely. Garza turned and rode away up Soldier Hill with the Apache and Arenas riding behind him.

Hannibal got up and grabbed the Henry Rimfire rifle from the gun-sleeve in Rip's saddle in the back of the wagon. He jumped off and hurried over to Cadence who was out of the water and up on the dock at the water's edge. Cadence holstered his revolvers and took the long rifle from Hannibal. He methodically leaned on the ferry crank-wheel to steady his aim and after exhaling a long breath, took one shot and hit in the middle of Garza's back from over a hundred yards away and halfway up Soldier Hill.

Hannibal handed Cadence another cartridge, which he loaded and then aimed and took a long deep breath, and halfway through his exhale, shot the Apache. He loaded for a third shot and aimed for the one remaining Comanchero, Arenas. As he rode hurriedly up the hill road, Cadence fired.

"You got him!" Hannibal proclaimed.

Cadence shook his head. "I missed."

They both heard Rip in his hushed voice behind them, "You winged him. But he will die soon." Then, looking at the puddle of blood around him Rip smiled. "As will I, it appears."

It was not until Cadence turned and saw Blade bleeding out and heard Frederick in pain he realized the damage Hank's two shots had caused. Alongside Blade, sitting in a puddle of his own blood, sat Rip.

Cadence dropped the Rimfire and ran over to him. "Oh no, oh my God, Rip what have you done?"

Rip tried to lift his hand, but nothing seemed to work. "Cadence take my knife and pop that hot slug out of Frederick," Rip told him.

Cadence, shaking, grabbed Rip's Bowie knife and went over to Frederick on the bench seat and dug the bullet out of Frederick's leg. Frederick took a silk scarf from his front coat pocket and tied it tightly around his leg.

"I'm good, Cadence. Go take care of Rip." Cadence dropped back down beside Rip and handed him back his Bowie knife.

Rip shook his head. "It's yours now. You keep it. From Jimmy Bowie, to me, and now to you, Cadence. I think Captain Bowie would approve." Rip took a deep labored breath.

"Stop talking so much, Rip!" Cadence was scrambling for some clothing or cloth or something to soak up the blood that poured out of Rip. He quickly ripped off strips of his own shirt. "Oh my God, it just won't stop!" Cadence pressed the makeshift bandages into the gaping hole in Rip's back. "Just hold on and let me get you into town to the doctor. Oh no, please, Rip. You can't die on me..." Cadence cried as he watched the life spilling out of Rip's body.

Cadence shook his head as he sobbed.

"You made me everything I am," Cadence blurted out. "I was so angry at you Rip. I am so sorry. I should have sensed Nelson's presence, but my rage blocked me. I lost my balance. I should have been looking out for you, instead of putting all my hate on you. I'm so sorry, Rip. Look what I've done. I could never hate you, Rip." Cadence broke down into tears.

Rip struggled to lift his head enough to see the boy. He managed to whisper his sentiment. "Whenever I look at you," Rip stopped for a breath. "And see what you have grown into; suddenly I don't feel so bad about myself and all the things I've done in my life." Rip stopped and winced.

He took another measured breath. "Do I wish I had never lied to you about your father? Well, hell, I don't know. Something about it sure seemed to work." Rip tried to laugh but coughed up a glob of blood instead. It landed on his chest. Rip looked at the blood spread out across his shirt. He struggled to continue breathing. He looked up again as if he had just remembered something.

"You gave me more than you can imagine, Cadence. You were someone to teach, someone to look out for, and someone who taught me at the same time. You were just like a son to me. That's what you have always been to me. I'm sorry I never told you that before."

Rip's eyes slowly closed as he continued in a softer whisper. "You have a good heart in you, Cadence. You will do well as a man. Of that, I am sure. Just remember to be true to yourself. Listen to the Spirits. And try to help more people than you kill."

Then his eyes faintly re-opened as though he had remembered something. He reached up with his last bit of effort, grabbed the encircled silver star Texas Ranger badge and tore it from his tattered bloody shirt. He looked up at Cadence.

"This belongs to you. You're the Texas Ranger, now." He tried to hand the badge to Cadence but couldn't lift his hand. Cadence, between sobs, took it from the dying man's hand.

Rip looked over at Blade, whose breathing became louder and more disturbed.

"Now, fetch my gun belt." Rip could only whisper.

Hannibal scrambled over to the buckboard, retrieved Rip's gun belt from under the bench seat, then quickly climbed down. Rip took his revolver but struggled mightily to pull the hammer back. Cadence placed his hand over Rip's and pulled the hammer back for him. Together they held the barrel up to Blade's head. But they didn't have to shoot her.

Blade made one final expulsion from her lungs, flaring her nostrils outward and kicking up the dust around her head for the last time. At that same instant, Cadence felt Rip's grip on the revolver soften and fall away from under his. He turned to see that Rip was gone as well.

Cadence held them both and cried.

EPILOGUE

BY THE TIME they got back to D.C., it was in the wee hours of the morning.

Frederick handled the wagon reins and drove directly to the Senator Hotel, Hannibal beside him on the bench seat. Cadence sat in the back of the buckboard, his arms wrapped around Rip's dead body.

Lydia met them dutifully at the alley side door of the closed saloon. She struggled to take her sobbing husband out of the wagon. Frederick and Hannibal helped her pull Cadence away from Rip. He did not want to let go. It took some time to untwine the two.

Once done, Frederick and Hannibal rode off in the wagon with Rip's body sprawled out in the back. They headed over to Mr. Harry P. Cattell, DC's most prominent mortician, and woke him up. One year later, Cattell would be the one to embalm Lincoln's eleven-year-old son, Willie, who would die of typhoid fever. Three years after that, he would embalm President Lincoln himself.

Lydia tried her best to comfort the exhausted Cadence. He spent the night in her loving embrace, gently crying until he finally fell asleep just before sunrise.

Several days later, Inspector Eugene 'Earl' Barron, the station chief of the newly formed Metropolitan Police Department, invited Cadence in for a meeting. Lydia insisted she accompany him. When they got there the officer in charge, Sgt. J.W. Johnson, walked them immediately into the station chief's office. Inspector Barron was holding a Virginia arrest warrant and four death certificates. He looked up when they entered.

"We were made aware by courier this morning that an arrest warrant has been issued down in Richmond. This warrant names a certain Cadence Gatlin as responsible for the deaths of Foster and Hank Nelson and three Comancheros; Rudolphus Garza, Eduardo Arenas and an outlaw known as the Apache. Am I correct in assuming that the aforementioned, is you?"

The station chief looked squarely at Cadence. Cadence looked down at Lydia, who looked up at him and squeezed his hand as she did. He looked back at the chief constable.

"Yes, that is me. Are you charging me with murder?" Cadence stood tall. "I know my rights. I've been reading the law."

"Murder? Goodness, no." The chief looked over at his officer in charge, then back at Cadence and Lydia. "We are simply confirming the facts. I am afraid that down there you are wanted for murder. Up here, however, you are collecting a reward, young man." The stern chief couldn't contain his smile any longer. "A rather sizable one I might add."

He referred to his notes. "Both Nelson brothers had rather large rewards that have been accumulating for years. And those Comancheros were three of the most prolific cattle rustlers in Colorado. They pay $3,000 each, which was offered by the Lytton Springs Cattle Company.

"But as I said, the Nelson boys have been wanted in these parts for over twenty years. The reward on them stems from the C&O Railroad for several train hold-ups and other *assorted mischief,* it says here. They pay a combined reward of $10,500 for the arrest or confirmed death of both Foster and Hank Nelson."

The Hunt for Frederick Douglass
Terry Balagia

The chief set his notes down and looked at the expectant young mother as he handed them an envelope.

"Take this to Capital City Bank and ask for Mr. Tim Crowley, the bank president. I have already talked with him. He is expecting you. They are holding this money for you in an unclaimed account there. You are to give him this letter, which will transfer the funds into your name. A total of $19,500."

Cadence and Lydia looked at each other. He took the envelope, and they both turned and walked out in stunned silence. Lydia could barely catch her breath. Cadence was trying to take in what had happened; they now had more money than they could ever spend in a lifetime.

The couple made it outside onto Pennsylvania Avenue.

Cadence suddenly stopped and grabbed Lydia by the shoulders. He was the first to speak. "Do you think this is just some kind of mistake? Or a joke someone is playing on us?"

Lydia smiled up at him. "I think it is an answered prayer, Cadence. That's what I think."

He started to walk Lydia to the bank when it occurred to him, he might as well hail a hackney carriage. "We can certainly afford it." Cadence smiled and then screamed aloud "Whoopee!" and picked up Lydia by the waist and swung her around in the air. She laughed as well and suddenly it all seemed real.

Cadence set her down still laughing and waved at a line of carriages on the other side of the wide boulevard. The one at the front of the line instantly headed toward them. The hackney driver pulled his carriage up alongside them as Cadence formally extended his hand to his young wife. She elegantly placed her hand atop his as she stepped up into the carriage. She felt so light on her feet, she almost bounced off the carriage step. Looking at her loveliness brought Cadence back to reality.

"What on earth do we do now?" he asked Lydia. As he did, he thought to himself, *What would Rip tell me we should do?*

Lydia looked around at the hackney carriage and smiled at him as he climbed in. "First, we're going to buy the nicest buggy in all of Washington, DC."

He smiled and dropped down on the seat beside her.

"Driver, take us to a buggy dealer!" Cadence instructed. Then he remembered, "But first, stop by the bank!" he called out with a big grin. Lydia gave him a loving smile.

"Then we are going to drive it by the Senator Hotel and show off a little bit," Lydia added. Cadence nodded, smiled, and thought about how much he loved this girl.

"After that," she said as her face opened to let her true light shine on him. "We're going to Texas."

That's when it occurred to Cadence that Lydia was right. That is exactly what Rip would have told him to do.

THE END

AUTHOR'S NOTES

HAVE YOU EVER had something strange happen that you could not explain or understand? Something more than a simple coincidence.

This book results from one of those.

I have always been an early riser. I like to get up in the wee hours and meditate before writing.

Between my meditation and my writing, I will turn on the computer and momentarily scour the web, looking for any wild, esoteric, interesting factoid, historic event or stories about UFOs and stuff to wake up and excite my imagination; to open up my mind before I begin my day's writing.

One day, several years ago, I was getting ready to write and was closing all the windows on my computer when I came across a random page that I'd opened from somewhere.

As I quickly scanned it, I was struck by the modern train of thought and yet the use of archaic formal language. I recognized the value of the great contrast within the writing.

But also—and strangely—I had the oddest sensation that even though I know I had never read these words before, they were somehow familiar.

So, I kept reading, and the next paragraph had the same effect and blew me away. It sounded so current and so modern, so sensible, so grounded in a deep and intimate understanding and knowledge of the Constitution. Most important, it was relevant and informative as to what was going on in today's America. Yet the language was old and formal. I wondered who had written it and quickly looked down at the bottom of the page to see...and there it was written, Frederick Douglass.

I found that very interesting! Interesting because it made me realize I knew almost nothing about Frederick Douglass other than a few tidbits I'd retained from my eighth-grade social studies book. I remembered a section about a page and a half long, with that rather stern-looking picture of him. What I couldn't recall was whether he taught himself to read, or if he went to England, or what had made him famous.

I was struck by his words, and I wondered how I could never have been exposed to them before. What was it about a system where I would discover such profound writings and thoughts from such a great patriot only as an adult? Why had I not been exposed to his writings before? What did this new reality say about me—about everything?

This short half-page of writing I stumbled upon seemed to offer a lot of insight and wisdom regarding what's going on today. I was driven to search and read the amazing editorials he had written. And I was astonished at how contemporary they were. Though he was talking about pre-Civil War issues, Frederick's words sounded like he was talking about the things we are experiencing today. His writings were discussions of a nation being polarized around race and bigotry—only the phrases had been scribed in 1845 when he published his first autobiography.

Imagine, giving a speech entitled, 'What To The Slave Is The Fourth Of July' back in 1852. Read the words! He holds nothing back. I was shocked, yes... because it was such a profound speech. But mostly because I had never heard of it before. I had never heard or read the writings of Frederick Douglass.

How is that possible? I consider myself a well-read person. I love to read. Especially works filled with historical and biographical

The Hunt for Frederick Douglass
Terry Balagia

significance. I remembered he wrote his famous autobiography, but I had forgotten he wrote two more. And I had no idea he started two newspapers; and wrote such empowered speeches and editorials. Such profound words—from this heroic American writer, orator, and great patriot—yet it appears he is little known. We were never exposed to his writings in school. It seems. Admittedly, I read little in junior high and high school. So maybe I missed it. But I don't think so.

Considering this new awareness, I thought, *Man I wish someone would write a great movie or book about this guy and get his writings back out into the public. Help people discover this man's writings. Learn from them. Apply their lessons and wisdom. Discuss them.*

But it would not be me. I was not about to start a book. *I am in the middle of editing two unfinished manuscripts; the last thing I need is to start another book. They take years.*

So, though I loved the thought, I *was not* going to do it.

But my imagination took over and I thought, *if—and that's a very big IF—I were to do it, I'd style it somewhat like Saul's conversion on the road to Damascus from the Bible.*

I was suddenly so caught up in the idea I Googled the passage, opened a file, and added it to my notes—along with some great Frederick Douglass quotes. And here is where the thinking started again! *IF I were to write it would be about a ruthless bounty hunter who, by some event in the storyline, has to spend time with Frederick Douglass and during an intense and emotional time together, he develops great admiration for the one he was hunting.*

I remembered a book I read many years ago written by one of the prison guards of Nelson Mandela who hated Mandela at first, but over time became a devout follower of the great man. Another thought...*that would be another good way to approach doing a story about Frederick Douglass.*

But it *would not* be me. So I forgot about it.

Later that morning, out of the blue, my daughter sent me an email about a guy, Shaun King from Morehouse College, who was starting a podcast found at *TheNorthStar.com*, inspired by the writings of Frederick Douglass. She said she thought this would interest me. I was rather startled! *I haven't heard that name since the eighth grade, and I have heard it twice now in one morning. Someone is sending me a message from somewhere.*

But I *would not* start another book, so I blocked it out of my mind again. But I remembered thinking, *that's two!*

Then that evening, as I ate dinner and watched the news—a night early in the Trump administration when he came out on the news and referenced Frederick Douglass as though he were still alive. When I heard Frederick Douglass on the news that same day as the other two mentions my jaw dropped.

I thought, *okay, that's three!* As strange as that sounds, I felt like it couldn't be a coincidence. I wondered whether I was getting a message...someone trying to tell me something. That something was: *looks like I'm writing a book about Frederick Douglass.*

It *was* going to be me after all!

It took those three random Frederick Douglass pokes from the Universe—all in the same day—to convince me to write this book. And who was I to say no?

So, I made a deal with the Universe. I agreed, *I will gladly write the book, as long as the story comes to me and flows through me and I have only to write it down, like a scribe watching a movie.* And as long as I could include as many of Frederick's own words and great quotes as I could. That was the whole idea of doing the book.

My goal was to bring the works of Fredcrick Douglass back into public conversation. I have seamlessly integrated over twenty-three or maybe twenty-five Frederick Douglass quotes and parts of his most famous speech, "What To The Slave Is The Fourth Of July?" within the context of this story. I hope people will discover the parallels from pre-Civil War days to today's venomous discussions. And in doing so, they re-discover the stirring words of Frederick Douglass. Hoping we can excoriate the animosity and restore an effective public discourse. His writing contains so much passion and perspective very relevant to today's times. I intend to give his voice a new platform. So that is what I asked the Universe for.

I also asked the Universe that when I was done writing it, I not have to go through the humiliating ordeal of sending it around and begging people to read it. The Universe would have to get it published for me.

It's been over four years and I finished. And the first publisher I sent it to immediately decided to publish it. Crazy, right?

So, thank you God, and the Universe, and please bless the memory of Frederick Douglass and Harriet Tubman. And while you are at it, Lord, please continue to bless the United States of America.

The Hunt for Frederick Douglass
Terry Balagia

ABOUT THE AUTHOR

BORN AND RAISED in Austin, Texas, Terry Balagia, cut his teeth as an advertising copywriter in New York City, ultimately attaining executive creative director positions at large multi-national ad agencies in New York and Los Angeles.

During a celebrated 30-year advertising career, Balagia wrote and shot many national advertising campaigns and won more than his share of the industry's creative awards.

Terry's lifelong dream has been to write novels. He vividly remembers coming home from college one day and telling his mom, "I know now what I am here to do...I want to write books. I want to be a novelist." Throughout his career, Balagia would write after work and on weekends.

In 2017, while working on an earlier manuscript and being mentored and encouraged by an old friend, re-known worldwide bestselling author, Maxine Paetro, Terry was hit with a striking bolt of intuition. This incident led him on a four-year quest to scribe an adventure involving one of history's most influential American writers of his time—Frederick Douglass.

The end result: Balagia's page-turning debut novel, *The Hunt for Frederick Douglass: The Last Chance, Secret Mission to Avoid the Civil War*, and his conclusion to "never give up on your dreams."

Terry spends his time between Los Angeles, Miami, and Austin, with his girlfriend, partner, and best friend. When not remotely teaching Scriptwriting or Story Writing at the highly acclaimed Miami Ad School, Balagia spends his time writing and daydreaming about future stories.

Balagia is currently writing and preparing the stage adaptation of *The Hunt for Frederick Douglass*. Join his loyal fans; sign up on the author page: terrybalagia.com for updates.

The Hunt for Frederick Douglass
Terry Balagia

Made in the USA
Las Vegas, NV
14 December 2023

82838319R00216